To Wi
Hope you e,

Brian, His Granddad
& the Cup of Ages

Phillip J. Taylor

Pen Press

© Phillip J. Taylor 2012

All rights reserved

No part of this publication may be reproduced, stored in a
retrieval system, or transmitted in any form or by any means,
without the prior permission in writing of the publisher, nor be
otherwise circulated in any form of binding or cover other than
that in which it is published and without a similar condition
including this condition being imposed on the subsequent
purchaser.

First published in Great Britain by Pen Press

All paper used in the printing of this book has been made from
wood grown in managed, sustainable forests.

ISBN 978-1-78003-422-5

Printed and bound in the UK
Pen Press is an imprint of
Indepenpress Publishing Limited
25 Eastern Place
Brighton
BN2 1GJ

A catalogue record of this book is available from
the British Library

Cover design by Jacqueline Abromeit

For Mum. Nighty-night, shirty-shirt.

Chapter 1

A VERY PECULIAR LETTER

The first time Brian ever met his grandparents was at a funeral. It was a burial for a relative whom he had never heard of before. A rather well to do chap, by all accounts, called Bertie Snodgrass. He had been killed one evening when the house he was living in had suddenly taken upon itself to blow up. Apparently, the explosion had been enormous. Not only did it create a rather unsightly ten-foot deep crater that his posh London neighbours complained to the local council about long after his death, but the blast had also been so great that it had sent some of the bricks that had previously formed Bertie's front living room wall into the back garden of another house at least four streets away, injuring a cat. The investigators from the gas company claimed that the cause of the explosion had been a faulty pipe.

The second occasion on which Brian had met his grandparents was at another funeral a few years later, this time for his Uncle Meredith. A somewhat tall and bearded man, he too had passed away in rather unfortunate circumstances. You see, Uncle Meredith had been the chairman of quite a prestigious golf club called 'The Last Fairway'. It was the sort of golf club that you couldn't just apply to join. No, you actually had to be invited to become a member, and you were only ever asked to become a member if you had quite a lot of money. Anyway, the weather on this particular

1

August afternoon was downright awful. Yet the rumbling clouds and the howling wind and constant pouring rain did not affect Uncle Meredith's round of golf. In fact, if anything, it actually seemed to help. But as he walked up to take his final putt on the eighteenth green and win the tournament to the cheers of the few onlookers who were cowering bravely under their umbrellas, a huge and brilliant flash of lightning struck Uncle Meredith slap, bang, on top of his head. And in a blink of an eye he had gone. Nothing of him was left. Uncle Meredith had entirely combusted. The only proof that he had been standing there, on the putting green, just seconds earlier was an abandoned golf club lying next to a smouldering pair of scorched shoes.

In ten years Brian had met his grandparents only twice, at two funerals. The third time he met them was when he went to live with them.

His granddad was old. Really old. Brian wasn't sure exactly how old but he looked at least 120. He was a tall, thin man with very little hair whose eyebrows, in contrast to his balding head, were a mass of bushy white spindly hair that looked remarkably like two fat caterpillars had crawled upon his face and fallen asleep above his eyes. His glasses, which appeared as though they had probably been purchased sometime before the First World War, were fragile-looking and each arm, it seemed, had been repaired at one time or another with some sticky black electrical tape, whilst always hanging within his shirt pocket was a small, yellow screwdriver, which oddly he seemed to carry with him wherever he went.

His grandmother, on the other hand, was a much smaller person and a lot rounder too. She seemed to spend most of her time in the kitchen baking cakes, scones and jam tarts that she then forced upon anybody and everybody who happened to call at her door along with boiling hot cups of tea whether they wanted them or not. Brian wouldn't have minded so much if the cakes were actually nice but her rock cakes could be used to literally hammer nails into walls and her sticky toffee pie had been known to glue your mouth shut for up to four days.

Brian's grandparents lived at number 14 Pyrmont Grove and from the outside, at least, their small terraced house looked no different from any of the other houses that lined the road. It had two upstairs windows, a large bay window downstairs and an old wooden front door whose faded blue paint was beginning to peel in places. The tiny front garden, although neatly tended, consisted of nothing more than a square piece of patchy lawn with a thin surrounding border of colourful shrubs. A tall, green hedge grew on each side of the garden whilst in front of the house an ancient-looking stone wall had been built, inset to which was a very old and rusty iron gate. On either side of the gate a sturdy stone pillar had been erected and sitting upon the very top of these had once been two stone ornaments of some description. Unfortunately, what the ornaments once were you couldn't tell for over the years the wind and the rain had altered them considerably and now they were completely unrecognisable.

'This house, y'know, is well over 200 years old,' his granddad informed Brian when Brian first arrived one summer morning with his mother.

And it certainly looked like it too, thought Brian as he followed his granddad through the gloomy hallway. The dreadfully thin carpet was a crazy maze of dark crimson and purple circles whilst the faded wallpaper, which was beginning to shed itself in places, had images of pink and violet flowers sprouting from it in almost every direction. The miniature glass chandelier hanging from the ceiling was covered in dust and, unbelievably, propped up in an alcove by two sets of stairs, one leading upwards and one leading down, was an old suit of armour covered in a thin layer of dust and cobwebs.

The living room into which he and his mother were led was, if anything, even worse. To Brian it actually looked like some sort of strange antique shop. Huge and dark wooden bookcases crammed full of different-sized books lined almost every wall and where there wasn't a bookcase there was an unfashionable table or an old-fashioned wooden sideboard, which usually had an ornate gold-painted lamp sitting upon it. An imposing stone fireplace stood opposite the living room door and decorating this were various china ornaments of dogs, birds and unknown figures.

'And you must be Brian,' said his grandmother with a pleasant smile; she had been sitting on the edge of a huge cherry flower patterned settee with a very large teapot in one hand and a china cup and saucer in the other, waiting for him. 'My, how you've grown' she remarked happily, handing Brian the cup and saucer she had just overfilled with tea.

'Oh, er… thanks,' said Brian, doing his utmost not to spill any more of the tea and at the same time sitting uneasily in an identical settee opposite her.

'Hasn't he grown, Henry?' said his grandmother aloud to her husband as she poured a second cup. 'Brian's still only eleven years old but, do you know, I think he'll soon be as tall as you! Here you are, Elizabeth,' she said, eagerly offering another overfilled cup to Brian's mother, who quickly took a sip, preventing any further tea from spilling into the saucer.

'It looks like you've grown at least ten inches since we last saw you, Brian,' said his granddad, sinking into a large purple armchair next to him.

Brian smiled awkwardly. He was having immense trouble squeezing his tiny fingers through the even tinier handle of his china cup.

'It runs in the family,' said his granddad.

'What does?' asked Brian.

'Tallness,' answered his granddad.

'Oh,' said Brian, still trying unsuccessfully to hook one of his fingers through the cup's tiny handle.

4

'That's right,' his grandmother said, nodding in agreement. 'That's right. Now I come to think of it, your Uncle Meredith, God rest his soul,' she said, tracing an imaginary cross upon her chest, 'was exceptionally tall.'

'Over six foot,' remarked his granddad.

'And each time poor Meredith visited us he'd always bang his head on that glass chandelier that's hanging in the hallway. Do you remember?' she said, pouring another cup of tea and handing it to her husband. 'Thank heavens I always had plenty of plasters handy!' she added, laughing. 'Now who wants to try one of my rock cakes?'

Uncertainly, Brian took one from the plate that his grandmother was now offering him. Blimey, he thought as he went to take a bite, his cake really did feel as heavy as a rock. And it tasted like one too. The cake's surface seemed hard enough to break your teeth on. Whilst the inside of the cake, which he expected to be soft and fluffy, was all mushy and crumbly and tasted like soggy chalk. Except for the raisins, that is, which tasted like bits of gravel.

'Well, how is it?' asked his grandmother enthusiastically, as she watched Brian swallow his first piece.

'Oh, it's… er… very nice,' Brian somehow managed to lie.

His grandmother looked pleased. 'Splendid' she said, delighted. 'Here, have another one'

'Oh. Erm… thanks,' said Brian, who rather reluctantly felt obliged to take a second cake.

'And when you've finished those two by all means have a third or even a fourth if you like. In fact, Brian dear, you can have as many of them as you like. I've got another two tubs of those in the kitchen ready to be eaten,' she said, offering the plate to Brian's mother.

'Great,' said Brian weakly; he was having a bit of difficulty in balancing both the cakes and his tea all on one saucer.

Brian's mother shook her head. 'No thank you, Doris,' she said, sipping her tea hastily and refusing a rock cake. 'I really do need to get back to town before it gets dark.'

'Oh, it's just that I thought you might stay for a bit of tea,' said Brian's grandmother, disappointedly. 'We haven't seen each other for such a long time. Well, not since Richard…'

At the mention of her husband's name Brian's mother immediately choked on her tea and began to cough. 'No, no, Henry, I'm fine,' she spluttered, waving at Brian's granddad to sit down; he had got up to help. 'There's-a-couple-of,' she managed to say between coughing fits, 'flats that I've arranged to see this evening.'

'Oh, right. Of course,' said Brian's grandmother a little sadly. 'Well, if you're sure. But you'll stay for lunch though, won't you?'

'I can't,' apologised Brian's mother, sipping quickly at her tea again.

'Sandwiches probably. Some crisps and…'

'Really, Doris, I can't.'

'A bit of salad…'

'Doris, stop it, please!' snapped Brian's mother suddenly, tea spilling over into her saucer, making Brian jump which, in turn, made him spill some of his tea too.

For a moment nobody spoke. Brian stared at his mother as she ran her fingers despairingly through her hair, and then at his grandparents who were staring at their daughter-in-law in complete surprise and shock. Brian sipped some more of his tea.

Eventually, Brian's mother said apologetically, 'I'm sorry. I didn't mean to snap. It's just that it's been a long drive down here this morning and I really do need to get back before five o'clock. Henry, you know what the traffic can be like on the motorway, especially in the rush hour and on a Friday?'

Brian's granddad nodded sympathetically. 'It's all right, Elizabeth,' he said, smiling a little sadly. 'We understand.'

Brian's mother rubbed her forehead and sighed wearily. 'It's not that I don't appreciate what you're doing. I do. Really I do. Looking after Brian for me until I've found a place to live and got settled in my job is a huge weight off my mind. It really is.'

'Oh my dear, that should be the least of your worries,' said his grandmother supportively, passing a plate to her husband upon which sat three very large rock cakes. 'It's the least we could do. After all we are his only grandparents. It'll be no trouble, no trouble at all. Will it, Henry?'

'No, of course not. Glad to have him staying with us,' replied her husband, smiling cheerfully. 'Just one rock cake for me, please, Doris,' he added, doing his utmost to avoid taking the plate from his wife.

'Nonsense,' said Brian's grandmother, forcing the cakes into her husband's hand. 'You hardly touched your breakfast this morning. And besides these rock cakes are your favourite.'

'But…' protested her husband.

'They've got extra raisins,' said Brian's grandmother.

'But…'

'And they're still warm,' added his wife.

'Oh, very well,' said Brian's granddad, finally accepting the plate. Then, placing it upon his lap, he picked up one of the cakes, dipped it into his cup of tea, and took a bite. 'So Brian, how do you feel about coming to live with us for a few months?' he mumbled.

Brian fidgeted uncomfortably in his seat. 'Erm… I'm looking forward to it,' he said, trying to sound and look as convincing as he could. But in reality he hated the idea. In fact he had hated the idea from the very first moment his mother had suggested it. Unfortunately for Brian, though, he hadn't really had much choice in the matter. Ever since his father had left them, almost a year ago, life for him and his mother had changed considerably. Unlike before, they now had very little money. For Brian this meant very few new clothes, no new trainers, no video games (they had had to sell his games console) and, worst of all, no mobile phone. His mother, who had previously worked for a firm of solicitors before raising Brian, had needed to find a job to support them both almost immediately. But that, of course, was easier said than done. It had taken quite a few months, much longer than she had hoped, and when eventually Brian's mother had found a similar position, at another firm of solicitors, all her savings had run out and the bank were in the final stages of repossessing their house.

To make matters worse his mother's job was to be based in a completely different part of the country because the company that she was going to work for was in the process of relocating. So not only would Brian's mother have to find a new home for them both to live in, but she would have to find Brian a new school too. And when she had successfully done that, there was still the problem of who was going to look after him each day after school until she came home from work. After lots of discussions (most of which did not include Brian) and many phone calls the only really sensible solution seemed to be for Brian to go and live with his grandparents, temporarily.

'He's been really looking forward to it, haven't you Brian?' said his mother, sipping at her tea again, trying to sound more cheerful.

Brian smiled and did his best to look enthusiastic for his mother.

His granddad burped loudly.

'Henry!' exclaimed his wife, mortified. 'Please, not in front of…'

'Oh, it's all right,' said her husband, patting his chest noisily. 'It's only Brian and Elizabeth and anyway, it's better out than in, isn't it?' he said, burping loudly again.

'Oh, Henry, for goodness' sake!' said his wife reproachfully.

Brian's granddad dipped his rock cake into his tea again and took another mushy bite. 'How was your journey down, Elizabeth?' he asked, spitting crumbs all over his trousers. 'Did you get caught in the rain?'

'Not for long,' replied Brian's mother. 'And the traffic wasn't too bad. Er... did you know you've got paint on your hands?' she said, staring, as Brian's granddad dipped another piece of rock cake into his tea before somehow managing to squeeze it all into his mouth at once.

'And on your trousers too,' scolded his wife, shaking her head disapprovingly. 'Goodness knows they were clean on today!'

Brian's granddad tried to say something, which sounded rather like 'Meen detorating'. But each time he opened his mouth to speak tiny bits of mushy rock cake flew everywhere.

'And, Henry, how many times have I told you not to speak with your mouth full?' reprimanded his wife, wiping away a piece of rock cake that had just landed beneath her left eye.

Brian's granddad gulped some of his tea and swallowed. 'Been decorating,' he finally managed to say. 'Only finished this morning as a matter of fact. The spare bedroom hasn't been decorated for years, y'know? Last time was probably just after the war.'

'Well, I'm sure it wasn't quite that long ago, Henry,' disagreed Brian's grandmother. 'Oh, and that reminds me,' she added, getting up and opening a door to an ancient-looking sideboard. From it she removed a thin parcel wrapped neatly in dark blue paper and tied loosely with a thick navy ribbon. 'This is for you, my dear,' she said, handing the gift to Brian. 'It's something for your room,' she explained a little nervously. 'From your granddad and me. We hope you like it.'

Brian carefully placed his cup and saucer upon an old wooden table in front of him and quickly began unwrapping his present. 'It's... er, a picture frame,' he said, trying to hide the sudden disappointment in his voice.

'Turn it over,' said his grandmother, twirling one of her hands at him, indicating that the picture frame was upside down. 'Turn it over. No, the other way, the other way. That's it.'

Brian flipped the wooden frame over in his hands and stared at it in pleasant surprise. Secured tightly behind its glass front was an old black and white photograph, which was bent and creased in places. It pictured a young man with long black hair, dressed in faded jeans and a scruffy T-shirt, standing outside a terraced house. In his hands he was holding some sort of trophy.

'It's Dad,' said Brian excitedly, lifting the frame to show his mother. 'Look, Mum, it's Dad!' he repeated, beaming. 'Doesn't he look young? And just look at his hair!'

'Well, that picture was probably taken when your father was about... let's see now... about fifteen years old,' said his grandmother, reminiscing. 'Not much older than you are now, dear. Isn't that right, Henry?'

Her husband nodded, dipping a second rock cake into his tea.

'And what's that he's holding in his hands?' asked Brian curiously, studying the old photograph more closely. 'It looks like some sort of cup.'

'It is,' confirmed Brian's granddad, spitting mushy crumbs all down his shirt. 'He was good at cricket, your father. Crikey, he couldn't 'arf hit a ball. Almost killed half a dozen people one year with all the balls he whacked into the stands! That trophy your dad's holding he won with the local cricket team. Got the highest innings too in the final if I remember rightly. 226 or 227 not out, I think.'

'Wow! Look, Mum,' said Brian excitedly again. He turned towards his mother. 'Doesn't Dad look strange with that long hair...?'

But his mother didn't answer. She was crying. Tears were streaming down her cheeks, her cup and saucer wobbling in one hand as she placed them upon the nearest table whilst in the other, clutched between her fingers, was a gold chain and locket. Brian knew what the locket held, a tiny photo of him and his mum and dad on holiday from a few years ago, but his mother hardly ever wore the locket now. Instead, and for a reason he didn't quite understand,

10

she simply kept it in one of her pockets, removing it every now and then to look inside.

'Oh my poor dear,' said Brian's grandmother, immediately getting up and trying to comfort her. 'It's all right,' she said soothingly. 'There now, it's okay. Henry, why don't you do something useful rather than just sitting there and show Brian around?'

'Right-o,' mumbled her husband, sending mushy cake crumbs flying in all directions once again. 'Come on then, Brian.'

Brian got up and followed his granddad out of the living room. He stared forlornly as he slipped past his mother. She was attempting to dry her eyes with a handkerchief that his grandmother had removed from one of her sleeves.

She had never used to cry, although he could vaguely recollect her getting upset once at somebody's funeral. It was only since his father had left them that his mother had begun to get upset more often, and usually at night when she was alone in her bedroom and thought Brian couldn't hear her.

'Now, what did you really think of your grandmother's rock cakes?' whispered his granddad, gently closing the living room door behind Brian.

'What?' said Brian distractedly, still worrying about his mother.

'Your grandmother's rock cakes,' repeated his granddad. 'What did you really think of them?'

'Oh, erm… they were nice,' answered Brian awkwardly.

'Come off it,' said his granddad, raising his eyebrows and pulling a face which looked like he'd just been poisoned. 'They were horrible. Everyone says so. So, what did you really think of them?'

'Well, they were a bit hard!' admitted Brian truthfully.

'Right you are,' said his granddad, chuckling. 'There's only one way to really enjoy your grandmother's rock cakes,' he said, descending a tiny flight of stairs that brought them to a small dining room. 'And that's to drown them in your tea for a few minutes. It softens them up, y'see. Otherwise they're only good for doorstops!'

Brian laughed.

'Er… best not tell your grandmother I said that, though, eh?' said his granddad, a worried look spreading across his face. 'Something we'd better just keep between us,' he added, glancing nervously over his shoulder.

Brian nodded in understanding and stared around the musty-smelling dining room. It didn't look much better than the living room. The floor was covered by a thin grey carpet whilst four brown wooden bookcases, crammed full with dull-coloured books, almost entirely concealed two of the room's four walls. Underneath a window on another wall was a large antique-looking chest of drawers, sitting upon which was a gold-painted table lamp, whilst at the centre of the dining room stood a traditional round wooden table with four chairs encircling it. Two further doors led away from the dining room. The first led into a pokey old-fashioned kitchen whilst a second, smaller door led into a basement.

'What's down there?' asked Brian curiously.

'Junk mostly,' said his granddad, climbing back up the stairs to the hallway and ascending a second flight of stairs, which brought them on to the first landing. Two doors led from it. The first into a bathroom, which, Brian was surprised to see, compared to the rest of the house, actually looked quite modern. 'We had to get it refitted a few years ago,' explained his granddad. 'Lots of leaky pipes.'

The second door led into what was going to be Brian's new bedroom. It was actually quite a bit bigger than Brian had thought it was going to be and the smell of fresh paint still dominated the room even with the window wide open. The walls were white, the curtains were blue and even the navy patterned carpet was bearable. In fact the only things that Brian really disliked about his new room were the two unfashionable wooden bookcases that were standing on either side of the bed and the large antique wardrobe positioned next to the open window.

'What do you think?' asked his granddad.

'Yeah, it's all right,' replied Brian, flopping on to the bed, which he found a little hard.

'Really?' said his granddad, visibly relieved. 'Because I only finished giving the walls a second coat of paint this morning, so they might still be a little wet, and those curtains, your grandmother made them. Fortunately, she makes better curtains than she does rock cakes,' he said, chuckling, then glancing quickly behind him to make sure he was out of earshot. 'And there should be plenty of room on the walls for you to stick up any posters now that I've taken down the shelves.'

'Thanks' said Brian, peering up at some of the oddly-shaped books in the old-fashioned bookcases.

'Couldn't do much about those though,' said his granddad. 'The bookcases, I mean; nowhere else to put them, y'see. They're antiques, you know? So I couldn't really paint them, and the wardrobe, well, you'll need somewhere to hang your clothes, won't you?'

'Oh, that's okay,' said Brian honestly. 'I mean, at least this room's bigger than my old one.'

'Good, well I'm glad you like it,' said Brian's granddad, smiling and stepping back out on to the landing. 'Come on, let me show you the rest of the house.'

Brian followed his granddad up another small flight of stairs, which brought them on to a second landing from which three doors led into three more rooms. 'This is your grandmother's and my bedroom,' said Brian's granddad, opening the first door. 'This is the second bedroom,' he said, opening another door, 'and this is my study,' he said, tapping on the third door, which he did not open. Opposite the study door a further, much steeper, flight of wooden stairs led upwards.

'What's up there?' asked Brian, gazing up at the ceiling where the stairs ended quite abruptly.

'The loft,' replied his granddad. 'Nothing much up there, though, apart from a few pigeons.'

Together, they walked back down the three flights of stairs and into the kitchen. It was a long, thin room with a muddle of units attached to just one wall. Standing at one end, and quite out of place, was another brown bookcase crammed full of hardback books whilst opposite it, at the other end of the kitchen, was a door that led to the back garden. There was only one window in the kitchen and sitting underneath it was probably the largest and deepest ceramic sink that Brian had ever seen.

'Do you want something to drink?' asked Brian's granddad, opening the fridge door. 'Only I bet you don't normally drink much tea at home, do you?'

'No, not really,' replied Brian, who was suddenly feeling quite thirsty.

'Well, what would you like?' asked his granddad, gazing in to the back of the fridge. 'We've got orange juice, apple juice, a bottle of red stuff,' he said, squinting at its label. 'Hmm, not sure what that is – oh, it's ketchup – and lemonade or Coke. What do you fancy?'

'Lemonade please,' said Brian.

'And I think I'll have one with you too,' said his granddad, taking two glasses from a cupboard above his head and filling them both with lemonade. 'Do you want to see the garden?' he asked, putting the bottle back into the fridge.

'Yeah, okay,' said Brian absentmindedly; he had already drunk half his drink.

His granddad opened the back door and Brian followed him outside. It was a beautiful August afternoon and the sun was shining brightly. The back garden, like the kitchen, was long and thin. A flowerbed of brightly coloured plants surrounded each side of the sunburnt lawn, whilst running through the grass were small stepping stones of concrete, which led up to a large wooden shed. And just like the front, the back garden was separated from its neighbours by two very tall green hedges.

'Got much to unpack?' asked his granddad, sitting on a rickety wooden bench next to the back door.

'No, not really,' said Brian, joining him. 'One suitcase, that's all.'

'Well, there's some drawers inside that wardrobe if you run out of hanging space,' said his granddad, sipping at his lemonade. 'And there's some more under your bed too, I think, that your grandmother emptied for you,' he added.

'Oh, okay,' said Brian, finishing his lemonade.

'Not sure there's anything worth reading in those bookcases next to your bed though,' remarked his granddad thoughtfully. 'Mostly history books, I think, and folk's recollections about the Second World War. Mind you, there might be a book or two on some of the fighter planes used in the Battle of Britain. You might like those.'

Brian nodded dolefully. They sat together in silence for a moment, the sun beating down upon their faces, his granddad occasionally sipping at his lemonade, Brian watching as a thin, ginger cat crept out from underneath the shed.

'Do you think he'll ever come back?' Brian asked eventually.

'Who?' asked his granddad.

'Dad,' said Brian.

'Oh,' said his granddad, shifting awkwardly in his seat. 'Well, er… what do you think, Brian?'

Brian shrugged. 'Dunno,' he answered glumly. 'Still don't know why he left. Mum doesn't talk about it. I've asked her but, well, you see how she gets. Mum cries a lot. So I don't really bother asking any more.' The ginger cat that Brian had spotted earlier padded towards him and began curling itself between his legs, rubbing its face affectionately against his knees. 'It's just that everything seemed okay, you know?' said Brian. 'I tried ringing him at work a few times. I found the number in a drawer in the kitchen. Don't tell Mum. But I think it must have been the wrong number because each time I phoned the same woman always answered and said that they didn't have a Mr Pankhurst working for Harvey & Norris.'

'Harvey & Norris?' repeated Brian's granddad. 'Who are they?'

'The accountants Dad worked for,' replied Brian.

Brian's granddad frowned and scratched his head thoughtfully. He drank some more lemonade and then, rubbing his whiskery chin, whispered, 'Listen, Brian, it's probably not my place to tell you this but, well, I thought you already knew.'

Now Brian frowned. 'Already knew what?' he asked.

'It's just that we thought your father would have told you before now.'

'Told me what?' asked Brian.

'Your mother was against it, I know,' continued his granddad, shaking his head, seemingly unaware of Brian's question. 'She didn't understand. But, nevertheless, your grandmother and I assumed that your father would have explained at least a little to you. But it's quite apparent that he did not and that would explain a great deal indeed.'

'What do you mean?' interrupted Brian, curiously. 'What should my dad have told me?'

For a moment Brian's granddad looked as though he was afraid to say anything more, as if he had already said too much. But then, peering over his spectacles and taking a deep breath, he whispered, 'Richard, I mean your father, did not work for a firm of accountants, Brian.'

Suddenly Brian's grandmother called out from somewhere inside the house. 'Henry! Brian! Where are you? Your mother's about to leave.'

Brian's granddad stared at him. 'Do you understand what I just told you, Brian?' he asked softly. 'Your father did not work for a firm of accountants. He never has.'

Brian found himself slowly nodding but he certainly didn't understand. As he got up and followed his granddad back into the kitchen his head was spinning madly. His father had been employed as an accountant almost all his adult life and Brian was sure that he had worked for Harvey & Norris for at least ten years. In fact he was certain that he had been promoted within the firm about two years ago. So why then would his granddad tell him that his father had never worked for a firm of accountants?

'Right then,' said his granddad, finishing his lemonade. 'We don't want to keep your mother waiting, do we? Come on.'

Brian placed his empty glass into the kitchen sink and was just about to follow his granddad into the dining room when he found himself lingering by the kitchen door. A strange hissing-like noise had caught his attention. He glanced over his shoulder and was surprised to see the ginger cat, which only moments earlier had been rubbing its face so affectionately against his knees, was now hissing and spitting angrily at something large and dark squatting upon the hedge just above it. It was a bird. But not just any bird. It was enormous! With scruffy black feathers, it looked almost as big as the angry cat which was sputtering so venomously at it from below. And, curiously, clasped within the bird's curved beak was what appeared to be a folded piece of paper.

As Brian stepped back into the garden the huge bird began to fidget uncomfortably, flapping its massive wings and hopping nervously about from one stick-like leg to the other. Its piercing black eyes seemed to stare first at Brian and then, rather more cautiously, at the furious cat below.

Brian edged a little closer to the bird, all the time wondering what the piece of paper was that it carried in its beak. But this only seemed to unsettle the massive creature and it flapped away from him, landing a little further along the hedge.

Undeterred, Brian stepped slightly nearer. But, just as before, the enormous bird hopped and then ran along the hedge's branches, stopping only when it seemed a safer distance away from him. Then, folding its massive wings, the bird cocked its head and stared at him suspiciously. The piece of folded paper still tightly locked in its sharp-looking beak.

Then three things happened at once. As Brian took another step forwards and the enormous bird flapped its wings, as if to take flight, the ginger cat that had been silently following it from beneath the hedge pounced. There was a sudden flurry of feathers, noisy squawks and a few *meeoowws* and a moment later the enormous bird had miraculously escaped the cat's clutches. It soared high into the air, swooping dangerously close to Brian's head, before landing uneasily on the branch of a nearby tree. The ginger cat, meanwhile, which looked to be bleeding, bolted back down the garden and disappeared underneath the wooden shed.

Brian stared at the hedge where the brief fight had just taken place. Caught amongst the leaves was the piece of folded paper that the bird had been carrying. After tugging it free, Brian quickly examined it. Unbelievably, it appeared to be some sort of letter. For on one side of the piece of paper, written in odd, wiry gold handwriting that seemed to positively glow, was his granddad's name, 'Henry Pankhurst'. Even more strangely, the letter looked as though it had, at one time, been sealed with red candle wax, although the scarlet seal was now broken.

Brian stared at the piece of paper in wonder. Birds didn't deliver letters! The very idea was completely crazy, and yet clutched in his hands was what appeared to be a letter addressed to his granddad. Brian ran his fingers over the almost warm, fiery letters and wondered if he should open it. Nobody would know if he stole a quick peek inside.

To his surprise, when he unfolded it, the piece of paper appeared to be blank. But then, in the top left-hand corner, Brian noticed three vertical lines of very tiny interlocking gold circles. He counted them. The first line had two gold circles. The second line had five and the third line had a total of eight gold circles, and these, for some reason, looked slightly larger than the others did. Whilst at the foot of the letter, towards the right-hand corner, were two tiny, ornately printed initials, B and W.

'All right, Brian?' asked his granddad, who was suddenly standing behind him. 'What's that you got there then?'

'Oh, er... nothing,' replied Brian, quickly refolding the peculiar letter. 'I found this lying in the garden,' he explained, handing over the piece of paper to his granddad.

Taking it from him, his granddad stuffed it into his shirt pocket next to his yellow screwdriver without even glancing at it. 'Probably rubbish blown into the garden by the wind,' he said casually. 'Come on, your mother's waiting for you upstairs.'

Brian followed his granddad back up the stairs and into the living room where his mother was chatting to someone on her mobile phone.

'Oh, that's really great news!' she said, looking pleased. 'Well, if I leave now I should hopefully be there by about four o'clock, depending on traffic. Okay, that's great. I'll see you at four then. Bye.'

'Who was that?' asked Brian.

'Mr Bracknell,' replied his mother, rubbing her eyes, which looked red and puffy. 'From Bracknell and Felch, the estate agent's in Bermondsey. They've had a three bedroom house come on the market today at a really good price and it's only a stone's throw from where I'll be working.'

'Oh, how wonderful,' said Brian's grandmother, pleased.

'So, does that mean you're leaving now?' asked Brian.

'I'll have to if I'm going to view this house at four o'clock,' she said, nodding and blowing her nose. 'But look at it this way,' she added, seeing her son's disappointed face. 'If this house is really nice and I put in an offer and it's accepted then you might not have to stay with your grandparents for as long as we thought.'

Unfortunately, this didn't make Brian feel any better. Somehow he felt as though his mother was leaving him just as his father had done almost a year before.

'Come on,' said his mother, snapping shut her mobile phone and slipping it back inside her handbag. 'It won't be that bad,' she whispered. 'Your room's bigger here than it was at the flat, isn't it? Let's get your suitcase from the car.'

Very reluctantly Brian followed his mother to the car and watched sullenly as she unlocked its boot and struggled with a large blue suitcase.

'Good grief, what have you got in here?' asked Brian's granddad, helping her. 'It looks like Brian's packed almost everything, including the kitchen sink,' he said, pulling the bulging suitcase along the uneven footpath and then somehow squeezing it through the front gate.

'Knowing Brian he probably has,' said his mother, shutting the car boot and giving her son a kiss. 'Now don't forget, whilst you're living with your grandparents you're to be on your best behaviour. Understand?'

Brian nodded.

'I mean it,' said his mother more sternly. 'No backchat.'

'Yeah, okay,' said Brian miserably, nodding again.

'Well, have a safe journey back, Elizabeth,' said Brian's granddad as they watched her climb into her car and start the engine.

Brian's grandmother tapped on the driver's window. 'And here's a couple of rock cakes,' she said as the driver's window began to lower, and she handed Brian's mother a large foil package that looked suspiciously like it contained quite a few more than just two cakes. 'In case you get hungry,' she added.

'Oh, right, thanks,' said Brian's mother, reluctantly placing the silver parcel on the passenger seat. Then, as she switched on the indicator lights, the car rolled forwards and she waved goodbye.

Brian waved goodbye too and so did his grandparents. As Brian watched his mother's car gradually drift out of sight and disappear up the terraced road and round a bend, his attention was curiously drawn to the black and white road sign. It appeared to have been damaged or, perhaps, vandalised, because every single letter was warped and grossly misshapen like ink smudged upon a letter. Almost as if an incredible, intense heat had suddenly consumed it. Almost as if the road sign had melted…

Chapter 2

THE BOOK OF NOTHING

Brian stared at himself unhappily in the wardrobe mirror. He was trying on his new school uniform for the very first time and he didn't like it. He was wearing one of five new, white shirts, which was badly creased as it had only just been unwrapped from its plastic packaging, and the rough material felt all prickly on his skin, like coarse sandpaper, which made him want to constantly itch his arms and chest. The shirt collar, which was a little tight and as stiff as cardboard, kept bending upwards, pointing to the ceiling and no matter how hard Brian tried he couldn't bend it back into shape. It just kept popping up again. His new school blazer, which had a blue and gold motif sewn upon its chest pocket, wasn't much better either. It was far too big for him. The arms were much too long and it was so baggy around his shoulders that it made poor Brian look as though he had shrunk, as if he had just tumbled out of a washing machine. His tie, which was a patchwork of green, red, blue and yellow stripes, looked like a two-year-old had been let loose with a paintbrush, and his trousers, which were unbelievably prickly, were about three inches too long.

'Now, how does that look?' asked his grandmother, who had been kneeling on the floor, busily fiddling with the legs to Brian's trousers. 'That's it, stand up straight, dear,' she mumbled, two pins hanging from between her pursed lips.

Brian studied his reflection against the wardrobe mirror and sighed dejectedly. The uniform was horrible. He hated it.

'Oh my, don't you look smart?' remarked his grandmother, pleased.

'But the shirt's really itchy,' complained Brian, scratching his neck irritably.

'Well, that's because it's new, dear,' replied his grandmother, who was once again enthusiastically adjusting one of the legs to Brian's trousers.

'And the collar's a bit tight too. Ouch!'

'Whoops! Sorry about that,' apologised his grandmother as she slipped another pin into the hem of Brian's trousers. 'Now, are you sure they're not too long, dear?' she asked anxiously. 'Only your trouser bottoms are almost touching the floor. I can turn them up a little more if you'd like me to? It won't be any trouble.'

Brian tugged at his tie, pulling it off grumpily. His shirt collar was pointing upwards again. 'No, they're fine,' he replied, trying to bend his collar back into shape.

'Are you sure, dear?'

'Yes, really,' he said a little testily.

His grandmother smiled pleasantly at him and pushed another pin into the hem of one of his trouser legs, which seemed to be on the verge of becoming undone. Then, using Brian's bed for support, she awkwardly climbed to her feet and gazed at her grandson's reflection in the wardrobe mirror. He was a skinny boy, not particularly tall, with wavy dark brown hair and deep blue eyes.

'Now, what *are* we going to do about that school blazer of yours?' she asked with a sigh, staring at Brian as though he had suddenly taken it upon himself to shrink before her very eyes. 'It really is much too big for you, my dear,' she said, tilting her head sideways and staring at him in disappointment. 'Much too big. Didn't you try it on in the shop, dear?'

'Mum didn't have time to go to the shops,' said Brian. 'She's been really busy. Y'know, with the new job and stuff. So she ordered it on the Internet.'

'The Inter-what, dear?' asked Brian's grandmother, looking slightly baffled.

'The Internet,' repeated Brian.

'And what's that then?'

'Oh right, erm… well, the Internet's sort of a massive electronic shop,' explained Brian. 'And, well, you can buy things on it using a computer and then get them delivered to your house.'

'Oh,' said his grandmother, still somewhat bemused. 'And what do you do if the clothes you've bought from this electronic shop don't fit, dear?'

Brian shrugged his shoulders. 'Well, you just send them back in the post.'

'You just send them back in the post?' repeated his grandmother, aghast and shaking her head in disbelief. 'Dear oh dear, it all sounds much too complicated. No, I think it will be much simpler to just pop into Kingsbury's in the high street and buy you another, smaller blazer. Yes, I'm sure your mother will be able to return this one,' she said. 'Now let me see, your granddad's popping out to see George Newtblaster this afternoon. He owns the second-hand book shop opposite the butcher's,' she explained. 'Yes, if you go along too, you'll be able to make sure that your granddad doesn't come back with anything other than the book he's actually ordered! Normally when he visits George Newtblaster he tends to sell your granddad at least four or five other books that he doesn't actually need. And goodness knows we have enough books in the house already!' she said in a slightly louder voice so that her husband might hear her.

Brian scratched his stomach. The bristly shirt was irritating his skin and his collar had popped up again.

'And then, after your granddad's collected his book, you can pop in to Kingsbury's on your way home and pick up your new blazer,' continued his grandmother. 'It's on the corner of Gargoyle Lane, opposite the chemist. Your granddad knows where it is. But do make sure you try the blazer on whilst you're there, dear, won't you? Now, where has your granddad got to? Henry!'

There was no answer.

'Henry!' Brian's grandmother shrilled again.

But there was still no answer.

She tutted. 'Do you know, I'm sure your granddad's going deaf,' she remarked, taking Brian's blazer from him and slipping it into a large white carrier bag. 'Be a dear, will you, and go see what he's up to? He's probably in his study.'

Leaving his grandmother to hang up his four remaining school shirts, Brian climbed the short staircase up to his granddad's study and knocked upon the door. Maybe this would be a good time to ask him what he had meant in the garden earlier when he had claimed that his dad had never worked for a firm of accountants.

'Hello? Granddad?'

There was no reply.

He knocked again, more loudly this time. But still no answer came. Cautiously Brian twisted the round, brass door handle. It was stiff and quite difficult to turn. But the door did not open. It was quite obviously locked.

'He's not there,' Brian shouted back to his grandmother, forcing his shirt collar back down again.

'What, dear?'

'I said he isn't here.'

'Oh? Well, he must be downstairs then,' his grandmother replied. 'Probably thieving some of my rock cakes,' she said, laughing.

Not likely, thought Brian as he trudged down the two flights of stairs and into the gloomy lilac-patterned hallway. He stopped

25

momentarily, peering curiously up at the ancient suit of armour that was propped up so precariously against the alcove wall. Cobwebs hung from it everywhere. Brian wondered why his grandparents owned such a strange antique and where it had originally come from. And, more importantly, what battles it had been worn in. He gazed admiringly up at the knight's dusty helmet and wondered if it might possibly fit him. But a loud THUD behind him, as if something very heavy had fallen upon the living room floor, instantly drove away all thoughts of Brian trying on the knight's helmet. Instead he swung the living room door open and poked his head inside.

'Hello? Granddad? Is that you?' he asked.

But the living room was empty. Which was very strange indeed. For Brian was almost certain – no, he was positive – that the loud THUDDING noise he had heard had come from somewhere inside. It was only when he was about to close the door and leave that he noticed the book.

It was lying on the patterned carpet just inches from his feet. In fact, if he had taken another step forwards he would surely have tripped over it. Brian bent down and picked the hardback book up. Unsurprisingly, it looked and smelt incredibly old. But then, thought Brian, everything looked and smelt incredibly old in his grandparents' house. The book's ripped sleeve was a dull, creamy colour and was so torn and shredded in places that it barely clung to its cover.

Brian carefully flipped the book over in his hands and tried to discern its title. In faded scarlet letters, it read '*Open Doors and How to Close Them – 4th Edition*', whilst beneath this was printed the author's name. But these words were even more discoloured than the writing above them and Brian couldn't work out what they said at all. Very carefully, so not to tear the book's sleeve any further, he opened it at the first page, which was blank. And so he turned to the next page. But, strangely, this too was blank. As were

26

the third, fourth, fifth and sixth pages. And when he quickly flicked through the whole book he discovered that all the pages were blank. There wasn't a single word or letter printed on any of them.

Why would all the pages of a book be blank, Brian wondered? What was the point? Maybe the pages had simply faded over time, because of the book's age, which was why the words were no longer visible? He quickly picked a page at random and studied it more closely. But it made no difference. He couldn't find or see a single word, nor a chapter heading or even a page number.

Puzzled, Brian closed the curious book and went to replace it in the bookshelf behind the living room door from which it must have surely fallen. But, oddly, he couldn't find an empty space for it. In fact, there were so many books crammed into the bookshelf he couldn't even pull a book from it, let alone squeeze another one in! So where had the book he was holding fallen from, he wondered?

Brian searched the next bookcase and then another. But each of these was exactly the same, so tightly crammed full of books that it was impossible to stuff another one in anywhere. Even more puzzled, he glanced at some of the other bookcases that lined the living room walls and there, opposite him, he suddenly noticed a shelf which, although overflowing with different-sized books, had the tiniest gap at one end. Brian stepped a little nearer. Had the book he was holding possibly fallen from here? The gap on the shelf wasn't very big. Brian glanced over his shoulder to where he had first discovered the book lying upon the carpet. He frowned, confused. The book he was holding couldn't possibly have fallen from this shelf, he thought. Brian measured the distance by pacing across the carpet. It was six feet. And yet when he gently slid the oddly titled book back on to the shelf it was a perfect fit!

Now thoroughly bewildered, Brian wandered into the hallway and downstairs to the dining room whilst still trying to figure out in his head how a book could have fallen from the bookshelf and then landed almost six feet away. The dining room was empty and his granddad wasn't in the kitchen either. Brian opened the back door and poked his head out into the garden but the rickety wooden bench against the kitchen wall was empty.

CRASH!

A sound like a mini explosion erupted from somewhere within the house. Brian whirled around and immediately ran back inside. He arrived at the now-closed living room door in the very same moment that his grandmother did, almost knocking her over.

'Oh, thank goodness,' said his grandmother, a bright pink handbag swinging madly from her arm and a worried look upon her face. 'You're all right, Brian. I thought for one dreadful moment that…'

A loud THUD against the living room door made them both jump.

Brian leapt backwards. 'W-what was that?' he asked, his voice shaking ever so slightly.

'I don't know,' replied his grandmother, uneasily. 'Where's your granddad?'

'I couldn't find him—' said Brian, who was interrupted by an even louder THUD against the living room door making it rattle within its frame. 'Is it burglars?' he asked uneasily. 'Are we being burgled?'

'Oh my, I do hope not,' replied his grandmother, the colour suddenly draining from her face. 'Whatever could they want? Quick, Brian, get that sword.' she said, pointing towards the suit of armour in the alcove behind them, her hand shaking badly.

Brian stared at his grandmother in alarm. Were they really being burgled? And, if so, how many burglars were there and what on earth could they be stealing? The living room was mostly full of dusty old books and not much else. Surely they weren't worth anything, or were they? Perhaps the burglars were after a piece of furniture? Some of the tables his grandparents owned looked at least a hundred years old. Maybe one was a really valuable antique?

'Not that I think we'll need the sword,' added his grandmother, seeing the worried look upon Brian's face. 'We'll just use it for, er... protection,' she said a little unconvincingly. 'To scare the burglars off.'

Brian grabbed the sword's cobwebbed hilt and, with difficulty, managed to pull the weapon free from the knight's grasp. It was much heavier than it looked and Brian struggled not only to raise the sword but also to keep it steady even when using both his hands.

More loud THUDS against the living room door.

'Oh my,' said his grandmother in alarm. 'Where on earth is your granddad when we need him?' she remarked anxiously.

Another THUD followed by another and then silence.

Brian's grandmother took a deep breath, stepped nervously forward, and turned the door handle. But the living room door did not open. She looked at Brian, puzzled. 'It can't be locked,' she said curiously. 'It doesn't have a lock.'

Balancing the sword unsteadily in one hand Brian tried opening the door himself. But much to his surprise he found that he couldn't open it either. Puzzled, he tried again. But this time he gripped the door handle more tightly and gave the door a heavy shove with his shoulder. It opened, but only ever so slightly.

'Perhaps if we pushed together?' suggested his grandmother hopefully.

So, between them, Brian and his grandmother heaved their shoulders against the living room door. It was slow work but gradually, inch-by-inch, the door eventually opened just enough for Brian to squeeze himself through, dragging the sword behind him. And what he found inside almost made his eyes pop out of their sockets!

For strewn across the whole of the living room floor were piles upon piles of books. Hardbacks and paperbacks of varying sizes and colours lay scattered all over the carpet like a massive jumble of topsy-turvy stepping-stones. It was as if every bookcase in the living room had suddenly somehow exploded, spewing books everywhere. There were books lying in the fireplace, books lying amongst the cushions on the sofa, books that had knocked over lamps and ornaments, breaking them, and there were even books hanging from the curtain track!

Behind him Brian heard somebody groan. And there slumped against the living room door, half covered in books, was his granddad, his thin-rimmed glasses hanging haphazardly from his nose whilst what little hair he had looked like it had just been combed with a firework. Dropping the sword, Brian helped him struggle to his feet and over to one of the cherry-patterned sofas.

'Brian dear, are you all right?' his grandmother called anxiously.

'Yeah, I'm okay,' said Brian, heaving away some of the books that had been blocking the living room door and yanking it open.

'Goodness gracious me!' exclaimed his grandmother, staring at all the books strewn over the carpet in horror. 'What on earth...' and then she spotted her husband, ashen-faced, sitting upon the nearest sofa. 'Oh my, what happened, Henry? Are you all right?' she asked, scurrying over to him.

'Yes, yes, I'm fine,' coughed her husband, who was busily trying to straighten his untidy hair. 'Just a little shaken, that's all.'

'You've got a cut on your head,' pointed out Brian, who was wondering how in the world his granddad had got into the living room. For, just moments earlier, when Brian had searched it, the living room had been empty. He was sure of it. So how then had his granddad got inside? There was only one door and the windows were far too small to crawl through. And, anyway, why on earth would his granddad crawl through a window to get into his own living room? That was ridiculous. Perhaps his granddad had been asleep on one of the sofas and he'd just never noticed? Old people, he had observed, were always falling asleep at odd times. But even more puzzling than this was why all the books in the living room had taken it upon themselves to fly off the shelves. None of it made any sense.

'Oh Henry, Brian's right, you're bleeding,' said his grandmother in alarm, suddenly noticing the cut above her husband's left eye.

'It's only a scratch, Doris. No need to fuss.'

'Nonsense!' exclaimed his wife sternly. 'That cut needs seeing to. Brian dear, could you pop up to the bathroom and fetch me the antiseptic cream from the cabinet and some plasters too, please?'

'Yeah. Okay,' said Brian, who, as he tiptoed around the fallen books and into the hallway, was still trying to work out how his granddad had got into the living room without him noticing.

'And can you also get me a bowl of warm water from the kitchen?' added his grandmother as Brian ran up the stairs and into the bathroom.

'Okay,' he shouted back.

A few moments later Brian had all the things his grandmother had asked for and, as he left the kitchen and slowly climbed upstairs, being careful not to spill any of the water, he could overhear his grandparents whispering.

'But we agreed, Henry, didn't we, that whilst Brian's staying with us we wouldn't use it,' scolded his wife. 'It's too risky. What if he had seen you?'

'I know,' replied his granddad. 'But…'

'And besides, that particular book is worn out,' his grandmother continued, ignoring her husband's protests. 'The amount of times I've warned you about it. Honestly! Remember last year when we were looking after Geraldine Simpson's cat. It opened on its own, didn't it, and we lost Cuddles for four days. If the manager of the Dragon's Claw hadn't found her when he did I don't know what we would have said to poor Geraldine! Goodness knows where her cat had been. Its hair had turned green and spiky and it smelt like a public toilet. And surely I don't have to remind you what was stuck all over its tail! Disgusting! I was so embarrassed!'

31

'But this was important, Doris,' argued her husband, more sternly now.

Curious, Brian quietly crept a little nearer to the living room door.

'Henry! For goodness' sake keep your voice down,' reprimanded his wife. 'Now what exactly was so important that you had to visit Barnaby Katobi? I assume that's where you disappeared to?'

'Yes, Doris,' his granddad replied. He took a long, deep breath before adding, 'The Diefromen was seen again last night.'

There was an uneasy silence for many moments and Brian found himself desperately straining to hear what might be said next. Cautiously he stepped just a little nearer. What in the world, he wondered, was a Diefromen?

'Where, Henry? Where was it seen?' asked his grandmother anxiously.

'Brute Close,' replied her husband, gravely. 'Monty Yatlor is pretty sure he saw it in Brute Close.'

'But, that's where Imelda Cumberbatch lives!' gasped his grandmother. 'Henry, we should have told Elizabeth. It's not safe here for Brian. We should have tried to explain…'

'And told her what exactly?' asked his granddad, sounding exasperated. 'We don't know anything for certain, and even if we did do you think Elizabeth would have believed us?'

Brian heard his grandmother sigh. 'No, I suppose you're right, Henry. What did Barnaby Katobi have to say when you saw him?'

'He thinks the melted road signs are possibly "markers" of some type,' whispered his granddad. 'He's arranging to send an emergency Appealcall for the Committee to meet later this afternoon and they'll make a decision then as to whether we should evacuate or not.'

Brian heard his grandmother gasp and whisper something to her husband that he couldn't quite hear. Somehow he had to get slightly nearer to the living room door. He took another careful step forwards and immediately wished he hadn't. A floorboard creaked noisily, giving him away, and at once his grandparents' whispering ceased.

'Mind your step,' warned his grandmother when Brian appeared at the living room door carrying in one hand the bowl of water and in the other the antiseptic cream and plasters.

Brian weaved his way carefully through the fallen books to where his grandmother was sitting on the cherry-patterned settee next to her husband, a worried look upon her face.

'Are you okay?' he asked his granddad

'Er, yes, I'm fine,' replied his granddad. 'But the living room is rather a mess, isn't it?'

Looking about him Brian nodded. The floor of the living room looked like an eruption of books had just burst forth from it. 'What happened?' he asked.

'Oh, well, it's, er… subsidence, Brian,' replied his granddad a little awkwardly as his wife pulled a handkerchief from the sleeve of her blouse and began cleaning the blood from his forehead. 'Lots of houses suffer from it. It's the clay soil. I mean, well, this house is over 200 years old, don't you know, and every now and then the walls move a little out of line, so to speak, and it makes the books fall out of their bookcases. Very annoying. And it's not the first time it's happened either. Why, it only happened last week to number 53 up the road.'

Brian's grandmother dipped her handkerchief into the bowl of water and dabbed it gently upon the cut above her husband's eye. 'You're lucky you only received a cut to the head,' she remarked, smudging some cream on to her husband's wound and making him wince painfully. Then, taping a plaster firmly over the cut, she kissed him softly on the cheek, forcing him to smile, and said, 'There, that should stop your brains from falling out for now. How do you feel? Do you want a hand getting up?'

33

'No, no, I'm fine, Doris,' replied her husband, climbing to his feet and staring unhappily at the piles of books strewn all over the living room floor. 'Better clear this lot up first before heading down to Newtblaster's. Will you give me a hand, Brian?'

'Yeah, sure,' replied Brian, bending down and picking up the nearest couple of books.

'Well, in that case, I'll go and make us all a nice fresh pot of tea,' said Brian's grandmother, tiptoeing around the books towards the living room door. 'And I'll get some rock cakes from the larder too. They're still lovely and fresh. How does that sound?'

'Oh... er... very nice,' said her husband, trying to sound enthusiastic. 'Only not too many for me though, Doris. Feeling a bit dizzy,' he added hastily.

'What about you, Brian?' asked his grandmother. 'Three rock cakes with your tea, dear?'

Brian nodded absentmindedly. He had been staring at one of the books lying on the floor. Straightening his shirt collar he bent down and picked it up. The book's cover was scorched as though it had almost caught fire. Black soot was rubbing on to his fingers. He turned the book over in his hands and as he did so parts of the spine began to crumble away and fall to the floor. Brian gazed at the book's dull sleeve in surprise. Its title, in faded scarlet letters, read 'Open Doors and How to Close Them – 4th Edition'.

Chapter 3

THE MEN WHO DISAPPEARED

Brian had rather been hoping that the brief walk to 'Newtblaster's Book Emporium' would give him the chance to ask his granddad some of the unanswered questions that were buzzing so madly, like angry wasps, within his head. What in the world, for example, was a Diefromen? It didn't even sound like a proper word. And what had his granddad really been doing in the living room when all the books had exploded from the shelves? He certainly didn't believe that story about it being subsidence. Subsidence, he knew, happened over a long period of time, years in fact. And, besides, why had nothing else in the house fallen from a shelf or toppled over? Why had it only happened in the living room?

He also wanted to know what that strange piece of paper was that he had discovered in the back garden. Had it really been a letter addressed to his granddad and had that massive, black bird really been trying to deliver it? Even now that idea sounded completely crazy to Brian. How could it have been a letter? The piece of paper had practically been blank. And yet it had been sealed with red candle wax. Not only that, but it had also been clearly addressed to his granddad, 'Henry Pankhurst'.

Other questions were puzzling Brian too. That book, *Open Doors and How to Close Them*? Quite apart from the extremely odd title Brian wanted to know why it was that every single page of the book had been empty. Not a single word was printed anywhere! And when he had come across it again, later that morning when he had helped his granddad tidy up the living room, how had the book become so scorched and burnt?

However, what was troubling Brian most of all, what he had wanted to ask his granddad more than any other question, was what he had meant earlier that morning when he had said that his father hadn't worked for a firm of accountants. Which was quite ridiculous, because Brian's father had always been an accountant! Every morning for as long as Brian could remember his father would always leave for work at eight o'clock sharp with his umbrella in one hand and a battered, black leather briefcase in the other, which in worn silver lettering had the words 'Harvey & Norris – Chartered Accountants & Registered Auditors' printed on one side.

'Granddad?' began Brian as they waited for a motorbike to pass them by before crossing a road, 'You know this morning, in the garden, what did you mean exactly when you said that Dad didn't work for a firm of accountants?'

'Been wondering when you'd ask me about that,' replied his granddad, awkwardly.

'It's just that, well, Dad's always been an accountant,' said Brian matter-of-factly.

'That's what you were meant to believe,' said his granddad.

'But he's worked for Harvey & Norris for years and years,' argued Brian. 'And he even had a briefcase with the company's name printed on it.'

'I'm afraid that isn't true,' said his granddad, rubbing his chin apprehensively, as they waited for a car to reverse out of a drive. 'This isn't going to be easy for you to accept, Brian, but Richard – sorry, I mean your father – is not an accountant. I'm afraid he never has been and I doubt very much that he ever will be. Actually, to be honest, maths was never really one of his stronger subjects when he was at school. I reckon your father told you that he worked as an accountant simply because that's what he and your mother wanted you to believe.'

'What?' said Brian, feeling utterly confused. 'I don't understand. What do you mean that's what my mum and dad wanted me to believe?'

'Er, well, you see, Brian,' began his granddad uncomfortably, 'your mother found it very difficult to accept certain, erm... aspects about your father's life.'

'Like what?' Brian asked, following his granddad round a bend, into another road.

'Oh dear. This is really is quite tricky,' his granddad mumbled, more to himself than to Brian. 'Let me think. Okay, right. Like a lot of people in the world, Brian, your mother doesn't believe in things that can't easily be explained. She's what some people would call a sceptic. Which basically means that she has difficulty in accepting that certain things exist or even the possibility that they might exist. And because of this she had trouble, at first, in accepting what your father did for a living and, more importantly, what he believed in.' A girl on a bicycle shot past them both along the pavement, only narrowly missing his granddad. 'Which is why your mother,' he continued, stumbling on the kerb, 'wanted you to lead a life far away from all the things that... couldn't easily be explained by modern science. She wanted you to experience what regular children of your age experienced, to have the same opportunities as them. But she conceded that a time would eventually come when she and your father would sit you down and explain exactly what he really did every day when he pretended to go to work at Harvey & Norris. I had wrongly assumed that when your father left, or perhaps I should say disappeared, your mother might have explained a little of this to you.'

'Wait a minute!' said Brian, his head spinning madly as if a tornado had suddenly been let loose within it. 'Are you trying to tell me that my dad had some sort of secret job?'

'Yes, Brian, he did, in a manner of speaking'

'And that he didn't leave me and my mum? That he just... sort of... disappeared one day?'

His granddad nodded. 'Yes, that's right, Brian,' he said quite calmly, as if people disappearing off the face of the planet was an everyday occurrence. 'Your father certainly never left you of his own free will. That I know for certain. He loved you and your mother very much!'

Brian was suddenly speechless. He couldn't believe what he was hearing! Was it really true? That his father, who for as long as he could remember had always worked as an accountant for Harvey & Norris, had, in fact, left each morning for another, completely different job? A secret job that, for some reason, his parents did not want him to know anything about? It sounded ridiculous. And what did his granddad mean when he said that his father had disappeared?

As they turned into the high street Brian was about to ask all these questions and more when his granddad stopped and announced, 'Here we are.'

Newtblaster's Book Emporium was a tiny and old-looking building squeezed between two modern and much taller shops. Its misshapen slate roof was bowed and sunken and its faded red brick walls leant so dangerously inwards that it almost looked as if the ancient structure might collapse in upon itself at any moment. It looked completely out of place next to its more fashionable neighbours.

Brian followed his granddad through the unusually small shop doorway, staring curiously through its grimy front window at the display of ancient leather-bound books whose pages had grown yellow with age. Who, he wondered, would ever want to read *The Essays and Miscellanies of Ebenezer Gruntdiggle: Comprising All*

His Works Collected Under the Title of – Conversations with Angry Dragons or *The Complete and Utter Book of Bat Droppings* and *How the Crazy Cows of Cuttlemead Turned Completely Crazy*?

A brass bell above the shop door rang out shrilly, announcing their entrance.

'Hello, Henry,' said a cheerful, ginger-headed man suddenly springing up from behind a high, wooden counter.

'All right, George?' said Brian's granddad. 'How's business?'

'Oh, not too bad,' he said, adjusting his thick-rimmed black glasses. 'Can't complain. Finally managed to sell the Ivan Chestacoff book this week.'

Brian's granddad blew a silent whistle, seemingly impressed. 'Not the first edition?'

The ginger-headed man nodded.

'Blimey, George! I never ever thought you'd ever sell that. Who on earth bought it?'

'A woman. Never seen her before. Not local anyway. She bartered me down. Made me knock off £25. I don't know what came over me. Must have been feeling in a very generous mood. Can't say I'm not glad to see the back of it though. Brought me nothing but bad luck, that book. Now who's this with you today?' he asked, smiling pleasantly at Brian who was hovering a few feet behind his granddad.

'This here's my grandson, Brian,' said Brian's granddad, turning proudly towards him. 'He's going to be staying with me and Doris for a bit, George. Brian, this is George Newtblaster. He owns this book shop.'

The ginger-haired man leant over the counter and held out his hand, which Brian shook.

'Pleased to meet you,' said Newtblaster enthusiastically. 'Oh, by the way, Henry,' he said, peering guardedly at the nearest aisle of bookshelves as if to make sure that nobody else could hear what he was about to say. 'Been keeping this by for you' he whispered with a tap on his nose and a knowing look, and he immediately disappeared through a door behind the counter

The brass bell above the shop door rang loudly again making Brian jump, and a very tall man with a curly moustache, wearing a long black coat, stepped inside. It must have started to rain because he was carrying a dark blue umbrella.

'Afternoon,' shouted the tall man in a loud, booming voice to Brian's granddad. 'Wasn't expecting to see you here, Henry. Only got the Appealcall myself not five minutes ago. Left Margaret looking after the shop. Thought it best not to mention any of this to her. No sense in worrying the poor woman. But this is a bad business, Henry, it really is,' the tall man remarked, brushing the rain from his coat and trying to shake his umbrella dry. 'First Sneaky Hollow, then Gargoyle Lane and even Brute Close. Can't remember the last time such a thing occurred. Apparently Monty Yatlor claims to have spotted a Diefro…'

'This is Brian, my grandson,' cut in Brian's granddad.

'What's that?' bellowed the tall man.

'I said this is Brian, my grandson,' repeated Brian's granddad, a little more loudly this time.

'I can't hear you.'

'I said this is Brian my… is your hearing aid switched on?'

'What are you saying? Speak up!'

'Your hearing aid!' shouted Brian's granddad hoarsely. 'Is it switched on?'

'Oh, hang on a minute,' shouted the tall man. 'I haven't got my hearing aid switched on. Trying to save the batteries. Ah, that's better. Hello there, Addison Aldwinkle at your service,' he announced, shaking Brian's hand vigorously. 'Oh my! Don't tell me this is Richard's son,' he said, fiddling with his hearing aid and turning excitedly to Brian's granddad, who nodded in return.

'My dear boy, why, I knew your father very well indeed. We were in the same cricket team. He was one hell of a batsman, a hell

40

of a batsman,' he repeated before adding, 'And not a bad bowler either for that matter! Afternoon, George.'

George Newtblaster had reappeared behind the shop counter carrying in his hands an incredibly old-looking, leather-bound book. 'Oh, er, hello there Addison,' he said a little sheepishly, immediately pushing the dusty-looking book underneath the counter. He turned to Brian's granddad and whispered, 'Has he got his hearing aid switched on?'

'What was that?' asked Aldwinkle.

'I said I see it's started to rain,' said Newtblaster.

'What?' said Aldwinkle following Newtblaster's gaze out of the shop window. 'Yes, typical, isn't it? No sooner do I get the Appealcall and step outside than the heavens open up upon me. Doesn't bode well, does it?' he remarked, shaking his head and curling his long black moustache tightly between his fingers. 'Anyway, must dash,' he said suddenly, and he strode purposefully off down an aisle signed 'History & Transport'.

'Poor fellow. Lost most of his hearing in an accident a few years ago,' explained Brian's granddad regretfully as the bell above the shop door rang again.

A very portly fellow dressed in an ill-fitting brown suit who seemed to be as wide as he was tall stood before them. And he was soaked to the skin.

'Dreadful weather!' he puffed whilst mopping his brow with a handkerchief that he had retrieved from somewhere within his jacket pocket.

'Hello, Gordon,' said Newtblaster.

'Oh, hello there George, Henry and...'

'Brian, my grandson,' said Brian's granddad, proudly. 'Brian, this is Gordon Grubshackle.'

'Hi,' said Brian.

41

Grubshackle shook Brian's hand weakly. 'Dreadful weather! And in August too,' he remarked in distress as a sudden flash of light momentarily filled the sky outside.

Brian, whose hand was now unpleasantly wet, wiped it uncomfortably on the back of his jeans.

'That weathergirl on the television last night didn't mention a single word about rain, let alone thunderstorms!' complained Grubshackle. 'I just pray my carnations will be all right. Didn't have time to bring them in from the back garden when I got the Appealcall,' he said as a booming clap of thunder rolled noisily somewhere far above them, making the shop lights momentarily dim.

'Nothing to be frightened of,' said Newtblaster reassuringly to Brian, who must have looked a little nervous as the shop about him suddenly fell dark. 'I'm afraid the wiring is very old. Happens all the time when there's a thunderstorm.'

'Entering the Homefield flower show this year, Gordon?' asked Brian's granddad.

'Of course,' replied Grubshackle, thrusting his chest out importantly. 'Have to defend my title, Henry. If, or rather I should say when, I win the Homefield Trophy next month it'll be my third consecutive victory! Nobody's done that before. Not even Hilary Gegglesworth! And my roses are looking especially good this year too, even if I do say so myself.'

'And what's your secret?' asked Brian's granddad.

Grubshackle smiled slyly. 'Now that would be telling, Henry. Usual row, I assume, George?'

Newtblaster nodded. 'That's right, Gordon,' he said, gesturing towards the aisle signposted 'History & Transport'. And with that the small, round man disappeared down it, still wiping his brow and still complaining, presumably to himself, about the unseasonal weather.

42

In between the continual dimming of the shop lights and the pouring rain outside a further six customers came into the bookshop and, very strangely, all of them, Brian noticed, with the exception of a woman who was lost and looking for a village called 'Tumbleton', either asked for or were directed to the aisle marked 'History & Transport'.

Brian had absolutely no idea why this particular aisle of books was proving so popular. It wasn't as if 'History & Transport' was even an interesting subject. It sounded about as appealing as watching paint dry! And what exactly, wondered Brian, was an Appealcall? At least four of the customers who had been directed to the 'History & Transport' aisle had mentioned one. And where, thought Brian suddenly, had all the customers disappeared to? For none of them had returned. None of them had actually bought anything. Something strange was going on and Brian was determined to find out what it was. And five minutes later, when yet another customer came into the bookshop enquiring about 'History & Transport', Brian got his chance.

'Afternoon, Stanley,' said Newtblaster cheerfully as a thin-looking man dressed in a long brown cloak entered the shop.

'Oh, hello, George,' the man replied with a long yawn. 'Oh my, I do apologise!' he said politely, placing a hand over his open mouth. 'That was rather rude of me, wasn't it? But, well, to be honest I've had rather a night of it, I'm afraid. Ah, Henry, I'm glad I've bumped into you,' he said, stepping towards Brian's granddad. 'Because it would seem that I have acquired a rather unwelcome lodger.'

'A lodger, you say?' remarked Brian's granddad, enquiringly.

'Yes, that's right,' the thin man said, yawning again. 'And all my attempts at making it... er... leave have so far failed. So I thought it was about time I called upon the assistance of an expert in such matters, so to speak.'

'Oh, I see,' said Brian's granddad, nodding. 'By the way, this is my grandson Brian. Brian, this is Stanley Clutterbucket.'

'I'm very pleased to meet you, Brian,' said Clutterbucket, smiling warmly.

'And what exactly do you think this lodger of yours is?' asked Brian's granddad curiously.

'Well, I'm by no means certain, you understand,' murmured Clutterbucket, leaning forwards. 'But I think,' he said in barely a whisper, 'it's a... howling hamster!'

Newtblaster drew a sharp intake of breath.

'Pesky little blighters,' remarked Brian's granddad.

'Very tricky,' added Newtblaster with a knowing look. 'Henrietta Hopkirk had one hiding in her cupboard under the stairs last year. Took a month to catch it, or so I heard.'

Stanley Clutterbucket's face blanched. 'Goodness,' he managed to stammer. 'I do hope it doesn't take quite that long. It's been bad enough these past three nights. I haven't had a wink of sleep and I'm nowhere near to catching it. So I was wondering, if it's not too much trouble, Henry...'

'Not at all,' replied Brian's granddad. 'Shall we say tonight? About 7.30pm?'

'Oh, that would be perfect,' said Clutterbucket, looking very relieved indeed and shaking Brian's granddad's hand gratefully. 'Usual row, I take it, George?'

'That's right, Stanley,' Newtblaster said with a nod, pointing towards the 'History & Transport' aisle.

'Mr Newtblaster,' began Brian, spotting an opportunity to follow Stanley Clutterbucket. 'Do you have any books that I might like to read?'

'Why, of course,' replied Newtblaster enthusiastically, pointing to another aisle further along the bookshop marked 'Children's Books'. 'Everything's in alphabetical order,' he explained.

'Okay. Thanks,' said Brian, heading off towards the children's aisle. Behind him he could hear Newtblaster rummaging under the shop counter and saying to his granddad in a hushed tone, 'Well, I discovered it in a house clearance last week, Henry. Found it in a box with a load of cookery books. A tenth edition of *Ghosts – Why They Can Never Leave the Scene of Their Death* by Gipper Taylor. I just couldn't believe it. Not seen a copy as good as this for almost twenty years. Thought of you immediately.'

Brian glanced casually over his shoulder. His granddad and Newtblaster were busy poring over the old, leather-bound book that Newtblaster had been concealing under the shop counter. Hastily slipping past the aisle signposted 'Children's Books', Brian ducked into a different row filled with what looked like geography books. He peered through them, into the 'History & Transport' aisle that Clutterbucket had entered moments earlier.

Not far ahead of him Brian could just make out Stanley Clutterbucket. He could see that he'd already reached the end of the opposite aisle and appeared to be busily searching a row of books. However, Brian was too far away to see exactly what Clutterbucket was up to and so, very carefully, he tiptoed gradually nearer, until he was finally standing behind him, peering at the thin, cloaked man through a large collection of folded maps.

Brian stared curiously as Stanley Clutterbucket gently ran his fingers over a row of different-sized hardback books, stopping only when he reached a large white book with scarlet letters, which was tightly squeezed between two even thicker books. Brian gawped at the book's title, which he could just make out: *Open Doors and How to Close Them – 134th Edition*. It was the exact same book that his granddad owned, except for the edition.

Clutterbucket began pulling the book from the shelf but stopped after a moment, as if changing his mind, leaving the pale volume hanging precariously from a row above his head. But instead of pushing the book back into place Clutterbucket's hand wandered to

45

the row below, this time lingering upon a very large black hardback book entitled *A Door for Every Room*. Clutterbucket started to remove this book from the shelf too. But, just as before, he suddenly stopped, leaving the book protruding awkwardly from the shelf.

Brian stared at Clutterbucket in puzzlement. What on earth was he doing, he wondered as he quietly watched him half-remove two further books from a lower shelf. He squinted at their titles, trying to discern what each was called. One book was titled *Great Ways to Cook Fish* whilst the other was called *He Who Seeks Council*.

However, before removing a fifth book, this one green and entitled *The Secret and Mysterious Chambers*, Clutterbucket first glanced cautiously up and then down the aisle he was standing in. It was only then, when Clutterbucket seemed to think that he was completely alone, that he began to remove it. And instantly the bookshop was thrown into complete darkness. A strange whooshing noise momentarily filled Brian's ears. A stale-smelling breeze brushed against his face. Everywhere around him was completely and utterly black. But then the shop lights began to splutter before suddenly springing back to life. And not for the first time that day Brian found himself frowning in puzzlement. Clutterbucket wasn't there. Brian pushed apart the maps that he'd been spying through and stared awkwardly up and down the 'History & Transport' aisle. It was empty. Clutterbucket, it seemed, had completely disappeared.

Chapter 4

SAM & HADLEY

By the time Brian and his granddad had returned from Newtblaster's Book Emporium and Kingsbury's, where he had successfully managed to purchase a much smaller school blazer to replace the one that his mother had bought on the Internet, his grandmother was already busy in the kitchen preparing dinner.

'Won't be long now, Brian dear,' she said, looking up at an antique clock hanging from a wall and wiping her brow. 'About another fifteen minutes. I hope you like roast beef. Oh Henry! For heaven's sake, what else did George Newtblaster sell you this time?' she asked, annoyed, spying the white plastic bag her husband was trying to conceal under his arm.

'But Doris…' he began.

'I mean, it's not as if we don't have enough books in the house already without you buying another one every time you visit George Newtblaster. Honestly, we have so many books I often wonder why we don't open our own bookshop! What is it this time?' she demanded, crossing her arms irritably.

'Er… I think something's boiling over,' said Brian, gesturing towards the oven where hot water was spilling out over the lip of a saucepan and onto the hob underneath.

'Oh my goodness!' cried Brian's grandmother, immediately turning down the gas and grabbing a dishcloth to mop the water up

47

with. 'On second thoughts, Henry, I don't want to know what it is you've bought. Just put it away and wash your hands ready for dinner. I've already laid the table. You too, Brian dear.'

Brian followed his granddad up the two flights of stairs to the bathroom and waited impatiently outside to wash his hands. He was feeling exasperated and annoyed. After leaving Newtblaster's Book Emporium his granddad had stubbornly refused to say any more about his father or even discuss where all the customers had mysteriously disappeared to in the bookshop. 'I'm sorry, Brian, but I really do need to telephone and speak to your mother first,' his granddad had said. It was as if he had suddenly regretted telling Brian anything at all. Even that his father hadn't left them as his mother had always implied.

Later, after they had eaten dinner, which to Brian's surprise was actually quite nice and not anywhere near as bad as he had feared, his granddad announced he was leaving to go to Stanley Clutterbucket's.

'Do you want to take some rock cakes with you, Henry?' asked his wife as her husband got up from the dinner table. 'Only I still have plenty left,' she remarked as she retrieved a large see-through plastic tub, which was so crammed full of rock cakes that Brian wondered how the lid could possibly stay on. 'And I always think poor Stanley looks so thin. He needs fattening up if you ask me.'

'Good idea,' said her husband; he winked at Brian and whispered, 'It'll mean less rock cakes for us,' before adding, 'But be quick, Doris, because I said I'd be at Stanley's for 7.30 and I want to get back tonight before it gets dark.'

After his granddad had left, Brian helped clear away the plates and cutlery and after drying up the dishes as his grandmother washed he went upstairs to the living room and flopped unhappily into one of the large cherry-patterned armchairs.

No sooner had he done this, however, than his grandmother came in carrying two cups of tea. 'Thought you might like another one, Brian dear,' she said sympathetically, handing him a china cup and saucer and sitting opposite him.

'Oh. Er, thanks,' said Brian, doing his best to sound enthusiastic, although secretly he was quite pleased and rather relived that his grandmother hadn't felt the need to bring any rock cakes with her too. He wasn't sure that his teeth could take many more of them.

His grandmother retrieved some knitting from a bag next to her and began noisily threading maroon wool between two long needles. 'Now, what's the matter, dear?' she enquired.

'What? Oh. Er…' said Brian distractedly, trying not to spill any of his tea into the saucer.

'You haven't been yourself all evening. Are you missing your mother?'

'No,' said Brian. 'I mean, yes, I am missing Mum but…'

'Well, it won't be for long, dear,' said his grandmother, smiling understandingly. 'Once your mother's settled in to her new job—'

'It's not that,' interrupted Brian.

'Oh?' said his grandmother, looking up from her knitting, somewhat surprised, and setting it aside to take a sip of her tea. 'Then what is it, dear?' she asked.

'It's Dad. It's what Granddad said about my dad.'

'And what did your granddad say exactly?' she asked, arching her eyebrows suspiciously.

'He said that Dad never left us, me and Mum, I mean. That he just, er… sort of disappeared. Is that true?'

His grandmother nodded and with a heavy sigh said, 'Yes, Brian dear. It's true, and that's really as much as your granddad and I or anybody else knows.'

'But nobody just disappears,' remarked Brian. 'Where did he go?'

'I'm afraid the only thing we know for certain, Brian, is that your father left for work one morning in August last year, but what happened to him after that… well, we just don't know.'

'But he was reported missing, right? I mean my mum reported him missing, didn't she?'

His grandmother smiled and took another sip of tea. 'Tell me, Brian dear, what did your mother say that your father did for a living?'

'Well, he doesn't work for a firm of accountants if that's what you mean,' said Brian. 'Because Granddad's already told me that.'

'Oh, did he?' said his grandmother rather disapprovingly. 'Hmm, well, your granddad's quite right of course, your father's job wasn't anything remotely like an accountant.'

'So what *was* my dad's job?' asked Brian.

His grandmother smiled uncomfortably and sipped her tea again. 'I think it's best, Brian dear, if we spoke to your mother first,' she said, picking up her knitting once more.

Instantly, Brian felt a sudden surge of anger rise within him. What was the big secret? Why would nobody tell him what his father's job was? Why wouldn't anybody explain anything to him? He wasn't stupid. He was eleven years old. He'd understand.

'This isn't fair!' he exclaimed, standing up so furiously that he spilt hot tea into his saucer and over his hand, scalding it.

His grandmother looked quite taken aback.

'He's my dad!' cried Brian angrily, his voice rising. 'So he wasn't an accountant. Big deal. And he had a different job. So what? I don't care. I really don't care. I just want somebody to tell me the truth!'

'Oh, Brian dear, it's just not as easy as that,' replied his grandmother, awkwardly.

'Why isn't it easy?' shouted Brian. 'I don't understand! What's so difficult about telling me the truth? What's so secret about Dad's job? What did he do every day when he pretended to go to work as an accountant? He wasn't a spy or something, was he?'

'Good heavens, no,' replied his grandmother.

'Well then, why can't you tell me what he did?' asked Brian.

'It's complicated, dear.'

'Complicated?' exclaimed Brian, growing more upset. 'What's complicated about telling me the truth?' he asked, angry tears forming within his eyes. 'What's complicated about telling me what my dad's real job was, where he is now and why he disappeared? He hasn't phoned. He hasn't written. It's like my dad's dead!'

'Oh Brian, your father isn't dead.'

'But how do you know that?' cried Brian. 'How can you be so certain?

'I'm so sorry, Brian dear. I can't—'

Brian banged his cup and saucer on to the coffee table so hard that he almost broke them, sending spilt tea flying everywhere. 'It isn't fair!' he exclaimed, wiping away his tears with the cuff of his sleeve and heading towards the hallway.

'Brian dear, where are you going?' asked his grandmother, concerned.

'To bed!' Brian shouted back angrily, and he slammed the living room door so hard behind him that the suit of armour in the hallway actually rattled. Then, after climbing the stairs to his bedroom, he kicked his door shut with a bang, changed into his pyjamas and climbed into bed. It was seven o'clock in the evening and much earlier than Brian would normally have gone to bed. He pulled the quilt tightly about his neck and even though he tried as hard as he possibly could it still took him a very long time indeed to fall asleep.

When Brian awoke it was with a sudden jolt. He had been dreaming and, although he couldn't remember exactly what his dream had been, he felt sure it had been about his father. Sleepily, he rolled over and stared, bleary-eyed, at the digital display of the alarm clock. It was 2.15am, the middle of the night. Yawning, he was just about to close his eyes again when the screaming began.

Brian sat up, his heart beating frantically. The screaming was coming from somewhere inside the house, from downstairs. Somebody somewhere sounded absolutely terrified. Was it his

51

grandmother? Brian leapt out of bed and skidded towards the bedroom door. He tugged at its handle. But immediately had to snatch his hand back, staring at it in shock. It was burnt. His palm and fingers were blistered and throbbing painfully.

Brian tried the door handle again, but this time found he could hardly touch it. The handle was now too hot, glowing a burning orange. He stared, astonished, as tiny strips of paint began to curl and peel from the door, dribbling onto the carpet.

Brian hooked the sleeve of his pyjama top over his hand for protection as he tried to open his bedroom door again, but as he did so the temperature within his bedroom rose dramatically. With a loud popping noise the bulb in his ceiling light suddenly exploded, spraying shards of broken glass all over his bed and carpet. His alarm clock began buzzing furiously as the green-numbered display flashed once, twice, and then both the sound and the display faded to nothing as smoke began pouring from it. At the very same moment a tremendously bright and flickering light shone through Brian's window, filling his bedroom with such an intense and powerful heat that, for the briefest of moments, he was certain that his pyjamas would actually catch fire.

But as the light quickly passed by his window and out of sight so the heat gradually began to lessen and Brian's bedroom once again fell into semi-darkness, the temperature steadily growing more bearable. The screaming too, he realised, had stopped. Sweat trickled down Brian's face; his hair was damp and sticking to his forehead. He dashed over to his bedroom window and, reaching out with his un-burnt hand, pulled back the curtains to see what could have caused such heat. He stared in amazement. His window had melted. Although still in one piece the glass had become so warped and distorted that he could see nothing through it except a very fuzzy image of the moon outside.

He dashed back to his bedroom door again and tentatively touched its handle. It felt surprisingly cool. He turned it, pulled open the door and went to step onto the landing. Only he couldn't. Something was in his way, blocking him. Something big and something hairy and something that smelt not too dissimilar to rotten cabbage. Brian gazed upwards, rooted to the spot, his mouth hanging open in terror.

It was a monster! There was no other word for it. It was a fully-fledged real life monster and it was standing in front of him, right now, blocking the doorway, stopping his escape! Brian's heart began to race, for the monster was absolutely enormous and covered from top to toe in a mass of thick brown hair! Brian staggered backwards; he couldn't help himself, for his legs had suddenly turned all wobbly, like jelly. He tried to scream, to call out to his grandparents, but each time he opened his mouth nothing came out. His feet dragged awkwardly along the carpet as he found himself gawping at the massive creature that completely filled the doorframe like an enormous hairy wall. Brian had to run. He had to escape, but how? Not by the door. There was no way he'd get past the hairy whatever-it-was! His only chance was through the bedroom window. If he could just open it in time he'd have a chance to climb down the drainpipe. But just as he was about to make a dash towards it, the monster moved.

The fearsome creature was bending forwards. It was going to enter his bedroom. Brian stumbled in panic, almost losing his balance, grabbing desperately at a bookcase for support. His chest was hurting badly now. As if his heart might burst from it at any moment. Was that a head? As the monster ducked and squeezed itself through the bedroom doorway Brian thought he had caught the briefest glimpse of two horns amongst the hair. The monster scraped noisily against the doorframe, splintering wood in all directions, and it seemed to snort unhappily to itself as one of its massive legs grazed the door, pulling it off its hinges. It stared at Brian and stalked towards him, lifting one of its arms threateningly as it did so. Brian was certain that he was about to be killed. He was absolutely

53

sure of it. Even if he could get to the window now he'd never have time to open it. He stared in utter horror as the monster, now only a few feet away from him, raised its arm higher and higher ready to strike and, instead... waved at him!

Brian frowned as the monster did it again, almost cheerfully this time. It grunted. And Brian had the distinct impression that it was saying 'hello'.

And then another voice, quite high pitched, said irritably, 'Gerrrofff! You're standing on my foot, you great big hairy oaf!' And from behind the furry monster a much smaller creature emerged. About half the size of Brian, it wore black wellington boots, with tights over its legs and what looked like a very long woolly jumper, which at one time had probably been white, hanging all the way down to its knees. Its head was bald and its face was grey and sunken-looking whilst its ears were large and pointy, like a cat's. 'Now where's the list?' it asked, looking up at its companion, annoyed.

The hairy monster seemed to shrug as it grunted something back at him.

'What do you mean you haven't got it? I gave it to you before we left! And what do you mean by lumbering into the poor boy's bedroom like that? You probably scared him half to death, charging at him in that way. He probably thought you were going to eat him. What were you thinking? And I won't even mention what you've done to his door!'

The hairy monster mumbled something in return.

'No, I don't think he does like you. I'm dreadfully sorry,' he said, turning towards Brian. 'I do apologise. My friend here, well, he gets easily excited.'

Brian nodded back dumbly. He couldn't quite believe what he was seeing, or hearing for that matter. It was the middle of the night and he was listening to two monsters bickering with each other.

'Now, what did you do with that list? It's got the names on it.'

His companion grunted again.

'Well, you'd better have a look for it right away because we can't go anywhere until you find it, you useless hairy rug!'

The massive monster scratched its head with an enormous hairy arm and began rummaging within its long brown matted fur, presumably for the list its companion was seeking.

'I'm ever so sorry,' apologised the small creature again. 'It's not normally like this. But we left in a bit of a rush, you see. Didn't even know you were here until an hour or so ago. A dustpan and brush,' he suddenly exclaimed, irritably, as his hairy companion removed the two items from within his fur, dropping them onto the carpet. 'Why in the world are you carrying those two things around with you?' He stared at the brush, which, Brian noticed in some alarm, seemed to be twitching and trying to sweep up his carpet all of its own accord.

The large monster seemed to shrug repentantly but continued to rummage within its fur, moments later removing an old iron kettle, a deck of loose playing cards and a half-eaten packet of sherbet lemons.

His smaller companion, sighed, exasperated, picked up the bag of sherbet lemons, popped one into his mouth and offered the bag to Brian.

'Er… thanks,' said Brian, who was slightly unsure if he should actually take one but did so anyway. He knew he shouldn't take sweets from strangers but nobody had ever said anything about taking sweets from… monsters?

'Prefer Flying Frisbees myself,' the little creature remarked, as he watched his huge, hairy friend successfully extract a rubber chicken from the depths of its fur and then drop it upon a growing pile of other curiosities. Which now included a multi-coloured scarf, a broken yo-yo, a half-eaten loaf of bread and a jar of something green, which looked disturbingly to Brian like it might actually be alive.

Brian stared at the rubber chicken curiously.

The smaller monster looked embarrassed. 'Don't ask,' he said awkwardly, bending down and picking up the jar and shaking it. The glass container began to smoulder ever so slightly, which seemed to make the room a little brighter. 'Glow worms,' he explained.

The large monster grunted.

'Well, it's about time! Give it here!' said its smaller companion, jumping up and snatching at the roll of badly creased parchment and subsequently unravelling it. 'Right, let me see. Yes, here we are. That's right. This is 14 Pyrmont Grove, isn't it?' he asked, looking up at Brian.

Brian nodded. Something about the sherbet lemon tasted funny.

'And you're Brian Pankhurst, aren't you?' he asked, taking a pen from the inside of his wellington boot and ticking something off his list.

Brian nodded again. The sherbet lemon didn't taste like a sherbet lemon any more.

'The grandson of Henry and Doris Pankhurst?' he asked with another tick.

'Yes, look…' began Brian, but as he opened his mouth to ask what was going on, a jet of sparkling, yellow smoke whizzed from it, quickly encircling his neck and swirling under his chin. 'W-w-what's happening?' he cried as steam began pouring from his ears. But before either of the two monsters could reply a strange fizzing noise began to crackle about Brian's head and the wispy smoke, which was now a golden pulsing hue, began to twist about him faster and faster, making Brian feel quite dizzy. Then, as the crackling noise intensified and the smoke glowed even more brightly there was a blinding flash of light. And instantly the smoke disappeared. It had been replaced, however, by a chain of what looked like mini lemons, which hung around Brian's neck.

Brian stared down at the odd-looking necklace in surprise and puzzlement and went to remove it.

'I wouldn't do that if I were you,' warned the small monster, taking a careful step backwards. But too late! No sooner had Brian gone to remove the chain of lemons then they all exploded with a pop, one by one, showering each and every one of them with sticky, gooey lemon juice!

'Exploding sherbet lemons,' explained the small monster, thrusting the pack of sherbet lemons excitedly towards Brian. 'See, there's one in every pack!' he said, licking some of the yellow goo that had been hanging from his nose.

Brian took the half-eaten packet of sweets and, wiping his eyes, this time examined it more closely. And, sure enough, above the words '*sherbet*' and '*lemons*' was the word '*exploding*' which, itself, kept magically exploding into different colours over and over again. Whilst towards the bottom of the packet in smaller flashing letters it said, '*There's one in every pack – which one will it be?*' and, underneath this, printed in even smaller writing, '*WARNING! Although not dangerous, it is recommended by the Sweets Standards Agency that "Exploding Sherbet Lemons" should not be given to children under 3 years of age, dragons or any other type of monster for that matter.*'

Brian handed the packet of sweets back to the smaller monster, wiping some of the sticky yellow goo from his pyjama top. 'Who exactly are you?' he asked.

'Well, my name is, or rather I should say I am called Sam, and this big furry rug is called Hadley,' he said, gesturing to his much taller companion whilst popping another sweet into his mouth and sucking.

The larger monster grunted and, rather reluctantly, its smaller friend pushed another sherbet lemon into its huge, outstretched furry hand. Brian watched curiously as it deposited the sweet somewhere in amongst its long strands of hair and wondered what the monster looked like underneath all its fur.

'We were sent here to collect you and…' said Sam, checking his list, 'Norman Crabtree and Audrey Jenkins.'

'Collect me?' repeated Brian, confused. 'But I don't understand. Where are my grandparents?'

Sam shrugged.

Hadley grunted and mumbled something back at him.

'No, you can't have another sweet,' said Sam, disapprovingly. 'You've had six already! I've only had three and Brian's only had one. Besides, you're meant to be losing weight! Just look what you did to poor Brian's door, you great hairy oaf!'

Brian squeezed past the two bickering monsters and dashed upstairs to his grandparents' bedroom. The door was already open and when he peered inside it looked like a tornado had torn through it. A wardrobe had fallen or been pushed against the bed, its clothes half hanging out. Drawers had been pulled open, their contents spilling out all over the floor. Ornaments had been broken, books ripped from the shelves and thrown upon the floor. Brian called out to his grandparents but no answer came. He ran downstairs and checked the living room, dining room and kitchen, still calling after them. But each room was empty. When he climbed back up the stairs to the living room Sam and Hadley were already waiting for him.

'Nice suit of armour,' remarked Sam admiringly, giving the jar of glow worms he was carrying another shake. 'Did you find them, your grandparents I mean?' he asked.

But before Brian had time to answer there was a massive explosion in the kitchen! Brian staggered. It felt as though the whole house was shaking. Pictures fell from the walls. A china ornament crashed onto the floor somewhere. The suit of armour next to Sam wobbled dangerously as though it were about to fall on top of him. And then, quite suddenly, it stopped.

Grabbing the banister for support Brian peered over his shoulder and stared into the dining room and kitchen below. It was clear that the kitchen was on fire, but it was not this that had caught his attention. It was the figure standing at the bottom of the stairs. Consumed in flame the creature silently stared up at Brian and the two monsters. Bits of its flame, almost like liquid, dripped from its body, landing on the carpet without burning it, whilst the doorframe picturing the creature, which should have erupted in flame, simply smouldered. Brian stared, open-mouthed, as the creature slowly grabbed the banister and began climbing the stairs.

'We need to leave!' shrieked Sam. 'Like now!' and he grabbed Brian's hand, pulling him into the living room. Hadley followed, slamming the door shut and twisting its handle so that it broke within the lock. Then, grabbing one of the cherry-patterned sofas, he pushed it up against the door.

'What *was* that?' asked Brian.

But Sam wasn't listening. Instead, he was busy poring over the bookcase nearest the door. 'Quickly Brian, pull that book off the shelf!' he instructed, jumping up and down and pointing frantically to a row of books above his head.

'What?' said Brian, confused, staring at all the different-coloured volumes.

'There's no time to explain!' said Sam urgently. 'Just pull that book off the shelf!'

'Which one?' asked Brian. 'Which book?'

'The white one!' said Sam, still pointing and glancing back at the living room door which now had a fiery glow surrounding it.

Brian hastily ran his fingers over the row of books, stopping at a pale hardback entitled *Open Doors and How to Close Them – 4th Edition*. He stared at it in surprise. It was the exact same book that he had found lying on the living room floor that afternoon, all burnt and scorched. Only now it looked brand new, the cover unblemished, perfect in fact.

'Hurry, Brian,' urged Sam, as flames began seeping through the edges of the door.

Brian began to tug the book free from the row.

'Stop!' cried Sam suddenly when the book was no more than half way out. 'That's enough. Now, Hadley, grab that big brown book,' he ordered, pointing to another volume on a higher shelf. 'Quickly! Quickly!'

Hadley did as he was instructed and pulled the tall leather book from the top row so that it too hung rather precariously.

By now wisps of flickering gold flame were coiling themselves under and around the living room door, tugging at the sofa, peeling the paint from the walls, seemingly alive and desperate to get in. The heat from the fire, which up until then had been hardly noticeable, suddenly became unbelievably intense, as though the living room had, all at once, transformed into a gigantic oven and Brian, Sam and Hadley were going to be roasted alive. There was a loud popping noise, which made Brian jump as all the living room light bulbs suddenly exploded simultaneously.

'Quickly, Hadley,' said Sam, jerking a smaller, blue book free from the shelf in front of him. 'That thick black book in front of you, pull that one! Pull it!'

Brian glanced at the shaggy-haired monster as he wrenched the book from its row. The temperature in the living room was almost unbearable now. Brian's whole body felt as though it were on fire. Where the living room door and the sofa had once been was an enormous pulsating and burning light. Brian stared at it, bewitched. Burning flamelike tendrils poured from it, edging across the carpet, wrapping themselves around the legs of furniture, pulling themselves towards him.

'Brian!' cried Sam, tugging at Brian's pyjama trouser leg. 'That green book!' he said, pointing frantically as wisps of fire began spreading under the antique tables and across the bookcases. 'It's the last one. Pull it free! Quickly! Do it now!'

Finding the tatty, green book that Sam had been pointing at Brian snatched it from the shelf and immediately all the books in front of him sprang to life. They began moving of their own accord, sliding to the left and shuffling to the right, seeming to disappear, one after another, into the very bookcase itself. Brian stared in wonder as each of the books withdrew further and further into their shelves until eventually there were no books left.

'Quickly Brian, through you go,' cried Sam, pushing Brian forwards, as the shelves of the bookcase began to shrink away too.

'But—' began Brian.

'No time to explain,' cried Sam, staring fearfully up at the ceiling as spirals of pulsating light began to descend the walls towards them. 'Take a big deep breath, that's it, and try to keep your arms at your sides.'

'But—' said Brian again.

'Don't want you losing a hand,' Sam remarked, and with that he and Hadley pushed Brian into the empty bookcase.

Chapter 5

THE SOOBIUS SYSTEM

As Brian stumbled into the bookcase he half-expected to hit his head, almost immediately, against its hard, wooden back, but he didn't. Instead he was instantly engulfed in a swirl of warm, musty air that seemed to lift him up and somehow jerk him forwards, pulling him further inside. His stomach lurched as he felt his feet quite suddenly abandon the bookcase floor, leaving Brian momentarily suspended in midair, weightless and in utter blackness, his legs and arms flailing about him as if he were trying to swim. No sooner had this happened, however, than Brian found himself being dragged forwards at a tremendous speed, as if somebody had tied one end of an invisible rope around his waist whilst the other end had been tied to a galloping horse. A pinprick of light became visible ahead of him; it instantly engulfed him, and Brian suddenly felt himself falling.

He landed on his knees, in what appeared to be somebody else's living room. It certainly wasn't his grandparents'. The furniture was too sparse and much too modern and on a mantelpiece were photographs of family members and friends whom he did not recognise.

A shuffling noise made Brian scramble to his feet and spin around. From an empty bookcase behind him Sam emerged, looking quite shaken, quickly followed by Hadley.

'Here,' he said, offering Brian the bag of sherbet lemons which was trembling badly in his hand.

'Look, what exactly is going on?' Brian demanded, waving away the offer of another sweet and staring at the empty bookcase as it began to somehow magically refill itself with lots of differently shaped and coloured books.

But before Sam could reply a voice from the darkness demanded, 'Who's there?'

Brian and the two monsters froze and Brian felt his heart begin to pound painfully in his chest. He stared fearfully as the living room door swung slowly open. The floorboards creaked. There was a gleam of metal and Brian was sure that, in the semi-darkness, he could just make out what looked like some sort of wheel.

'Oh, it's you, Hadley!' said the voice, sounding quite relieved, as a small boy in a wheelchair, wearing a grey dressing gown, rolled into the living room. 'Jeez, you almost gave me a heart attack! For a minute I thought somebody had broken in. There's been some right funny stuff going on tonight. All right, Sam?' he said, waving at the smaller monster. 'Mum and Dad aren't here. Don't know where they are. Who's that with you?' he asked, suddenly spotting Brian and gliding forwards curiously.

'This is Brian,' announced Sam, sticking a finger in his mouth as he attempted to prise out some sherbet lemon that had got stuck between two teeth. 'Brian Pankhurst. And this,' he mumbled, gesturing towards the blonde-haired boy in the wheelchair and licking his fingers after successfully dislodging the yellow sweet, 'is Norman Crabtree.'

'Wotcher,' said Norman, nodding in Brian's direction and going to switch the living room light on.

But Hadley suddenly stepped forwards, almost knocking Sam over in the process, and, reaching out an enormous hairy arm, shielded the switch with one of his gigantic hands.

'Hey! What's going on?' cried Norman indignantly.

'Best not switch the light on,' warned Sam, still licking his fingers and kicking his taller companion in the leg for almost knocking him over.

'Why?' asked Norman in surprise. 'What's up?'

'A Diefromen!' replied Sam.

'You're joking!' said Norman, sounding both excited and impressed. 'Blimey! Where?'

'Brian's house,' said Sam, jerking a thumb towards the bookcase that was now full of books again. 'Only just escaped. And we're not really meant to be using the Soobius System. We were warned not to.'

The bigger monster confirmed what Sam had just said with a loud grunt and held out his hand, presumably for another sherbet lemon.

'We've been instructed to collect you, Brian and Audrey,' Sam said, tipping another two of the yellow sweets into Hadley's outstretched palm and consulting his roll of creased parchment again. 'Gotta take you to the Committee Chambers as soon as possible. Got given strict orders from Barnaby Katobi himself. Hey, you got any Flaresuction potion?'

'Dunno,' said Norman with a shrug.

'Er... sorry, but what's a Flaresuction potion?' asked Brian.

'It's a baffling brew,' replied Sam. 'It duplicates our trail, for at least a while anyway. So if anybody *is* watching or following us through the Soobius System it'll take them twice as long to find us. It doesn't last for very long though. But I don't reckon it's safe to wander about outside with a Diefromen on the loose. What do you reckon, Hadley?'

The hairy monster mumbled something in agreement and stepped past Brian and Norman, ducking and somehow squeezing himself through the open door and into the hallway. Sam popped the last sherbet lemon into his mouth and, with difficulty, mumbled, 'Where's the kitchen?'

'Downstairs,' replied Norman.

'Won't be long,' he said, giving the glass of glow worms he was still carrying a quick shake and popping it on a table before following Hadley out of the living room. 'Won't take five minutes to make some Flaresuction potion,' he said on his way out, before asking as an afterthought, 'I don't suppose you've got a jar of beetles lying about, have you?'

Norman screwed up his face in disgust and said, 'No!'

'Oh well, not to worry,' mumbled Sam, disappearing downstairs, into the kitchen. 'I'm sure we'll be able to find another insect to use, maybe a dead ant or a fly.'

Brian and Norman both grimaced.

There followed an uncomfortable silence where, for a few moments, neither boy said anything to the other. Brian shifted uncomfortably, transferring his weight from one foot to the other, staring down at his own bare feet before Norman finally said, 'So, did you really get attacked by a Diefromen?'

'What?' replied Brian, distractedly. 'Oh, yeah; well, at least I think we did.'

'What do you mean?' Norman asked with a frown, rolling his wheelchair slightly nearer. 'Don't you know?'

'Well, I've never seen a Diefromen before,' explained Brian. 'In fact, until tonight, I'd never even heard of one.'

'You're joking!' exclaimed Norman in surprise.

'I'm not,' said Brian. 'I honestly don't know what a Diefromen is.'

'Are you serious?' said Norman. 'Jeez, I thought everybody knew what a Diefromen was.'

'Well, I don't,' said Brian. 'What are they?'

'They're fire demons, of course,' said Norman matter-of-factly.

For a moment Brian thought he had misheard Norman. 'They're what?' he repeated, a little stunned. 'Fire demons? Don't be ridiculous!'

65

'No, it's true,' said Norman. 'Never seen one myself, of course. But that's because they're very rare and very, very dangerous too. They mostly live underground, really deep down, and can only be controlled by a very powerful magician or warlock.'

Brian stared at Norman in disbelief and laughed. 'Sorry, but did you just say "magician or warlock"? Because... well, magicians and warlocks don't really exist, mate!'

'Actually, I think you'll find they do,' said Norman seriously.

'Yeah, in books maybe, but not in real life.'

Norman pushed his wheelchair even closer to Brian, a wounded expression upon his face. 'And what about fire demons?' he whispered. 'Do they exist in real life? Or do they only appear in books too? Because I'm assuming then that you can explain what attacked you tonight if it wasn't a fire demon?'

Brian opened his mouth to reply but suddenly realised that he didn't know what to say because he honestly didn't know what had actually attacked him. The fire that had engulfed his grandparents' living room was like nothing he had ever seen before.

'And what about Sam and Hadley?' continued Norman. 'Are they real or just monsters from your imagination? Because right now I can hear your imagination rummaging around in my parents' kitchen downstairs. What's that smell?'

'What smell?' said Brian, sniffing.

'It smells, well, like lemons,' remarked Norman, spinning his chair around Brian.

'Oh yeah, that'll be me,' admitted Brian, a little uncomfortably.

'Exploding sherbet lemon?' asked Norman with a knowing look upon his face.

'Yeah,' said Brian.

Norman laughed. 'Well, there's one in every pack!' he said, mimicking the words that were printed on the packet of sweets. 'Y'know, I had one once that exploded so loudly that I went deaf in my left ear for a month. Faulty packet. Mum was furious. Wrote to

66

the manufacturers and everything. She even threatened to visit them in person using the Soobius System!'

Brian rubbed his eyes and sat down on one of the sofas, yawning. 'None of this is making any sense,' he said. 'What's the Soobius System?'

'It's how you got here tonight,' said Norman.

'What?' said Brian.

'Well, I'm assuming you travelled from your house to mine via a bookcase, right?'

'Er... yeah,' said Brian.

'Well, that's the Soobius System,' said Norman.

'But how is that even possible?' asked Brian. 'How can you travel from one bookcase to another?'

Norman frowned. 'You're not from around here, are you, mate?' he said, smiling.

'No,' replied Brian, sighing wearily. 'I'm staying with my grandparents for a while.'

'How come?' asked Norman.

'It's, er... complicated,' said Brian, who really didn't want to explain to a boy whom he'd only just met why he was living with his grandparents instead of with his mother and father. 'So, explain this Soobius System thing to me again.'

'Well, years and years ago, long before magicians and warlocks learnt how to perform the Comedango spell—'

'The Comedango spell?' repeated Brian, confused.

'Yeah, it's a spell that transports you from one place to another in, like, seconds,' explained Norman. 'It's wicked! Can't do it myself yet though. Mum won't let me. But I've tried. I know all words to the incantation off by heart,' he said enthusiastically.

'Right,' said Brian somewhat incredulously.

'Well, anyway, before wizards and magicians could do the Comedango spell,' continued Norman, undeterred, 'they used to use the Soobius System to get from one place to another. Augustine

Soobius created it. Took him years, almost his whole life to construct the magical pathways. He died not long after, I think. I'm not too good on magical history. But you see, before the Soobius System, magical folk had to travel from place to place just like regular people. I mean, can you imagine magicians travelling on public transport and whipping out their staffs and amulets on a bus or a train, or Sam and Hadley wandering up and down the high street?'

There was a sudden and very loud crash from somewhere downstairs, making both the boys jump.

'You great clumsy oaf! Sorry!' cried Sam from the kitchen. 'That was Hadley's fault! Just a couple of plates though. Not to worry, I can see your mother's got lots more!'

'Mum's going to go mental,' said Norman, shaking his head and grimacing. 'She doesn't like anybody in her kitchen. Least of all a couple of monsters!' he whispered.

'So let me get this straight,' said Brian, staring at the bookcase that he had fallen out of. 'The Soobius System is like a magical door from one place to another?'

'That's right,' Norman said, nodding. 'Now you're getting it.'

'But why a bookcase?'

'What do you mean?' asked Norman, puzzled.

'Well, why not just use a regular door?' suggested Brian. 'Why is this Soobius System connected by bookcases?'

'Dunno,' Norman said, with a shrug.

'And how does it work exactly?' asked Brian, getting up and studying the different-shaped books within the bookcase more closely.

Norman wheeled his chair around the sofa to be next to Brian and pulled a pale, cream-coloured book from the second-lowest shelf. Its title, Brian noticed, was *Open Doors and How to Close Them – 53rd Edition*.

'That book,' remarked Brian, taken aback. 'I've seen it before, at my grandparents' house and at Newtblaster's Book Emporium in the high street.'

'I'm not surprised,' said Norman, who was idly thumbing through its pages. 'Probably every magical household in the country has at least one copy of this particular book.'

'But why?' asked Brian, perplexed.

'Right, let me explain,' said Norman, seeing the confused expression on Brian's face. 'Nearly all the bookcases in this house and probably your grandparents' too are linked to the Soobius System. And the books within them are sort of... keys. Yeah, magical keys, and where you travel to depends on what books you remove from the shelf. I'll show you,' he said, pushing the copy of *Open Doors and How to Close Them* back into the bookcase. 'Right. Okay. So first let's pull that book back out again,' he said, gesturing to the pale volume that he had just replaced. 'But don't pull it too far. Just enough so that it's protruding from the rest.'

'Like this?' asked Brian, tugging the 53rd volume of *Open Doors and How to Close Them* free from the shelf.

'Yeah, that's right,' said Norman, scanning the shelves for the next book to remove. 'Perfect, now what you've got to remember is the first word of that book. Which is "Open", isn't it? So the second book you need to remove has to have a title where the second word is "Door". Like that one.' He pointed to a green paperback titled *A Door to Every Room*.

Brian pulled the ragged book from the shelf and watched patiently as Norman scanned the shelves for a third book.

'It's almost like we're constructing a sentence,' explained Norman. 'Do you see? So far we've pulled out two books. The first word of the first book was "Open". The second word of the second book was "Door" and the third book has to have a third word just like this,' he said, leaning forwards and pulling free a book called *Magic Tricks to Impress Your Friends*.

'So now we have three books and three words, Open, Door and To,' said Norman. 'There's some travel books towards the top of the bookcase. Pick a country you'd like to visit.'

Brian scanned the top row of books and removed a thin blue volume entitled *Rough Guide to France*.

'Now watch what happens!' said Norman.

Brian took a step back and once again stared in amazement as, one by one, all the books in front of him suddenly sprang into life. They scuttled backwards and forwards along their shelves as though being shuffled by unseen hands. Smaller books hovered between larger books whilst some thicker, hardback books floated back and forth, forcing less bulky books out of their path. Eventually, though, each and every book seemed to disappear deeper and deeper into the depths of the bookcase until only the shelves remained.

'So are you saying that if I stepped into this bookcase right now it would take me to France?' asked Brian, fascinated, as he watched the last of the shelves disappear into the bookcase.

'Yup!' said Norman, nodding. 'The Soobius System is connected to almost every country in the world. We save a right bundle of money when we go on holiday each year because we don't need to fly. And it's much quicker too. Although it does tend to make me feel a bit Soosick sometimes. But the magic in the books doesn't last forever. Some of the really old books get a bit unpredictable when their magic runs out.'

'What do you mean?' asked Brian, remembering the condition of his granddad's copy of *Open Doors and How to Close Them* when he had found it the day before.

'Well, usually their pages just go blank and they just don't work any more,' explained Norman. 'But sometimes they can fly off the shelves or spontaneously combust. My cousin had one book that, when its magic ran out, jumped off the shelf and hit him right in the face. Gave him a massive black eye!'

'What's "spontaneously combust"?' asked Brian.

'It's like when a book explodes or suddenly sets fire to itself!'

'What in the world are you doing?' cried Sam frantically as he and Hadley returned from the kitchen carrying two large cups of foaming green liquid. 'Didn't I just tell you that the Soobius System might be being watched? And here you two are opening the door to who knows where!' he continued, thrusting one of the foaming cups into Brian's hand and, at the same time, returning the books to their original positions within the bookcase.

'Sorry,' said Norman. 'I was just explaining to Brian how the Soobius System worked. He's never used it before.'

'Well, tonight is hardly the time for a Soobius lesson. Now, drink some of this,' Sam said, watching as Hadley handed Norman the second cup of foaming green liquid.

'Urghh, what is it?' asked Norman.

'Flaresuction potion,' replied Sam. 'Drink up. Not all of it though. Save some for Hadley and me. You too, Brian.'

'But it smells disgusting!' remarked Norman, wrinkling his nose up. 'Like sweaty socks that haven't been washed for a month!'

'Well, that's because we were short on time and Hadley could only find a dead spider.'

Norman heaved. 'I think I'm going to be sick!' he said, holding his hand over his mouth.

'It's an important ingredient,' explained Sam. 'Without a dead spider or some sort of insect you can't make the Flaresuction potion. Now, drink up!'

Brian looked at Norman, whose face was quite pale, and watched as he gripped his nose tightly with two fingers, put the cup to his lips and reluctantly swallowed.

'Oh man, that is so disgusting!' said Norman, almost gagging after he had finished and wiping the green foam from his lips. 'I think I've got a spider's leg trapped between my teeth!'

Brian laughed.

'It isn't funny!' protested Norman. 'Seriously, I think I'm going to be sick.'

Brian sniffed his cup and he realised that Norman had been right. The Flaresuction potion really did smell like sweaty socks. But, nevertheless, Brian took a couple of gulps and handed the cup back to Sam, who drained the glass completely and licked his lips appreciatively. Hadley did the same with Norman's cup.

'Yummy,' said Sam whilst Hadley burped loudly. Brian just felt very sick!

'And what happens now?' asked Norman. 'I don't feel any different apart from wanting to be sick everywhere!'

But no sooner had Norman said this than both Brian and Norman's feet suddenly lurched forward as if they had been possessed.

'W-w-what's happening?' said Brian, panicking; he had the distinct feeling that his feet were trying to escape from his legs as they unexpectedly leapt forwards again.

'D-d-don't worry,' said Sam reassuringly as his feet too started moving in such a way that he wouldn't have looked out of place on a disco dance floor.

Hadley's massive hairy feet, however, were a different matter. Every time they involuntarily kicked out he would knock over Norman's parents' coffee table or send one of their sofas flying across the living room floor and into the table and chairs at the opposite end.

'H-h-how long does this last for?' asked Brian, who looked like he was performing some sort of mad Irish tap dance.

'N-n-not long,' came Sam's reply, swiftly followed by a howl of pain as his left foot accidentally kicked Norman's wheelchair.

Brian's feet leapt forwards again, almost propelling him into the fireplace, but this time he had left two silver impressions, like footprints, on the carpet floor where he had just been standing.

'Mum's going to go spare!' cried Norman as a pair of silver tyre marks appeared under his wheelchair too. 'She only had this carpet cleaned last month!' he remarked rather weakly as he finally gained control of his twitching feet. His face grew even paler when, suddenly, his and Brian's silver foot and tyre prints started wandering around the living room of their own free will, leaving a trail of grey impressions wherever they went. He watched miserably as his tyre marks rolled casually past Hadley, out the living room door and into the hallway.

'Don't look so worried,' said Sam reassuringly to Norman. 'The Flaresuction potion isn't permanent. Those silver prints will soon disappear. Well, most of the time they do,' he added as an afterthought. 'But with more than one set of footprints to follow anybody who might be trying to trail us is going to take twice as long now. Unlike regular footprints our replicated ones will wander absolutely everywhere, even under doors if they want to get outside and explore.'

Brian watched curiously as his silver footprints seemed to circle Norman's wheelchair before ambling over to a large antique sideboard set in another corner of the room.

'Right then,' said Sam, picking up his jar of glow worms and giving it a shake. He headed over to the bookcase, leaving another trail of glistening footprints behind him, but unlike his magical footprints these ones did not move. 'Next stop is Audrey Jenkins!' he announced, and promptly tripped over Norman's wheelchair, dropping the jar of glow worms onto Hadley's foot, before crashing head first into the bookcase.

Chapter 6

THE ORDER OF WIZITCHES

Brian, Norman, Sam and Hadley arrived in Audrey Jenkins' hallway, via another bookcase, a few minutes later. Brian, who was not used to travelling in such a fashion, landed on his knees again, almost toppling headfirst into a hat and coat stand.

'You all right, mate?' asked Norman, wheeling himself out of the bookcase and doing his best not to laugh.

'Yeah,' said Brian, getting up, feeling more than a little embarrassed.

'You get used to it after a while,' said Norman, reassuringly. 'When I was younger and before I was in this thing' – he gestured irritably to his wheelchair – 'I used to fall over all the time when I used the Soobius System. One day when I was about seven or eight I pulled a wrong book out by mistake and fell right into the middle of some old lady's tea party in India. She went berserk because I knocked over all her drinks and her cake and everything. Which is why Mum always keeps the travel books on the top shelf now. Not that I can reach them in this!' he said miserably, pushing his wheelchair forwards.

'What's going on?' asked a small black girl suddenly, dressed in pink pyjamas and descending a flight of stairs into the hallway. 'And what are you all doing here?'

'Oh, wotcher, Audrey,' said Norman, who clearly had met this girl before. He wheeled himself towards her, two sparkling silver tyre marks following directly behind him.

'Norman!' scolded the girl. 'What on earth have you got on your wheels? Look what they're doing to the carpet! My parents are going to go nuts!'

'What?' said Norman, peering over his shoulder. 'Oh, yeah, sorry, it's the Flaresuction potion. Don't worry. It's not permanent. Sam said it would wear off pretty soon, didn't you?'

The smaller monster nodded. 'Yes, well, that's what usually happens,' he said, swiftly exiting into an opposite room, closely followed by Hadley.

'Usually happens!' exclaimed Audrey, her voice rising almost to a shriek. 'Well, it better had,' she called after him. 'Because if it doesn't disappear my mum and dad are going to go crazy! And who's this?' she asked, turning her attention towards Brian whilst at the same time removing a blue asthma inhaler from her pyjama pocket. She put the inhaler to her lips and pressed down upon it.

Norman introduced them both. 'Brian Pankhurst, meet Audrey Jenkins.'

'Hi,' said Brian.

Audrey smiled back at him awkwardly. 'So, what exactly are you all doing here?' she demanded, taking another puff from her inhaler and folding her arms.

'Brian was attacked by a Diefromen,' explained Norman matter-of-factly.

'Oh please!' said Audrey. 'You're so gullible! Diefromen aren't real. They just exist in fairy tales or are used to frighten younger children who don't go to sleep at night. My dad used to say it to me all the time.' Mimicking her father's voice, she said, 'If you don't go to sleep right this minute, Audrey Jenkins, then a Diefromen will come and snatch you from your bed!'

'Well, whether you believe us or not Brian's grandparents have gone missing and my parents seem to have too and I'm worried,' said Norman. 'Where's your mum and dad, by the way?'

'I don't know,' she admitted a little reluctantly. 'I heard a noise and got up to investigate. But my mum and dad aren't here. I don't know where they are.'

'So your mum and dad have gone missing too?' said Norman.

'Well, it's a good job my mum and dad aren't about! Because they'd go mental if they knew Sam and Hadley were here with you both.'

'Why?' asked Brian.

'Yeah, what's wrong with Sam and Hadley?' asked Norman, wheeling himself into the room the two monsters had just disappeared into.

'Because things have a tendency to go missing when they're about,' said Audrey as she, Brian and Brian's magical footprints followed Norman into her living room. 'Things disappear.'

'You mean they steal things?' asked Brian.

'No. Not steal exactly,' whispered Audrey uncomfortably. 'It's just that, well, whenever they're about things just sort of go missing. Like last time they were here some pictures disappeared. And I don't just mean small pictures. Large ones from right off the walls that I can't even carry myself. Oh, and a rubber duck went missing too along with a pair of my dad's slippers!'

'Well, they can have my old slippers any time they want! I could do with a new pair because my old ones stink!' remarked Norman as they joined Sam and Hadley who, not for the first time that night, were busy bickering.

'Well, look for it again!' said Sam irritably. 'It must be there somewhere! Have you checked under your ears?' he asked, pointing.

Hadley growled back at him.

'All right! All right! I only asked,' remarked Sam. 'No need to be so rude about it. And what's that sticking out from underneath your arm? No, not that one,' he said, jumping up and down excitedly and pointing again. 'The other one. Your left arm, you great hairy carpet!'

Hadley shrugged and from under his enormous shaggy left shoulder removed what looked like a black electrical plug. He tugged at it and a long loop of flex flopped out on to his fur, making him look like some sort of gigantic robot gorilla that needed to be plugged in.

'Well, don't just stand there, pull it again!' demanded Sam, and this time when Hadley tugged at the plug a small, silver toaster fell out of his fur.

'Hey!' exclaimed Norman. 'That looks like my mum's toaster!' He grabbed it out of Hadley's gargantuan hands and quickly examined it. 'It *is* my mum's toaster! What are you doing with it?' he asked, popping it into the satchel hanging off the back of his wheelchair.

The massive monster shrugged.

'Norman asked you a question,' said Sam, kicking his taller companion in the leg. 'What are you doing with his mother's toaster, you massive fur ball?'

Hadley shrugged again and grumbled something in reply.

'What do you mean you don't know how it got there?' said Sam, slapping his forehead in frustration. 'Well, it can't have got there on its own, now can it? Come on, what else have you got under there?'

Hadley grumbled again and after a few moments of rummaging under his left shoulder he removed a small and ornate silver photo frame that held within it a picture of Brian's grandparents, and also a large tub of rock cakes.

'I don't believe it!' exclaimed Sam, furiously kicking his taller companion in the leg again and stamping on his foot too just for good measure. 'Give them back at once!'

Remorsefully, Hadley held out his gigantic hands and Brian took back the silver photo frame, which was just small enough to slip into one of his pyjama pockets. However, instead of taking back the tub of rock cakes he pushed it back into Hadley's hands and said, 'It's okay, you can keep them.'

'What?' said Sam, surprised. 'Are you sure?'

Hadley mumbled excitedly.

'Yes. Definitely,' replied Brian, trying not to sound too eager. 'My grandmother's made loads and I'll never eat them all. I'm sure she'd only be too glad to share them with you.'

'Well, if you're sure,' said Sam, uncertainly.

Brian nodded. 'Absolutely!'

'Now just see how lucky you are!' the smaller monster said to his much larger companion. 'Brian's letting you keep all those cakes you've stolen. You're very, very fortunate. If it had been anybody else you and I would have been in so much trouble!'

Hadley mumbled something unintelligible.

'What did he say?' asked Brian.

'He said thanks a lot,' replied Sam. 'Now, where's Audrey's Flaresuction potion, you great hairy carpet? Check under your other arm,' he suggested as Hadley pushed the tub of rock cakes back into the folds of his fur. Hadley rummaged for a few moments under his right arm before eventually removing a tall glass of foaming green liquid, which he handed to Audrey.

'It smells disgusting!' remarked Audrey, grimacing.

'Yeah, and it's got spider's legs in it too,' said a beaming Norman.

'You're joking!' said Audrey, who was suddenly feeling quite ill.

'Drink up!' said Norman, smiling.

'Yes, drink up,' said Sam. 'We're rather behind schedule.'

Audrey held the frothy drink up to her mouth and quickly took two gulps, stopping only because she thought she was going to throw up. 'Yuck! It tastes like smelly socks,' she remarked, holding her hand over her mouth. 'I think I'm going to vomit!'

But before she had a chance to be sick her feet suddenly lurched forwards. They jumped again and then twice more and before she knew what was happening she had completely lost control of her legs and feet and she was dancing on the spot, looking as if her very life depended on winning first prize in a boogie competition, just like Brian had done earlier.

'That's so funny!' laughed Norman. 'You look like a keep-fit instructor!'

'W-w-was that meant to happen?' stammered Audrey as her legs finally seemed to stop twitching and a silver pair of her footprints began wandering off to investigate a newspaper rack.

'Oh yes, nothing to worry about,' said Sam reassuringly as Hadley began half-removing one book after another from the bookcase opposite them. 'Now, hurry through,' Sam instructed as the final books began to recede and disappear into the bookcase. 'That's it, quickly now, you first Hadley, then you next Brian.'

Moments later Brian emerged, yet again, from another bookcase, this time tripping over his own feet and stumbling into the back of Hadley.

'Er, sorry, Hadley,' apologised Brian, prising himself free from the massive monster's hairy legs and removing some clumps of fur from his nose and mouth.

Hadley mumbled something in reply, the monster's enormous shoulders shaking momentarily, almost as if he were chuckling to himself.

Norman, meanwhile, did his best not to laugh out loud.

'Where are we?' asked Brian, getting to his feet whilst removing more hair from his pyjama shirt collar. They had arrived in what appeared to be a large rectangular room that was lined from wall to wall with hundreds and thousands of differently shaped and coloured books. Large ones, small ones, old ones, new ones, paperbacks and hardbacks too. In fact the long rectangular room seemed to hold every type of book you could possibly imagine. To

Brian's left a staircase led steeply upwards, to a wooden balcony above him that stretched around the whole room and provided access to a second level of shelves where even more books were displayed. From this balcony another flight of stairs led up to a third level of books and then a fourth and a fifth too.

'Welcome to the Hall of Blooskstoof,' announced Sam, his voice echoing eerily around the enormous room.

'Wow!' exclaimed Norman, impressed. 'How many floors are in here?' he asked, staring upwards, trying to see the room's ceiling.

'Oh, not that many,' replied Sam, casually. 'Only about 500, I think.'

Norman whistled in astonishment, rolled his wheelchair to the nearest shelf and, bending his neck, began studying some of the books' many titles.

'And what sorts of books do they keep here?' asked Audrey, pulling out a faded green leather volume from the nearest shelf entitled *Felix Clearweather & His Amazing Talking Goat* by C. Mclune-Calvin and idly flicking through it.

'The Hall of Blooskstoof probably has every book you can possibly imagine,' said Sam.

'Even *Monster Cricket*?' asked Norman enthusiastically, looking up from the row of books that he was studying.

'Indeed, the whole of the 26th floor is devoted to it,' remarked Sam. 'From within this hall you can find any book that you desire. And if you can't find it then it probably means it has yet to be written. You can find everything from knitting and ballroom dancing to how to cut a dragon's toenails or how best to cook a dung worm with just a parsnip and a very large carrot.' And then in a hushed tone he whispered, 'And also, on some of the higher levels, they say, well… that you can gain access to some right nasty places, if you know what I mean. Isn't that right, Hadley?'

Hadley grunted and nodded his shaggy head in agreement.

'And what's on the very highest floors?' asked Brian curiously.

'Well, the 499th level is where, supposedly, you can find books that explain how to travel through time,' replied Sam. 'Imagine that! Travelling anywhere you wanted to at any time you wanted. Maybe even meeting your own great-great-great-great-great-grandfather!'

'Wow! Can we go there now?' asked Norman excitedly. 'I'd love to travel back in time.'

Sam shook his head. 'Can't, level 499 is restricted. All the floors above 395 are.'

'And why would you want to travel back in time anyway?' asked Audrey. 'I'd much rather be able to travel into the future. It would be so much more exciting, I think.'

'Oh, I wouldn't want to travel too far back,' replied Norman. 'Three years should be enough.'

'Why, what happened three years ago?' asked Brian.

Norman stared miserably at the wheelchair he was sitting in. 'Three years ago I had the accident that put me in this,' he said.

A moment's silence followed where nobody, not even Sam or Hadley, really knew what to say or do. Finally, Hadley burped very loudly, which made everybody laugh out loud, even Norman.

'Has anybody ever done that before?' asked Audrey, replacing *Felix Clearweather & His Amazing Talking Goat* upon its shelf. 'Travelled back in time, I mean?'

Sam shrugged. 'Dunno. I do know that not everybody can do it. Not sure why. And it has to be for a very special reason too. Like to prevent some sort of disaster or catastrophe. Oh, and you can't travel back in time for personal gain either. That's not allowed. Personally, I've never met anybody who's been higher than the 326th level.'

'So how do you know that there is such a floor, then?' asked Audrey, doubtfully.

But before Sam could reply a bell chimed three times within the hall.

Hadley grunted and pointed towards a pair of double doors at the opposite end of the room that Brian hadn't previously noticed.

'We're late,' remarked Sam, a worried expression upon his face. 'Now, follow me.' He ushered the children forward, the huge wooden doors somehow opening of their own accord as they approached.

Another, much smaller room lay beyond the Hall of Blooskstoof, filled with comfy-looking armchairs and large sofas all of which were occupied by children dressed in pyjamas or dressing gowns just like Brian, Norman and Audrey. Eager to see who had arrived, some of the children looked up expectantly as they entered, their faces tired and frightened-looking.

Some of the younger children, Brian noticed, were curled up and fast asleep in front of a small oval table with what appeared to be amber flames erupting from its surface, circling its centre like a horse on a merry-go-round. And yet the wooden table did not appear any worse for wear. Indeed, the antique table did not seem to be damaged by the peculiar fire at all.

Standing amongst the tired and sleeping children were other monsters just like Sam and Hadley. Creatures with scaly green skin and horns protruding from their foreheads, other monsters with four arms, some with only one eye and a few with teeth so sharp they looked like they could bite through metal. There was even one small creature with a white fluffy beard, wearing a red floppy hat with a gold bell hanging from it, which would have looked remarkably like a garden gnome if it hadn't been for its eight thin spidery legs.

'Is everyone here, Beatrice?' asked a tall black man with greying hair and a silvery goat-like beard as he suddenly emerged from a bookcase at the other end of the room carrying what looked like a notepad in one hand and a walking stick in the other.

'Yes, I believe so, Barnaby,' said a cold voice from behind Brian, making him jump. Brian glanced over his shoulder to see who the voice belonged to. And there, standing behind him, was a scary-looking woman dressed entirely in blood red. She was wearing a close-fitting top that was fastened so tightly from her neck to her waist that it looked almost as if it were impossible for her to breathe, whilst the skirt she wore billowed out beneath her, concealing both her legs and her feet. Her face was flushed, her curly black hair broken up with occasional streaks of scarlet. And there, sitting upon her left shoulder, squawking occasionally into her ear and staring suspiciously at Brian, was a large, scruffy black bird.

'Excellent,' coughed the bearded man, clearing his throat and untying a cloak from around his neck. He hung it on an invisible peg next to him so that, somehow, the cloak was completely suspended in midair. 'Excellent. Firstly let me introduce myself. My name is Barnaby Katobi and I am the head of the Coffinsgrave Committee. I feel I must apologise for bringing you all to the Hall of Blooskstoof at such a very untimely hour. The Hall of Blooskstoof is a vast and wonderful library of information and I would wholeheartedly recommend that you visit it at the very first opportunity you get. Especially the 34th floor. I regret very much, however, that you will not get the chance to do so tonight, or rather I should say this morning,' he said, peering at a large, golden clock that had just magically appeared in front of him, hovering a few feet away, its tick, tick, ticking echoing about the silent room. He smiled and coughed again before continuing, the clock suddenly disappearing with a tiny flash of light.

'Secondly I would like to thank all our friends in the monster community for their kind help and assistance tonight. They were given instructions to collect you all at very short notice and I think you'll agree that they have done a splendid job.' Katobi began clapping, as did the woman behind Brian, albeit more weakly. A few of the older children in the room clapped too.

When the clapping had subsided Katobi announced, 'Next, I feel an explanation is in order as to why you are all here. I am sure you all have many questions, just as I would have if I were you. And I shall endeavour to answer all of these for you now.'

Behind him Brian heard Hadley grunt something to Sam to which the smaller monster replied, 'No, I haven't got any more sherbet lemons! Now shut up and keep quiet!'

'I am very much aware that there are, perhaps, a few amongst us who may never have heard of Coffinsgrave and who, until tonight, had never travelled by bookcase or, indeed, even met a real life monster. I can imagine that it must have come as quite a shock to you all and I therefore apologise once again, unreservedly. Normally such things would have been explained to you by your parents, guardians or, in some cases, your grandparents. But as, regrettably, they are not here I will try to explain everything as best I can.'

One of the younger children began to cry. A small, furry monster standing beside the girl wrapped two of its four arms around her shoulders and gave her a hug.

'You have been brought tonight to the Hall of Blooskstoof which lies within an ancient building at the very centre of a hamlet, or should I say village, called Coffinsgrave. Unlike most villages, towns or even cities for that matter, Coffinsgrave is located very deep underground. And it can get rather uncomfortably hot in the summer. Although not unique, for there are five other villages such as this, Coffinsgrave has been kept secret from the outside world for a number of reasons. One of which I'm sure is quite apparent to you tonight,' said Katobi, gesturing towards the many monsters standing within the room.

'Many years ago the world was not as you and I know it now. It was a far more dangerous place full of mysterious creatures and beasts that roamed the land and swam in the seas. Most of these monsters, for that is what they were, were kind, friendly and, for the most part, good natured. Completely opposite to how most monsters are depicted and portrayed in ancient scripts and the modern books of today. There were, however, a few creatures… and I shall not call them monsters, for that would be both wrong and unjust to all our friends and colleagues who have brought you here tonight. These

84

creatures were different. Their only pleasure, it seemed, was to cause as much mischief and mayhem in the world as possible. Their only desire to possess the weak and control the vulnerable. In times past they were known as sprites or evil ghosts. Nowadays they are more commonly known as demons.'

A sudden murmuring broke out amongst some of the children within the room and Katobi raised his hands to quieten them before continuing.

'A millennium ago these demons numbered a great many indeed and they were not solely to be found within this country. Reports of demons were commonplace throughout the world no matter where you lived. But these creatures did not belong here. It wasn't their home and they were not from our world. Instead, they secretly travelled to us from their own realm, usually via portals or what we call gates. I am pleased to say that all of these gates are now inactive. A few have been destroyed whilst others have simply been, for want of a better term, switched off. Within our country there are, or were I should say, six such gates. All of which can be found deep underground. Indeed, you are standing upon one right now.'

Once again a nervous murmuring and chatter suddenly erupted within the room.

'But do not be alarmed,' Katobi reassured them loudly. 'For the gate which Coffinsgrave sits upon is not active. This village, like its five sister hamlets, was built solely for the purpose of ensuring that the gate remains forever closed. However, to make absolutely certain of this and to banish any remaining demons that refused to return to their own realm, for there were initially a great many, a special and secret order was created. The Order of Wizitches, formed almost a thousand years ago. These gifted individuals were trained in the ancient art of conjuring, enchantment and magic. For you see demons, unlike monsters, are magical creatures and to defend yourself against enchantment, to actually fight back against evil magic, you can and must only use magic. And very powerful magic at that. Thankfully, as each century drew to a close and another began, the number of demons within our world grew steadily less and less until eventually it was felt that the Order of Wizitches was no longer needed. So, over time, the Order gradually departed from the outside world and instead began constructing the hamlets, deep underground, that now protect each of the six gates that I have previously mentioned. There were a few Wizitches who remained, though.

'Now what has all this got to do with you and why are you here?' asked Katobi, smiling. 'Well, although you may not realise it, each and every one of you is connected to the Order of Wizitches in some way. For although the world above no longer needs protecting by the Order they still, even to this day, guard the six gates, the responsibility often being passed down from one generation to the next. You have been brought here tonight because your parents, guardians and, in some cases, your grandparents all protect the gate upon which Coffinsgrave sits. This is because they are all Wizitches.'

There were a chorus of gasps from some of the younger children in the room. But Brian noticed that some of the older children, including Norman and Audrey, didn't look particularly surprised. He guessed that, unlike him, they were aware of this news already.

Katobi raised his hands to quieten the children once again. 'But this does not explain why you have all been brought here tonight,' he said in a much graver tone. 'I'm afraid there is no easy way to tell you this, but you have been brought here tonight for your own safety. Unfortunately, it is my regrettable duty to inform you that each and every Wizitch who protects Coffinsgrave was scrobbled at 2.11am this morning!'

Chapter 7

THE DRAGON'S CLAW

At once there was an eruption of voices within the room as all the children simultaneously began to shout questions, talk amongst themselves or, in some cases, cry. Those who did get upset were comforted by the strange and peculiar monsters that had brought them to the Halls of Blooskstoof earlier that night.

'What exactly does scrobbled mean?' asked Brian, who had never heard of the word before.

Audrey sucked on her inhaler twice, 'It means,' she replied in between gasps of breath, 'kidnapped. It means our parents and your grandparents have all been kidnapped!'

'Blimey,' remarked Norman, who was pointing at the various bookcases dotted about the room as a number of important-looking individuals suddenly began emerging from them. 'Who do you think they are?'

Audrey shook her head. 'I don't know,' she replied.

Brian, however, recognised two of the men who had emerged from one of the bookcases to his right, Stanley Clutterbucket and Addison Aldwinkle whom he had met at Newtblaster's Book Emporium the day before.

Barnaby Katobi raised his hands once more and after a few moments the room fell silent again. 'I know this must have come as a shock to you all,' he said gravely. 'At present we do not know who has scrobbled your parents, guardians and grandparents or, indeed, why they should have been scrobbled at all. Rather regrettably, we also do not know where they are currently being held, undoubtedly against their will. But rest assured we are doing everything within our power to locate and rescue them as soon as possible. It was decided by myself and the Coffinsgrave Committee earlier this evening,' and at this point Barnaby Katobi gestured to the men and women who had just emerged from the bookcases, 'that you should all be brought here tonight not only to be given a full explanation of the events that have occurred so far but also for your own safety and protection. I have, therefore, arranged accommodation for you all at a number of taverns within Coffinsgrave, and when I call your names I would be most grateful if you would join the committee member who has an arrow floating above their head.'

Brian, Norman and Audrey watched intrigued as suddenly floating above the head of a rather large woman dressed mostly in green was a thin and golden arrow pointing downwards, spinning slowly about in midair.

'The Norris brothers, Dylan and Mason,' began Barnaby Katobi, who was reading from a curly piece of parchment that had just appeared, with a puff of smoke, in his left hand, 'Jade Saliba, Jake Allen, Sophie Ellis and Lucie Ellis. If you could all make your way over to Melissant Melchant.'

Once all the children had gathered by her the golden arrow above her head began to quickly fade whilst another arrow, this time a purple one, appeared over the head of Stanley Clutterbucket with a flurry of sparks.

'Excellent,' remarked Barnaby Katobi. 'Next the Hyland siblings, now where are you all?'

A tall girl with auburn hair popped her hand into the air, her younger sisters and brother crowding anxiously around her.

'Excellent,' repeated Barnaby Katobi. 'So that's Faune Hyland, Amy, Katie, Sophia and not forgetting little Adam,' he said with a smile. 'If you could all make your way over to Stanley Clutterbucket. That's right. Very good.'

Barnaby Katobi continued to call out the names of all the children present until, at last, he reached the final three names on his list.

'Well then,' he said with a satisfied sigh, 'that just leaves Brian Pankhurst, Norman Crabtree and Audrey Jenkins.'

The three children put their hands in the air but to Brian's dismay he couldn't see which committee member they should walk to. None had an arrow hovering above their head and each committee member, it seemed, had already been allocated their children.

'Ah yes, I see you are standing by Beatrice already,' remarked Barnaby Katobi, smiling pleasantly.

Brian turned around and was disappointed to find a scarlet arrow twisting silently over the head of the woman clothed in blood red who had been standing behind them, the large scruffy black bird still seated upon her left shoulder and still staring suspiciously at Brian with its dark, beady eyes. 'Follow me, children,' she said, smiling coldly.

As the other children began to leave the Hall of Blooskstoof, each waving goodbye to the monsters that had brought them, Brian along with Norman and Audrey found himself unexpectedly wrapped up in Hadley's massive arms as the enormous monster said goodbye with a hug that practically squeezed the very life out of them. Sam, who could hardly reach above the children's knees, just gave their legs a bit of a hug.

After getting their breath back and Audrey taking a puff from her inhaler the children followed the red-clothed woman back through the double doors and into the large rectangular room full of books.

'My name is Beatrice Waghorn,' said the woman as she walked briskly up to a tall bookcase and began removing various coloured volumes from it. She spoke quite slowly and clearly, almost as if she were addressing three very stupid ogres. 'You may call me Miss Waghorn. Is that clear?'

'Yes,' the three children replied, sullenly.

'Yes what?' snapped Waghorn, pausing as she removed the final book from the bookcase.

'Yes, Miss Waghorn,' they replied.

'That's better,' replied Waghorn, and she ushered the children through the empty bookcase.

The now familiar whoosh of warm, musty air lifted Brian off his feet and he was jerked forwards into the impenetrable blackness once more. This time he landed successfully on his feet in what appeared to be a very long passage lined with yet more bookcases. Oddly, each of the bookcases seemed to be filled with exactly the same type and shape of books. Norman and Audrey were already waiting for him and they watched together as Waghorn materialised from the bookcase, the shelves magically refilling almost immediately.

'Where are we?' whispered Brian as they followed Waghorn along a corridor, around a bend and into another, almost identical, corridor.

'The Coffinsgrave Soobius Station, I think,' replied Audrey, who was helping Norman to keep up with Waghorn by helping to push his wheelchair for him. 'It's a bit like a railway station,' she explained. 'From here you can travel to some of the most common destinations by the Soobius System.'

'Evening, Miss Waghorn,' said a grey-haired old man dressed in a long brown cloak who had been sitting behind a desk piled high with various burnt and scorched-looking books.

But Beatrice Waghorn didn't even glance at the elderly man as he got up politely from his chair to greet her. Instead, she marched rudely past him almost as if he were invisible and pushed open a large wooden door which brought the three children out onto a dark and cobbled street. From here, and still walking at a furious pace, Waghorn strode across the road and down a deserted and winding alley until she stopped abruptly at a tiny terraced building that was no bigger than Newtblaster's Book Emporium. It had a single, dirty green door set into its front which was accompanied by a grimy and stained glass window to one side. Above the door hung a sign. Much to Brian's disgust it appeared to be a very large and very real severed claw of some type. Blood was dripping from its dark green scaly skin and, Brian noticed, when it landed upon the cobbled street seemed to disappear. Almost as if the stones were somehow absorbing it.

'It's not real,' said Norman, who had been watching as Brian stared curiously at the evaporating blood. 'It's magic.'

'But it looks so real,' whispered Brian.

'It's just an illusion,' remarked Norman as Waghorn pushed open the tavern door and entered, the three children following close behind her.

Due to the lateness of the hour it was practically empty of customers. There was, however, one patron dressed in what looked like a very faded and once-flamboyant purple military uniform who was sitting within a corner, slumped against a wall, seemingly fast asleep, a tankard of brown liquid sitting untouched upon the table in front of him. Other tables and chairs were spread haphazardly across the drink-spattered floor whilst to the left were a bar and a flight of stairs that led upwards. To the rear of the tavern was a stage, probably used for some form of entertainment. Brian guessed that, at its busiest, the tavern must have had seating for at least several hundred customers and for those who didn't mind standing it probably had room at the bar for perhaps another hundred more. Which was weird because from the outside, at least, the tavern didn't really look that big.

'We're closed,' shouted a large bald-headed man irritably, suddenly appearing from behind the bar. He wore a dirty brown shirt over what looked like an even dirtier white vest. 'Oh, it's you, Miss Waghorn,' he said, apologetically, and put on the falsest smile that Brian had ever seen. 'Not seen you around these parts in a very long time. If you don't mind me saying so you're looking very well, and such a lovely perfume you've chosen to wear. I must get my wife a bottle. What is it called?'

Waghorn smiled, which, thought Brian, made her look like she was sneering rather than actually smiling. 'I believe I have a reservation, Mr Gillibottom,' she said, ignoring the tavern owner's question.

'For yourself, Miss Waghorn?' asked Gillibottom, wiping his sweaty forehead with the bottom of his filthy apron.

'No, for these children,' said Waghorn, gesturing to Brian, Norman and Audrey. 'They have had rooms allocated to them by Barnaby Katobi.'

Gillibottom reached over the bar and, from underneath it, removed a large, black book which he opened and hastily flicked through. The bird on Waghorn's shoulder squawked noisily at him.

'Morgan, Bluebottle, Grainger, Babette,' remarked Gillibottom, running his finger slowly down the most recent page of bookings. 'Patel, Boxwhippet, Smith. Ah, here's the booking, Katobi, three children and unknown length of stay. Room 44 is the only room we have free at the moment though, Miss Waghorn. But it's one of our very best, even if I do say so myself. Has a lovely view.'

'I'm sure it has,' remarked Waghorn, indifferently.

Just then, the door behind the bar opened. 'What's taking you so long?' asked a large ginger-haired woman who was busy consuming the last of what appeared to be an incredibly big slice of chocolate cake. 'Guests, at this hour?' she remarked, staring at Waghorn, the children and then up at the clock on the wall above her.

Gillibottom pushed the guest book towards his wife and said, 'Room 44, Elfrida my dear.'

'Room 44?' repeated the ginger-haired woman, frowning in surprise and somehow managing to force the last of the chocolate cake into her mouth. 'But that's next to...' she mumbled. But her husband had already disappeared into the kitchen. She shrugged and wiped her mouth on the cuff of her sleeve. Then, pulling the guest book towards her, she found a pen, peered at the children and snapped, 'Names?'

Waghorn pushed Brian roughly forwards.

'Pankhurst. Brian Pankhurst,' he said.

'Next?' sniffed the woman.

'Audrey Jenkins.'

'And you in the chair thing?' she asked, wiping her nose on the same sleeve that she had wiped the remains of her chocolate cake away with so she now had crumbs stuck all over one of her cheeks.

'Norman Crabtree,' said Norman, wheeling his chair forwards.

The ginger-haired woman sniffed again before finally looking up from the tavern register and saying, 'That'll be four silver pieces, in advance.'

Waghorn raised one of her eyebrows suspiciously. 'Isn't that rather expensive?' she remarked before adding, almost as an afterthought, 'For a tavern like this?'

'Take it or leave it,' said the ginger-haired woman, wiping the chocolate crumbs from her cheek and into her hand before popping them into her mouth.

Somewhat reluctantly, Waghorn removed the required fee from a small leather pouch that she'd had upon her person and placed the four coins, one by one, onto the grubby bar. The ginger-haired woman greedily took the money, shoving it hastily into one of her pockets. Then, walking over to the end of the bar, she looked down at what appeared to be a smooth stone slab embedded within it and cried at the top of her voice, 'Engleburt!'

Brian watched curiously, wondering if the poor woman had, in fact, lost her mind. What was she expecting to happen? Was she hoping to see some sort of head emerge from the stone slab? But that was exactly what did happen! The stone slab suddenly rippled just as water does when something splashes upon its surface and then very slowly a small bald and horned head emerged, seemingly also made out of stone.

'Engleburt, take these children to room 44,' said the ginger-haired woman sternly.

The stone head yawned grumpily. 'Do it yourself,' it said in a deep, gravelly voice.

'What?' cried the woman, aghast. 'What did you just say to me?'

'I said do it yourself!' replied the stone head irritably, trying unsuccessfully to shake the sleep from its stone skull. 'Do you know what time it is?'

'It doesn't matter what time it is or what time it isn't,' scolded the ginger-haired woman. 'It's your job to show guests to their rooms! That's what you're employed for!'

'But not at five o'clock in the morning I'm not!' it snapped, yawning again. 'We gargoyles need to sleep as well, you know!'

'I'm not the remotest bit interested in your sleeping habits,' shot back the ginger-haired woman. 'Just do your job and show these guests to their room!'

'Shan't,' said the stone head, sticking its tongue out unpleasantly at the woman and blowing a rude noise with its lips.

Furiously, the ginger-haired woman lunged at the stone head with her outstretched hands, but it was much too quick for her and instantly disappeared back into the slab of grey stone with a wicked cackle.

'Engleburt!' cried the ginger-haired woman irately. 'Engleburt, come back here at once! Do you hear me? Come back at once or so help me…' She cursed loudly a number of times and made a number of terrible threats, all involving the gargoyle's head and a particularly heavy hammer that she had secretly hidden somewhere within the bar, but the stone head did not resurface. Instead, she bellowed another name. 'Violet!' There was no response. 'Violet! Get down here at once!'

Somewhere far above them there was the noise of a door opening and closing followed by the sound of light footsteps hastily descending a number of stairs, which gradually grew louder and louder until eventually a girl with curly black hair, wearing a thin and ragged grey dressing gown, emerged from the staircase directly behind the bar.

'How many times do I have to call your name, you stupid girl!' snapped the ginger-haired woman and she struck the girl across the side of her face, the girl's left cheek instantly turning bright red.

The girl cowered and immediately tried to protect herself as the ginger-haired woman went to strike her once more. Brian stared in dismay at the mass of bruises upon the girl's wrists as the sleeves of her dressing gown rolled backwards.

'I would not do that again,' warned Waghorn, who had suddenly grabbed the ginger-haired woman's hand with her own.

'Here, what do you think you're doing? Let go of me!' demanded the ginger-haired woman, trying to shake her wrist free from Waghorn's grasp. 'Who is she to you?' she asked, gesturing to the young girl. 'She's no daughter of yours.'

'And neither is she a daughter of yours,' remarked Waghorn, sternly. 'Leave her be. Clearly she was asleep when you called for her and your fury should be directed at your disobedient gargoyle rather than this girl.'

Waghorn relaxed her vice-like grip upon the ginger-haired woman's wrist and finally she was able to snatch her hand free. She stared at Waghorn, an expression of anger mixed with fear upon her face. 'Take these guests to room 44,' she spat at the girl.

The girl nodded politely and gestured to the children to follow her towards a bookcase next to the stairs by which she had just descended.

'And you!' the woman said to Waghorn, venomously. 'Get out of my tavern!'

Beatrice Waghorn smiled, which once again, thought Brian, looked more like a sneer rather than an actual smile. Turning towards the children she said, 'Until I tell you otherwise you are to remain in your room at all times. Do not feel the need to explore or wander through the tavern, and under no circumstance are you to go outside. Do you understand?'

'Yes,' the children replied.

'Yes what?' snapped Waghorn, impatiently.

'Yes, Miss Waghorn,' replied the children, and they watched as she turned on her heel and left the tavern without giving any of them a second glance. Then, following the curly-haired girl into the bookcase, they emerged seconds later in a very small corridor apparently on a higher floor within the tavern.

'This room's yours,' said the girl, and she pointed at the door opposite them. 'I sleep in the next room, number 45.'

'Thanks,' said Brian.

'Are you all right?' asked Audrey, concerned as the girl's cheek was still visibly quite pink from where the ginger-haired woman had slapped her.

She nodded, rubbing her face painfully. 'I guess I should have come down a bit quicker.'

'Nonsense!' said Audrey, firmly. 'That woman downstairs needs a good kicking!'

Norman laughed. 'A good kicking!'

'Well, not a good kicking,' said Audrey, awkwardly. 'But, well, she needs reporting! Horrible woman!'

'Was Waghorn right?' asked Brian, tentatively. 'When she said she wasn't your mother?'

The girl nodded her head. 'Yes, my parents are both dead.'

'Oh,' said Brian, suddenly feeling very uncomfortable indeed.

'It's okay,' said the girl, sensing Brian's obvious discomfort. 'They died a long time ago and I can hardly remember them. Elfrida, I mean, Mrs Gillibottom and her husband took me in when I was very young and now I work for them. I should be grateful really. If they hadn't taken me in then I would probably be dead too.'

'What do you mean you work for them?' asked Audrey, surprised. 'You're the same age as us, aren't you? Eleven, a little bit older maybe? How old are you? When's your birthday?'

The girl shrugged.

'You don't know how old you are?' asked Audrey, shocked.

'Don't you go to school?' asked Norman.

The girl shrugged again.

'Cool!' exclaimed Norman. 'I wish I didn't have to go to school!'

Audrey glared at him. 'Norman Crabtree! The fact that she does not go to school is not cool at all. It's wrong. Completely wrong!' she said, turning to face the girl again. 'How long have you worked here, then, exactly?'

'I don't know,' the girl replied. 'I guess since I was about this high,' and she held out her hand so that it was just above her waist.

'You can't have been more than about five or six,' remarked Audrey in disgust.

'And what do you do here?' asked Norman.

'Anything the Gillibottoms ask me to do,' replied the girl. 'Wash the floors, make the beds, do the laundry, clean the dishes, unblock the toilets...'

'But you get breaks, don't you?' asked Audrey. 'Time off?'

Violet shook her head. 'No. Besides, why would I want any time off?'

'To relax,' said Audrey. 'To have fun and to go out and play with your friends!'

'But I don't have any friends,' said the girl.

Audrey stared at Violet, open-mouthed. How were the Gillibottoms getting away with this? Violet was being treated as though she were a slave. And from the bruises on her arms she was being beaten too! How could she have no friends? How could she not even know when her birthday was? Didn't anybody care?

'Right, let's do this properly then,' said Audrey.

'Oh, Audrey, do we have to?' began Norman, rolling his eyes upwards.

'Yes, we do have to,' argued Audrey.

'But I really need—' protested Norman.

'It's not about what you need!' snapped Audrey and then, turning towards Violet, she said very politely, 'My name's Audrey Jenkins,' and shook the girl's hand. 'Pleased to meet you!'

'Violet Armstrong,' said Violet. 'And I'm pleased to meet you too!'

'And this is Brian Pankhurst,' said Audrey, nodding at Brian and gesturing to Norman. 'And he's Norman Crabtree.'

'Pleased to meet you,' said Brian.

Violet beamed.

'Brilliant!' said Norman. 'Now we've got that sorted and we're all friends, where's the toilet? Because I'm busting!'

Chapter 8

ARNOLD BLOODLOCK AND THE CUP OF AGES

When Brian awoke Norman was already up and peering through the bedroom window. After saying goodnight to Violet earlier that morning, for it had been very late indeed when the three children had been brought to Coffinsgrave, they had wearily climbed into their beds, tired and exhausted, without even discussing any of the night's events, and within minutes they had all been soundly fast asleep.

Brian had slept almost undisturbed. However, he did awaken once, although he couldn't be sure exactly what time it had been because the room that he, Norman and Audrey were sharing had no alarm clock and he was not wearing a watch. He was also not entirely sure of what had actually awoken him. He couldn't be certain but he'd had the distinct impression that someone or something had been scratching at the bedroom door, trying to get in. But when he had strained to hear more clearly the peculiar scratching noise had ceased.

Their room at the Dragon's Claw was small and basic. Brian guessed that it was normally a twin room and the Gillibottoms had somehow managed to squeeze in a third bed. It was sparsely furnished with just a couple of wardrobes and some random pictures hanging on the grubby walls. The children's bathroom, meanwhile, adjoining their bedroom, had no towels or soap and the toilet was blocked.

'What's going on?' asked Brian with a yawn, stretching his arms. Outside he could hear all sorts of strange popping sounds which, he assumed, were probably what had just woken him up.

'It's raining,' replied Norman.

'What?' said Brian, confused. 'It can't be raining. We're underground, remember?'

'I know, but it's still raining,' said Norman matter-of-factly.

'But how can it be?' asked Brian, climbing out of bed and joining Norman at the window. He peered through the dirty glass and stared in amazement. Norman was right. It was raining. Outside it was, quite literally, raining cats and dogs! Tiny, miniature cats and dogs of all shapes, sizes and colours were falling slowly, like bubbles, from somewhere high above, and as they landed gently on a roof or a path or bounced upon the cobbled street each one exploded with a tiny bark or meow!

'The cavern roof is enchanted,' explained Norman, watching as a white poodle exploded with a woof on the windowsill in front of him. 'Coffinsgrave was built in a huge natural cavern and the roof is cursed. Can't remember how it happened, some demon or something or other years and years ago. Like I said, I'm not too good on magical history, and besides it's all very boring! Anyway, it usually rains here every day. Some days it rains cats and dogs like today. Other days it rains balloons or coat-hangers and once when I visited here with Mum and Dad it actually rained rabbit droppings! Nasty!' he remarked, wrinkling his nose in disgust and pulling an unpleasant face.

Brian stared out the window and sighed. In just a single day and night his whole world had been turned completely upside down and now he just didn't know what to believe any more. He'd witnessed amazing things, seen incredible creatures and listened to fantastic stories. Things that normally he would have scoffed and laughed at and yet here he was, deep underground in a tavern whose sign dripped magical blood, staring through a window, watching as tiny cats and dogs exploded in the street below him. Brian wondered where his mother was right now and what she was doing. How much did she know about all this? Was she even aware of Coffinsgrave's existence and the demon portal that it had protected for hundreds of years? Brian suspected that she probably was, and that this was partly the reason why, until now, he'd had so little contact with his grandparents. And what of his father? What had his real job been? He certainly hadn't been an accountant, Brian was certain of that. Had his father, like his grandparents, been a Wizitch? Did his disappearance, almost a year ago now, have something to do with Brian's grandparents being kidnapped? Even if he could have spoken to his mother right there and then Brian doubted that she'd have the answers that he wanted.

'It must have come as quite a shock for you,' said Audrey, also awake and sitting up in bed. She took a puff from her inhaler. 'All this, I mean. Norman and I have grown up with it. We knew what our parents did for a living. But for you everything must seem so completely unbelievable.'

'That's it exactly,' said Brian, moving from the window to the end of Audrey's bed. 'It's almost too unbelievable to be true. But last night I saw walking, talking monsters, creatures that for me used to only exist in books! I've travelled by bookcase from one place to another in just a blink of an eye, drunk a potion that gave me silver footprints with a mind of their own, able to wander anywhere they wanted to of their own free will!'

'That was so funny!' laughed Norman as three ginger cats all exploded on the windowsill in front of him at the same time. 'Audrey looked like she was doing the tango!'

'I used to think magic was just pretend,' continued Brian. 'That it was just card tricks and men in strange costumes cutting pieces of rope in half. But it's real, isn't it? All of it is real.'

Audrey nodded and climbed out of bed to peer out of the window at the falling cats and dogs herself. 'It's real all right,' she said, more to herself perhaps than to Brian or Norman. 'Magic is real and so are demons. Our parents, your grandparents, all the Wizitches are missing. We don't know why or where they've been taken. We don't even know if they're alive or dead.'

'Well, that's a cheerful thought,' said Norman, wheeling his chair back to his bed.

'Norman Crabtree, aren't you in the least bit worried about your parents?' asked Audrey anxiously.

'Yeah, I am,' he said grimly, dragging himself from his wheelchair and on to the end of his bed, so that he was facing her. 'Of course I'm worried, Audrey. My mum and dad have been kidnapped and I'm worried sick! But what can we do?' he asked, throwing his hands up into the air in frustration.

Audrey sat down next to Norman and put her hand on his shoulder. 'I'm sorry,' she said. 'I didn't mean to snap. I guess we've just got to hope that Barnaby Katobi can rescue them.'

'Looks like somebody's been here whilst we've been asleep,' said Brian, walking over to his bed and picking up a brown sack lying at its side. 'I don't remember seeing this here last night!'

'What's in it?' asked Norman, finding a similar sack next to his bed. There was one by Audrey's too.

Brian loosened the rope sash that had been fastening his sack and tipped the contents onto his bed. Out fell his trainers, a pair of jeans, T-shirts and all sorts of other clothes as well as a toothbrush, soap and other toiletries. 'Looks like we're going to be here for some time,' he remarked thoughtfully.

There was a knock at the door and Audrey got up to open it.

'I see you've found your clean clothes,' remarked Violet, who was standing outside. The curly-haired girl was dressed in a pair of torn trousers and a shabby T-shirt, both of which looked as though they hadn't been washed for quite some time. Her arms, the children

102

noticed, were covered in painful-looking bruises. 'I brought them in this morning whilst you were still asleep,' she giggled. 'Norman was snoring like a pig!'

Norman's face flushed.

'Are you hungry?' asked Violet.

All three children nodded.

'I'm starving!' said Norman, his belly suddenly rumbling furiously.

'You're always hungry,' remarked Audrey.

'Well, if you get dressed quickly there's just enough time to have your breakfast downstairs before the tavern opens,' said Violet. 'Mr Gillibottom says you've got to be back up in your room during opening hours, which means you'll have to have your other meals up here I'm afraid. I'll wait for you out in the hallway.'

A few minutes later Brian, Norman and Audrey joined Violet and they passed into the bookcase opposite their bedroom door, reappearing moments later in the bar downstairs. And just like the previous night the bar was empty. Well, almost empty. In the furthest corner, still slumped against the wall, was the man dressed in purple they had seen the night before when they had first arrived, his tankard of ale still sitting on the table before him, apparently untouched. Which was strange, thought Brian, as Violet had just informed them that the tavern wasn't even open yet.

Noticing the children emerging from the bookcase the man waved and beckoned them over.

'That's Major Arnold Bloodlock,' whispered Violet, waving back at him. 'Good morning, Major! How are you this morning?'

'Can't complain, my dear,' he replied cheerfully, his aristocratic voice revealing a privileged upbringing. 'And whom do you have with you today?' he enquired, gesturing towards the other children.

'This is Brian, Norman and Audrey,' said Violet, introducing each one of her new friends to the major. 'They're staying at the Dragon's Claw for a while.'

Although old, Brian guessed that Major Bloodlock was probably younger than his granddad, possibly in his sixties. However, the flamboyant purple military uniform that he wore looked very much older indeed. In fact it was quite unlike anything Brian had ever seen before. With his matching purple hat it looked more like some sort of fancy dress outfit than an actual uniform. Somewhat oddly, Brian also noticed that the major appeared to be covered from head to foot in a thin layer of dust, almost as if he'd been sitting within the tavern in exactly the same chair and position for many years.

'I'm right pleased to meet you all,' said Bloodlock, getting up and bowing politely. But as he did so a cloud of dust fell from him like an avalanche. It poured over the table and onto the floor, covering each of the children's feet. In an attempt to halt the flow of the dust Bloodlock removed his hat and flapped it about, doing his utmost to clear the air. It didn't work.

'I'll go and get your breakfasts,' said Violet, disappearing through the door behind the bar as Brian and Audrey each took a chair and, with Norman, joined Arnold Bloodlock at his table.

'Sorry about that,' apologised Bloodlock, awkwardly, replacing his hat. He coughed and sat down. 'So, why are you young children staying at the Dragon's Claw?' he asked. 'I suspect that there are more hospitable taverns than this to visit.'

'The other taverns were all fully booked,' explained Audrey.

Bloodlock nodded in sudden understanding. 'No doubt because of the Coffinsgrave Fair, my dear,' he said, sitting back in his chair and adjusting his hat to a more satisfactory angle which, in turn, sent another avalanche of dust straight into his tankard of ale. 'But that still does not explain why Miss Waghorn brought you to the Dragon's Claw at such an unfashionably late hour last night. I watched you arrive.'

'Our parents—' began Norman.

'And my grandparents,' added Brian.

'Have all been scrobbled,' said Audrey.

104

'Scrobbled, you say!' remarked Bloodlock, curiously. 'Why, what happened?'

Audrey, with help from Brian and Norman, explained all that had happened to them since they had been collected by Sam and Hadley and taken to the Halls of Blooskstoof. When she had finished recounting their tale Bloodlock whistled, seemingly impressed by the children's story. Behind them Violet reappeared, carrying three surprisingly appetising plates of cooked breakfast, which she carefully placed in front of the children whilst handing them each a knife, a fork and a napkin. Then, glancing cautiously over her shoulder, she joined the children at Bloodlock's table.

'My, those breakfasts do look lovely,' remarked Bloodlock, licking his lips hungrily as if he hadn't eaten for a very long while.

'Would you like some of mine?' asked Audrey. 'Only there really is too much here for me to eat. Here, have a sausage.' She offered her plate to the major.

'No, no, I couldn't possibly, my dear,' said Bloodlock, tipping his hat politely at her and forcing another cloud of dust on to the table. 'But I thank you so kindly for asking.' In barely a whisper, he added, 'I suppose you do know that this is not the first time an attempt has been made to scrobble the Wizitches?'

'What?' mumbled Norman in surprise, half-choking on a piece of bacon.

'You mean this has happened before?' said Brian, shocked.

'Indeed it has, my dear boy,' said Bloodlock, nodding. 'It was a very long time ago now, but there were some Wizitches who died in the attempted scrobbling. Died right here in Coffinsgrave, if you'd believe such a thing could happen!'

Audrey gasped and put a hand to her mouth, suddenly frightened for her parents.

'Oh, I didn't mean to scare you, my dear,' apologised Bloodlock. 'I'm sure whatever has happened to your parents and the other Wizitches has no connection with the Demon Lord.'

105

'The Demon Lord!' exclaimed Norman in shock, missing his mouth with his fork and prodding himself in the cheek with half a fried tomato.

'I've never heard of any attempt to scrobble the Wizitches before,' remarked Audrey, sucking on her inhaler.

'It's in the very old history books,' said Bloodlock, nodding.

'What happened exactly?' asked Brian, fascinated.

'Unfortunately, my memory is not what it once was,' remarked Bloodlock, rubbing his forehead and sending another eruption of dust into the air. 'Let me think; I'm trying to recall the Demon Lord's name. Its real name, that is, and not the name its followers used to call it by. Let me think. Ah yes, I have it, Deevilmon.'

'I've never heard of a demon by that name before,' said Audrey.

'Me neither,' said Norman, forcing half a slice of toast into his mouth all in one go.

'Well, as I said, this all happened a very long time ago indeed,' said Bloodlock. 'I do not think that it is an overstatement to claim that Deevilmon was probably the most powerful demon to have ever entered our world. Like many others of its kind, when it was given the opportunity to leave and return to its own realm, it outright refused. Demons, as I'm sure you're already aware, are magical creatures and revel in causing as much mischief and mayhem as possible. But Deevilmon was different. It didn't want to simply cause as much chaos as it could. Oh no, it wanted much more than that. It craved something entirely different. Power! Not only did Deevilmon want to rule over its own kind, bending each and every other demon to its own will, but it wanted to govern our world too. It wanted to rule and live forever. It wanted to become immortal.'

'But nobody can live forever,' pointed out Brian matter-of-factly.

Bloodlock smiled. 'There is a way to become immortal,' he said in barely a whisper, 'It isn't easy of course. Attempting to live

106

forever never is. But all Deevilmon would really need is the Wizitches and, of course, the Cup of Ages!'

'What's the Cup of Ages?' asked Norman, who was mopping up the last of his fried egg with his final slice of buttered toast.

'Why, the Cup of Ages is the source of the Wizitches' powers!' remarked Bloodlock, apparently surprised that the children didn't know this. 'To signify that a person is a Wizitch each Wizitch carries a ruby stone. When I was a Wizitch I had a stud in one of my ears, quite fashionable at the time. Forget which one it was now though. I think it was the left, or was it the right? No, it was the left.'

'But you're not a Wizitch any more?' enquired Audrey.

Bloodlock shook his head and both Brian and Violet sneezed violently.

'No, not any more,' replied Bloodlock a little sadly. 'Each magical stone that a Wizitch bears is usually carried by them in the form of a piece of jewellery, which in turn, disguises its true purpose. It might be a ring, necklace, bracelet or some other trinket.'

'My mother has a ring that she wears all the time,' remarked Audrey, wiping her lips clean with her napkin. 'On her right hand.'

'And my dad wears a gold chain on his wrist which has a tiny red jewel hanging from it like a charm,' said Norman, thoughtfully.

'My grandmother has a broach that she wears,' said Brian. 'It has a red stone at its centre, and my granddad wears a ring on his little finger that's got a red stone in it.'

'So the stones signify who is a Wizitch,' said Norman in understanding. 'I get that, but lots of people wear jewellery with ruby stones in them. What's so special about the rubies that the Wizitches carry?'

'Isn't it obvious?' said Bloodlock. 'They're magical. Not only do the stones enhance the user's magical powers but they also allow the Wizitch to age at a much slower rate than normal people. They hardly age at all.'

'So by scrobbling the Wizitches this demon, Deevilmon, would have obtained all the magical stones,' said Violet, who had been listening intently to the major's story.

'Exactly!' exclaimed Bloodlock. 'And can you imagine how powerful all the stones would be collectively?'

'But why would Deevilmon also need the Cup of Ages?' asked Brian.

'Because the Cup of Ages and the ruby stones the Wizitches carry are, in effect, one and the same thing,' explained Bloodlock. 'Oh dear, I'm not explaining this very well, am I?' he said, seeing the children's confused faces. 'The Cup of Ages was at one time and still is to this day a very magical and powerful artefact. In years gone by it was thought by some to be too powerful; in the wrong hands it could have been used as a weapon. It was therefore decided long ago that its power should, instead, be shared and so, very carefully, the twelve ruby stones that contained the majority of the Cup's power were removed from its outer edge...'

'And these are the stones that the twelve Wizitches carry today,' finished Violet.

'Exactly!' said Bloodlock, punching the table with his fist and sending an explosion of dust into the air. 'For Deevilmon to become immortal it would have needed not only the twelve ruby stones but also the Cup of Ages. One without the other would not have been enough!'

'There's still one thing that I don't understand,' said Brian. 'If Deevilmon only needed the Cup of Ages and the twelve ruby stones that the Wizitches carried to become immortal then why didn't it just steal the stones? I mean, why go to all the trouble of trying to kidnap the Wizitches in the first place? It doesn't make any sense.'

'Because, my boy, to become immortal Deevilmon needed three things,' said Bloodlock.

'The Cup of Ages?' said Violet.

'And the twelve Wizitch rubies,' added Norman.

'But what else?' asked Brian, puzzled.

Bloodlock leant forward and in a hushed tone said, 'Deevilmon would have also needed a substantial amount of blood from each of the Wizitches!'

Chapter 9

COFFINSGRAVE

'Why you good-for-nothing lazy little girl!' cried Elfrida Gillibottom fiercely from behind the bar, her face instantly glowering red with rage. 'What do *you* think you're doing?' she demanded, staring at Violet, who was still sitting at the table with Brian, Norman, Audrey and Major Bloodlock.

'Nothing. I—' replied Violet, jumping up to her feet in fright.

'Exactly!' screamed Elfrida Gillibottom, storming over to Violet and grabbing her ear painfully with two of her fat fingers, dragging her back towards the bar. 'There's work to be done and you're sitting idly, doing NOTHING! You should be ashamed of yourself after all my husband and I have done for you!'

'But I—' cried Violet, trying to explain.

'Do *not* raise your voice to me, you little MONSTER!' shouted the tavern owner's wife, pinching Violet hard on the arm and slapping her across the face. 'Now get into that kitchen and start washing them dishes before I really lose my temper! And you three,' she snapped, glaring at Brian, Norman and Audrey, 'you better get to your room double-quick if you know what's good for you!'

A few minutes later, as the three children emerged from the bookcase opposite their bedroom door, Audrey said, 'I don't know why we didn't do anything. I mean, how *could* we have just sat there and let that horrible woman slap Violet? Did you see her face? Her cheek was so pink! I feel awful. We should have done something. I can't believe we just sat there and watched it all happen and didn't even get up from our chairs! I'm going to tell Barnaby Katobi. I'm going to report her! That awful Gillibottom woman isn't going to get away with this!'

They did not see Violet again until later that afternoon when she brought them their lunch, which was an unpleasant-looking sandwich on dry bread that had mouldy cheese inside and smelt horrid. Violet apologised for their meagre meal before immediately disappearing back downstairs and presumably into the kitchen. Her cheek, the children noticed, was still very pink.

For most of that morning and afternoon Brian, Norman and Audrey discussed Major Bloodlock's tale concerning Deevilmon and the Wizitches. Audrey was convinced that the demon had returned and that this was the only explanation as to why all the Wizitches had been kidnapped, although she had no evidence to actually back this theory up with. Norman thought she was quite mad and Brian, frankly, didn't know what to think.

'So explain how Deevilmon managed to get through the portal then?' asked Norman, sceptically. 'It's been closed for years!'

'I can't,' replied Audrey. 'Not yet! But every locked door can be opened if you have the right key.'

'But if this demon has returned then why hasn't it stolen the Cup of Ages already?' continued Norman. 'Surely if it wanted to become immortal then its plan would have been to scrobble the Wizitches and steal the Cup of Ages at the same time. It doesn't make any sense to steal one without the other. Barnaby Katobi must know about Deevilmon's previous attempt to steal the Cup of Ages and he would have had it locked away or put it under armed guard as soon as the Wizitches were scrobbled! And that's assuming the Cup of Ages is even in Coffinsgrave. It might have been taken away from here long ago. What do you think, Brian?'

Brian shrugged. 'I don't know,' he replied, honestly. 'It does seem unlikely that Deevilmon could get through a portal that's been closed for more than a century, but I can't think of any other reason why all the Wizitches would have been kidnapped.'

'Who's to say that Deevilmon even came into our world through this portal?' said Audrey, thoughtfully. 'Barnaby Katobi said there were six in total. Maybe it got through one of the other ones?'

'And aren't there other portals in other countries too?' suggested Brian.

Audrey nodded enthusiastically.

'Hang on a minute,' said Norman, taken aback. 'You're not actually buying any of this demon nonsense, are you, Brian?'

'I don't know what to believe,' Brian replied, shrugging his shoulders again. 'But it's the only theory we have. Until a better one comes along I think we've got to assume that the Wizitches have been taken against their will, don't you?'

For the rest of that day the children remained in their room, Norman and Audrey arguing about other possible and farfetched theories as to how and why the Wizitches had been kidnapped with Brian occasionally chipping in with an idea himself when he could get a word in edgeways.

Later that evening Violet brought them their dinner, which was an unpleasant-looking and -smelling stew of some type, but she did not stay for long.

'What's in it?' asked Norman, staring at the three bowls of stew suspiciously.

'You don't want to know,' replied Violet, placing the tray carrying the bowls of stew onto a bedroom table. 'I can't stay. If I'm away from the kitchen for more than five minutes Mrs Gillibottom will notice and I'll be punished again. Oh, and I got these for you.' She handed each of the children a small wrapped biscuit. 'It's not much,' she said, turning towards the bedroom door to leave. 'But I thought you might like it if you didn't enjoy the stew.'

'But you'll get into so much trouble, Violet,' said Audrey, attempting to hand the chocolate biscuit back to Violet.

112

Violet shook her head. 'Mrs Gillibottom won't notice. She has a secret cupboard full of them,' she said, pushing the biscuit back into Audrey's hand. 'That's why she's so fat. She eats about twenty bars a day!'

Next morning, the children were disappointed to learn that they were now to have all their meals in their room, including breakfast. Brian, who once again had been woken during the night by a strange scratching noise at the bedroom door, was still half asleep when Norman read out the note that he had discovered, slipped underneath their door.

'Breakfast will now be left outside your room each day at 8.00am sharp,' Norman read. 'EG.'

'What's EG mean?' asked Brian, taking the note and reading it himself. In the top left-hand corner he noticed three vertical lines of tiny interlocking circles. He had seen something like this before. On his first day at his grandparents' house his granddad had received a letter which, coincidentally, had also had three lines of interlocking circles printed in one corner. He quickly counted the circles. The first line had two circles. The second line had seven and the third line had a total of eight circles which seemed to look slightly larger than those in the other two lines.

'I'm guessing EG stands for Elfrida Gillibottom,' said Audrey, pulling an unpleasant-looking face almost as if the very name itself had left a nasty taste in her mouth.

'And what do these mean?' asked Brian, showing Norman and Audrey the note and pointing at the circles.

'That's the date when the note was written,' explained Norman. 'The first two lines signify the day. Two and seven, so that's twenty-seven, and the third line is the month,' he said, counting the circles. 'Eight, so that's August. Well, today's the 27th August so Gillibottom must have written that note sometime this morning.'

'What time is it now?' asked Audrey.

'Dunno,' said Norman.

Audrey got up and opened their bedroom door. Upon the filthy floor, outside, sat a tray with three plates of very cold cooked breakfast on it. 'Evidently, 8.00am has been and gone,' she remarked, disappointedly.

Over the next few days the three children saw Violet only when she brought them their meals. Occasionally, she brought them a chocolate sweet or a biscuit too. Quite how she was able to smuggle these out of the kitchen without anybody noticing, the children had no idea. As much as they enjoyed the delicious treats they were terribly worried that Violet might get caught and, in turn, suffer another beating at the hands of the tavern owner's wife.

As each day passed with no further news of the missing Wizitches or visits from Beatrice Waghorn and her scruffy black bird the children quickly grew more bored and restless. With the three of them unable to leave their tiny bedroom it began to feel more like a prison cell and soon they were all getting on each other's nerves with Norman and Audrey constantly bickering. Brian spent most of the time sitting by the window watching the falling rain, which so far had consisted of cats and dogs, feather dusters, picture frames and pink, fluffy rabbits. He wondered if his mother knew what had happened to him and his grandparents and whether she had reported their disappearance to the police.

On the evening of their fourth day Violet brought them their dinner, which once again consisted of three bowls of the unpleasant-smelling stew that they'd been given on their first night at the tavern. However, unlike the previous days Violet did not leave immediately.

'You must get really bored stuck in here all day,' remarked Violet, staring at Norman, who appeared to have been enthusiastically making some sort of strange figure from a discarded box of matchsticks, a broken pencil and an elastic band that he had found. 'I don't suppose you fancy a tour of Coffinsgrave, do you?'

'What?' said the children all at the same time.

'I've got to go on an errand for Mrs Gillibottom,' Violet explained. 'And I thought maybe you might want to come too.'

'It's a bit dangerous though,' said Audrey, nervously. 'What if we get caught? Waghorn warned us not to leave the tavern under any circumstances.'

'Oh come on, Audrey!' said Norman, rolling his eyes upwards. 'Do you do everything you're told? Besides, if I have to stay in here much longer listening to your crackpot theories about Deevilmon you won't have to worry about getting into trouble with Waghorn because I'll have killed you by then! What about you, Brian, you up for it?'

'Definitely!' said Brian, nodding enthusiastically.

'Well, you can't leave me here alone,' protested Audrey. 'So I'd better come too! But if we get caught then don't say I didn't warn you!'

'It's uncanny how much you sound like my mum sometimes, Audrey,' remarked Norman, wheeling himself towards the bedroom door.

Audrey pushed past him, forcing Norman to steer his wheelchair into the doorframe.

'Hey! Watch it!' snapped Norman, annoyed.

'I've only visited Coffinsgrave a couple of times before,' said Audrey, ignoring Norman's protests as she walked past him with Brian and Violet. 'And that was only with my parents, so it'll be nice to explore a little bit.'

From the bookcase opposite the children's bedroom Violet quickly removed a number of different-coloured books as Brian, Norman and Audrey looked on expectantly. Once the shelves were completely empty and had themselves disappeared into the bookcase Violet stepped inside quickly followed by her new friends.

They emerged, moments later, inside the Coffinsgrave Soobius Station. Unlike their previous visit, four nights ago, it was a lot busier with various people, some dressed in cloaks and pointed hats, disappearing into and appearing out of the numerous bookcases that formed the long and identical aisles.

'Where is everyone going to?' asked Brian as they turned a corner and weaved their way through the hurrying crowd.

'It's the rush hour,' explained Violet. 'It's like this every day. It's manic! Everyone's on their way home from work.'

'Sorry!' apologised Norman as one of the wheels of his chair rolled over a woman's foot.

As they reached the station exit Brian noticed the grey-haired old man whom they had seen on their previous visit to the Soobius Station, still sitting behind his desk but this time with even more burnt and scorched-looking books piled about him. Indeed, the mountain of books was so high that the old man could barely be seen behind them.

Once outside, Brian was amazed to see that the sun was shining, which, of course, it wasn't because they were, in reality, deep underground. He had forgotten that the cavern roof was cursed. He was thankful, however, that it wasn't raining rabbit droppings as it had once done when Norman had been here. Brian stared up at the cloudless sky, surprised at how realistic it looked. In the distance the sun was disappearing just as it would have been in the real world above them. In front of him the cobbled streets were just as busy as the inside of the Soobius Station with people, young and old, hastening to their respective destinations. Violet led them quickly along the main street which eventually curved inwards like a half-moon, revealing an underground harbour. A row of terraced houses ran alongside the street. The lopsided buildings were bent with age whilst their slated roofs appeared warped and uneven. Underneath some of the sunken windows and mounted upon the walls, Brian noticed, were baskets of different-coloured flowers.

Norman was struggling with his wheelchair over the uneven stones but Audrey and Brian helped push him to the harbour edge and they paused to peer into the murky water of the underground lake.

'This is Gravestone Harbour,' announced Violet. She pointed to somewhere far in the distance. 'There's an island out there somewhere where all the dead from long ago are buried.'

'Where? I can't see it,' said Norman, straining his eyes in the fading light. 'Can we visit it tonight?' he asked, eagerly.

'Of course we can't!' said Audrey. 'It's in the middle of the lake and it's getting dark and how exactly would we get there?'

'In one of those!' suggested Norman, pointing to some boats that were tied to the harbour wall and gently bobbing up and down in the muddy water.

'We're not going to visit the island tonight, are we?' enquired Audrey, nervously, but before Violet could reply something quite unexpectedly swooped down upon the four children, just missing their heads. Indeed, it caught Audrey so much by surprise that she almost toppled into the lake below.

'W-what was that?' she stammered, frightened, hurrying back from the harbour's edge and searching above her for whatever it was that had almost forced her to fall into the shadowy water.

But before Violet could reply something swooped towards them again, making all the children duck. It was small, square and flapping frantically. Violet snatched one of the pieces of paper as it hovered annoyingly in front of her nose. 'Just grab one as they fly past,' she instructed.

'What are they?' asked Brian, seizing the fluttering piece of paper that was encircling his head.

'They're flyers,' explained Violet. 'They're sort of like notices, information about what's happening in Coffinsgrave, and you have to take one because if you don't they'll just continue to flap about you until you do take one! They're so annoying. Some days there are so many of them that when I pop out to do an errand for Mrs Gillibottom I come back with about twenty of the things!'

117

Brian unfolded the flyer that he had just plucked from midair and looked at the picture printed upon its front cover. It was a colour drawing of a large red tent which, as he stared at it, magically began to open before his very eyes, almost as if it were real. From inside the tent letters emerged, one by one, and began floating up towards the top of the flyer to spell the word 'WELCOME', which was followed by the word 'TO' and then the words 'COFFINSGRAVE' and 'FAIR'. Underneath the tent more words materialised revealing a date, '1st SEPTEMBER', which kept exploding in yellow and orange puffs of real smoke that made Brian cough. Inside the flyer, when he opened it, were lists of all the different types of stalls that were going to be at the fair. There were stalls that would be selling monster teeth, monster masks, potions, charms, musical instruments, books, cakes and sweets among other things. There was also a list of games and competitions you could enter from Yeti Shoe Throwing to Hook a Bat.

'What's the fair like?' asked Brian, folding up the flyer and slipping it into one of his trouser pockets.

'Is it any good?' asked Norman, eagerly.

'I've never been,' replied Violet, disappointedly. 'I've never been allowed. I've always had to work. But it's meant to be fabulous. There's three fairs here every year. One in the spring, one in the summer and one in the winter too! Loads of people travel to Coffinsgrave for it from all over the county and lots of them stay at the inns and taverns, which is why all the really nice ones were already fully booked and why you got stuck with a room at the Dragon's Claw.'

'But if we weren't staying at the Dragon's Claw we wouldn't have met you and made a new friend,' said Audrey, smiling.

After leading them along the harbour wall, Violet guided the three children down a number of twisting side streets until she finally arrived at the Halls of Blooskstoof. Although Brian, Norman and Audrey had already been inside the Halls of Blooskstoof they had not yet had the opportunity to see the building from the outside and they were in for a bit of a surprise. For the building in front of them looked very much like a regular terraced house.

'Are you sure this is the right place?' asked Norman, staring up at the building confused.

Violet laughed and pointed to a wooden sign screwed upon the wall by the building's front door which clearly stated that they were, indeed, standing outside the Halls of Blooskstoof.

'But it's so small!' remarked Audrey, her mouth hanging open in wonder. 'The building's just so incredibly small!'

'It doesn't look any bigger than my grandparents' house,' said Brian, amazed.

'But it's got 500 floors!' exclaimed Audrey, suddenly remembering what Sam had told them when he and Hadley had brought them to the Halls of Blooskstoof four nights ago. 'How can it fit 500 floors inside?' she asked.

'Magic!' said Violet simply. 'Lots of buildings in Coffinsgrave are built using a bit of magic as well as stones and bricks. Some buildings can look really, really small on the outside but on the inside they're completely enormous!'

'Hey, what are they?' asked Norman, pointing to some tiny lights in the darkening sky that were weaving their way around chimneys and over building roofs. The four children watched as more lights began appearing from almost every direction, darting through the streets at a tremendous speed whilst, at the same time, somehow avoiding all the people rushing back and forth.

'They're flying into those glass boxes on top of the lampposts!' exclaimed Brian, in wonderment.

'They're fairies,' explained Violet. 'They live inside the lampposts and at night it's their job to light the streets for us. You've heard of fairy-lights before, haven't you?' she asked.

The three children all nodded and watched, smiling in amazement, as hundreds upon hundreds of sparkling little fairies all

119

disappeared into the lampposts one by one until, eventually, every lamppost in Coffinsgrave glowed brightly.

Leaving the Halls of Blooskstoof behind them, Violet led the children into an alley opposite and then up a particularly long cobbled street which brought them into a tiny square that was surrounded by a number of different shops, one of which had quite a large number of people queuing up outside.

'Can we stop for a moment?' asked Norman, who was red-faced and out of breath. 'These cobbled streets aren't made for wheelchairs,' he remarked, puffing.

The children sat down upon one of the many benches situated around the square, next to a marble statue of a man wearing a tunic and sandals and carrying a bow and a quiver of arrows. They watched silently as the crowd of people queuing excitedly outside the shop opposite them grew steadily more and more.

'I wonder what's going on over there,' said Brian to the others, curiously.

The stone statue next to the children suddenly yawned and said, rather dully, 'It's Abner Antiques. It's got its grand opening this evening.'

Chapter 10

ABNER ANTIQUES & THE DOOR OF PEALING

Poor Brian almost jumped out of his skin. 'W-what did you just say?' he stammered, staring up at the white marble statue as it yawned lazily again before climbing off its platform and sitting down on the bench next to him, which groaned disagreeably from the additional weight.

'They're all queuing outside Abner Antiques,' the statue repeated, uninterestedly. 'It has its grand opening tonight. Frankly I don't know what all the fuss is about. It's only an antique shop and it will only be selling very old bits of furniture at very expensive prices to customers with far more money than sense! You don't mind if I sit next to you, do you? Only my legs tend to get a little stiff from standing on that platform all day every day,' he said, gesturing towards the now empty block of cream-coloured marble that the children were sitting next to.

'But you're a statue and you're talking,' said Brian, flabbergasted.

The statue sighed monotonously. 'Yes, I know,' it replied before adding quite sarcastically, 'How very observant of you.'

'Sorry, it's just I've never met a talking statue before,' apologised Brian.

'Clearly,' the statue remarked, bored.

'These are my friends, Norman, Audrey and Violet,' said Brian.

The three children, who evidently already knew that the statues in Coffinsgrave could magically walk and talk, waved back. The statue nodded in their direction, displaying no more interest than before, and scratched the back of its neck. 'Quite why I have to carry these awful arrows over my shoulder I don't know. They keep rubbing against my back and it's very irritating. On top of which I don't even know how to use a bow and arrow, so quite why I was sculpted carrying such things I'll never know.'

'Yeah, I can see how that would be annoying,' said Brian.

'Are you trying to be funny?' asked the statue, tetchily.

'No, I really mean it,' said Brian. 'Having to carry stuff about all day every day that you can't even take off must be really annoying. I'm guessing that because the bow and arrow are made out of stone, like you, you can't take them off?'

The statue sniffed, disgruntled. 'No, I can't,' it replied.

'My name's Brian, by the way,' said Brian, extending his arm. 'Pleased to meet you.'

For a moment it looked as though the statue was trying to decide whether it could be bothered to shake Brian's hand or not, but in the end it must have decided that it could because it took Brian's hand in its and with a vice-like grip almost broke every bone in his fingers. 'Sir Rodney Applegate. Well, not the real Sir Rodney Applegate obviously, because he's dead, but I'm the statue that was built in his honour.'

'And who was Rodney Applegate?' asked Brian.

'Sir Rodney Applegate,' corrected the statue.

'Who was Sir Rodney Applegate?' repeated Brian.

'Haven't the foggiest,' replied the statue, blankly. 'They don't bother to tell you these things when they make you.'

'What time does it open?' asked Norman.

'Excuse me?' said Applegate, peering round at Norman. 'What time does what open?'

'Abner Antiques,' said Norman. 'What time does it open?'

'I have no idea,' replied Applegate. 'I'm just a statue and nobody tells a statue anything.'

'Oh,' said Norman.

After a moment's silence Applegate said, 'Do you want me to find out for you? I suppose I could if you really wanted to know, if it was really important?'

'Could you?' asked Norman. 'That would be great.' Then, turning to Audrey, he said, 'I mean, it wouldn't hurt to have a quick look around, would it? We might not get the opportunity again.'

'We're not even meant to be out,' warned Audrey. 'If we get caught...'

Having no interest in the argument which was about to erupt between Norman and Audrey, Applegate sighed and climbed back on to his podium, then, putting his stone hands to his stone lips, he called, 'Lord Benfleet? Excuse me, Lord Benfleet!'

A few seconds later a voice from amongst the crowd of people queuing outside Abner Antiques shouted back, 'Ahoy there matey and shiver your timbers, Sir Rodney. How goes it?'

Sir Rodney Applegate shook his head and appeared to roll his eyes skywards out of boredom, but Brian couldn't be completely sure of this because the stone statue didn't really have any eyes, just two round, smooth pieces of stone that had been expertly sculpted to look like a pair of eyes. 'I was just wondering, Lord Benfleet, if you knew what time the grand opening of Abner Antiques was this evening.'

From amongst the queue of excited people standing outside the antique shop a large grey, granite statue suddenly emerged. Unlike Sir Rodney Applegate this statue was dressed in or rather sculpted so that it had the appearance of wearing a uniform of sorts, with big, baggy boots and a hat adorned with a feather on one side. Carved upon the statue's waist was a curved stone cutlass. 'Ahoy there, you landlubbers, and let me introduce myself. I am Lord Benfleet, captain of the *Courageous*, and I am at your service!'

123

'I only asked what time Abner Antiques was due to open,' remarked Applegate, irritably, as each of the children introduced themselves. 'You didn't have to march all the way over here and familiarise yourself!'

'Nonsense,' said Benfleet, attempting and failing to puff out his stone chest importantly. 'It would be rude of me not to introduce myself. Now, what was it that you wanted to know, landlubbers, for, without a doubt, I am sure that I can be of some assistance?'

'What time does Abner Antiques open?' asked Norman.

Lord Benfleet attempted to remove a pocket-watch from one of the stone pockets of his stone waistcoat, which of course he couldn't because, like him, it was carved out of stone and so, instead, he glanced up at a clock that had been built upon one of the tallest buildings within the square. It was almost seven o'clock. 'Why, Abner Antiques should be opening its doors at any moment,' he exclaimed, cheerily. 'But there's a mighty queue of people waiting to get inside before you, I'm afraid.'

'Oh,' said Norman, disappointed.

'Such a shame,' remarked Benfleet. 'For I've heard tell that the shop's shelves are laden with many an ancient and mysterious artefact, some magical too or I'm not the greatest sea captain to have ever lived!'

'No, you're not,' said Applegate, matter-of-factly.

'What?' said Benfleet, clearly flustered.

'I said no, you're not the greatest sea captain to have ever lived,' repeated Applegate, deprecatingly. 'You're merely, as some have claimed, a statue of the greatest sea captain to have ever lived.'

'Nonsense!' exclaimed Benfleet, placing his hands upon his hips and striking an impressive pose. 'What poppycock! Look at the likeness, Sir Rodney! Look at my eyes, my chin and the scars upon this rugged seafaring face. Why, I even carry Lord Benfleet's cutlass and do you know why that is? It's because I am Lord Benfleet!' he bellowed heartily before adding, 'Swash, swash, buckle, buckle!'

Applegate shook his head. 'Whatever,' he said, becoming clearly bored with the conversation.

'I tell you what, shipmates,' said Benfleet, rubbing his stone chin thoughtfully. 'I think I might have a plan forming in my swashbuckling seafaring brain to help get you to the front of the queue.' He gave a sly wink.

'You're a statue!' pointed out Applegate, evidently finding this immensely tedious. 'You don't have a brain.'

Benfleet ignored him. 'So, what do you have to say to that, shipmates?'

'That would be brilliant!' exclaimed Norman, his disappointment from moments earlier instantly replaced with sudden excitement.

'But what if we get caught?' warned Audrey, nervously taking a puff from her inhaler. 'We weren't supposed to leave the Dragon's Claw, were we? Waghorn warned us. We shouldn't even be out now. I don't know, what do you think, Brian?'

'Well, it wouldn't hurt to have a quick look inside, would it?' said Brian who, like Norman, was quite eager to see what supernatural and magical artefacts the antique shop was selling. 'I mean, we might as well have a look whilst we're here.'

'And what about you, Violet? Haven't you got that errand to do for Mrs Gillibottom?' Audrey reminded her.

Violet nodded. 'Yes, but I don't have to be back until eight o'clock,' she said, clearly enjoying her brief bit of freedom from the drudgery of the Dragon's Claw. 'I can easily do it after we've checked out the antique shop.'

Audrey frowned. 'Well, I just hope we don't get caught!' she complained, waving goodbye to Sir Rodney Applegate and joining the others who were now following Lord Benfleet across the square, towards the queue of people standing impatiently outside the antique shop. 'Because if we do then I'm never talking to any of you ever again!'

'Don't get my hopes up, Audrey!' remarked Norman.

'Make way! Make way you scurvy dogs!' cried Benfleet as he began pushing his way up towards the front of the queue. 'Sir, out of the way, that's it, let me through. Please, there's really no need for that sort of language, madam.'

'And where do you think you're going?' asked a suspicious voice once Benfleet had led the children through the excitable crowd and up to the front door of the antique shop.

'It's me, Lord Benfleet!' said Benfleet, bowing politely to the horned head of the gargoyle that had magically appeared from a slab of stone, protruding from the wall next to the shop's doorway.

'Oh, sorry, Lord Benfleet,' said the gargoyle apologetically and in a much less distrustful tone. 'Didn't realise it was you, sir. How can I be of assistance?'

'Well, my friends here,' he said, gesturing wildly towards the children with a wave of his stone arm that made Brian leap backwards and duck just in time so that his shoulders were not parted from his head, 'would like to visit Abner Antiques. Only there is rather a large queue, as I'm sure you can see. And, well, I was rather hoping that they could join the front of the queue.'

'The front of the queue?' repeated the gargoyle, quite taken aback. 'But Lord Benfleet, some of these people have been queuing for almost two hours, sir!'

'I know, I know,' said Benfleet, nodding in understanding. 'Only this poor boy was a sailor until his unfortunate accident,' he fibbed, pointing at Norman's wheelchair before adding in a hushed tone, 'Lost the use of his legs in a dreadful shipping disaster, and lost his father at sea too, I might add.'

'And my mum,' chipped in Norman.

'Bit young to be a sailor, wasn't he?' suggested the gargoyle a little suspiciously.

'Well, you'd be surprised how young they start these days,' remarked Benfleet, matter-of-factly.

The gargoyle's thin, grey arms appeared from out of the stone slab and he used them to push himself up and peer over at Norman sitting in his wheelchair below. 'Shipping accident, you say?' it said, raising one of its stone eyebrows at Benfleet sceptically.

'Did I mention his sister is currently missing at sea too?' said Benfleet, sadly. 'Presumed dead, poor lass.'

The gargoyle sniffed dubiously before nodding its head. 'All right,' it said. 'You can be the first in the queue. I'm going to be opening the doors shortly.'

'Excellent!' roared Benfleet. 'Do you hear that, my hearties, you're going to be first in the queue!'

'Hey, what about us?' complained two gentlemen dressed in matching silver cloaks who, until the children had arrived, had been the first in the long line of prospective customers.

'Shut yer faces!' snapped the gargoyle. 'Can't you see the poor boy's lost the use of his legs? He fought a four-eyed sea monster with more tentacles than you've had hot dinners for three whole days and nights at sea.' It winked deviously at Lord Benfleet. 'You two ought to be ashamed of yourselves, complaining about a poor boy that not only lost his father and mother in the battle but lost his sister too. You two make me sick.' It spat at the two cloaked men, who jumped aside only just in time to avoid the gargoyle's phlegm.

'We're ever so sorry,' said the taller of the two cloaked men, apologetically. 'We really didn't know, did we?'

'No we didn't,' said his companion meekly, stepping aside. 'By all means go ahead of us. We insist!'

'So that's settled then,' roared Benfleet, pleased with the positive outcome, and he patted Norman so hard on the back with his thick, stone hand that it sent him hurtling into the shop's front door with a loud crash. Thankfully, Norman's wheelchair saved him from any permanent damage. 'If you need anything else just let me know, shipmates. Now, out of my way, you scurvy dogs,' cried

Benfleet, making his way back to his podium, which was situated in front of another shop within the square.

As the front door to Abner Antiques opened inwards the children all waved goodbye to Lord Benfleet and disappeared hastily inside, eager to see what magical artefacts were for sale.

Amazingly, Abner Antiques was exactly the same as the Halls of Blooskstoof in that it was much, much bigger on the inside than it was on the outside. Shelves of unusual ornaments lined the walls, some in glass cases whilst others were free to be picked up and examined by curious hands. Each little knick-knack had a little handwritten card next to it detailing exactly what the ornament was, its history and, of course, its price. Large pieces of furniture filled most of the ground floor and, much like the ornaments sitting upon the shelves, each one had its own piece of history written upon a card that had then been fastened to it in some manner. Brian leaned over an antique table to peer into a large glass bottle which seemed to contain some type of long-dead beetle lying on a bed of sand. He leapt back in fright when the creature suddenly scampered towards him, its black pincers snapping furiously through its glass prison!

Norman meanwhile was staring curiously at an odd-looking door still within its frame but completely freestanding, almost as if it had been sucked out of the wall into which it had once been secured. He wheeled his chair around it in a circle and wondered exactly what the point was of having a door that led precisely nowhere. Who, in their right mind, would want to buy it?

'Ah, I see you are admiring one of my Doors of Pealing,' remarked a green-suited man, smiling pleasantly and shaking each of the children's hands. 'My name is Barrington Abner and this is my shop, Abner Antiques. And as you appear to be my first visitors I shall give you each one of these,' he said, cheerfully handing each of the children a paper coupon that offered them up to 30% off a number of items within his shop.

'What does the door do?' asked Norman.

'What does any door do?' returned Abner. 'Except allow you to leave one place and enter another.'

'But it's just an ordinary door, isn't it?' remarked Audrey, running her hand over its smooth wooden surface, curiously.

'It looks just like one of the doors in the Dragon's Claw,' said Violet.

'Just a door it certainly isn't, my dear,' said Abner, smiling and chuckling at the children. 'Open the door and step through. See where it takes you to.'

Audrey shook her head. 'No thank you,' she said, distrustfully, and taking a puff from her inhaler she stepped a little further away from the green-suited shop owner.

'There's nothing to be afraid of,' said Abner.

'Is it magic?' asked Norman.

'Why not find out for yourself?' suggested Abner, turning the handle and letting the door swing slowly open so that the children could see through it and to the other side of the shop, where lots of customers were eagerly examining many of the curiosities that filled the shelves. 'Step through it. I dare you to.'

'But it doesn't lead anywhere,' pointed out Norman, wheeling his chair round to the other side of the door for a closer inspection and waving through it at Brian, Audrey and Violet.

'Is that so?' said Abner, smiling as Norman wheeled himself back to where his friends, like him, had been staring at the door most curiously. 'Well, if doesn't lead anywhere then you have nothing to fear, my young friend.' He beckoned Norman a little closer. 'It's just a door, after all.'

'What will happen to us if we step through it?' asked Violet.

'Who knows?' replied Abner, shrugging in mock innocence. 'But more importantly, who has the nerve to find out?' he asked, drawing closer to Norman and gesturing to the children with an outstretched hand. 'Which one of you is brave enough to take up my challenge, I wonder?'

Norman spun his chair backwards, away from the shop owner's reach and straight over Brian's foot, making him cry out in pain.

'Ah, I see that one of you is brave enough after all,' said Abner, clearly delighted. 'And what's your name?' he whispered.

'Brian,' said Brian, glaring madly at Norman.

Abner cleared his throat. 'Ladies and gentlemen, can I have your attention please?'

The customers who were busy studying the various antiques on display suddenly stopped what they were doing to stare at the green-suited shop owner, their interest aroused to see what he was going to say next. Indeed, some customers hastily made their way over to where Abner was firmly hugging Brian in the hope that, perhaps, the shop owner might be giving away some antiques for free, and very soon a small crowd had gathered around them.

'Ladies and gentlemen, can I firstly thank you all so much for visiting Abner Antiques on its opening night?' continued Abner. 'Because of you I am certain that it will be an absolutely tremendous success! There are some real bargains to be had, even if I do say so myself, and if you haven't yet received one of my coupons offering up to 30% off your purchase this evening – that's right, your ears are not deceiving you, I did say 30% off – then please see me after this brief magical demonstration. For my young friend, Brian, is going to test, before your very eyes, one of my four Doors of Pealing!'

The crowd of customers, which was rapidly growing, clapped and cheered noisily.

'Now, there's nothing to be afraid of,' he whispered to Brian whilst out of earshot of everyone else as he brought him face to face with the open door. 'Just step through it as you would do any normal door. Rest assured that you are in no danger and that you will reappear momentarily. You have my word.' Then, turning to face the crowd before him, Abner cried, 'Now watch as young Brian steps through the Door of Pealing and disappears before your very eyes!'

130

Once more the crowd of eager onlookers clapped and cheered enthusiastically, some even whistling with excitement.

As Abner pressed Brian towards the open doorway he again whispered softly into his ear, 'Do not be afraid. There is nothing to fear.' But Brian *was* afraid and, what's more, there was something about Barrington Abner that he didn't like. There was something about him that made Brian feel decidedly uneasy. As ridiculous as it sounded it was almost as if Abner was too nice. As Brian felt the shop owner push him nearer to the door he immediately felt a terrible sickness erupt within the pit of his stomach. Where would this mysterious door take him to? He was certain that it was no ordinary door, but where would he emerge once he had passed through it? For a brief moment he had the frightening image of stepping into the open doorway and suddenly emerging over the mouth of a massive volcano or, perhaps, ending up on a tiny, deserted island in the middle of nowhere. He wanted to turn back. He didn't want to go through with it, but by now there were too many people watching him, willing Brian to step through the magical door and he dared not change his mind and turn back. Brian glanced over his shoulder one last time. He stared at Norman, Audrey and Violet and, taking a deep breath, stepped through the door.

Chapter 11

AN UNEXPECTED ATTACK

The gathering of excited customers who had been encircling Barrington Abner and the Door of Pealing, many of whom had had their mouths hanging open in amazement as Brian had disappeared, instantly erupted into tremendous applause with more whistling and the occasional whoop of 'bravo' and 'hurrah'. But Brian heard none of this. Instead, as he had stepped nervously into the open doorway his world had begun to change dramatically. The customers, the shop and everything in it had suddenly become blurred and distorted as if his eyes were having difficulty focusing. Sounds became muffled and voices seemed distant. Images swam before him as though caught in some sort of magical maelstrom. Feeling momentarily dizzy he emerged from the other side of the door and wandered, disorientated, straight into a large, antique sideboard, bruising his knees.

Gradually the world about him began to stop spinning, which allowed Brian to finally release his grip upon the sideboard. Little by little he turned around and stared at the door before him. It looked no different to the one he had just entered. In fact the door before him looked identical in every respect. It was still within its frame and still eerily freestanding. Brian took a step towards it and immediately wished he hadn't. His stomach heaved and he fell back against the sideboard. Taking a deep breath he glanced briefly at his surroundings. He appeared to be in a room completely filled with furniture. Tables, wardrobes and cupboards packed every aisle. Then to his left he noticed a balcony and he realised that he was not in a room at all but rather on some sort of floor. Feeling less queasy he stepped towards the ornate wooden balcony and as he did so a thunderous roar of applause erupted from somewhere beneath him.

'And here he is,' exclaimed Abner, smiling up at Brian from the floor below. 'Magically transported from one floor to another and completely unharmed!'

The crowd of enthralled customers, who were all staring up at Brian in complete amazement, cheered loudly and began clapping enthusiastically again. Norman, Audrey and Violet waved at him. Brian, still feeling ever so slightly sick, waved weakly back.

'Now, who would like to join Brian up on the first floor to see what other bargains there are to be had on this, the opening night of Abner Antiques?' cried Abner, grinning haughtily.

Immediately, a whole host of hands shot up into the air and within seconds a queue of excited people had formed in front of the Door of Pealing, all eager to pass through its wooden frame so that they could reach the floor of antiques above them.

Brian watched as Norman, Audrey and Violet disappeared into the open door whilst Abner marched up and down the queue of customers, eagerly handing out his paper coupons to each and every one of them.

Unlike the other buildings that Brian had visited so far in Coffinsgrave, Abner Antiques had only a ground and first floor. However, what it lacked in floor numbers it made up in size as each floor seemed to be as large as two football pitches! After joining Brian the children wandered idly up and down the aisles of furniture, occasionally stopping to examine a particular piece they thought interesting or to inspect one of the more unusual objects that they found resting upon the many shelves that lined the shop walls.

'Wow, a Norsip Ball!' remarked Audrey, picking up and examining a small black and golden orb that she had discovered sitting upon an antique desk. 'I've never seen a real one before!'

'What's a Norsip Ball?' asked Norman, taking the orb from Audrey and examining it himself. It was about as big as a snooker ball but weighed a good deal more.

'They don't use them any more, thank goodness,' said Audrey, taking the ball from Norman and putting it back on the desk where she had found it. 'Warlocks used to use them years ago. Kept people in them. Prisoners. Not very nice. Alessandra Slugworth was famous for using them. It was rumoured that she had a collection of over twenty-five.'

'Hang on,' Brian said, frowning. 'I thought all warlocks were supposed to be male?'

Audrey gave Brian a very reproachful look indeed. 'Did you seriously just say what I think you said? Because that's so incredibly sexist! Warlocks can be male and female y'know. Admittedly, there aren't an awful lot of female warlocks but that's not the point.'

Another item caught Brian's attention. It was a battered, wooden mask that when he held it in his hands seemed to somehow mysteriously keep changing shape. 'What's this?' he asked the others, studying the mask curiously.

'Wow, that's a Mirrormask!' exclaimed Norman, who up until then, like Brian, had been feeling rather sick since passing through the Door of Pealing.

'A Mirrorwhat?' said Brian.

'It's a Mirrormask,' repeated Audrey, taking it from him and having a closer look at it herself. 'If used with the right potion it will mirror the face of another person right down to the freckles on their nose.' She held the mask over her face and, as if to prove what she was saying was true, the mask quickly began to change shape until eventually it looked just like Audrey. Incredibly, even its eyes blinked and its lips moved at exactly the same time as Audrey's did!

134

'That's amazing!' remarked Brian, impressed. 'But it doesn't make a particularly good disguise, does it? I mean, it's made out of wood.'

'Yes, but with the right potion the mask's colour and texture can be altered too so that it looks exactly like a normal person's face,' she explained. 'I could make myself look like Norman and you'd not be able to tell us apart. We'd be identical!'

'Here, let's have a go,' said Norman, who pressed the mask upon his face and stuck out his tongue and then picked his nose.

Violet giggled.

Audrey shook her head in disgust. 'That's gross, Norman!'

Norman laughed and was about to hand the Mirrormask to Violet so that she could try it on herself when Audrey suddenly exclaimed, 'Waghorn's here! Look!', and there, standing beside the Door of Pealing in the next aisle and chatting to Barrington Abner, was none other than Beatrice Waghorn, the dishevelled black bird still sitting upon her shoulder, its head cocked to one side, staring suspiciously at anyone and everyone who walked by. 'I'd recognise that nasty perfume anywhere!' remarked Audrey, wrinkling up her nose in disgust.

'If she sees us we're dead!' exclaimed Norman, hastily wheeling his chair behind a cupboard and out of sight.

'I told you we shouldn't have left the Dragon's Claw,' complained Audrey as she, Brian and Violet rushed to join him. 'But oh no, you never listen to me, do you…'

'Put a sock in it, Audrey,' said Norman. 'Jeez, you're starting to sound like my mum again!'

Audrey ignored him. 'Well, has anybody got any ideas as to how on earth we're going to get back down to the ground floor without Waghorn catching us?' she asked, peering round the wardrobe at Waghorn and Abner who now seemed to be having a heated debate rather than making polite conversation.

'We could start by throwing you over the balcony?' suggested Norman, unhelpfully.

Audrey had opened her mouth to say something nasty back to Norman when Brian snapped, 'We haven't got time for one of your arguments! So can you please both put a sock in it? We need to come up with a plan! Somehow we've got to get back to that Door of Pealing without any of us being seen.'

'I've got an idea,' volunteered Violet. '*You're* not supposed to be out tonight but there's nothing stopping me from being at the opening of Abner Antiques. If I can cause a distraction, maybe I can get Waghorn and Abner to move away from that door long enough so that you can get through it and get back downstairs. What do you think?'

Brian considered Violet's suggestion. The only way back down to the ground floor was via the Door of Pealing, for they had discovered no flight of stairs that linked the two floors, and the only way they could get to the Door of Pealing was if Waghorn and Abner were somehow coaxed away from it. 'I can't think of a better plan,' he finally admitted. 'Can either of you two?' he asked Norman and Audrey.

Norman shrugged whilst Audrey, with a shake of her head, took a puff from her inhaler.

'Well, we need to get as close to that door as possible,' said Brian, thoughtfully. 'If we work our way carefully down this aisle and keep out of sight behind some of those larger pieces of furniture then we can probably hide behind that big wardrobe next to the cabinet right at the very end.' He pointed at an odd cabinet that kept opening and closing its doors all of its own accord as if it were attempting to eat each customer that wandered by. 'Then, once Waghorn and Abner are out of the way, we can make a dash for the Door of Pealing!'

'What sort of distraction are you going to make?' asked Audrey.

136

'Oh, I've got one or two ideas,' admitted Violet, with a mischievous grin, and with that she quickly disappeared down one of the other aisles and out of sight.

'Come on then, quick, follow me,' said Brian, and he left their hiding place with Norman and Audrey close behind him. The three children made their way very slowly along the aisle, all the while keeping their eyes firmly fixed on Waghorn and Abner, who were now clearly arguing over something. Three times the children had to suddenly stop and hide behind some piece of furniture when it looked like Waghorn or Abner were looking in their direction. But, eventually, they reached the enormous wardrobe at the end of the aisle without being seen and remained secretly hidden behind it, waiting nervously for whatever distraction Violet had planned. Next to them the peculiar cabinet which kept magically opening and closing its doors was doing its very utmost to actually eat a woman dressed in a glittering blue cloak and sparkly hat. Fearful that the cabinet might give their hiding place away Brian kept peering around the side of the wardrobe, praying that neither Waghorn nor Abner would have the urge to rescue the customer who, by now, had been half swallowed by the strange cabinet so that only her legs could be seen dangling from its doors.

Thankfully, they did not have to wait very long for Violet's distraction as, a few minutes later, there was the sound of breaking glass followed by frightened screams from a number of customers as something large, black and exceedingly hairy and which appeared to be growing at a very alarming rate suddenly galloped down another aisle sending furniture and antiques flying in all directions, not to mention quite a few customers too!

Waghorn and Abner stopped their argument to see what all the sudden commotion was about.

'Oh dear,' the children heard Abner sigh, irritably. 'It looks as though one of the manticores has escaped. However did that happen, I wonder? How annoying! I'll have to recapture it before it gets too big! I'm afraid we'll have to finish this conversation another time, Beatrice.'

'You'll regret this, Abner,' they heard Waghorn say to the green-suited shop owner before Abner, looking slightly alarmed at this remark, hastily disappeared down another aisle to take charge of the rampaging beast that was still rapidly growing in size and which now had what looked like a coffee table hooked upon one of its three horns, which it was vigorously trying to shake off. Waghorn meanwhile turned on her heel and, with a squawk from the scruffy black bird sitting upon her shoulder, disappeared back through the Door of Pealing.

A moment later Violet reappeared, still giggling at Abner's attempts at recapturing the beast that she had let loose, and then, when they thought it was safe to do so, the children quickly made their way to the Door of Pealing and, one by one, disappeared back through it.

Instantly re-emerging on the ground floor, the children quickly ducked behind an antique sideboard. The four of them watched as Waghorn stormed furiously through the aisles, pushing eager customers aside so forcefully that some actually fell over pieces of furniture, and out through the shop's front door, which she closed so violently behind her that its glass window actually splintered.

'What on earth do you think they were arguing about?' asked Brian.

But before Norman, Audrey or Violet could answer him there was a terrific explosion from somewhere outside, shattering every window within the shop and sending shards of glass flying in all directions. Fires immediately erupted throughout the ground floor and customers began screaming hysterically as they clambered over the fallen and broken furniture in a desperate bid to escape the shop. Brian staggered backwards, finding Norman's wheelchair behind him and leaning against it for support. He felt dizzy and when he wiped his forehead with the back of his hand it felt oddly wet. It was only when he stared at his fingers that he realised that they were covered in blood.

In the square outside people were running frantically about in every possible direction, screaming and shouting, disappearing down the many side streets and alleyways whilst in the pavement outside Abner Antiques there was now a massive, fiery crater. Rubble and cobblestones were strewn everywhere. Other shop fronts were badly damaged too, some with their windows smashed or with their front doors completely blown apart. Some shops, like Abner Antiques, were on fire and these were quickly getting out of control.

'Run for your lives, shipmates!' cried Lord Benfleet, galloping past the children as they emerged from Abner Antiques, their faces and hair covered in black soot and dust.

'Some hero he is!' remarked Norman, disappointedly, as Lord Benfleet disappeared amongst the fleeing crowd.

On the opposite side of the square a burning ball of orange flame plunged into the front of a butcher's shop which immediately exploded with an almighty bang sending burning debris flying in all directions.

People began screaming again, some bumping into each other in their panic to escape the explosion whilst others were pushed to the ground or simply fell over in their rush to flee the square, which was now beginning to look more and more like some sort of battle ground.

'What's happening?' mumbled Brian, who was still feeling dazed from the explosion outside Abner Antiques.

'I don't know,' replied Audrey. 'I think we're being attacked!'

'But by what?' asked Brian.

They did not have to wait long to find out.

'Diefromen!' cried Norman in terror, and he pointed towards a creature covered in flame as it directed another fireball towards a building opposite the children, which immediately collapsed in a plume of smoke and dust.

The fire demon that had entered the square was enormous and much bigger than the creature that had attacked Brian's grandparents' house. As tall as the buildings that surrounded it, the Diefromen, covered in head to foot by a fierce, raging fire, emerged into the square, moving very slowly but with such massive steps that it stood towering before the frightened children in a matter of mere seconds.

Brian felt himself shake with fright as it opened its colossal, fiery jaws and roared so loudly that some of the shop windows that up until then had still been intact exploded inwards.

'What are we going to do?' yelled Violet, stumbling backwards, terrified.

'We can't escape!' shouted Brian over the noise of the bellowing flames that were engulfing the demon.

Norman couldn't say anything; he was still pointing at the demon before him in complete and utter shock, his mouth hanging limply open in horrified amazement.

By now the square was practically devoid of people and the children could clearly see the trail of burning footprints left by the demon, still smouldering, as very slowly it began to lift one of its burning arms and, from within the palm of what passed as a hand, released another fireball but this time towards *them*! The children all ducked and miraculously the ball of flame passed harmlessly over their heads, exploding into Abner Antiques behind them, which was instantly consumed in flames.

Then, out of thin air, a white-robed warlock materialised beside the children. Brian recognised him immediately. It was Addison Aldwinkle.

'Get back!' he bellowed to the children, waving at them to get behind him.

The children didn't need to be told twice. As the Diefromen began to raise one of its blazing arms again, ready to launch another fireball, a second robed warlock suddenly materialised next to

Aldwinkle; this was followed by a third and then a fourth and then a fifth until, eventually, there were seven white-robed warlocks all standing between the children and the demon. This seemed to confuse the Diefromen and for a moment it seemed unsure what to do next. Its indecision did not last long, however, and with a swing of one of its burning arms it released another massive fireball.

Brian was certain that he was going to die right there and then. He was absolutely positive about it. The fireball was heading straight at him. He and his friends were going to be burned alive and killed. But, unbelievably, the children were not killed. Instead, Brian watched in utter amazement as one of the white-robed warlocks, a black woman whom he did not recognise, held up what looked bizarrely like a wooden school ruler. As she waved it in front of her a surge of jagged blue lighting suddenly shot from it, immediately encircling the demon's ball of flame and entrapping it in midair. Then, with a flick of her wrist, the female warlock was somehow able to control the fireball and propel it back towards the demon. It missed, however, and instead exploded, with a tremendous bang, straight into another shop on the other side of the square.

'Sorry!' she cried over the ferocious roar of the fire demon as it angrily stamped its enormous legs upon the cobbled street, sending flame, stone and dirt high into the air about them.

Audrey coughed and began fumbling for her inhaler; Brian, Norman and Violet watched as the seven warlocks quickly surrounded the Diefromen, each one apparently wielding some form of unusual magical weapon. One warlock was carrying a woolly hat, another a pair of scissors; there was a tall warlock wearing a single red glove, a fat warlock holding up a ballpoint pen rather threateningly and another warlock who was carrying a broom whilst Addison Aldwinkle was clearly wielding an umbrella.

As the seven warlocks raised their unusual weapons together a strange, silvery smoke-like substance began to drift from the end of each one. It seemed to start with the warlock who was carrying the ballpoint pen. A wispy white tendril had leapt from the end of the biro. It floated momentarily in midair before suddenly splitting in two and instantly merging with each of its neighbours; the same happened with every one of the weapons until each warlock was joined by a silver circle of pulsing light.

Seemingly unaffected by the heat from the demon's flaming body the seven warlocks edged nearer still to the Diefromen, their ring of silver light clearly not only protecting them from the terrible creature but also somehow weakening it, for as the throbbing silver light between the warlocks grew momentarily brighter the flames that engulfed the fire demon seemed to subside. But the Diefromen was not so easily defeated. It roared furiously and, once again, raised its enormous fiery arms. Two balls of flame immediately burst from its hands, exploding with a deafening boom just above the heads of the seven warlocks, breaking their protective circle and sending the warlocks flying through the air like rag dolls. Some were more fortunate than others and were just blown off their feet whilst others were sent flying so far through the air that they landed upon the other side of the square. Two of the warlocks, Brian noticed, did not get up again.

'There are not enough of us!' cried one wizard, scrambling desperately for his magical broom and dodging a ball of flame which exploded upon the street just where his head had been, creating another massive crater and sending cobblestones flying in all directions.

'We must try to contain the creature,' yelled another of the warlocks, staggering to his feet and aiming his scissors at the fire demon as it sent another massive fireball in his direction. But with a flip of his wrist a red beam of fizzing light shot out from the end of his scissors, capturing the ball of flame and immediately bouncing it back towards the Diefromen. It crashed into the creature's chest in a flurry of flame and sparks but appeared to have no effect whatsoever. Instead of hurting the fire demon the massive ball of flame simply seemed to be absorbed into the creature! It roared noisily and raised its fiery arms again.

'One of us must reach Katobi,' said the female warlock with the ruler. 'We must have help! We cannot hope to defeat the Diefromen alone!'

Addison Aldwinkle leapt aside just as another ball of flame exploded in front of him; he ran back towards Brian, almost tripping over his umbrella in his haste. 'Oh my!' he said, puffing. 'This is a right pickle, a right pickle! Brian, I need you to find Barnaby Katobi, do you think you can do that for me?'

'Yeah, I guess so,' replied Brian as the warlock with the ruler caught another ball of flame with a bolt of magical blue lightning and flung it back at the fire demon.

'What did you say?' bellowed Aldwinkle, cupping his hand to his ear.

'I said I guess so,' shouted back Brian.

'Excellent, excellent!' cried Aldwinkle, firing two shots of green light at the Diefromen's head from his umbrella, one of which missed and disappeared up into the cavern's enchanted roof. 'Only we can't defeat this demon alone. We badly need some help. Do you think you can get to a Soobius Station?'

'I'll go,' volunteered Violet.

'What?' shouted Aldwinkle.

'I said I'll go,' repeated Violet.

'What, speak up dear?' cried Aldwinkle, cupping a hand to his ear again. 'Oh, hang on, I haven't got my hearing aid switched on. Ah, that's better.'

'I said I'll go!' shouted Violet.

'All right, my dear, no need to shout,' said Aldwinkle, firing another three shots of green light at the fire demon all of which hit the creature in the chest, making it roar furiously at him. 'Are you sure?'

'Yes, I know the way back to the Soobius Station better than Brian,' said Violet. 'And I'll be quicker!'

'Excellent, excellent!' said Aldwinkle again. 'Find Barnaby Katobi as quickly as you can, my dear. Tell him we need help! The rest of you should get out of here immediately. It's too dangerous!' And with that Aldwinkle, almost tripping over his umbrella again, ran back to join the other four warlocks who were now encircling the demon once again whilst doing their very utmost to avoid being hit by one of its fireballs.

'I'll be as quick as I can!' said Violet, and with a quick wave she weaved her way through the burning rubble before disappearing down an alleyway. Brian, Norman and Audrey went to follow her but with so much debris now scattered all over the square it was proving difficult for Norman in his wheelchair to get anywhere. Brian and Audrey were helping him when there was another massive explosion as yet another fireball thundered over their heads and straight through a shop frontage, immediately setting the building alight and sending its façade collapsing on to the street below, blocking the alleyway the children had been making for.

'We're trapped!' exclaimed Norman, irritably. 'And all because of this stupid wheelchair! That building's blocked our only escape!'

'Do you think Violet made it through the alley okay?' shouted Audrey over the roar of the burning building, taking another puff of her inhaler.

'I'm sure she did,' Brian reassured her. 'Quickly, let's get behind here,' he said, gesturing to the mouth of the crater outside what used to be Abner Antiques but was now completely ablaze. Brian and Audrey helped push Norman towards a massive wall of fallen bricks and rubble next to the crater and they quickly hid behind it, peeking out occasionally to stare at the Diefromen and the five warlocks who were trying desperately to control it.

'They're circling the Diefromen again!' cried Audrey, coughing from the smoke and dust of the burning buildings.

144

Brian and Norman peered over the rubble to watch as all five warlocks, their robes now scorched and filthy, began simultaneously to raise their magical weapons. Then, just as before, a wispy, silvery smoke-like substance began to drift from the end of each one, quickly merging with their neighbours until each warlock was connected by a shimmering circle of silver light which throbbed and pulsed like a living, breathing thing. The Diefromen staggered backwards, the fires that had been ravaging its entire body momentarily dimming. The ring of light that encircled the fire demon grew brighter and for a moment, at least, it looked to the children as though the five warlocks had won, as though the Diefromen, entrapped before them, had been defeated. But they were wrong. The Diefromen, raising its enormous arms high above its head, roared fiercely, before bringing its gigantic hands thundering down upon the cobbled street below which instantly erupted, just like a volcano!

Brian would never clearly remember what exactly happened next. He could recall seeing Norman, curled up on the floor amongst the bricks and the rubble desperately calling his name, his face covered in dust and dirt; Audrey, lying pale and motionless at the bottom of the crater, her arm bent at a horrible, unnatural angle.

But how Brian had ended up standing all alone before the Diefromen in the middle of the square he could never truly say. Around him buildings were ablaze, some had partially collapsed whilst others had already been burnt to the ground. The five warlocks who had almost defeated the fire demon were lying amongst the rubble, their faces burnt, cut and in some cases bleeding.

The only two things that Brian could clearly remember, later, were the Diefromen and the woolly hat. He found the warlock's hat, which was partially burnt, lying at his feet, half hidden by some bricks and stone. Although he could not explain why, he knew that he wanted it, that he must have it. And so, kicking the burning rubble off the hat, he pulled it free. But he was surprised at how heavy it felt in his hands. It felt incredibly heavy, as though, impossibly, something were inside it. What an odd thing to be doing, thought Brian as he slipped his hand inside the hat. He knew he should have been running, that he should have been trying to escape from the Diefromen which towered above him and which was surely about to kill him. But, instead, he wanted to know what was inside the hat. He wanted to know what it was that felt so cold to the touch.

He gasped when he removed the icicle. For although he had not known what to expect Brian had certainly not been anticipating a freezing spear of ice. He stared at it almost as if hypnotised, turning it over in his hands. Its surface was smooth and as clear as crystal and yet, oddly, it did not reflect even the merest hint of flame from the fire demon that stood before him.

The Diefromen roared triumphantly above him and Brian raised his hands protectively over his head knowing full well that it would do little either to shield or to save him. He was going to die.

It was then that the icicle that he was holding in his hands began to shake so furiously that it felt almost as if it were actually alive. Indeed it wriggled and shook so violently that, for one dreadful moment, Brian thought it might actually escape from his grasp and take off like some uncontrollable rocket. Having to use both hands just to keep the wriggling icicle under some form of control, Brian stared in astonishment as a jet of freezing blue ice suddenly burst forth from its tip, hitting the Diefromen upon its chest and sending the demon, unexpectedly, staggering backwards. It roared furiously as it raised its arms and roared even louder when it realised that it could not bring its burning arms down upon the boy and kill him. Instead the creature's arms remained fixed and unmoving, somehow frozen above its flaming head.

The fire demon stared at Brian in both confusion and bewilderment. Below it, the unstoppable stream of blue ice

146

continued to hurtle from the tip of the icicle. It coursed through the creature's magical body, engulfing and quenching the flames upon its chest, and quickly spread to each and every one of its other limbs. The Diefromen attempted to move its legs, to get away from this boy and his odd, silver wand, but by then it was already too late. The fire demon's legs, just like its arms, had become frozen and it was now rooted to the spot.

Brian stared up in amazement as the Diefromen's flames were soon completely extinguished. In just a few seconds its whole appearance had completely altered. Gone were the demon's burning flames, the roaring fires that had consumed its entire bulk. Instead it now towered above Brian in complete and utter silence, its remains encased in a tomb of white, sparkling ice. The Diefromen was frozen solid.

'Look out!' shouted a voice suddenly.

For a moment Brian thought he recognised the voice but he could not see who it belonged to. He turned around just in time to see Barnaby Katobi materialise in front of one of the burning shops, his right hand clutching his walking stick. Other people had magically appeared in the square too; some of them were pointing at Brian whilst others were gawping up at the frozen Diefromen in both awe and shock.

'Look out!' cried the voice again. 'The fire demon is about to collapse!'

Brian stared up at the Diefromen and watched, terrified, as its body began to gradually crack and splinter. First, one of its arms fell off, then part of its head before finally a leg gave way and, very slowly, it began to topple forward. The fire demon was going to kill him after all. The huge statue of ice was falling… and it was falling on top of Brian!

The creature that rescued him was unbelievably fast. As the ice began to break apart and fall towards Brian a very dark and long-haired monster suddenly burst into the square, galloping past

147

Barnaby Katobi so fast that its wiry tail actually brushed his walking stick, knocking it out of his hand. It raced towards Brian at an astonishing pace, leaping over the fallen rubble and springing over the burning fires.

Brian heard the creature before he actually saw it. The first chips of ice began to shower down upon him, and Brian heard the monster howl as it swiftly scooped him up in its large, hairy arms and bounded over a smouldering crater to the other side of the square.

Moments later Brian found himself lying on his side in the remains of a partially collapsed shop. The creature that had rescued him was standing in the shadows, panting heavily as the last chunks of the frozen fire demon collapsed into the square to form a massive mountain of ice. Dropping to all fours it crept slowly forwards, into the partial light, and Brian stared at it fearfully. It had the head of a bird, a falcon or an eagle perhaps? But it was the size of a man with feathers that covered its face, merging into long, shaggy hair just below its neck which seemed to cover its entire body. Its legs and arms were long and nimble-looking whilst its feet had claws that looked as sharp as knives.

'Are you okay, Brian?' the monster asked, concerned, crouching at his feet.

Brian sat up. 'Yeah, I'm okay,' he replied, realising that, unlike a week ago, he now found that a talking monster was nothing out of the ordinary.

The monster reached towards him and Brian recoiled, momentarily afraid that the creature might hurt him, but instead, the monster simply stroked Brian's hair with one of its massive paws. 'Your head is bleeding,' it said, almost in a whisper.

'Yeah, it got cut when Abner Antiques got attacked,' replied Brian. 'I'm okay though.'

The monster glanced over its shoulder. Behind them a number of warlocks were busy clambering over the mass of ice towards Brian.

A few warlocks, Brian noticed, kept slipping over and scrambling to their feet again only to then slip a second or third time.

'I must go,' said the monster, standing up.

'But...' began Brian.

'If I am caught...' remarked the creature, turning to leave.

'But you've saved my life and I don't even know your name,' said Brian.

The monster smiled and Brian noticed that it had teeth within its beak that looked almost as sharp as its claws. 'You do know my name,' it said with a grin. 'It's just my face you don't recognise.'

Brian watched silently as the monster slipped into the shadows just as the first warlock scrambled over the fallen shop towards him. But it wasn't a warlock. Instead it was an old man with bushy white eyebrows and glasses.

'Brian, my boy, are you all right?' asked his granddad, kneeling beside him.

Chapter 12

THE BROWN WOOLLY HAT

Brian rolled over in his bed and yawned sleepily. He'd been having such a weird dream. He had dreamt that his grandparents had been kidnapped and that in a cavern, deep underground, there was a magical village filled with warlocks, monsters and talking statues and that he'd been attacked by a huge demon which had been able to conjure balls of flame from the very palms of its hands. Not only had he dreamt that he'd somehow defeated this demon by turning it to ice, no less, but he had also dreamt of being rescued from certain death by an enormous talking bird-like monster! Brian yawned again, rubbed the sleep from his eyes and very slowly opened them.

Sitting on a chair beside Brian's bed, half asleep, with his ankles crossed and his spectacles hanging haphazardly from his nose, was his granddad. His face was cut and grazed and he had a nasty-looking black eye but a broad smile immediately started to spread across his face when he saw that Brian was stirring.

'Oh, thank goodness!' he said, visibly relieved and pushing his spectacles back up his nose. 'You're awake at last. We've been so worried. This has been a frightful business. Poor Addison Aldwinkle broke both his legs during the Diefromen attack and how you managed to defeat the fire demon all on your own is almost too incredible for words! If I hadn't seen you do it with my own eyes then I would never have believed it. But you did it, my boy!' remarked his granddad before adding as an afterthought, 'Although quite what your grandmother would say if she were here I don't know. After you passed out—'

'I passed out?' interrupted Brian, frowning and sitting up in bed.

'Why yes, don't you remember?' asked his granddad. 'That Jackerbot was trying to scrobble you, Brian.'

'Jacker-what?' asked Brian.

'Jackerbot,' repeated his granddad. 'Don't you remember? A monster with the head of a bird and the body of a wolf.' He pulled the scariest face he could. 'I reached you just in the nick of time. I dread to think what would have happened if I had arrived a few minutes later. You were barely conscious when I reached you.'

'No,' protested Brian. 'The Jackerbot rescued me.'

Brian's granddad shook his head. 'It may have saved you from that frozen demon,' he remarked gravely. 'But believe me, Brian, if I had not escaped and found you when I did, it would certainly have scrobbled you too! Now, how do you feel? You look pale.'

Brian yawned again. Although he had no recollection of passing out he felt certain that his granddad was wrong and that the Jackerbot who had rescued him had had, in fact, no intention of actually kidnapping him. But he felt too tired to argue and did not pursue the matter any further. 'I feel a bit sick,' he admitted, staring at his surroundings. He appeared to be in a small cubicle of sorts, an oval space more than an actual room which was enclosed by two curtains that were pulled shut like makeshift walls. 'But what happened to you? Where are all the other Wizitches? Barnaby Katobi said you'd all been kidnapped!'

'I'll explain everything later, my boy,' said his granddad, getting up and looking about. 'First I need to find the nurse. Now where's she disappeared to? She wanted to know the moment you woke up. I'll be back in a minute,' he said, disappearing through a slit in the curtains.

A moment later one of the curtains next to him was pulled back and Norman, who had apparently been lying in the bed next to him,

151

peered round its side and said with a grin, 'Blimey! I didn't think you were ever going to wake up!'

'What is this place?' asked Brian, who could now clearly see that he was actually in a much larger room altogether, full of beds, many of which had curtains drawn around them just like his. 'Where am I?'

'You're in the Monster Ward of the HAPPI,' replied Norman.

'The monster what?' said Brian, confused.

'The Monster Ward of the HAPPI,' repeated Norman. 'The Hospital for the Afflicted and Poorly People with Injuries. We were all brought here after the attack by the Diefromen. Normally we'd be in the Warlock Ward, but so many people were injured after the attack yesterday that they only had beds available in the Monster Ward. Audrey had an asthma attack and broke her arm and I had some slug-stitches put on my ankle.' He rolled up his pyjama leg to proudly show off his wound that, rather oddly, appeared to be held together by five very thin and sticky squirming black slugs.

'Are those things real?' asked Brian, recoiling in disgust. 'I mean, are they really slugs?'

'Yup, and there's five of the little beauties,' said Norman, counting each slug individually. 'This first one's called Bob, the second one's called Bernard, then there's Bill, Bart and that tiny one at the bottom, he's called Basil.'

'You've actually named them?' asked Brian in astonishment.

Norman nodded. 'Yup, reckon I'll get a scar too!' he said, enthusiastically. 'How cool is that? You've got one less than me, mate,' he remarked, pointing at Brian's head.

'What?' asked Brian in alarm, and he quickly ran his fingers through his hair, finding four of the tiny creatures wriggling upon a nasty gash just over his forehead. 'How long will they be there for?' he asked, weakly.

'Only a couple of days,' replied Norman in evident disappointment. 'Three if you're lucky! Once your wound's healed they'll just drop off!'

'So the battle with the fire demon wasn't just a bad dream after all,' stated Brian, sighing dejectedly.

'Hardly,' replied Norman. 'Most of the shops in the square have been destroyed. Over fifty people and monsters were injured too! Most of them are in here, of course, in the Warlock Ward. And you know that Barrington Abner? He was killed. Found him in his shop. So badly burnt that he was unrecognisable, they say.'

'But where did the Diefromen come from?' asked Brian, shaking his head sadly. He hadn't taken a particular liking to the green-suited shop owner, but to be burnt alive was a horrible way to die!

'Dunno where it came from,' replied Norman. 'I guess from the portal. Oh, and Audrey's got another crackpot theory about that one too,' he said, rolling his eyes skywards. 'But I'll let her tell you about that when she comes back.'

'Comes back?' repeated Brian. 'Where from?'

'She's with Katobi and the Coffinsgrave Committee,' explained Norman. 'We've all got to go, to explain what happened yesterday and everything. You know, with the Diefromen and why we were there. I'm next and you're after me, mate. Violet went this morning. Can you believe she was with them for over an hour and half?'

'And is Violet okay?' asked Brian.

'Well, she wasn't hurt in the attack if that's what you mean,' replied Norman. 'She was here earlier but she didn't stay for long. Said she had to get back to the Dragon's Claw. You know, had some chores and stuff to do.'

Brian nodded in understanding but a few moments later he asked, 'Do you think she was punished?'

'What, for being out with us last night, you mean?' suggested Norman, awkwardly.

'Yeah,' said Brian.

153

'Well, when she was here this morning she had a few scratches on her face,' explained Norman, uncomfortably. 'Reckon she got them when Abner Antiques exploded though. Like how you got that cut on your head.' He pointed at the four slugs that were wriggling over the wound within Brian's hair.

Brian sighed. 'We should have listened to Audrey,' he said, regretfully. 'We should have stayed in our room and not gone out. We should never have left the Dragon's Claw.'

'What?' said Norman, aghast. 'Don't be daft, mate! If we hadn't been out last night or, more importantly, if *you* hadn't been out last night then that Diefromen would have probably killed loads of people! Because of you thirty, forty, maybe a hundred lives were saved! Do you really think Aldwinkle and those other warlocks who were knocked unconscious by the Diefromen would be alive right now if it weren't for you?'

'But I didn't really do anything,' admitted Brian.

'What are you talking about?' cried Norman, his eyes staring wide at Brian in amazement. 'You defeated the Diefromen! You turned it to ice! What you did was unbelievable! Everyone's talking about it!'

'Yeah, but that was all just luck,' said Brian, awkwardly. 'All I did was put my hand into that Wizitch's hat. The icicle thing was already in there. I just pulled it out. After that it just sort of came alive in my hands. To be honest it was all I could do just to keep hold of the thing!'

'Yes, but not everybody can do that!' remarked Audrey, who had just returned to the ward after her inquisition by the Coffinsgrave Committee. She sat on the end of Norman's bed, her arm in a sling which was clearly barely concealing a large black slithering mass. 'What you were able to do with that warlock's hat is almost unheard of,' she explained. 'Normally one warlock's weapon is utterly useless in the hands of another warlock. You see, it's unique to that warlock. But, for some reason, *you* were able to use it

154

and that's very, very strange. In fact I can't think of another warlock in the last hundred years who could do what you did yesterday!'

'Is that what I think it is?' asked Brian, staring at the giant slug that was clutched to Audrey's arm.

Audrey nodded. 'Disgusting, isn't it?' she said, pulling an unpleasant face. 'But the nurse said it should drop off in about a week. It smells awful too!' she added, wrinkling up her nose.

'How'd it go with Katobi?' asked Norman.

But before Audrey could reply Brian's granddad reappeared with the ward nurse, a pink-haired woman with six arms and a long orange tail, who was carrying three glasses of foaming blue liquid on a plastic tray.

'Ah, Master Pankhurst, your granddad was right I see. You're awake and looking remarkably well after your ordeal,' she remarked, pleasantly. 'Excellent! Now if you could just stick your tongue out for me?' She bent down to examine it. 'That's right, and if you could say "ah" for me?'

'Ahhhhhhh,' said Brian.

'Again,' said the nurse. 'A bit more loudly.'

'Ahhhhhhh,' repeated Brian.

'Excellent! Excellent!' said the nurse, smiling pleasantly. 'You certainly don't appear any worse for wear after your adventures. Now, I want you all to drink this down nice and quickly,' she ordered, handing each of the children a glass of the foaming blue liquid that she had brought with her.

'What is it?' asked Norman, sniffing the contents of the glass suspiciously.

'It's a little pick-me-up,' replied the nurse, tucking a loose bed sheet back under Brian's mattress with her long, furry tail. 'It'll have you all feeling better in no time at all.'

Brian sipped at the potion, which, surprisingly, tasted rather like lemonade and was so fizzy that it made his eyes water. Once he, Norman and Audrey had all finished their potions the nurse, still

155

smiling cheerily, took the empty glasses from them and said, 'Now, you'll be pleased to know that you'll probably be able to leave the hospital tomorrow, once the doctor has made his rounds in the morning.'

'Brilliant!' cried Norman. 'I want to show everyone my scar!'

'You haven't got a scar yet! And what about my arm?' Audrey asked irritably, staring at the wriggling mass within her sling.

'It'll drop off soon enough, my dear, don't worry,' said the nurse, reassuringly.

Suddenly there was a deafening crash that echoed so noisily throughout the whole ward that it woke almost every patient within it. This was followed, a moment later, by a high-pitched voice which screamed irately, 'I told you to open the doors gently! Gently is what I said. You do know what gently is, don't you? What do you mean that was gently? Here, pick that door up off the floor and prop it up against the wall. No, the other way. That's it. And now the other one too. Hurry up, before somebody sees us! You've put the door upside down, you great hairy oaf! Quickly, turn it around before that nurse turns up! Now, what's the matter? Oh no, not your tooth again. I wish you'd stop complaining about that. That's all you've gone about for the past two days! Your tooth! Your tooth! Your tooth! It's all about you, isn't it? You're like a broken record. Change the subject, you great hairy carpet! No, I don't care that it's hurting. It serves you right for eating all them rock cakes!'

As the two bickering monsters emerged into the ward Brian recognised them immediately; one was small and wore a very long woolly jumper and black wellington boots whilst his much larger companion was literally covered from head to toe in brown, messy hair. It was Sam and Hadley!

'Oh no you don't!' complained the nurse, striding purposefully over to the larger of the two monsters and snatching back a grey stethoscope that had become half-hidden within Hadley's fur. 'And

I'll take these back too,' she said, removing a pair of crutches from under one of the monster's massive arms.

'Wotcher!' said Sam, pulling himself up on to the end of Brian's bed. Hadley waved and everyone waved back at him, except the pink-haired nurse who, with her three pairs of hands, was still busily rummaging under the giant monster's hairy arms, having discovered a deck chair and computer keyboard to go with the stethoscope and crutches that she had already reclaimed.

'Do you want to see my scar?' asked Norman, rolling up his trouser leg excitedly.

'You don't have a scar yet,' Audrey reminded him.

Norman ignored her.

'Wow!' gasped Sam, staring at Norman's ankle, impressed. 'Five slug stitches. That's almost as many as I had once.'

'You've had more than five slug stitches?' asked Norman, disheartened.

'Yup, on my arm,' said Sam, rolling up his sleeve to reveal a curved scar upon his elbow. 'Had to have six slug stitches after me and Hadley got into a bit of a disagreement in the Witch's Hat a few years ago.'

'The Witch's Hat?' said Brian, who hadn't heard of such a place.

'Yeah, it's a tavern or rather it used to be a tavern in that square where you had that fight with the Diefromen,' said Sam. 'Everyone's talking about it, aren't they Hadley?'

The bigger monster, who was still being searched by the nurse, mumbled something in return.

'I said everyone's talking about the fight Brian had with the fire demon, aren't they? I do wish you'd get those big ears of yours cleaned!' complained Sam, irritably.

Hadley grumbled a reply.

'Oh, who cares about your tooth?' snapped Sam.

'What's the matter with Hadley's tooth?' whispered Brian.

157

'Chipped it on one of them rock cakes you gave us,' he replied, smiling wickedly.

Brian and his granddad both did their best not to laugh.

'Well, I think that's everything!' declared the nurse tetchily, placing the bicycle tyre she had just removed onto a pile of other oddments which now included an electric kettle, a furry orange moneybox that growled if you got too near it and an alarm clock that kept jumping up and down and shouting at the top of its voice, 'Wake up! It's time to wake up!'

'Here, you can have this back,' said the nurse, irritably handing the noisy alarm clock back to Hadley. 'Now what are you two doing in my ward?'

'We've been sent by the Coffinsgrave Committee,' replied Sam. 'To collect Brian,' he added.

'But I thought I was next,' said Norman, disappointedly. 'I wanted to show Barnaby Katobi my scar!' he said, flashing his wounded ankle at anyone who happened to be looking.

Hadley, tucking the shrieking alarm clock back into the folds of his fur, raised an enormous arm and pointed at a large cabinet full of bottled potions, mumbling something to his smaller companion as he did so.

'You don't happen to have a potion in that cabinet to cure toothache, do you?' Sam asked the nurse, hopefully. 'Only my friend here…'

'No, I do not,' replied the nurse, curtly. Then, turning to Brian, she asked, 'Now, are you sure you're well enough to walk, Brian, or would you like to use a wheelchair?'

'You can borrow mine,' suggested Norman.

'And I can push you,' suggested his granddad.

'You're coming too?' asked Brian, looking up at his granddad expectantly.

'Of course,' replied his granddad, smiling. 'I'm not going to let you face Barnaby Katobi and the Coffinsgrave Committee alone.'

Brian beamed, glad that his granddad was going to accompany him. 'But I don't need a wheelchair,' he said, climbing out of bed and throwing on his dressing gown and slippers, which he found next to his bed.

'And I'll have that back too, thank you very much,' said the nurse, snatching back the clipboard that Hadley had inadvertently picked up and was just in the process of slipping under his arm whilst nobody was looking.

'Good luck!' cried Norman and Audrey together as the nurse, with her six arms and furry ginger tail, began to hurriedly usher the two monsters out of her ward. Brian, trying hard not to laugh, and his granddad followed Sam, Hadley and the nurse down a long, brightly lit corridor which appeared to have a number of private rooms branching off it. When they eventually stopped, the nurse seemed to have some sort of fit at the sight of Hadley having to lift up one of the broken ward doors to let Brian and his granddad pass under it and into a small 'waiting room' which, unsurprisingly, sported a number of bookcases upon one of its four walls.

Leaving the nurse, who was now swearing dreadfully, in the corridor behind them, Brian watched as the two bickering monsters quickly removed a number of different-shaped volumes from one of the bookcases. Then, just as before, the books that had filled it began to rapidly disappear until very soon the bookcase was empty. As Brian followed Sam and Hadley into it he immediately felt the familiar tug upon his waist and was jerked sharply forwards before being engulfed by the blackness within.

Moments later Brian found himself standing in a circular room in front of an oval table seated at which were a number of individuals dressed in variously coloured cloaks and shawls. He recognised some of the faces seated at the table. One of them was Addison Aldwinkle who, Brian noticed, was seated in some sort of wheelchair that appeared to have a number of brown, scaly legs attached to it instead of actual wheels. At the head of the table was

Barnaby Katobi, whilst seated next to him and, rather unusually, without her scruffy, feathered companion was Beatrice Waghorn, the scent from her unpleasant perfume filling the room.

'Brian, thank you so much for coming and at such short notice,' said Barnaby Katobi, getting up and walking towards Brian with the aid of his walking stick. 'You look remarkably well for somebody who only yesterday was locked in battle with a Diefromen,' he remarked, shaking Brian's hand warmly and then his granddad's. 'Tell me, how do you feel?'

'Okay. But I don't like these slug things,' he said, pointing at the four tiny creatures that were wriggling amongst his hair.

'Yes, unpleasant little beasts, aren't they?' agreed Katobi, who began limping back to his chair with Brian and his granddad following behind. Sam and Hadley remained standing by the bookcase which had magically begun to refill itself. 'But they do have a quite remarkable healing quality, which means they are preferable to regular creams and stitches. Now, I believe you already know some of the Coffinsgrave Committee,' said Katobi, easing himself back into his chair and gesturing to his colleagues seated around the wooden, oval table. 'You've met, I think, Stanley Clutterbucket, Addison Aldwinkle, Gordon Grubshackle and, of course, Beatrice Waghorn. The other members of the Committee whom you may not have been formerly introduced to are Melissant Melchant, Helga Braithwaite, Winifred Hogfoot, Benjamin Brewster, Winston Zillion, Monty Yatlor and Kuchinska Chang.'

With the exception of Beatrice Waghorn all the committee members either smiled or nodded politely in Brian's direction. Waghorn, however, simply stared at Brian as though she were extremely bored.

'Would I be right in thinking that you have already spoken to Master Crabtree, Miss Jenkins and Miss Armstrong,' asked Katobi, 'and, therefore, know why you have been brought before the Committee this morning?'

'Norman said that you wanted to know what happened yesterday,' replied Brian, nervously.

'Correct,' said Katobi. 'And I suspect that you also have a great number of questions. First let me assure you, in case you are wondering, that neither you nor your friends are in any trouble whatsoever, quite the reverse in fact. But I, and the rest of the Committee, do need to know exactly what happened to you yesterday, starting from the moment when you left the Dragon's Claw. Leave nothing out, even if you may think it trivial. A demon, let alone a Diefromen, has not been seen in Coffinsgrave for a very long time indeed and it is, therefore, imperative that we know as much as possible.'

So, taking a deep breath, Brian began telling Katobi and the rest of the Coffinsgrave Committee exactly what had happened to them after he, Norman, Audrey and Violet had left the tavern the previous evening, pausing only to answer an occasional question when one was raised. However, when he reached the part about the opening night of Abner Antiques and witnessing the apparent argument between Beatrice Waghorn and Barrington Abner he saw that Waghorn looked absolutely furious. Indeed, if looks could actually kill a person then Brian was absolutely positive that he would have died right there on the spot!

Once Brian had finished telling his tale Katobi immediately turned to Helga Braithwaite and asked, 'I wonder, would you mind if I borrowed your hat for a moment, Helga?'

'Of course not, Barnaby,' replied Braithwaite and from within her cloak she produced a brown and woolly hat which she passed to Waghorn who, in turn, passed it to Katobi.

Brian recognised the burnt hat immediately. It was the exact same one that he had used to defeat the Diefromen.

'I'm curious, Brian,' began Katobi, turning the hat over in his hands thoughtfully. 'For, as I'm sure you're aware, this hat, although extremely well made by the way, is by no means a normal hat. It is, in fact, magical. Indeed, as I'm sure you've already guessed, it's the very same hat that you defeated the Diefromen with yesterday. I do not know if you are aware of this, Brian, but every warlock, witch and magician who resides in Coffinsgrave has some form of magical artefact that acts as a conduit for their magical abilities. And I say artefact rather than weapon for we are certainly not soldiers. We are merely protectors, keepers of the peace if you will. Now, I imagine that you must find it quite odd that a woolly hat has magical properties. Perhaps you're wondering why we don't use wands as depicted in so many films and books of the outside world?'

Brian nodded, more than a little confused.

'Regrettably, we do not presently have the time for me to recount to you the rather unpleasant altercation between Rula Rupolla and the twenty-two possessed and very angry shopping trolleys in broad daylight outside a supermarket in Edinburgh during the summer of 1953.'

'Very nasty business,' remarked Benjamin Brewster, nodding gravely.

'Indeed,' agreed Katobi. 'Another time, I think. But suffice to say, Brian, that carrying a wand can, and quite often does, raise far too many questions. Would you not find it odd to see somebody walking along the street casually carrying a magical wand in their hand?'

'Yeah, I guess so,' replied Brian.

'I suspect, however, that you would not look twice at somebody carrying a pen or perhaps an umbrella or maybe somebody wearing a woolly hat?' suggested Katobi. 'And it is for this reason and this reason alone that our magical artefacts are created in this way, to look like simple, everyday objects. We call them Fizzlesticks.'

'But Audrey said that one warlock's weapon, I mean Fizzlestick, could not be used by another warlock,' said Brian.

'Did she?' said Katobi, raising his eyebrows in surprise before smiling. 'Well, Miss Jenkins is not only very well informed but she is also absolutely correct. Each Fizzlestick is unique to each and every warlock, witch and magician. Which *usually* means that one magician cannot use another's Fizzlestick. Let me try and explain this in a slightly different way,' suggested Katobi, seeing the confused expression upon Brian's face. 'Imagine, if you will, your front door key. I'm sure that it fits and works perfectly well when you insert it into the lock of your own front door, doesn't it?'

Brian nodded.

'So what would happen if you used this same key to try and open your neighbour's front door?' asked Katobi.

'It wouldn't work,' replied Brian.

'And why is that?' asked Katobi.

'Because it doesn't belong to that door,' replied Brian. 'It wouldn't fit.'

'Exactly!' said Katobi. 'A magician's Fizzlestick is very much like your own front door key, Brian, in that each one is specifically made for that magician. It's tailored to their own needs and their own abilities. In the hands of another magician someone else's Fizzlestick, just like someone else's front door key, won't work. It would be like trying to open your own front door with, say, Beatrice's front door key. However, very occasionally and for reasons that we do not fully understand, even after a thousand years, there are certain individuals who *are* somehow able to use another's Fizzlestick. This ability is very rare, which is why, after the events of yesterday, we are so curious about you, Brian, for when you defeated the Diefromen you did it by using another magician's Fizzlestick!'

Katobi ran his fingers through his greying beard thoughtfully. 'I wonder, Brian,' he said eventually. 'Would you mind terribly if I asked you to satisfy an old man's curiosity and attempt to repeat yesterday's phenomenon?'

Brian shrugged. 'Sure. Okay. But seriously, what happened yesterday, well, that was just luck,' he said, feeling a little uncomfortable at suddenly being under such scrutiny from everyone sitting at the table.

'Perhaps,' said Katobi, contemplatively, and he handed the hat to Brian, but not before tipping it upside down and folding it inside out to prove to everyone who was watching that there was nothing already concealed within it.

Unlike yesterday the hat did not feel particularly heavy in Brian's hands. In fact it felt and looked just like any normal woolly hat that you might buy in a high street shop. Brian peered into it. The hat, as he had suspected, appeared empty. Slowly, he slipped his hand inside, expecting to find absolutely nothing at all just as Katobi had proved to everyone who had been watching moments earlier. But he didn't. Instead, his fingers touched upon something quite unexpected.

Brian ran his fingers over the surface of the object inside the hat. Oddly, it seemed to be slightly larger at one end than the other and at first Brian thought it was, perhaps, another icicle like the one he had retrieved from the hat yesterday. But the object he was touching now did not feel cold. Indeed, when he felt all along the object properly, from one end to the other, he discovered that the thinner part seemed to have what felt like leaves or, perhaps, petals sprouting from it. Very cautiously, Brian wrapped his hand around one end of the object and, to the sudden gasps of the Coffinsgrave Committee seated before him, removed it from the hat.

Chapter 13

THE MONSTER IN ROOM SEVEN

'I don't believe it,' gasped Helga Braithwaite, staring at Brian as he stood before Barnaby Katobi and the Coffinsgrave Committee with what appeared to be a stick of celery clutched in his hand.

Immediately, an eruption of voices all began talking and shouting at once with Gordon Grubshackle crying out the loudest, 'By golly he's done it again!' and Winston Zillion yelling, 'Unbelievable!' whilst Kuchinska Chang declared Brian to be 'A natural magician!'

'This really is quite extraordinary!' remarked Katobi enthusiastically, once the room had gradually begun to quieten down. 'As I suspected, Brian, you clearly have the rather rare and exceptional capability of being able to use another magician's Fizzlestick.'

'But, it's, er... a stick of celery!' exclaimed Brian, staring disappointedly at the rather limp vegetable in his hand.

'Indeed it is,' agreed Katobi. 'And very nice with a hot salsa dip it is too!'

'But I don't understand,' said Brian. 'What's so amazing about a stick of celery?'

Katobi smiled. 'What's so amazing,' he began, passing Helga's hat back to her, 'is the fact that you were actually able to conjure anything at all from the hat, because I can assure you that other than

Helga, whose hat it is, nobody else here present can replicate what you have just achieved.'

Brian felt his granddad's hand rest upon his shoulder. 'It seems you have inherited some of your father's talent,' his granddad remarked, smiling proudly.

'My father?' exclaimed Brian, turning to face his granddad. 'You mean my father had this ability too? He could use other magicians' Fizzlesticks?'

'No, not exactly,' replied his granddad, grinning. 'But like you, Brian, he had a rather unique magical ability.'

'Like what?' asked Brian, suddenly desperate to know more. For, up until now, his granddad had hardly spoken of his father; somehow he'd always managed to avoid the subject when Brian had raised it. Occasionally his granddad had hinted at something more, something secret, but each time he had done so he had seemed to suddenly change his mind and attempted to change the subject. As if he almost regretted saying anything at all.

'Your father had an uncanny ability to detect demons without the use of conventional magic or Fizzlesticks,' explained Brian's granddad. 'He could somehow sense where a demon was and when one was present without the need of casting a spell. He could see past their disguises and locate their secret hiding places using merely the impressions and images that would appear to him within his mind's eye.'

'A quite remarkable gift,' remarked Katobi. 'And with such an ability your father became a very formidable opponent indeed when battling a demon.'

'And does this have something to do with why my dad disappeared?' asked Brian.

'Undoubtedly, it was for this very reason that your father was scrobbled,' said Katobi gravely.

For a moment Brian didn't know quite what to say. He felt numb, as though he'd been suddenly slapped in the face. For although his mother had always implied that his father had left them both Brian knew that wasn't true. In fact, after his grandparents had been kidnapped, Brian had even wondered if his father had suffered a similar fate. But to have this fear suddenly confirmed by Katobi still came as a dreadful shock to him.

'So who kidnapped my dad?' asked Brian.

'He was scrobbled by a demon,' said Katobi. 'When your father first disappeared I suspected as much although I had no actual proof. I made some investigations, of course, but, unfortunately, discovered very little. It wasn't until yesterday, when your granddad escaped and was able to confirm my worst fears, that I knew for certain which demon it was that had returned. A demon that many of us thought had long since perished.'

'And what is this demon's name?' asked Brian, although he thought that he could probably guess.

'Its name is Deevilmon!' announced Brian's granddad, to sudden gasps of shock and wonder from some of the committee members who were seated at the oval table; Winifred Hogfoot looked like she might actually faint. It was then that Brian noticed that his granddad's gold ring, the one with the ruby stone at its centre, was missing from his little finger.

'What are we to do?' demanded Benjamin Brewster, standing up and bringing his clenched fist down upon the table in frustration. 'There are so few of us,' he said, looking at his fellow committee members. 'We cannot fight Deevilmon alone!'

'We can and we will,' said Brian's granddad, determined. 'What other choice do we have? Deevilmon is not all-powerful. The demon was defeated before and it can be defeated again. Its followers are few in numbers. It does not yet have enough, for if it did then I would surely not have escaped.'

'And exactly how *did* you escape?' bellowed Aldwinkle, who clearly didn't have his hearing aid turned up high enough. 'I've been stuck in the Wizarding Ward of the HAPPI since the Diefromen

167

attack, horrible hospital food I might add, and have not heard anything about your remarkable escape!'

'There's nothing much to tell, Addison,' replied Brian's granddad. 'Before I was captured I managed to conceal my Fizzlestick in the top of one of my bed socks, and when the demons who scrobbled me couldn't find it they wrongly assumed that I must have dropped it during the scrobbling.' He tapped his shirt pocket where, normally, his yellow screwdriver always sat. 'It was only when I was being transported from the cell I was being held captive in that I was able to retrieve my Fizzlestick and use it to overcome the demon guards and escape!'

'But where were you being held prisoner?' bellowed Aldwinkle, fiddling with the knob that controlled his hearing aid. 'And how did you return to Coffinsgrave?'

'I do not know where I was being held prisoner,' he replied, unhappily. 'I recognised nothing and neither saw nor found any doors or windows within the building in which I was being held captive which could even remotely suggest where I was.'

'And what of your son and the other Wizitches who were scrobbled?' asked Aldwinkle, a little less loudly this time as, evidently, he had adjusted the volume of his hearing aid to a more satisfactory level.

'I did not see anybody other than my captors,' he replied, shaking his head regretfully. 'I tried casting the Comedango spell but each time I attempted the spell it simply would not work. I guessed then that Deevilmon's cells were somehow magically protected. I thought I was trapped. You can imagine my surprise, therefore, when I finally stumbled upon a hidden bookcase which was connected to the Soobius System within one of the walls and it was through that I was able to return to Coffinsgrave.'

'No doubt it was by this method that Deevilmon's followers were able to control the Diefromen to spy upon and capture all the Wizitches,' said Katobi, knowingly, and a number of the

Coffinsgrave Committee members nodded their heads, muttering in agreement.

'But I ask again,' repeated Aldwinkle, 'what are we to do? How do we fight such a demon, for we surely cannot fight it alone?'

'I do not believe Deevilmon desires such a confrontation,' remarked Katobi. 'Not yet.'

'What do you mean?' demanded Aldwinkle, puzzled.

'Deevilmon desires eternal life,' explained Katobi. 'With the exception of Henry here,' he said, gesturing towards Brian's granddad, 'it has already successfully scrobbled all the Wizitches and, therefore, already has in its possession each of the precious stones that every Wizitch carries. It now has two further obstacles to overcome. Firstly, it must recapture Henry, for without him Deevilmon's plan is doomed to certain failure. And secondly, of course, it must also obtain the Cup of Ages!'

'Then what should we do?' asked Aldwinkle, desperately.

'Three things!' replied Katobi. 'First we must ensure that Henry is not scrobbled again, for, undeniably, Deevilmon will attempt further scrobblings, and secondly we must also make certain that the Cup of Ages does not fall into Deevilmon's clutches.'

'And what is the third thing?' asked Aldwinkle.

'Somehow, we must locate and rescue both Brian's father and all the other missing Wizitches,' announced Katobi.

Once again a sudden outbreak of voices all began talking and shouting ideas at once, with Benjamin Brewster suggesting to Helga Braithwaite, who was seated opposite him, that they attempt to actually conjure a demon themselves in an effort to track down Deevilmon. Stanley Clutterbucket, however, declared this to be a far too risky idea and immediately began narrating the troubles he'd recently been having with the howling hamster that had taken up residence somewhere within his attic. Melissant Melchant, meanwhile, had conjured, on the table they were all seated around, a

169

three-dimensional map of Coffinsgrave and was busily pointing out various buildings and dwellings that Deevilmon could be hiding in.

As the committee members continued to heatedly debate what should be done next, Katobi, with the aid of his walking stick, got up from his chair and with Brian's granddad escorted Brian back to the bookcase by which he had arrived earlier that morning. Unsurprisingly, Sam and Hadley, who up until then had been waiting patiently for the meeting to finish, were once again busy bickering, which had resulted in Sam kicking his bigger companion twice in the leg and stamping on his furry toes.

'What you have heard here today, Brian,' began Katobi as they approached the two arguing monsters, 'is not common knowledge. Nobody in Coffinsgrave with the exception of those here present knows the full story of what has happened to your father and the Wizitches and of the return of Deevilmon. As I have already said, I do not believe Deevilmon desires a confrontation. That is not the demon's plan. For the moment it seeks only immortality. And, rightly or wrongly, it is for this reason that the Committee has voted overwhelmingly to suppress certain information in relation to the Diefromen attack. They do not wish to cause the residents of Coffinsgrave any unnecessary panic. Therefore, an announcement will be made later today detailing a slightly different version of the attack.'

'But Norman said that there were over fifty people and monsters injured,' said Brian, heatedly. 'Barrington Abner was killed!'

'I did not say that I agreed with the Committee's decision,' said Katobi, gravely. 'But, nevertheless, I must abide by their judgement. And I hope that you will abide by their decision too and keep to yourself what you have learned today?'

'You mean I can't even tell Norman, Audrey and Violet?' asked Brian, disappointed.

Katobi thought for a moment before conceding, albeit reluctantly, 'Very well, if you feel that your friends can keep what you've learned today just between yourselves then I see no harm in you telling them. But now I must say goodbye, Brian. We still have to interview Norman Crabtree and there is still a great deal to be discussed by the Committee and I rather fancy a nice cup of tea and one or two digestives. I shall leave you in the capable hands of Sam and Hadley, who will escort you back to the Monster Ward of the HAPPI.'

'But you're coming back too, aren't you?' asked Brian, turning to face his granddad.

Brian's granddad shook his head and smiled a little sadly. 'You must understand, Brian, that Deevilmon will do absolutely everything within its power to scrobble me again,' he explained. 'As well as the Cup of Ages it must have me to succeed in its plan to become immortal. Without me it will fail. For the time being, at least, it's probably better that I remain here. It'll be safer for me and I'll be better protected. The last thing in the world I want is for you to be hurt in any way if an attempt is made to scrobble me again.'

'But I've hardly seen you,' complained Brian, who could suddenly feel himself getting upset.

'I know, but it won't be for long,' his granddad promised, giving him a hug.

Brian wiped his eyes and wondered why it was that he felt so upset, for until recently he'd only ever met his grandparents twice before, at two funerals. He hardly knew them and yet he felt a bond, an attachment to them that he couldn't quite explain or understand. He desperately wished his granddad were coming back with him to the HAPPI but he understood the reasons why he wasn't. As much as he hated to admit it, his granddad was right. If Deevilmon's plan was to be a success then the demon would undoubtedly attempt to kidnap him again, and what on earth could Brian do to stop that? He could hardly help protect his granddad with the stick of celery that he'd just pulled out of Helga Braithwaite's woolly hat.

Albeit very reluctantly Brian nodded his head in agreement and watched in unhappy silence as Sam and Hadley began removing the various volumes needed for the bookcase to magically empty itself again.

'Shall we bring Norman back with us?' asked Sam, as his bigger companion removed a faded blue book from the very top shelf of the bookcase.

'No,' replied Katobi. 'We'll interview him this afternoon, I think. If you could escort him here at, let's say, about three o'clock. How's that?'

Sam nodded and disappeared into the empty bookcase, closely followed by Hadley. But as Brian went to follow the two monsters he paused momentarily and, instead, turned and gave his granddad a massive hug before running to the bookcase and disappearing inside.

Moments later Brian emerged in the waiting room of the Monster Ward. Sam and Hadley were already there waiting for him. Seated at a desk on the opposite side of the waiting room was the same pink-haired nurse, her six arms not only busily scribbling notes on what appeared to be various patients' charts but, at the same time, holding a mug of coffee from which she took occasional sips whilst filing away some paperwork in a large, green cabinet behind her. Sitting upon a sofa next to the nurse Brian was pleased to see Norman, Audrey and Violet, who evidently had been waiting for his return.

'Stop right there!' demanded the nurse, leaping up from her chair in alarm and marching crossly over to Sam and Hadley. 'Where do you think you're going?'

'We're escorting Brian back to the Monster Ward,' replied Sam.

'I don't think so! This is quite far enough! Just look what you've done to my ward doors!' the nurse cried, jabbing all seventy-two of her fingers in the direction of the two massive doors that had previously separated the Monster Ward from the waiting room, one of which had fallen back upon the corridor floor again, its round glass window clearly smashed. 'Brian's friends can escort him back to the ward,' she said, gesturing to Norman, Audrey and Violet. 'You two, meanwhile, can both turn about and step right back into that bookcase!'

'But—' began Sam.

'Quickly, quickly!' ordered the nurse. 'Before it refills itself!' and she ushered the two monsters back inside the bookcase just as the first shelves and books began to magically reappear.

'Now then, how are you feeling, Master Pankhurst?' enquired the nurse, returning to her desk and swallowing a mouthful of coffee.

'Yeah, I feel okay,' replied Brian, watching as the nurse, once again, began performing a number of tasks all at the same time.

'Excellent!' she replied, pinning up some paperwork on a notice board behind her whilst at the same time stapling a large pile of notes together and then punching holes through them. 'Now, are you able to return to the ward yourself, do you think? You know the way, don't you? Straight down that corridor and through the doors... only... one of the doors won't open now and the other one, well, you'll have to climb over that,' she remarked with an unhappy tut and a shake of her head.

'It's okay, we can take him,' replied Audrey.

'Excellent!' said the nurse again, with a sigh of relief. 'Only I do have a dreadful amount of paperwork to complete after that awful business with the Diefromen!' As she spoke, she opened a filing cabinet with her tail and slipped a number of folders inside.

'You okay, Violet?' asked Brian, who hadn't seen Violet since the Diefromen attack.

'Course I am,' replied Violet.

'I mean, did you get into much trouble with the Gillibottoms?' said Brian. 'For being out with us during the Diefromen attack?'

'No, not really,' she replied before adding as an afterthought, 'Well, no more than usual.'

173

As the children left the waiting room and the nurse continued to staple, punch and file her paperwork Brian began recounting all that had occurred during his meeting with Barnaby Katobi and the Coffinsgrave Committee, whilst Norman was a little disappointed to learn that he wouldn't be able to show them his scar until later that afternoon. As they made their way through the corridor, clambering over the fallen door and helping Norman wheel his chair over it, Audrey told Brian about her theory.

'It's Waghorn!'

'What?' said Brian, incredulously.

'Waghorn's behind it all,' said Audrey.

'Waghorn is in league with Deevilmon, you mean?' remarked Brian, unconvinced.

'See, told you it was a crackpot theory,' said Norman.

Audrey shot Norman a venomous glance and flicked his ear with one of her fingers.

'Ouch, that hurt!' cried Norman, who then tried to run Audrey over in his wheelchair.

'Don't you see, it all adds up,' said Audrey, easily sidestepping Norman's attempt at mowing her down so that he crashed into the corridor wall instead, scuffing the paint. 'Waghorn's on the Coffinsgrave Committee, right?'

'Yeah,' said Brian.

'So she's got access to nearly everywhere in Coffinsgrave.'

'Okay.'

'And we saw her arguing with Barrington Abner, didn't we?' said Audrey.

'That's true,' said Violet.

'And I don't like her hair!' remarked Norman.

'What?' said Audrey, tetchily.

'I don't like Waghorn's hair,' repeated Norman.

'I'm being serious, Norman!' said Audrey, annoyed.

'So am I,' replied Norman. 'I don't like those red streaks in her hair. It looks nasty. And I don't like her perfume or that pet bird of hers either or the fact that when she smiles it looks like she's chewing a wasp!'

'But none of that means anything!' said Brian, sceptically. 'You can't seriously suggest that Waghorn is in cahoots with Deevilmon just because she's on the Coffinsgrave Committee and because we saw her arguing with Abner. You and Norman argue all the time, don't you? But that doesn't mean I think you're up to no good!'

'But don't you think it's odd that the very moment Waghorn left Abner Antiques the Diefromen appeared and pretty much destroyed the square?' asked Audrey. 'Barrington Abner's dead and the last person he was seen talking to... no, arguing with, before he was killed, was Waghorn!'

'Audrey does have a point,' said Violet. 'I wonder what they were both arguing about?'

But before anybody could offer any theories a door to the children's left swung open, almost knocking Norman out of his wheelchair, and a massive, white furry monster carrying what looked like an enormous bundle of food dashed from it and into a room opposite.

'Hey, he's dropped something,' remarked Violet, bending down and picking up what appeared to be a packet of chocolate chip muffins. As she did the children couldn't help but notice the fresh bruises on her arm.

'That flippin' monster almost killed me!' complained Norman, wheeling his chair over to the room the monster had just disappeared into. 'Blimey, what's happened to the door number?'

The children stared at the silver number 7 screwed to the middle of the door. It was covered in ice and so was the door handle. In fact the door handle was covered by so much ice that tiny, thin icicles were hanging from one end of it. Audrey stood on tiptoe and peered through the door's oval window and gasped in amazement.

'What can you see?' asked Norman.

'It's snowing!' exclaimed Audrey, shocked.

'What do you mean it's snowing?' said Norman, disbelievingly. 'How can it be snowing? We're in a hospital, remember?'

Brian laughed. 'Well, it rains in Coffinsgrave even though it's I-don't-know-how-many miles deep underground,' he remarked with a grin.

'Here, let's have a look!' said Violet, joining Audrey at the window and peering through it. Audrey was right; it was indeed snowing, not particularly heavily but snow was drifting steadily down from somewhere within the room, covering not only the floor but also the bed and other furniture too! Large footprints led away from the door to a cabinet beside the bed where the massive white-haired monster, with a bandage covering half his head, appeared to be busily putting away various tins and packets of food. Suddenly, he turned around and stared in alarm at the faces of the two girls spying upon him through the door's oval window. After quickly concealing what appeared to be a packet of biscuits and a cake under one of his pillows, the monster plunged through the snow towards them.

'What's your game?' demanded the monster, throwing open the door and growling angrily before any of the children had even thought of hiding. 'Spying on me, were you?'

'Er... you dropped this,' said Violet, holding up the packet of chocolate chip muffins nervously.

'Oh, did I?' said the monster, his tone of voice completely changing. 'Well... er, don't just stand there,' he added, clearly flustered. 'You'd better come inside. Quickly, before somebody sees you.' He glanced up and down the corridor anxiously. 'And make sure you shut the door behind you!'

The children followed the monster through the snow, which was quite difficult as they were all in their slippers except for Violet, who was wearing a pair of old trainers, and the four of them

176

watched as the monster climbed back into bed, unwrapped a packet of biscuits and began scoffing them three and four at a time.

'The food in here is terrible,' it remarked, finishing the packet of biscuits and unwrapping a very large slab of walnut cake. 'Only I was so hungry and my belly was rumbling so loudly that I thought I might actually wake up the monster in the next room. So I, er... borrowed a bit of grub from the hospital kitchen.'

'A bit!' exclaimed Norman, staring at the monster's bedside cabinet, which was covered in snow and so crammed full of packets of food that its two doors couldn't shut properly.

'You won't tell the nurse, will you?' asked the monster, fearfully.

'Of course not,' said Violet, admiring the snow falling from the ceiling.

'Phew!' exclaimed the monster, visibly relieved. 'Do you know what they gave me for breakfast this morning?'

The children all shook their heads.

'Twelve eggs, ten sausages, twenty slices of bacon, six tins of mushrooms, a bowl of baked beans, two loaves of bread and three tankards of coffee!' said the monster.

'Blimey!' exclaimed Norman, impressed.

'That wouldn't feed a mouse!' exclaimed the monster, indignantly.

'Depends on the size of the mouse,' remarked Norman, under his breath.

'Well, that does sound rather a lot!' said Violet.

'Not for a yeti,' remarked the monster, licking the last crumbs of walnut cake from his furry fingers. 'To a yeti that's just a snack! The name's Willy Googalak, by the way,' he said, holding out a massive sticky hand, which the children all shook, somewhat reluctantly, as they introduced themselves one by one.

177

'It's a bit cold in here,' remarked Audrey, wiping her now sticky hand on the side of her dressing gown and pulling it a little more tightly about her.

'Yeah, it's freezing!' said Norman, making a snowball and throwing it at Brian; it hit him on the side of his face.

'Well, I'm from the Himalayas,' explained the yeti. 'Can't stand the heat. Gives me a right headache! So the doctors gave me this private room. It's a bit small!' he remarked, glancing about at it. 'Well, small for a yeti, I suppose, but they cast a snow spell upon the ceiling so that I'd feel a bit more at home.'

'How long have you been in here?' asked Violet.

'Oh, only since yesterday,' replied Googalak as he tore open a massive bag of multi-pack crisps. The children watched as he emptied the different-flavoured packets onto his lap before selecting eight of them, which he then ripped open with his large, clawed fingers and emptied, one by one, into his gaping and fanged mouth. 'Would you like a packet?' he asked the children, sending tiny bits of crisp flying from his mouth in all directions and gesturing to the four remaining packets on the bed in front of him.

'Yes please!' said Norman, hungrily.

Googalak swallowed some of the crisps that he was munching on and chucked one of the packets over to Norman, which he caught. 'Only I don't like Troll's Toenails,' said the yeti.

'What?' said Brian, throwing a snowball back at Norman which caught him on the ear.

'That's the only flavour left,' remarked Googalak, pointing at Norman's packet of crisps and the other three unopened packets lying upon the bed. 'Troll's Toenails. Horrible flavour.'

'On second thoughts I think I'll pass,' said Norman, throwing the packet back on to the yeti's bed. He'd had Troll's Toenail flavoured crisps once before and had been violently sick immediately afterwards.

'How'd you hurt your arm?' asked the yeti, staring with a repulsed expression at the wriggling slug within Audrey's sling.

'Disgusting, isn't it?' remarked Audrey.

The yeti nodded in agreement.

'We all got hurt in the Diefromen attack,' said Audrey. 'Is that why you're in here too?'

'No,' replied Googalak, pouring a bowl of fruit into his mouth. 'Whilst the Diefromen attack was happening I was being robbed.' He pointed at the bandage covering a large portion of his head. 'Which is how I got this!'

'Oh dear,' said Audrey. 'That does look painful. Is your head very sore?'

'Just a few stitches,' said the yeti.

'Did you have to have slug stitches?' asked an excited Norman, who had been secretly rolling another snowball ready to throw back at Brian when he wasn't looking.

Googalak nodded and immediately, from his expression, wished he hadn't. 'Got a dreadful headache too!' he said, rubbing the bandaged fur above his eyes, soothingly.

'I've had to have slug stitches too,' said Norman, pulling up his pyjama trouser leg enthusiastically. 'Five of them, look!'

'Looks painful,' remarked Googalak.

'Yeah, I lost loads of blood,' said Norman, proudly and then pointing to the slugs attached to his ankle he said, 'Look, this one's called Bob, the second one's called Bernard, then there's Bill, Bart and that tiny one at the bottom is called Basil.'

'You've actually named them?' said Googalak, surprised.

'Yup, and I reckon I'll get a scar too!' replied Norman, happily. 'How many stitches did you have?'

'Twelve,' replied Googalak.

'Oh,' said Norman, a little disheartened.

'What happened?' asked Brian. 'I mean, how did you get robbed?'

179

'I've got a shop on the other side of Coffinsgrave,' said Googalak. 'It's called the Snow Shack. You've heard of it maybe?'

All four children shrugged and shook their heads.

'Oh well, it doesn't matter,' said Googalak, handing a Danish pastry to each of the children before swallowing another seven himself, all in one go. 'I sell anything and everything to do with snow and ice,' he said, wiping his mouth with the back of his furry hand. 'Christmas is my busiest time of year of course, the summer's always quiet. Not much call for snowboards and sledges during a heat wave,' he remarked with a chuckle. 'Although some of my ice potions are quite popular. You know, to cool yourself down when it's really, really hot! My Ice Explosion potion is always a big hit! Makes you burp snowflakes and sneeze ice cubes and when you go to the loo...'

'Yeah, I think we get the picture,' said Audrey, flicking some snow off the end of the yeti's bed and sitting down.

'You should come and visit my shop when I get out of here,' suggested Googalak. 'You can each try an Ice Explosion potion for free!'

'Brilliant!' exclaimed Norman, excitedly.

'Anyway,' continued Googalak, 'I had just closed the shop up and was busy re-stocking some of the shelves when I see somebody or something standing by the potion counter!'

'What was it?' asked Norman.

'Dunno,' said Googalak, with another shake of his head which made him groan and rub the fur above his eyes again. 'It was difficult to tell because they kept changing shape. There were at least two of them. Maybe three?'

'What do you mean, changing shape?' asked Violet.

'Well, I suppose I might as well admit it' said Googalak, reluctantly. 'I reckon they were demons!'

'Demons!' exclaimed Audrey, shocked.

'Shh, not so loud. Yeah, demons and in my shop too!'

180

'And what happened then?' asked Brian.

'Not really sure, to tell you the truth,' said the yeti. 'Everything happened so fast! I don't think they realised I was still in the shop. I think they thought I'd already locked up and gone home. Well, normally I would have but like I said I had some shelf filling to do and a bit of stock take too. Been putting it off. Hate doing a stock take. Anyway, like I said already, they were at the potion counter when I must have disturbed them because as soon as they saw me they immediately stopped talking, if you can call it talking. Was more like they were whispering or hissing to each other.'

'What did they look like?' asked Audrey, gripped.

'Hard to say,' replied Googalak, trying to remember. 'They were dark shadowy things. They kept changing shape and leaping about. Well, not leaping about exactly. More like transporting themselves from one place to another. They didn't seem to walk or even have legs for that matter. They just seemed to appear and then disappear again. One moment they'd be in front of me and then the next they'd be behind me. Each time I blinked they'd be in a different place, a different position! They must have cast a spell or put a curse on me because I don't recall anything else. The next thing I remember is waking up on the shop floor with a badly cut and bruised head!'

'And what did they steal?' asked Norman.

'Well, that's the funny thing,' remarked Googalak, puzzled. 'I didn't think they'd stolen anything at first because I couldn't find anything missing. The expensive potions, artefacts, charms and relics I keep in stock hadn't been touched at all. But just before I got taken to the HAPPI I realised that one particular potion was missing. The cheapest potion in the whole shop, would you believe. All of it had been taken. Every last drop!'

'Which one was it?' asked Brian.

'The Freeze-a-Friend potion,' replied the yeti. 'Children buy them mostly to play practical jokes on each other. You see, within

181

about ten seconds after drinking one you suddenly freeze to the spot!'

'How long for?' asked Violet.

'Oh, only for a couple of minutes,' replied Googalak, laughing. 'But usually, that's just enough time to draw a purple moustache on the person's face or maybe colour their eyebrows bright red!'

'Sounds excellent!' exclaimed Norman, smiling. 'I'm going to have to buy some of those!'

'You said the demons were talking about something when you disturbed them,' said Audrey, returning to the matter at hand. 'Can you remember what it was?'

Googalak shook his head and groaned painfully again. 'It's like I said already. They don't really talk like you or me. They speak a strange hissing speech. I'm afraid I only caught a little of what they were saying.'

'I don't suppose they happened to mention the Cup of Ages, did they?' she asked.

'The cup of what?' repeated Googalak, bewildered. 'No, they weren't whispering about no cup or trophy. I did hear something about the sea though.'

It was Audrey's turn to be puzzled. 'The sea?' she repeated, confused.

Googalak nodded again and immediately, again, wished he hadn't. 'Yeah, they were whispering about the sea and collecting some sort of stone I think. Seems a strange thing to be whispering about, don't you think?'

Chapter 14

AUDREY'S PLAN

When Brian awoke it was raining again. Outside he could hear the now familiar 'popping' noise as the magical drops of rain burst upon the tavern roof and on the cobbled streets below. He, Norman and Audrey had all been discharged from the hospital the day before. They had thanked the nurse for looking after them, said their goodbyes to Willy Googalak and promised to visit him in his shop, the Snow Shack, as soon as they could. Norman it seemed was already up, sitting in his wheelchair by the window ledge and examining the wound upon his ankle.

'One's fallen off!' he said a little sadly.

'What?' said Brian with a yawn, rubbing the sleep from his eyes. Although he had slept reasonably well Brian had, yet again, been awoken during the night by the same peculiar and persistent scratching noise at the bedroom door. This time, however, he had got up to investigate, but after managing to successfully creep across the floorboards without waking Norman or Audrey Brian had been disappointed to discover nothing actually behind the door. The corridor outside had appeared empty and the bookcase opposite undisturbed. It had only been when Brian had gone to close the bedroom door that he had noticed the unusual claw marks at its base, almost as if something had been trying to get inside.

'Bernard's dead!' said Norman, pointing forlornly at his ankle. 'He's fallen off!'

'Oh,' said Brian, who didn't really know quite what to say for the best. He brushed a hand through his hair and was disappointed to find that all four of his stitches were still wriggling away quite happily. Unlike Norman, Brian hated the horrible slimy slugs. Norman meanwhile had grown quite attached to his.

'I suppose they'll all drop off soon!' said Norman, despondently.

'What's it raining today?' asked Brian, climbing out of bed and desperately wanting to change the subject.

'Mice,' replied Norman, without even looking up from his ankle.

Brian joined Norman at the window and pulled back the grubby curtains to peer outside. The magical sky above them looked dark and thunderous. It was early and there were very few people wandering the streets below.

'Where's Audrey?' asked Brian, suddenly realising that he and Norman were alone.

Norman shrugged. 'Dunno,' he replied, unconcerned, and he began to affectionately stroke each of the four remaining slugs that were attached to his ankle.

Feeling less than sympathetic to Norman's unexpected loss Brian shook his head, rolled his eyes upwards and disappeared into the bathroom to get washed and dressed. When he returned about twenty minutes later Audrey had still not materialised and Norman, who was still sitting by the bedroom window, was now whispering lovingly to each of the slugs, saying things like 'Good slug', 'There-there, it'll be okay' and 'Who's a clever slug?' as well as stroking them.

A few moments later, and much to Brian's relief, the bedroom door opened and in stepped Audrey, already fully dressed and carrying a bundle of different-coloured papers all of which seemed to be twitching of their own accord.

'Where have you been?' he asked, glad to finally have some more cheerful company.

184

'I quickly popped to the Halls of Blooskstoof,' replied Audrey, placing the pile of convulsing paper onto her bed.

'But we're not meant to leave the tavern,' Brian reminded her, surprised. 'It was *you* who kept telling me and Norman that before the Diefromen attack, remember? We mustn't do this, we mustn't do that...'

'I know, I know!' replied Audrey, irritably, 'Which is why I went by Soobius System this morning, on my own, and without you two. There was less chance of me being seen that way.'

'And what exactly did you go to the Halls of Blooskstoof for?' asked Brian, puzzled.

'To find out a bit more about Deevilmon, of course,' she replied.

'Oh, and did you?'

Audrey shook her head and sighed disappointedly. 'No, apart from a few references to demons in some of the history books I couldn't find a single thing about Deevilmon. And when I asked one of the members of staff they said all the books about demons were on the Mind Your Own Business Floor.'

Brian laughed. 'You're joking!' he said. 'They really have a floor called Mind Your Own Business?'

Audrey nodded. 'Yes, and it's in the "secret section" too which I wasn't allowed to visit,' she replied tetchily. 'But I did find out that the Cup of Ages is definitely kept in Coffinsgrave.'

'Wow!' said Brian, impressed. 'Whereabouts exactly?'

'It's locked in a vault deep under the Committee Chambers,' replied Audrey, staring curiously at Norman who hadn't yet acknowledged her return let alone joined in their conversation. 'You know, where we were interviewed yesterday by Katobi. What's up with him?' she asked, pointing at Norman.

'Bernard's died,' replied Brian.

'Who's Bernard?' asked Audrey.

'One of his slugs.'

'Oh good grief!' said Audrey, as one of the coloured pieces of paper she'd carried in with her began to flap and attempted to crawl across her bed.

'What are those?' asked Brian, nodding towards the crumpled pile of paper.

'Flyers!' replied Audrey, snatching back the folded red sheet that had been trying unsuccessfully to escape. 'There are loads of them in Coffinsgrave today! You can't turn a corner without being dive-bombed by three or four of them! Most of the flyers are about the Diefromen attack. I watched one woman run into a lamppost as she tried to get away from a whole swarm of the things, knocked herself out cold!'

'I think Basil's dying too!' declared Norman, wheeling himself away from the window ledge and disappearing into the bathroom. 'He's not moving any more!'

Audrey ignored him. 'But I did manage to find out what those demons were discussing in Willy Googalak's shop,' she said, looking rather smug.

'You mean about the sea and the stone?' said Brian.

Audrey nodded and handed Brian a yellow flyer that she took from the very bottom of the pile on her bed, which twitched feebly in his hands as he read it. Brian recalled having seen something similar a few days earlier when Violet had shown them all around Gravestone Harbour. On the front of the flyer was a drawing of a large red tent which, as he stared at it, magically began to open before his eyes. From inside the tent letters emerged, one by one, and began floating up towards the top of the piece of paper, spelling the words 'DUE TO HUGE PUBLIC DEMAND THE COFFINSGRAVE SUMMER FAIR WILL BE GOING AHEAD AS NORMAL NEXT WEEK', whilst underneath the tent the date '1st SEPTEMBER' kept exploding in yellow and orange puffs of smoke. Inside the flyer, just as before, was a list of all the different stalls that were going to be at the fair.

'What's this got to do with the robbery at the Snow Shack?' asked Brian, confused.

Audrey jabbed her finger at one of the stalls being advertised inside the flyer. 'Look!' she said, and between a large advert for 'Hook-a-Vampire Bat – It's Fangtastic!' and a new body cream 'made from real sewer worms – it'll make you look 100 years younger!' was a much smaller advert for 'Madame Shinny's Wondrous & Incredible Seeing Stone'. Next to it was a drawing of an extremely old woman wearing a golden turban and in very tiny writing, underneath, was the following message:

Hello, my name's Madame Shinny and at some time in everyone's life there comes a point when the support and advice of family, friends and monsters just isn't enough. Perhaps you're secretly in love with a particularly ferocious Minotaur or you need to make an important career decision and you feel that a shufti at what might happen in the future is needed?

Well, don't despair because I, Madame Shinny, have had over 165 years' experience in helping monsters and humans alike. By using my astonishing psychic powers in conjunction with my wondrous and incredible Seeing Stone I will be able to give you a clearer picture of what your future holds and how you can make the right changes. See me and see what my third eye can see too...

*(available at the Coffinsgrave Fair all week except
on Thursday afternoon due to unforeseen
circumstances)*

'Do you think she really does have a third eye?' asked Brian, trying to picture where exactly on Madame Shinny's face it might be located.

'Of course she doesn't,' said Audrey. 'Well, not in the way that you're thinking. She's talking about her psychic ability. That's what she means by her third eye!'

'Oh,' said Brian. 'But what's Madame Shinny got to do with the robbery at the Snow Shack?'

'Isn't it obvious?' said Audrey, tetchily.

'Er…' began Brian.

Audrey sighed, exasperated. 'Willy said that when he caught the demons in his shop he overheard them whispering about the sea and some sort of stone, didn't he?'

'Right,' said Brian, nodding in agreement.

'Only I don't think they were just whispering about pebbles on a beach,' said Audrey, jabbing her finger at the psychic's advertisement once again. 'I think they were discussing Madame Shinny's Seeing Stone!'

'What?' exclaimed Brian, in amazement. 'You think Deevilmon's after this woman's magical stone?' He frowned. 'No, Deevilmon's after the Cup of Ages. Barnaby Katobi told me that himself, and my granddad too! Anyway, what could Deevilmon possibly want with this… Seeing Stone?'

Audrey shrugged. 'I don't know,' she admitted. 'Which is why we're going to see her next week!'

'What?' exclaimed Brian in surprise. 'When?'

'On the third day of the Coffinsgrave Fair,' she replied, looking remarkably pleased with herself. 'Normally I'd suggest going to see

Katobi straight away and tell him everything about Willy Googalak and the Seeing Stone, but I'm not too sure he'd believe us!'

'Yeah, I can see how he might think we've lost our marbles!' remarked Brian. 'Anyway, don't psychics usually charge money to see people?'

'That's right,' replied Audrey. 'They do and Madame Shinny charges nine bronze pieces for each thirty-minute reading.'

'Right, but we haven't got any money,' Brian pointed out, confused.

'We haven't got any money *yet*,' Audrey corrected him.

'Oh, don't tell me, you've already got a plan to make some money too, haven't you?' said Brian.

'Yup!' said Audrey, beaming. 'We're going to have a stall at the fair!'

'We're what?' exclaimed Brian.

'It's free!' explained Audrey.

'Free!' repeated Brian, dubiously.

'Well, okay, technically it's not free,' Audrey explained. 'What I mean is that there's nothing to pay up front. The cost of actually hiring a stall is taken from any money you've made at the end of each day. It's about 5%, I think.'

'But we're not allowed out of the tavern,' said Brian, matter-of-factly. 'How would we run the stall and what on earth would we sell?'

'We're not going to be running the stall,' said Audrey, slyly. 'Sam and Hadley will be. Once I've asked them, that is,' she added.

'What?' exclaimed Brian; it was a question he seemed to be asking quite a lot in this conversation, but he felt it was justified. 'Are you serious? Because you know what Hadley's like! He'll nick it all! Anything we try and sell will disappear under each of his arms in a matter of minutes! We'll have nothing left!'

'But we'll be at the fair too,' explained Audrey.

'We will?' said Brian, puzzled.

'Yes,' replied Audrey. 'We'll be hiding under one of the tables at our stall. That way we can keep an eye on Hadley and also make sure that they sell everything for the right price.'

'Right,' said Brian, somewhat unconvinced. 'And what exactly was it that you were planning to sell? Only we don't exactly have an awful lot here, do we?' he remarked, looking about their sparse bedroom.

'All our old toys, books and clothes,' replied Audrey.

'You mean jumble?' said Brian. 'And that'll mean using the Soobius System to get back to our bedrooms in our own houses?'

Audrey nodded.

'And who exactly is going to buy all our jumble then?' asked Brian, sceptically.

'Monsters!' replied Audrey. 'Monsters love anything to do with humans and the outside world. They're fascinated by our stuff. Trust me, we'll make a fortune! Well, maybe not a fortune but certainly enough to go and see Madame Shinny!'

Just then Norman reappeared from the bathroom and, if it was actually possible, he was now looking even more forlorn than before.

'Hey, what's up?' asked Brian, nodding in his direction.

Norman unfolded one of his hands. Lying quite still upon his palm was a thin, black slug. 'It's Basil,' he said, upset. 'He's dead!'

After doing their best to console Norman, which was actually quite difficult as neither Brian nor Audrey had any real liking for their slugs, especially Audrey who still had a particularly massive and sticky one wrapped around her broken arm, they explained Audrey's plan to him. Unsurprisingly, Norman thought it completely ridiculous, especially the part about Madame Shinny and her wondrous and incredible Seeing Stone. Besides, he pointed out, how exactly was he, whilst sitting in his wheelchair, meant to hide underneath one of the tables at the fair? That, said Audrey, was something they'd figure out nearer the time.

After Norman had got dressed and cleaned his teeth Audrey informed both him and Brian that Sam and Hadley lived somewhere in Stermon Passage, which was on the eastern side of Coffinsgrave. This, apparently, was where most of the monsters in Coffinsgrave lived.

'But isn't Stermon Passage meant to be a bit dodgy and a bit dangerous?' said Norman. 'I mean not all the monsters in Coffinsgrave are very nice, y'know? My mate Robbie Scott got lost once and wandered into Stermon Passage by mistake and almost got eaten by a Gungoo.'

'What nonsense!' said Audrey, shaking her head irritably. 'Do you know how big a Gungoo is meant to be? About the size of a house! Robbie Scott never went near Stermon Passage. He made that story up so that he wouldn't get into trouble with his parents after getting lost in the Maze of Nessdam. Honestly, Norman, you'll believe anything!'

'Well, even so, I've heard some funny stories about Stermon Passage,' he remarked, gravely. 'How do you know for sure that Sam and Hadley live down there?'

'Well, after I went to the Halls of Blooskstoof this morning I popped into the HAPPI and visited Willy Googalak. It was him who gave me their address.'

'Do you think we should tell Violet what we're doing?' suggested Norman. 'I mean, she might want to come with us.'

Audrey shook her head. 'It's probably best that we don't tell her,' she said. 'What if we get caught or get seen? She'll just get another beating from those awful Gillibottoms! I couldn't bear that.'

Norman nodded reluctantly in agreement and he and Brian watched as Audrey quickly removed five different-shaped and - coloured volumes from the bookcase opposite their bedroom until, one by one, all the books and shelves had, once again, disappeared into its murky depths. Then they followed her inside.

Moments later Brian emerged behind Norman and Audrey at another Soobius Station and, although it looked identical to the one they had passed through a few days before, Audrey, taking a puff from her inhaler, assured him that it was a completely different Soobius Station on the other side of Coffinsgrave. It was then, as they wandered down a long and straight corridor of bookcases, that Brian remembered that Audrey, as well as breaking her arm during the battle with the Diefromen, had had an asthma attack and that he had never once asked how she was and if she felt fully recovered. Feeling bad he said, 'How long have you been asthmatic, Audrey?'

'Ever since,' Audrey replied between taking another two puffs from her inhaler, 'I was a baby. It's inherited. My mum's got it and her grandmother had it too. It's worse when I get stressed or when I worry. Especially when I have exams at school.'

At the mention of Audrey's mother Brian suddenly wondered what his own mother was doing and where she was. He missed her and suddenly wished she was with him now. She may not have liked or agreed with the world in which his grandparents and father had been brought up, but he was certain that she would have helped in any way that she could have against Deevilmon. Like Norman, Brian wasn't completely convinced by Audrey's plan and her 'bonkers' theory (as Norman had put it) about Madame Shinny, but his mother would have known what to do for the best. If only he could somehow contact her. But how could he? There was certainly no way of reaching her from Coffinsgrave. He'd not even seen or spoken to his granddad since his meeting with Barnaby Katobi and the Coffinsgrave Committee two days before. So what chance was there of seeing or speaking to his mother?

'Norman said that you had an asthma attack when the Diefromen destroyed Abner Antiques,' Brian said to Audrey as he and Norman followed her round a corner and into another corridor full of dull-coloured bookcases. 'You feel okay now?'

'Yeah,' replied Audrey. 'I'm used to it. I've had asthma all my life.'

'And that inhaler you use,' said Brian, pointing at the blue and silver tube that Audrey had just tucked away into her jeans pocket. 'That helps you breathe more easily?'

Audrey nodded as she pushed open the doors to the Soobius Station and stepped out onto a thin and curved street of old and grey-looking houses and shops, the raining mice having seemingly stopped some time earlier. 'The inhaler clears the airways to my lungs. They get swollen and inflamed when I'm stressed, which makes my chest tighten; it gets real hard to breathe,' she explained.

'But you can't die from it, can you?' asked Brian.

'Actually you can,' replied Audrey, matter-of-factly. 'If you have a really bad attack and it's not treated quickly enough. But that's pretty rare.'

'Oh,' said Brian, more than a little shocked. 'And have you had many asthma attacks?'

'A few,' replied Audrey, helping Norman negotiate his wheelchair over the cobbled street and to the other side. 'But I've only been admitted to hospital with it once. Because I've had asthma for so long it doesn't really seem like a big deal any more.'

'But you're okay now though?' asked Brian, genuinely concerned. 'I mean, are you feeling all right since the Diefromen attack?'

'Oh yeah, I feel fine,' replied Audrey, smiling. 'Here we are, Stermon Passage,' she announced, bringing Norman's wheelchair to a halt in front of a very thin side street of old and rickety buildings that seemed to lean so far inwards that if there was a sudden breeze it might actually make them topple forwards and collapse in on each other. Above the children the cavern roof still looked dark and menacing as if it might begin raining again at any moment. Brian prayed it wouldn't rain rabbit droppings or, perhaps, something even nastier. He stared into Stermon Passage and, even though it was lit

193

by a number of street lamps, it didn't look particularly inviting. Although it was, in fact, still early morning the thunderous clouds above them made it seem and feel to the children as if it were the middle of the night. In the distance Brian could hear strange growls and high-pitched screams whilst in the shadowy darkness on either side of the passage he could see different-coloured eyes staring and blinking at them. He did not dare wonder what sorts of creatures the eyes belonged to.

'See, I told you Stermon Passage was dangerous! Can you see them horrible eyes staring at us?' Norman said, pointing into the darkness.

'Shh, keep your voice down, Norman,' said Audrey. 'Monsters can't always help the way they look and they certainly can't help what colour eyes they have!'

'What do you think's making that growling?' asked Brian.

'I don't know and I don't want to find out,' remarked Norman, as he did his utmost to avoid staring at a pair of blazing red eyes that seemed, rather disconcertingly, to be staring straight back at him. 'You're mad, Audrey!' he said. 'Do you honestly think Sam and Hadley live down here?'

'Oh, don't be such a girl,' said Audrey, a little unconvincingly, and she stepped forwards into Stermon Passage. 'There's nothing to be afraid of!' But no sooner had she spoken than something suddenly leapt from the shadows. The hooded figure which had been secretly watching the children grabbed Audrey's throat, lifting her off the floor, and flung her into the side of the nearest building so that she fell to the floor in a crumpled heap.

Norman immediately spun his wheelchair forwards, towards the hooded figure, trying to run it over, but the figure before him simply kicked Norman's wheelchair with such force that it somersaulted twice in midair, sending Norman crashing to the floor and his wheelchair hurtling into a row of dustbins on the opposite side of the street.

Then the hooded figure turned towards Brian and before he had time to run or even think about fighting back it had stretched out an arm and with an old, bony hand it had grabbed Brian around his throat too, lifting him physically up off the floor so that his feet began kicking against thin air as he struggled in vain to free himself from the hooded figure's monstrously tight grip.

'Give me the ring!' it rasped as Brian desperately tried to recoil from its foul-smelling breath.

'W-what?' stammered Brian, almost choking.

'Give me the ring!' repeated the hooded figure coldly.

'I d-don't know w-what you're t-talking about,' spluttered Brian who, as the figure's grip upon his throat began to tighten, began struggling to breathe.

'Give me the ring,' the hooded figure rasped again.

'I d-don't have your ring,' gasped Brian, choking.

'I will not ask again. If you do not give me the ring then I shall kill the girl. Then I shall kill the cripple and then I shall kill you,' hissed the figure and, as it began to raise its other arm towards Audrey, Brian saw that its aged and gnarled hand had suddenly become consumed by a silver and pulsing light which crackled and fizzed dangerously over its twisted fingers.

Chapter 15

AN UNWANTED VISITOR

Brian gasped, almost choking for breath. Even as he frantically tried to suck in another lungful of air he could feel the hooded man's grip tighten dangerously about his throat. Brian was suffocating! He was in agony! His chest was burning so badly that it felt as though it had been set on fire. Whilst his eyes, streaming with tears, felt like they were going to explode at any moment!

He coughed and spluttered uncontrollably as he desperately fought for breath, but each time Brian opened his mouth instead of sucking in air he would only gag and choke as the hooded man's grip began to squeeze upon his throat even tighter. Brian tried to say something, something that might save his life, something that might save the lives of Norman and Audrey too. He pressed his lips together but the words were painfully slow in forming and when eventually they managed it each word left his mouth in nothing more than a whisper.

'I... haven't... got... your... ring...'

But whether the hooded man actually heard what Brian had said he would never know. For as the terrifying figure had turned and pointed one of its crooked fingers towards Audrey, as if to cast a spell or to release a deadly bolt of lightning at her, a large and very hairy creature had leapt upon him, forcing the figure to the floor and, in turn, releasing Brian from his lethal grip. The Jackerbot howled furiously as the hooded figure, pinned beneath it, struggled in vain to escape.

'Who are you?' growled the Jackerbot, angrily. 'And what do you want with these children?'

But the hooded figure did not reply.

'Who are you?' repeated the Jackerbot even more angrily this time.

But, once again, the hooded figure did not answer. Instead, the man beneath the Jackerbot continued to relentlessly struggle in an attempt to somehow break free from the furious creature's grasp. But it was to no avail as the weight of the Jackerbot upon him meant that the hooded man was well and truly trapped.

The Jackerbot laughed, although it sounded to Brian more like a howl. 'There is no escape,' it said, bearing its teeth menacingly towards the man's concealed face so that long slivers of drool dripped upon him from its open jaws.

Then one of the figure's bony hands began to crackle and fizz as, once again, it became consumed by the same silver, pulsating light.

'I don't think so!' roared the Jackerbot, and it brought one of its huge paws down upon the man's outstretched hand so hard that it made him cry out in pain and instantly extinguish the deadly ball of magic that had been manifesting itself over his twisted fingers.

'Are you all right, Brian?' the Jackerbot growled.

Brian coughed and managed to rasp, 'Yes.'

'Then let us see who is concealed under this hood,' said the Jackerbot, bending forwards, its teeth bared, ready to tear off the man's disguise.

But no sooner had the enormous Jackerbot opened its beak than the hooded man beneath it began to mumble something under his breath. Then, with a dull flash of grey light, he completely vanished leaving behind nothing more than a few wisps of black, sinewy smoke that very soon had disappeared also.

197

The Jackerbot growled unpleasantly. 'He's escaped! Teleported to who knows where,' it said angrily, standing up on its two hind legs, walking over to Brian and helping him to his feet. 'He must have used the Comedango spell.'

Brian coughed. 'Who was he?'

The Jackerbot shrugged. 'No doubt one of Deevilmon's followers.'

'You know about Deevilmon?' said Brian, surprised.

Behind them Norman groaned and managed to sit up. He had a nasty-looking bruise under his right eye. With the Jackerbot's help, Brian retrieved Norman's wheelchair and helped him back into it. Audrey, meanwhile, was also back on her feet, although she looked a little unsteady and for a couple of minutes used Brian's arm and shoulder for support.

'Is this the same Jackerbot who rescued you from the Diefromen?' she whispered to Brian, whilst checking inside her sling for the slug that was wrapped around her broken arm. Disappointingly, when she prodded it, the slug seemed to be no worse for their encounter with the hooded man.

'Yes. At least I think it is,' rasped Brian, his voice not yet having fully returned.

'Thank you for saving us,' said Audrey, nervously extending her hand, which was shaking badly. She did not mean to be afraid of the Jackerbot, but when it was standing on its hind legs, as it was now, the creature was almost twice as tall as she was.

The Jackerbot looked down its dark beak rather uncertainly at Audrey before gently shaking her hand. Its massive paws were about four times the size of Audrey's hand and its claws looked lethal! And yet the creature's actual paw was smooth and felt quite soft to the touch. Its palm, if you could call it that, Audrey noticed, was slightly scalded but not very badly, probably caused, she guessed, by the hooded man's magical ball of light.

'You shouldn't have come here,' the Jackerbot remarked, pacing uneasily up and down in front of the children. 'Stermon Passage can be very dangerous, especially this, the eastern side.'

'Who are you?' asked Audrey.

'And how did you know we were even here?' enquired Norman.

The Jackerbot looked at the children and frowned. 'What were you doing in Stermon Passage?' it asked.

'We were looking for Sam and Hadley,' replied Brian.

'The two monsters who work for Barnaby Katobi?' questioned the Jackerbot.

Brian nodded. 'They're supposed to live here.'

'They do,' said the Jackerbot, nodding. 'Most monsters live in Stermon Passage, but Sam and Hadley do not live on this side. They live on the western edge. If I were you, I'd go back to the Soobius Station you came here by and use it to get to the other side of Coffinsgrave. Walking from here through Stermon Passage would not be wise.' It turned to leave.

'Hey, where are you going?' asked Brian.

'Like you, I should not be here,' replied the Jackerbot. 'It isn't safe.'

'But we don't even know your name!' cried Audrey, as the Jackerbot fell to all fours and disappeared into the shadows.

The Jackerbot, however, did not reply. Instead, it continued into the darkness, pausing only once to briefly glance over its shoulder at the three children to ensure their safe departure from the cobbled street.

'Did you see the size of its teeth?' asked Norman a few minutes later, as the three children made a hasty retreat out of Stermon Passage and back into the Soobius Station by which they had arrived previously. 'I reckon it could have torn that hooded man to pieces if it had wanted to!'

'Your neck looks really sore, Brian,' remarked Audrey. 'Are you okay?'

Brian rubbed his throat tenderly. 'That man or whatever it was very nearly strangled me!' he complained.

'Do you think he really was in league with Deevilmon, like that Jackerbot suggested?' asked Norman, as they made their way along one of the many corridors of coloured books within the Soobius Station.

Brian shrugged. 'Dunno,' he replied, honestly. 'One thing's for certain though, you're going to have a really black eye!' He pointed at the swelling above Norman's right cheek, which was already turning a nasty darkish blue.

'Do you reckon it'll need slug stitches?' asked Norman, excitedly.

'What, for a black eye?' scoffed Audrey, dismissively. 'I very much doubt it! Anyway, what do you think this ring was that the hooded man was after?'

'No idea. I don't even own a ring!' said Brian, holding up his hands and wriggling his bare fingers. 'You're wearing a ring though,' he remarked, nodding at Audrey. 'Why didn't he want yours?'

'He didn't want just any old ring,' said Norman.

Audrey nodded in agreement. 'Norman's right,' she said. 'That man, or whoever he was, was after a very specific ring.'

'But why did he think I might have it?' asked Brian.

Norman and Audrey both shrugged and the three children disappeared into one of the bookcases, re-emerging moments later in another, identical Soobius Station but this time on the western side of Coffinsgrave.

They found Sam and Hadley's home relatively easily; it was a small (from the outside at least) square building which seemed to have only one floor, but when they knocked at their door there was no reply. Fortunately, Audrey had a pen and paper with her and she hastily scribbled a note that she popped through the letterbox, which, much to Brian's surprise, burped loudly and said in a strange and unusual accent, 'Ta very much.' Then, returning to the Soobius Station, they disappeared into another bookcase just as it began to rain pink umbrellas outside.

The children knew something was wrong as soon as they stepped out of the bookcase. Their bedroom landing was not as they had left it earlier that morning; far from it. Books, were now lying absolutely everywhere, many with their pages ripped out, whilst the few grubby pictures that had been hanging on the walls had been torn from their hooks and thrown to the floor, their facades smashed and broken. As the bookcase attempted to refill itself the children were alarmed to see that only twelve books were able to magically re-materialise. These then proceeded to wander up and down their respective shelves as if searching for their missing neighbours. All the other books, it seemed, were now lying scattered over the landing floor. Of course, it was not the first time that Brian had seen something like this. On his very first day at his grandparents' house he had witnessed something very similar when a bookcase had apparently exploded in their living room, sending books flying in every possible direction. He was about to mention this fact to Norman and Audrey when Norman suddenly pointed at their bedroom door.

When they had left for Stermon Passage earlier that morning their bedroom door had been closed and locked. But now it was ever-so-slightly open. And inside their bedroom they could hear footsteps. Audrey pushed a finger to her lips, signalling for Brian and Norman to be absolutely quiet. The gap between their bedroom door and its frame was not particularly big but it was just wide enough for all three children to peer through. Inside they could see the figure of a woman. A woman dressed entirely in blood red. She seemed to be bending over, examining something. But the children could not see what. Then, all at once, she stopped what she was doing and twisted her head.

'We have visitors,' she announced to nobody in particular, turning about and suddenly standing up. And with a flick of her wrist the children's bedroom door was magically yanked open.

'You!' cried Brian in both shock and amazement.

It was Beatrice Waghorn who stood before them, the scent of her unpleasant perfume hitting the children full in the face. Her scruffy pet bird, which had been secretly acting as a lookout somewhere on the landing, flew obediently to its mistress's shoulder, cocking its head to one side and staring distrustfully at the children as they entered.

'What's happened?' cried Audrey, gawping at their bedroom in utter dismay. For, just as with the landing outside, somebody had been inside the children's bedroom and turned it completely upside down. The mattresses from their beds had been dragged to the floor, stripped and then torn apart by something so sharp that most of the stuffing now lay all over the floorboards. The same thing had been done to their pillows too. Feathers were everywhere! Their table had been overturned and the drawers to their wardrobes emptied and then discarded, whilst their clothes which had been neatly folded or hanging in a wardrobe were now lying in a messy pile in a corner.

'You were told not to leave the tavern!' exclaimed Waghorn, her eyes burning with undisguised fury. 'What part of DO NOT LEAVE THE TAVERN did you not understand? Where have you been?'

Brian shifted uncomfortably from one foot to the other, accidentally stepping upon and breaking the glass covering a picture that, until earlier that morning, had been hanging upon one of their bedroom walls. He didn't want to tell Waghorn where they'd been but he couldn't think of what else to say. 'W-we went to Stermon Passage,' he admitted, rather reluctantly.

Waghorn's face immediately flushed so red with rage that it very nearly matched the streaks of scarlet within her hair. 'But Barnaby Katobi himself told you to remain here,' she snapped.

'But—' began Brian.

'Do you want to get yourselves all killed?' snapped Waghorn.

'No, but—'

'Because I can arrange a particularly painful death for you all right now.'

The toilet flushed. 'Oh, don't be so hard upon them!' remarked Brian's granddad, suddenly emerging from the bathroom. 'Sorry, drank too much tea at breakfast,' he admitted, smiling pleasantly at all the children whilst cleaning his spectacles with the end of his chequered shirt. 'Besides, Beatrice, it looks as though it was a jolly good job they weren't here. Don't you agree? Just look at all this mess!'

Waghorn's scruffy black bird twisted its head towards Brian's granddad, flapped its wings and with a squawk hopped on to its mistress's other shoulder and appeared to nibble her ear. Although Brian had the distinct impression that it was, in fact, telling her something.

'What's going on?' asked a voice suddenly from the landing, behind the children. It was Violet and she gasped in amazement when she saw the state of the children's bedroom. 'What's happened?'

'That's exactly what I want to know,' demanded Waghorn. 'I assume that you did not leave your bedroom in this sorry state when you ignored Barnaby Katobi's specific instructions and left for Stermon Passage this morning?'

'No, of course we didn't,' replied Audrey.

'And *what*, may I ask, were you doing in Stermon Passage?' asked Waghorn.

'Er… we were just visiting friends,' replied Norman.

'Is that so?' said Waghorn, suspiciously. 'And is that how you got the black eye?'

Norman did his best to avoid Waghorn's gaze.

'Good grief! What's happened to your neck, Brian?' exclaimed his granddad, putting his spectacles back on and staring at Brian's throat, which was now quite red and swollen.

'Got it during the Diefromen attack,' Brian lied. He certainly wasn't about to tell his granddad the truth about how he, Norman and Audrey had been attacked in Stermon Passage with Beatrice Waghorn still in the room with them.

'But I don't remember seeing it before,' said his granddad, crouching down to carefully examine Brian's neck. 'It looks painful. And you say you got this during the Diefromen attack?'

Brian nodded but he could tell from the look on Beatrice Waghorn's face that she didn't believe a word of it. 'What are you doing here?' Brian asked his granddad, trying to change the subject. 'I thought you weren't allowed to leave the Committee Chambers.'

'Well, technically, I'm not really meant to,' agreed his granddad, pushing his spectacles back up his nose and standing up, seemingly satisfied with Brian's story about injuring his neck during the Diefromen attack. 'But I wanted to see how you were, my boy. I wanted to see if you were all right. Beatrice was kind enough to... accompany me, so I was in safe hands. And I think I was right to be worried, don't you? Just look at this room! I wonder what in the world it was that they were looking for. Is there anything missing?'

Brian shrugged. 'I don't know,' he replied. The room was in such a dreadful mess he doubted very much that they would really know if anything had been stolen until they had actually tidied it all back up.

'Do you have any idea what they could have been looking for?' asked Waghorn inquisitively, stepping closer to the children. The bird seated upon her shoulder flapped its wings to steady itself as she leant forwards.

'No,' said Norman and Audrey a little too quickly whilst Brian just shook his head. He knew already that whoever it was that they had encountered in Stermon Passage had also been here, in their bedroom, searching for a ring.

'If you have any suspicions it would be wise to tell me now,' warned Waghorn. 'Clearly, if whoever broke into your bedroom was unsuccessful in finding what they were looking for then it's quite possible that they may return. If you know who did this or you think you know then it would be wise to tell me now!'

Brian glanced uneasily at Norman and Audrey and then back at Waghorn. For the very first time he began to wonder if Audrey's theory about Waghorn was right. Was she in league with Deevilmon? Was she, in some way, connected with the hooded figure that the children had encountered in Stermon Passage?

'We've got no idea who did this or why,' said Brian.

Waghorn raised an eyebrow suspiciously. It was perfectly clear from the expression on her face that she didn't believe a word that he had said.

Chapter 16

A HIDDEN THREAT

The tidying up of the children's bedroom took a lot longer than Brian had thought it would. He had hoped that it wouldn't take any longer than, perhaps, a couple of hours, but even with the three of them (Violet had been ordered back into the tavern's kitchen by a shrieking Elfrida Gillibottom) it had taken most of the day. Not only had their bedroom been turned completely upside down but their bathroom had suffered a similar fate too. The shower curtain surrounding the bath had been torn to shreds and the bathroom cupboard had been ripped from the wall and completely pulled apart, its contents scattered deliberately all over the floor, whilst the mirror that had previously been hanging above the bathroom sink had, it seemed, been smashed into a thousand pieces.

Of course their goal would have been achieved a lot quicker if they'd had some form of magical help. In particular, the re-stuffing of their mattresses, which with the aid of a simple magical spell would have taken mere seconds, had instead taken many hours. But no such help had been forthcoming from Beatrice Waghorn and Brian's granddad was unable to offer any real magical assistance as he didn't have his yellow screwdriver with him. He did, however, say that he would explain everything to the Gillibottoms and set things right before he left the tavern. But, even so, when the children's meals arrived outside their door later that evening the portions were even colder and even more meagre than usual.

206

'Sorry about your dinner,' said Violet, apologetically, when she had knocked at their bedroom door later that evening. The children's plates, she noticed, appeared untouched.

'Oh, that's okay,' replied Norman. 'We've got our own stash of food.' He waved half a packet of digestive biscuits in the air.

'Where did you get these from?' asked Violet, taking the biscuit which Norman offered her.

'Willy Googalak,' replied Audrey, who was half way through eating a rather large packet of crisps. 'He... er, obtained some more food from the hospital store room and, well, he gave us a few packets of biscuits, crisps and things to take back with us when we left the hospital. In case we got hungry.'

'Think he was a bit worried that we might tell the nurse what he'd been up to.' Norman pushed a whole digestive into his mouth all at once. 'So he shared some of the food that he nicked with us,' he mumbled.

'Borrowed!' corrected Audrey.

'Nicked!' repeated Norman. 'You can't borrow food, Audrey. You can borrow a game and you can borrow a book but you can't borrow food.' He stuffed another digestive into his mouth all at once. 'Because once you've eaten it, it's gone, forever!'

'Here, have some apple pie,' said Brian, offering Violet a slice which she happily took. As she did, he noticed a burn mark on her hand. 'How did you do that?' he asked.

'Oh, it's nothing,' replied Violet, hiding her arm behind her back. 'It was my fault. I wasn't looking at what I was doing in the kitchen. One of the handles to the cooking pots was hotter than I realised. It's okay. Hardly sore at all.'

'Oh my goodness!' exclaimed Audrey, concerned. 'Have you put anything on it?'

'I've put some magiseptic on it and it's fine,' replied Violet. 'Doesn't sting or hurt at all now!'

Brian stared at Violet dubiously and wondered if she was being completely honest with them. Her burnt hand looked sore and painful and he sincerely hoped that Violet's injury had not been inflicted by one of the Gillibottoms as punishment for some mistake.

'Don't the Gillibottoms give you oven gloves to wear in the kitchen?' asked Audrey, as she studied Violet's blistered hand.

'They only have one pair and Elfrida Gillibottom uses those,' replied Violet.

'Do you know I've got a good mind to go down to the Gillibottoms right now and tell them exactly what I think about them both!' exclaimed Audrey, thrusting her hands upon her hips angrily.

'Oh, please don't!' begged Violet.

'But they treat you like a slave!' said Audrey, crossly.

'I know they don't treat me as well as they could,' agreed Violet. 'But please don't say anything. It'll just make things much worse for me. Elfrida will make me clean the toilets with a toothbrush or something unpleasant like that!'

'But the Gillibottoms shouldn't be able to get away with this!' said Audrey, angrily.

'You don't know what they're like!' said Violet. 'If you do say anything to them then they'll just make my life even more miserable than it is already!'

'But—' protested Audrey.

'Please,' implored Violet.

'Okay,' agreed Audrey, albeit reluctantly. 'But they just make me so mad. It's wrong! They shouldn't be allowed to get away with how they treat you. When this is all over I'm going to speak to Barnaby Katobi about it!'

'So, anyway, what are you doing here at this time of night?' asked Brian. 'I mean, it's not like we're not pleased to see you or anything but the Gillibottoms normally have you working in the kitchen or waiting tables.'

'Well, since your granddad told them that somebody had broken into your room they've told me to keep an eye on you.'

'Why?' asked Norman.

'Let's just say that if word got out that somebody or something had broken into the tavern then that would not be good for business. The Gillibottoms have already tried to get you moved to another tavern but everywhere is pretty much booked because of the Coffinsgrave Fair. Oh, and I almost forgot,' she said, rummaging in her trouser pocket and handing Audrey a folded envelope. 'This arrived for you this afternoon.'

Audrey took the envelope, which had been addressed to her in what appeared to be a thick green crayon and sealed with candle wax of a similar colour. Inside was a letter which she quickly read.

'Who's it from?' asked Norman, as he stuffed another digestive into his mouth.

'Sam and Hadley,' replied Audrey. 'They've agreed to run our stall at the Coffinsgrave Fair next week.'

'But you're not meant to leave the tavern!' exclaimed Violet, in surprise.

'Oh dear, I think you'd better explain your plan to Violet,' suggested Brian, finishing the piece of apple pie he had been eating and licking his fingers clean one by one. 'If the Gillibottoms expect her to keep a close eye on us all then you'd better tell her everything. Including what happened in Stermon Passage this morning.'

So, taking a deep breath, Audrey began recounting to Violet everything that had happened to her, Brian and Norman earlier that day in Stermon Passage and the likelihood that whoever had attacked them had also been the person responsible for breaking into their bedroom and ransacking it. Lastly, she showed Violet the Coffinsgrave Fair flyer and the advertisement inside for Madame Shinny's Wondrous & Incredible Seeing Stone.

'So you think that this Seeing Stone is what Willy Googalak overheard those demons whispering about when they broke into his shop?' said Violet, dubiously. 'When they stole the freezing potions?'

Audrey nodded.

'Admit it,' said Norman. 'It's a bonkers theory, isn't it?'

'Well, it does seem a bit of a long shot,' admitted Violet.

'That's what I thought too, at first,' agreed Brian. 'But I can't come up with a better theory and I'm also beginning to think that Audrey's right about Beatrice Waghorn too. It just seems too much of a coincidence that she was here when we got back this afternoon, on the very same morning that our bedroom got broken in to!'

After breakfast the following morning, the children gathered on the landing outside their bedroom. Before them the bookcase that had been emptied of nearly all its enchanted books the day before was now magically re-filled.

'Right then,' began Audrey, sucking on a pen and studying a piece of paper upon which she had made a list of what needed to be done. 'We'll go to my house first and then we'll go to Norman's and Brian's grandparents' last of all, and remember we need things that we can *sell* at the Coffinsgrave Fair. Not useless junk like computer game magazines or trading cards or jigsaws which have got pieces missing or action figures that've lost their heads or an arm or a leg.' She handed each of them an empty sack that Violet had provided as she spoke before beginning to remove the first book from a shelf in front of her.

By the time the children had rummaged through Audrey and Norman's bedrooms they had, incredibly, managed to completely fill three sacks of different items all of which Audrey was positive that they would be able to sell at the Coffinsgrave Fair. In Audrey's bedroom, amongst other things, they had found some old glittery make up that she no longer used, some old scarves and hats, a wooden instrument called a recorder, some stuffed toys, a few board games, a skipping rope and some juggling balls, whilst in Norman's bedroom they had discovered, in the back of a wardrobe, two toy helmets that when you wore them managed to somehow alter your voice so that you sounded like a strange and scary alien. They also found a guitar (which, miraculously, still had most of its strings), a Frisbee, some small metal model cars and planes, a jigsaw of a spaceship (which Norman assured Audrey had no missing pieces as he had completed it himself only the previous month), a pair of binoculars, a few comics and a ridiculously large amount of Lego.

They arrived at Brian's grandparents' house after about an hour and Brian was feeling more than a little awkward. He had absolutely no idea what he might have that he could possibly sell at the Coffinsgrave Fair. He had literally only just moved into his grandparents' house and he had brought so little with him from the flat that he and his mother had been previously sharing that he doubted that he had anything useful to sell at all. However, as the four children emerged into the darkened hallway of his grandparents' house all thoughts of finding something to sell at the Coffinsgrave Fair were immediately forgotten.

'What a mess!' remarked Audrey, staring at the walls where large sections of the flowery wallpaper had been burnt away or had fallen upon the carpet, scorching it in a number of places. In the centre of the hall, lying in a heap was the crystal chandelier that had previously hung from the ceiling. Its droplets of cut glass were smudged and dirty and in some places cracked and badly damaged.

'What happened here?' asked Violet, running her hand over the blackened banisters by the stairs; when she lifted her fingers, they were covered in soot.

'A Diefromen,' replied Brian, who briefly explained again what had occurred on the night that Sam and Hadley had come to collect him and escort him to the Halls of Blooskstoof.

211

'But why didn't the whole house burn down?' asked Violet curiously, gazing into the room below where she could clearly see large, black footprints leading from the kitchen, up the stairs and into the living room.

'A Diefromen is a very magical creature,' explained Audrey. 'Even though it's a demon fashioned from fire its flames will only consume what the person controlling it instructs it to consume.' She pushed open the living room door and peered inquisitively inside. 'Goodness, just look at the mess in here!'

Brian followed Audrey into his grandparents' living room and stared in amazement. It looked just like a tornado had torn through it! As well as all the burnt wallpaper and soot there were books strewn absolutely everywhere. Not a single volume remained upon its shelf or within its bookcase. Tables had been upturned, cupboard drawers pulled out and ripped apart, curtains torn from their poles and ornaments deliberately smashed and broken.

'Did the Diefromen do all this?' asked Violet, shocked.

'No, I don't think so,' replied Audrey gravely, staring at the dreadful chaos all about them.

'I think somebody's been here before us,' said Norman matter-of-factly.

'Yeah, I think you're right,' agreed Brian. 'And I think it's probably the same person who broke into our bedroom!'

'Hey, what's this?' said Audrey, bending down and removing a partially burnt piece of paper that had been trapped under the living room door.

'It's just another piece of wallpaper, isn't it?' said Norman, lifting a very sooty picture that had previously hung upon the living room wall from the path of his wheelchair.

'No, I don't think it is,' replied Audrey, unfolding the paper. 'It's a letter,' she announced in some surprise. 'And it's addressed to your granddad, Brian.'

Equally taken aback, Brian carefully took the letter from Audrey and examined it closely. Parts of it, he saw, had been completely burned away. However, on one side, written in gold, almost fiery handwriting was his granddad's name, Henry Pankhurst, which even through the thick layer of soot seemed to somehow glow as he read it aloud. Whilst the other side of the letter appeared almost blank. Almost, but not quite. The first thing that Brian noticed was three vertical lines of very tiny interlocking gold circles in the top left-hand corner. Within the first line there were two gold circles, the second line had five and the third line had eight. 'Hey, I recognise this letter,' exclaimed Brian excitedly. 'I think this is the same note that was delivered to my granddad on the day I arrived here with my mum!'

'So?' said Norman, dropping the picture frame that he'd just picked up and wiping his now filthy fingers on his trousers in an effort to rid them of soot.

'Well, the letter's different,' replied Brian, gently turning the piece of paper over in his hands, examining it even more intently.

'Different?' repeated Audrey, confused.

'Yes,' said Brian, as Norman, Audrey and Violet gathered round him. 'When this letter was originally delivered I, er... opened it,' he admitted, somewhat awkwardly.

'You did what?' cried Audrey, aghast.

'Not now, Audrey!' said Norman, impatiently.

'Anyway, when I first saw this letter it was practically blank,' explained Brian. 'But just look at it now.' He jabbed his finger towards what appeared to be a number of random words that had materialised upon it.

'I've seen something like this before,' declared Audrey.

'You have?' asked Brian, surprised.

Audrey nodded. 'I think that when this letter was originally sent it was magically sealed, and that somebody's tried to break the seal and read it by using something like the Readtoneed spell.'

213

'I don't understand,' said Violet. 'How can a letter be magically sealed and what's the Readtoneed spell?'

'Well, some letters are sealed by the sender using a particular magical spell or an enchantment,' explained Audrey. 'It's not difficult. I've done it myself before. There are lots of reasons to seal a letter but usually it's to stop the wrong people from reading it. You know, just in case the letter gets delivered to the wrong address or maybe falls into the wrong hands, if you know what I mean. Anyway, this letter was clearly only meant to be read by your granddad, Brian.'

'But you just said that you thought somebody else had already tried to read the letter,' said Violet.

Audrey nodded again. 'Well, if you happen to know the spell or enchantment with which a letter was originally sealed then you can easily reverse it. The trouble is there are literally hundreds upon hundreds of different spells and enchantments that can be used to seal a letter,' she explained. 'The most common way, though, is by using the Readtoneed spell. It looks to me as though somebody other than your granddad has tried reading this letter and failed, which is why only a few of the words have appeared on it.'

'So what do the words say?' asked Norman, curiously.

'It's private!' exclaimed Audrey.

'But it might be important,' retorted Norman, irritably.

'Norman's right,' agreed Brian, and he began reading aloud each of the twelve words that had appeared on the letter. The first word was 'FEAR'. A few lines further down were the words 'DEMONS' and 'DEEVILMON'. Below these were three more words, 'RETURNED', 'MEET' and 'TONIGHT'. The next five words appeared all on the same line, 'IF', 'NOT', 'WILL', 'BE' and 'GRAVE', whilst the final word, below this, was 'CONSEQUENCES'. The remainder of the letter was too badly burnt to be able to read any more.

'Is it just me or do those words, when read together, sound like a threat?' suggested Norman.

Violet agreed. 'Does it say who the letter's from?' she asked.

'No, it's too badly burnt,' replied Brian. 'But I do know who delivered it!'

'You do?' said Audrey, in some surprise.

'Who?' asked Norman.

'It was delivered by a bird,' said Brian.

'A bird?' repeated Violet, puzzled.

'Yes, it was delivered by a crow,' said Brian, carefully refolding his granddad's letter and slipping it into the pocket of his trousers. 'And we all know who has a pet crow, don't we?' he remarked, gravely.

Chapter 17

THE 736TH COFFINSGRAVE SUMMER FAIR

Later that morning, after the children had investigated the rest of the rooms in Brian's grandparents' house, which, much to Brian's dismay, had been completely ransacked just like the living room, they returned to the Dragon's Claw with Brian carrying a tub of his grandmother's rock cakes and Audrey steadfastly claiming that she had caught a whiff of Waghorn's perfume in almost every room they'd visited.

As they emerged from the bookcase Brian was surprised to see Sam and Hadley waiting for them, bickering as usual and fighting over what appeared to be a small and rather battered cardboard box.

'Hiya!' said Sam, clearly pleased to see the children and waving at them eagerly. Then, giving up the tug-of-war he'd been having over the cardboard box, he promptly kicked Hadley twice in the ankle before running to meet the children, his overlarge wellington boots smacking noisily against his legs as he did so.

'What are you doing here?' asked Brian, who was as pleased to see the two monsters as they were to see him and his friends.

'We brought you this!' said Sam, jumping up and down excitedly and thrusting a finger at the cardboard box that Hadley was carrying in his gigantic hands. 'It's for the Coffinsgrave Fair!'

'Oh, that's, er… great,' said Brian, doing his very best to sound as enthusiastic as possible. It was, after all, just a cardboard box.

'Yeah, that'll be useful all right!' added Norman, doing his best not to laugh.

'It's, er… really kind of you, but I'm not too sure we can really sell that,' remarked Audrey as tactfully as she could so as not to hurt the two monsters' feelings.

Hadley shook his enormous hairy head and mumbled something to his smaller companion, who nodded in agreement. 'No, you don't understand,' said Sam. 'We didn't bring you the cardboard box to sell at the fair.'

'Oh?' said Audrey in some surprise. 'Then, er… why have you brought it?'

'You said in your letter,' said Sam, searching one of his wellington boots and finding Audrey's note, which he unfolded and quickly re-read, 'that you wanted a way to get to the Coffinsgrave Fair undetected and in secret.'

'That's right,' said Audrey, nodding.

'Well, this is it!' exclaimed Sam triumphantly, stuffing Audrey's letter back into the boot he had just retrieved it from and pointing at the tiny cardboard box excitedly.

'He's gone mad!' whispered Norman to Brian in disbelief.

'Okay,' said Audrey, more than a little confused. 'And how exactly is the cardboard box going to help us get to the Coffinsgrave Fair?' she asked as delicately as she could.

Sam frowned almost as if the answer were as obvious as the plume of smoke that drifts up from a dragon's nostrils. 'Why, you just climb inside it, of course,' he said, matter-of-factly.

'Now I know he's gone mad!' exclaimed Norman in amazement. 'That box isn't large enough to carry a gargoyle in, let alone the four of us! It's way too small!'

'No, it is big enough,' argued Sam. He began waving his arms frantically at Hadley, which seemed to be some sort of instruction for Hadley to place the box on its side upon the landing floor.

217

'Look,' said Norman, rolling his wheelchair forwards and grabbing hold of the lid of the open box. 'How can any of us possibly fit inside it when it's so small? I mean, I can't even...' But as Norman went to pick the cardboard box up a very strange thing happened. Rather than lifting off the floor as he had intended, the cardboard box remained firmly fixed where it was, as if it had been magically nailed to the floorboards. And, instead, the cardboard box suddenly stretched upwards so violently that it almost knocked Norman out of his wheelchair.

All four children stared at the battered box in complete astonishment for, miraculously, it was now exactly the same height as Norman! But that was not the only surprise! Because when Norman tugged at one of its sides the cardboard box instantly began to stretch wider and wider until it grew so wide that it was actually touching the landing wall!

'It's an Expandobox!' exclaimed Violet, excitedly.

'It's a what?' asked Norman, staring at the cardboard box in amazement. It was now so big that he could actually wheel himself inside it, which he did.

'It's an Expandobox!' repeated Violet, following Norman into the box and looking about it curiously. 'It's magic,' she said, her voice echoing oddly from within it. 'You can make an Expandobox as big or as small as you want, and you can put anything in it too because it never gets any heavier!'

'But for all of us to fit inside the box it's going to have to be huge!' pointed out Brian. 'It may not weigh anything but look how large it is now with just you and Norman inside it!'

'That won't be a problem,' said Violet, confidently. 'An Expandobox is just like some of the buildings in Coffinsgrave. It's a lot larger on the inside than it is on the outside. Try pulling the walls together to make the box thinner whilst Norman and I are still in it,' she instructed.

Brian looked at Violet dubiously.

'Honestly, Norman and I will be fine,' Violet reassured him. 'Go on, try it!'

So, albeit rather reluctantly, Brian did as Violet had instructed and tugged at one of the box's cardboard walls, which instantly began to shrink. He watched in silent wonder as it quickly glided effortlessly back to its previous width.

'Now make the box smaller,' Violet instructed from inside.

'How do I do that?' asked Brian.

Violet poked out her head out of the box and pointed above her. 'Just pull the lid of the box down,' she said.

'But you'll get squashed!' said Audrey, fearfully.

Violet giggled. 'I've already told you,' she said. 'It's magic! Even though the box will look much smaller on the outside, on the inside it will still be the same size as it was when Norman and I first got in!'

Brian gave the roof of the cardboard box a little tug and, sure enough, just as the wall had done seconds earlier this also began to shrink until the cardboard box was exactly the same size as it had been when Brian had first seen Sam and Hadley squabbling over it.

'Can you still hear me?' squeaked a mouse-like voice from inside the cardboard box which was just barely recognisable as Violet.

'Yeah!' replied Brian in amazement.

'Are you and Norman okay in there?' asked Audrey, concerned, crouching down beside the box and tapping it.

'Yes, we're fine!' squeaked Violet. 'Now pick the box up, Brian, and you should find it's not heavy at all!'

Brian knelt down and was surprised to find that Violet was absolutely right. The box weighed almost nothing. In fact it felt practically empty when he lifted it up. He shook it gently and immediately heard Norman cry out in alarm, 'Hey, what are you doing? Be careful, I almost fell out of my wheelchair when you did that!'

'Sorry,' apologised Brian, replacing the cardboard box upon the floor just as it momentarily expanded to let Norman and Violet both out before instantly returning to its original size.

'Will the cardboard box be okay?' asked Sam, hopefully. 'Only we've also got to visit Lillian Goosestrangler this morning and help set up her flower stall for the fair tomorrow and we're already late.'

'It's absolutely perfect!' exclaimed Audrey, excitedly picking up the box and examining it more closely herself. 'Not only can we all fit inside it but we'll be able to bring everything we're going to sell at the fair too and the box won't be any heavier than it is now. It's brilliant! Where did you get it from?'

'We sort of... found it,' said Sam, a little awkwardly. 'A few months ago.'

'You found it?' repeated Audrey, sceptically. She knew only too well that for every five things that went missing in Coffinsgrave at least two of them would somehow end up in Sam and Hadley's possession.

'Well, I didn't personally find it, you understand,' explained Sam. 'Hadley did, didn't you?'

The taller monster grunted and mumbled something back to his smaller companion and appeared to scratch his hairy head. This, in turn, seemed to dislodge a golf ball from somewhere deep within his fur, which bounced along the landing towards Norman. But instead of eventually coming to a halt like a normal golf ball would, this one, clearly enchanted and doing its utmost to avoid recapture, kept bouncing around him in a circle, over and over again.

'That's right, Hadley, er... found the box in the street,' continued Sam, heading over to the bookcase and removing a number of different-coloured volumes from it. 'Fell over it actually and almost trampled that nice magician to death, didn't you?'

Hadley grumbled something unintelligible back at him.

'What do you mean what magician?' snapped back Sam, as all the books within the bookcase gradually began to disappear. 'The one with the pointed blue sparkly hat, you great hairy oaf! You remember! You fell on top of him and he nearly suffocated. He was moving into that new shop and had all those boxes piled up on the pavement outside. Honestly, your memory! Anyway, we'll see you first thing on Wednesday morning, Audrey,' said Sam before disappearing into the bookcase closely followed by Hadley, who turned and waved goodbye.

'I have a funny feeling that the wizard with the pointed blue sparkly hat is probably missing one of his Expandoboxes,' said Norman, managing to finally grab the annoying bouncing golf ball as it tried unsuccessfully to bounce over his head.

All the children laughed.

With their transport to and from the Coffinsgrave Fair now resolved the children's next job was to price everything that they had collected from each of their bedrooms. From the Gillibottoms' office Violet had secretly borrowed a roll of white stickers and some pens, which the children used to carefully print a price before sticking it on each item.

For Brian this particular task was not as easy as it had first seemed, for he was having quite a bit of difficulty in understanding how money actually worked in Coffinsgrave.

'It's simple,' explained Audrey, unpeeling a sticker and placing it on one of her old scarves. 'One hundred tin pieces are equal to one bronze piece and one hundred bronze pieces are equal to one silver piece. Are you following me so far?' she asked, seeing the puzzled expression upon Brian's face.

'Yeah, I think so,' lied Brian, who unlike Audrey actually thought that all the different types of money were quite complicated and far from simple.

'And twenty-five silver pieces are equal to exactly one gold piece,' said Audrey.

'So how much do you think I should sell these rock cakes for?' asked Brian, confused.

'You'll be lucky to give them away!' laughed Norman who, for the past hour, had been sorting out his various pieces of Lego into different shapes and colours.

'Let's see,' said Audrey thoughtfully. 'Well, we don't want to overprice them, do we? I think you should sell them for thirty tin pieces each,' she suggested, and she watched as Brian carefully wrote out a sticker and stuck it onto the lid of the tub of rock cakes.

The following day was Monday and the first day of the Coffinsgrave Summer Fair. Just like the two other fairs the village held each year its summer fair lasted exactly seven days, Monday through to Sunday. Brian was the first to wake up that morning and he peered out of the bedroom window excitedly. Even though he had never been to such a fair before he had, by now, heard so much about it that he was really quite looking forward to it. Although exactly how much he would actually get to see from the inside of an Expandobox he wasn't entirely sure. Outside it was raining as usual. A shower of baby and multicoloured cockerels were drifting down from the enchanted roof of the cavern, with each one happily chirping 'cock-a-doodle-doo' before suddenly exploding in a puff of orange smoke as they landed on the cobbled streets and pavements far below. Even at such an early hour the streets were already full of people dashing in and out of different shops and buildings with the majority appearing to be heading in the general direction of Gravestone Harbour, which was where the fair was located.

Later that morning, after everyone had got up, Norman emerged from the bathroom having washed and dressed and announced rather sadly to anybody who could be bothered to listen that his three remaining slug stitches, Bob, Bill and Bart, had all fallen off his ankle during the night and subsequently died.

'Are you going to bury them?' asked Violet, trying hard to suppress a giggle; she had arrived a few minutes earlier with the children's breakfasts.

222

'No, I just flushed them down the toilet,' replied Norman, forlornly. 'Thought it was the kindest thing to do.'

'Very nice!' remarked Audrey, wrinkling her nose up in disgust. 'I hope you'd remembered to flush everything away before you threw them in there!'

'Course I had,' snapped back Norman.

'It was a sort of burial at sea then,' remarked Brian, who was also trying hard not to laugh whilst feeling for his own slug stitches which, just like Norman's, had disappeared. But exactly when they'd dropped off he couldn't say. Much to Audrey's disappointment the slug within her sling was still very much alive and wriggling away quite happily.

Over the next couple of days the children remained mostly in their bedroom. They did sneak out occasionally but only when Violet informed them that the coast was clear which usually meant that the Gillibottoms were, for whatever reason, nowhere to be found. And, after having explored the tavern from top to bottom, the children headed towards the bar below where Arnold Bloodlock was always to be found, covered in dust, sitting in his usual chair and forever ready with another incredible tale or famous legend. Not for the first time Brian wondered why the major never seemed to leave the tavern. He was sure that there must be much nicer and more homely saloons within Coffinsgrave that he could frequent. It didn't seem to matter whether it was night or day; the major was always sitting in the same chair at the same table with the same unfinished tankard of ale in front of him.

Unfortunately, the children were unable to visit the major quite as often as they would have liked as, regrettably, the Gillibottoms did not leave the Dragon's Claw very often or for very long. The children, therefore, spent quite long periods of time confined solely to their bedroom. During these times Brian kept hoping that, perhaps, his granddad might visit him again even if that meant being escorted by the dreadful Beatrice Waghorn and her black bird. But nobody other than Violet ever knocked at their bedroom door.

To keep themselves occupied the children played some board games which Norman and Audrey had brought back after their visit to their bedrooms. However, more often than not, an argument would erupt between the two of them with each accusing the other of cheating and Brian having to read out the rules to every game at least half-a-dozen times. Thankfully, Violet had discovered a pack of cards and so the children were also able to play Snap, Old Maid and Stealing Bundles without too much bickering and squabbling.

Wednesday finally arrived and, as promised, Sam and Hadley turned up at the children's bedroom just in time to help them finish off that morning's meagre breakfast of semi-cold sausage, overcooked egg and very dry toast. Audrey expanded the Expandobox to an acceptable size and, with their sacks full of items to sell, the children stepped inside.

'I wish there was something to hold on to in here!' remarked Brian as he felt Hadley pick up the box, which lurched suddenly sideways and almost sent him and Violet flying into Norman's lap.

'How on earth does that light bulb stay on?' asked Audrey, pointing to the white electrical flex hanging from the cardboard box's ceiling. 'There's no electricity to power it.'

'I told you,' said Violet, 'it's magic.'

Brian, doing his utmost to hold onto the cardboard wall, peered over his shoulder towards the rear of the box, which was concealed in darkness. 'How big do you think it is in here?' he asked. 'I mean, how far back does this box actually go, I wonder?'

'I'll go see,' said Norman, who switched off the brakes to his wheelchair, spun it around and rolled cautiously forwards.

'Be careful!' said Audrey, who had already decided that she didn't like being in the Expandobox one little bit and couldn't wait to get out.

They watched as Norman disappeared into the darkness, losing sight of him only momentarily before suddenly another bulb flickered on above his head.

'I think the box must somehow sense where you are!' announced Norman, pointing up at the ceiling above him. 'That light bulb came on as soon I got near it. Just like a motion detector or one of them security lights that some people have on their houses,' he said, before rolling his wheelchair forwards and disappearing into the shadows again.

'Don't go too far!' warned Audrey, anxiously.

A moment later Norman reappeared a second time, but as the bulb above him spluttered into life the one between him and Brian, Audrey and Violet began to fade so that a patch of complete and utter blackness unexpectedly separated them.

'This box must be huge!' exclaimed Norman, as it suddenly teetered dangerously forwards, forcing him to throw on his wheelchair brakes whilst everyone else fell over.

'Sorry!' they heard Sam cry from somewhere outside.

'What happened?' shouted back Brian, picking himself up.

'What?' cried Sam.

'I said what happened?' repeated Brian, dusting himself down.

'Soobius System!' replied Sam. 'Bit rough coming out at the other end, sorry!'

'That can happen when the Soobius System is really busy,' explained Audrey. 'There are probably loads of people using it to get to the fair. It'll be worse later!'

In the time it took Norman to wheel himself back Sam had announced that he and Hadley had reached the outskirts of the fair and, in particular, the stall that Audrey had reserved, which was number 2010. It wasn't a particularly big stall but then the children didn't have a huge amount to sell. Audrey's plan was to make enough money to pay for the hire of the stall and for at least one of them to see Madame Shinny too.

After Hadley had put the box down Audrey poked her head out to see how busy the fair was. Although it was still early she was, nevertheless, quite surprised at how quiet it seemed.

'That's because you've got a high stall number,' explained Sam, who, with Hadley's help, began pulling the cardboard box this way and that until it was large enough for the children to exit from. 'The lower the stall number the more central your stall will be within the fair and probably busier too! Any stall number under 100 would cost you an absolute fortune to hire!'

The children emerged from the Expandobox and immediately began setting up their stall with all the items that they had collected from their bedrooms. Because there were so few people about Audrey thought it was probably worth the risk of doing it themselves. However, it proved to be much more difficult than she had anticipated as they kept getting attacked by lots of flyers, all of which were advertising other stalls within the fair. The first five flyers alone were promotions for various snacks and food. Peasmold Fortuna was offering a 10% discount on his famous fried, stewed and roasted bats' wings whilst Isobel Kuppala was selling fourteen different types of spider's leg at half price between the hours of 2.00pm and 5.00pm. The most unpleasant advertisement that Brian was forced to read was an invitation for an 'all you can eat' buffet of rats' tails, giant beetles' eyes, boiled worms and fly cakes!

In the end it took almost an hour to set the stall out to Audrey's satisfaction, and that included yet another argument between her and Norman about where he wanted his Lego to be positioned. Norman wanted it to take pride of place at the very front of the stall, which was where Audrey had already arranged her cuddly toys. Thankfully a compromise was reached where, for the first half of the day, Audrey could show off her stuffed toys whilst for the second half of the day Norman could exhibit his ridiculously large collection of Lego.

During the time it took the children to finish setting up their stall other stands and booths nearby had already opened and the fair was quickly growing busier. Sam and Hadley, meanwhile, had wandered over to investigate a stall that was selling cloaks and other outlandish clothing for magicians and sorcerers. Opposite it was a booth that was having a sale on fairy lights and next to this was a small stand which was selling gargoyles that would grumble and curse and make rude hand gestures at almost everybody who walked by.

Directly behind the children's stall a black tent had been erected which had a gold trim running about its centre and what looked like grey clouds very slowly encircling its roof, which would occasionally crackle and fizz with lightning. Written upon two boards that had been placed on either side of the tent's draped entrance were the words *'Come and visit Madame Shinny and her Wondrous & Incredible Seeing Stone – Just 9 bronze pieces for a 30 minute reading'*.

'I didn't realise Madame Shinny's tent would be so close,' remarked Brian, surprised.

'That's why I chose this stall. It's the nearest one I could get,' said Audrey. 'I couldn't risk being too far away in case we got seen travelling to and from it. Especially as we're not supposed to leave the tavern.'

Next to Madame Shinny's tent, which had just made a number of people jump, including the children, with a tremendous clap of thunder, was a very large stall indeed which, to Brian, looked more like an igloo than an actual stall for, incredibly, it appeared to be made out of huge blocks of ice whilst falling from above and around it was a steady sprinkle of magical snowflakes.

'Whose stall do you think that is?' asked Brian, impressed by the enchanted snow that was glistening upon the cobbled street and which some people, especially children, were picking up and making snowballs out of.

'That's my stall!' announced a very deep voice from behind the children.

'Willy!' exclaimed Audrey, pleased to see the yeti whom they had all met in the Hospital for the Afflicted and Poorly People with Injuries. 'How are you feeling and when did you get out of hospital? You look really well!'

Willy Googalak smiled. 'I'm feeling much better, thanks,' he replied. 'Got out of hospital yesterday and not a moment too soon, I can tell you. Got caught, didn't I, by that nurse, borrowing food from the kitchen. She went berserk. Kept shouting and waving all her fingers and arms at me! I was starving by the time I got out of there! And to make matters worse I lost my original stall that I'd reserved for the fair – y'know, what with being laid up in hospital and everything – so I've had to make do with this one, got it at short notice. Nowhere near the centre as I would have liked, but I guess I shouldn't complain. Reckon I'm lucky to be alive after what happened, you know, with them demons.' He whispered the word 'demons' ever so quietly so that the children could barely hear it, peering nervously over his shoulder to ensure nobody else had. If it ever got out that Willy Googalak had been attacked by demons in his own shop then the yeti was certain his business would collapse overnight. People would avoid shopping at the Snow Shack like a person avoids visiting a friend who's been cursed with the windybottom spell! 'And I haven't forgotten my promise to you either,' he added. 'You can each try one of my Ice Explosion potions for free! Or, if you like the look of one of my other potions, you can try that instead. My new Snowball Shooter potion is selling really well at the moment. Immediately after you drink it a snowball materialises in one of your hands and for a further fifteen minutes you can keep throwing it at anyone or anything you like for as many times as you like because it'll just keep rematerialising.'

'Wow, that sounds brilliant!' exclaimed Norman excitedly.

'Anyway, best be getting along. Looks like I've got some customers,' Willy remarked, rubbing his white, furry hands excitedly and gesturing to a man and woman, dressed in matching orange coats and wearing even brighter orange hats, who had just entered his igloo. 'Pop over whenever you like,' he added. 'I'm here 'til Sunday.'

A few minutes later Sam and Hadley returned, with the larger of the two monsters appearing to have an item of clothing partially concealed under his left arm. Written upon a price tag that was hanging from it were the words *'Green Hooded Cloak'* and *'Ten Bronze Pieces'*.

'For goodness' sake, put that away before somebody sees you!' exclaimed Sam through gritted teeth, pointing discreetly at the hood of the cloak which was swinging from Hadley's fur.

Hadley mumbled something unintelligible back at Sam and shrugged.

'What do you mean put what away?' snapped Sam, embarrassed. 'The cloak, you enormous hairy carpet, the cloak that's somehow found its way underneath your arm! No, not that arm, the other one!'

As Hadley began stuffing the cloak back into the folds of his long, straggly fur the children quickly disappeared back inside the Expandobox. The fair was rapidly growing busier and there were already a number of customers picking up and examining some of the items they had for sale.

Suddenly a puff of yellow smoke erupted near the children's stall, followed by the appearance of a bearded warlock dressed in grey and white and wearing a hat which covered both his ears. He coughed loudly as he stepped forwards, waving his hand briefly in an unsuccessful attempt to blow some of the smoke away.

'Good morning!' he said merrily to Sam and Hadley as it began to rain down pencil sharpeners from the cavern roof. 'My, what a lovely stall. I particularly like the cuddly toys. Very nice.' He coughed again. The yellow smoke that he had materialised from didn't seem to be disappearing. Instead it seemed to be lingering behind him, almost as if it were waiting for the warlock to return. 'Sorry I'm so late but we've had quite a few problems with our Penny Pots this week,' he said with a weary sigh. 'Ever had a stall at one of our fairs before?'

Sam shook his head.

'Well, it couldn't be simpler,' declared the warlock as he removed what looked like a miniature cauldron from the folds of his cloak, handing it to Hadley. 'That pot I've just given you is called a Penny Pot,' he explained, covering his mouth and coughing again. 'Basically, all you've really got to remember is that any money you make from what you sell today must always be deposited into your Penny Pot. Then, when you've finished, the Penny Pot will magically deduct 3% from all your sales. Normally it's 5% but there's a special reduced rate today. This, in turn, will cover the cost of the hire of your stall, quite simple really. Now, is that all clear?'

Sam and Hadley both nodded.

'Excellent,' said the warlock, untying a small brown money pouch from his belt. 'And please ensure that you deposit *all* the money you make into the Penny Pot. Trust me, we'll know if you don't.' He gave a knowing wink and then briefly touched the end of his nose with one of his fingers as if to say *you have been warned*. 'Now, I think I'll have one of those delicious-looking rock cakes, please.'

Climbing onto a stool that Hadley had found somewhere earlier, Sam peeled open the lid of the tub of rock cakes; the warlock selected one and then handed him two fifteen tin pieces which he had removed from his money pouch.

'Now, don't forget to pop those pieces into the Penny Pot,' he said, coughing again as he disappeared back into the yellow smoke behind him. Then, with a flash of light, the warlock vanished and so too did the smoke.

Surprisingly for the four children, the morning passed very quickly indeed. Even though they were confined to the inside of the Expandobox it was really quite exciting to watch Sam and Hadley as the two monsters yelled and shouted about what was for sale on the children's stall and it wasn't very long before quite a crowd had gathered around it.

Amazingly, Norman's Lego proved to be extremely popular with some of the monsters that stopped to see what Sam and Hadley were shouting about and by eleven o'clock all but one of Norman's buckets of Lego had been sold. The final bucket, and by far the biggest, was sold not long after to a tall, female monster that had small pointed horns running from her forehead, over her neck and all the way down her back. Audrey's cuddly toys were proving popular too and, incredibly, so were Brian's grandmother's rock cakes! By midday Sam and Hadley had also managed to sell three jigsaws, a hat, two scarves, some model aeroplanes, a football, some lipstick, a rugby shirt and even a rubber duck which was bought by a particularly fearsome-looking monster with eight hairy legs who thought the duck adorable, immediately naming it Colin.

Audrey had arranged to see Madame Shinny at two o'clock and it was clear from what Sam and Hadley had managed to sell so far that the children had made more than enough money to keep their appointment with the psychic. However, as the children were about to sneak out of the Expandobox a scruffy black bird landed on top of it, squawking noisily and picking at the cardboard box's roof with its sharp, pointed beak. The bird's owner, Beatrice Waghorn, dressed in a dark cloak and even darker hood, emerged from the bustling crowd and immediately made her way towards the children's stall.

'Well, well, well, what a lot of items you do have for sale,' remarked Waghorn, peering down her nose at the stall. 'And, oh my, your Penny Pot does look full. It certainly looks like you've had a very profitable morning.'

'Is there anything in particular that takes your fancy, Ms Waghorn?' asked Sam, nervously, as Hadley gestured towards the few remaining cuddly toys whilst at the same time stepping in front of the Expandobox in which the children were hiding, doing his best to conceal it from Waghorn's view.

'Dear me, no,' sneered Waghorn, with a rather disagreeable sniff. 'Everything here looks so very cheap and rather tacky, to be honest. Especially those awful stuffed toys,' she remarked, unpleasantly.

Inside the Expandobox Audrey's face flushed red with anger.

'No, I was just wondering where two monsters, such as you, obtained so many *human* things to sell on their stall?' asked Waghorn, suspiciously. 'Especially those rock cakes! They look very familiar!'

An uneasy silence followed before Sam suddenly finally said, 'They were donated. You see, we're raising money for MUPPET.'

'MUPPET?' snapped Waghorn, distrustfully.

'Yes, it stands for Monsters who are Under Privileged, Penniless and who may have suffered Extreme Trauma.'

'Never heard of it,' remarked Waghorn matter-of-factly, peering curiously underneath the children's stall.

'Well, that's because the charity's only recently been set up,' explained Sam, removing a handkerchief from one of his wellington boots and mopping his forehead nervously with it. 'I wonder,' he said. 'We're always looking for more donations. Any loose change you might have would be greatly appreciated, Ms Waghorn. Would you be interested in, perhaps, donating something to MUPPET?'

'No, I certainly would not!' scoffed Waghorn, glancing behind Hadley suspiciously.

'Then are you sure you wouldn't like to buy something?' asked Sam, enthusiastically picking up Norman's red football shirt. 'Scarlet is so your colour...'

'No!' snapped Waghorn, irritably.

232

'Not even a rock cake?' suggested Sam, picking up the plastic tub and shaking it, temptingly. 'They're absolutely delicious!'

'I seriously doubt that!' said Waghorn, unpleasantly. 'No, I have other business to attend to. I am on my way to the Dragon's Claw. And if I find those children have disobeyed Barnaby Katobi's instructions *yet again* and are not in their bedroom as they should be then I will endeavour to ensure their punishment is most... *severe.*' She turned on her heel and disappeared back into the busy crowd with her pet bird immediately taking flight and duly following.

'Phew, that was close!' said Sam, a few minutes later when he poked his head inside the Expandobox. 'She wouldn't even buy a rock cake!' he complained, wiping his forehead again before returning the handkerchief to the inside of one of his wellington boots.

'What are we going to do?' asked Norman, panicking. 'You heard what Waghorn said! She's on her way to the Dragon's Claw and when she finds we're not there she's going to go absolutely nuts!'

'Hadley can take you all back right now,' suggested Sam. 'Can't you?'

Hadley mumbled something unintelligible and appeared to nod in agreement.

'And if Waghorn gets there before us we can just say we were in my room,' suggested Violet.

'But we've not seen Madame Shinny yet,' complained Audrey. 'That was the whole point of having a stall at the fair in the first place!' She threw her arms up into the air in frustration. 'No, you three go back with Hadley. I'm going to see Madame Shinny. I'm certain that her Seeing Stone is somehow vital to Deevilmon's plan!'

'But...' began Brian.

'Sam, will you be okay running the stall on your own until Hadley returns?' asked Audrey.

'You betcha!' said Sam, excitedly.

'And if Waghorn asks where I am,' said Audrey to the others, thoughtfully, 'you can tell her that... er, I've gone back to the HAPPI because I was complaining about my arm and that I thought I might need a new slug sling! Okay?' She got up to leave. And that was when the screaming started.

By the time all the children had clambered out of the Expandobox to see what was happening an old woman, dressed in black and wearing a golden turban, was being carried out of Madame Shinny's tent on a stretcher, shaking and crying uncontrollably. 'It's gone! It's gone!' she shrieked frantically, screaming even more loudly than before and pushing off the blanket that had been covering her as she tried in vain to sit up.

'Who's that?' asked Norman, peering at the woman through the crowd of eager onlookers that had quickly gathered about the tent.

'I think that's Madame Shinny!' replied Audrey, shaken.

'What do you think's happened?' asked Brian, as the psychic grabbed the arm of one of the onlookers and screamed again at the top of her voice, 'It's gone! It's gone!'

'I don't know,' replied Audrey, starting to feel frightened.

'Is she hurt?' asked Violet, trying to squeeze past a woman in front of her who seemed rooted to the spot.

'I can't tell,' said Norman, rolling his wheelchair a little nearer in an attempt to get a better look at the psychic, but in doing so he bumped into a blue-cloaked magician who had been standing next to him, accidentally running over one of his feet. 'Whoops, sorry!' he apologised. But the magician did not reply. Instead, he simply wobbled. Just as though he were a cardboard cut-out. Norman stared up at the magician in alarm as, very slowly, he rocked first forwards and then backwards before finally toppling over.

A woman behind Norman screamed. For the blue-robed magician whom she had just watched collapse did not get back up again. He couldn't. His entire body was covered in ice. The magician was frozen solid!

To Audrey's left another more elderly woman began screaming now, pointing frantically at the two white-robed wizards who had been carrying Madame Shinny out of her tent. For they too were now covered from head to foot in ice! And already icicles were forming upon their hands, arms, chins and even their noses!

'It's gone! It's gone!' shrieked Madame Shinny to the crowd of onlookers, completely oblivious to the fact that the mysterious ice which had just frozen the two wizards carrying her had also spread to her legs. 'My Seeing Stone,' she cried, desperately, as she began to feel the effects of the approaching ice upon her frail body. She tried to sit up, to turn her head but found that she could do neither. The last six words the psychic managed to utter before the ice finally overcame her were, 'My... Seeing... Stone... has... been... stolen!'

Immediately a wave of panic began spreading through the crowd of onlookers and indeed the whole fair as more and more people found that, for some inexplicable reason, they could no longer move. Stall holders discovered that their feet had become frozen to where they stood. Crowds of eager shoppers found that their bags had become stuck to their hands, a thin layer of ice forming within their palms which began rapidly spreading to each of their fingers and up their arms. Mayhem quickly ensued as those who were still able to move attempted to run to safety, often bumping into and knocking over those who were already frozen and immobile. People screamed in terror and shouted in confusion. Younger children cried uncontrollably.

A very tall man in front of Violet who looked as though he had been trying to run away had become frozen in mid-step so that he was now standing on only one leg, like a statue, at an impossible angle, whilst the boy next to Brian had begun crying hysterically as the finger he'd been using to pick his nose with had now become permanently stuck up his right nostril.

'I can't believe I didn't see this coming!' cried Audrey suddenly as a four-legged monster on the opposite side of the street attempted to leap upon one of the nearby buildings and, presumably, to safety but instead froze in midair before crashing into one of the stalls below, sending magical ornaments of all different shapes and sizes flying in every direction.

'See what coming?' cried Brian.

'Yeah, what are you on about, Audrey?' shouted Norman over the pandemonium.

'There isn't time to explain!' she shouted, grabbing hold of Norman's wheelchair and pushing him past a woman, frozen solid, whose mouth was hanging open in a constant, never-ending scream. 'Just follow me before it's too late!'

They ran after Audrey and followed her into Willy Googalak's igloo where, to their horror, they discovered the giant yeti already frozen like a statue and apparently in the process of handing over some change to a customer who, like him, was also motionless.

'Here, drink this!' ordered Audrey, shoving a curious glass of foaming liquid into everyone's hands.

'What is it?' asked Norman, sniffing the glass's contents suspiciously.

'Just drink it!' shouted Audrey frantically, in between swallowing gulps of the sapphire liquid herself. 'There's no time to explain. Just drink it now, all of you! Before it's too late!'

Whatever the potion was that Audrey was forcing them to drink, it didn't taste quite like Brian had expected it to. He had wrongly assumed that because the glass was cold the blue liquid inside would also be cold. But it wasn't. Instead it tasted rather warm, with a flavour similar to orange. He finished it in three massive gulps and wiped his lips with the cuff of his sleeve. Norman burped after finishing his drink but nobody laughed. Instead all four children suddenly became aware of how very quiet it had become. It was deathly quiet.

They peered out of the igloo and stared at the scene before them in complete and utter astonishment. Everything and everyone they could see was covered from head to foot in a thin layer of sparkling ice. It was as if time itself had become frozen. With the exception of the children, every man, woman, child and monster in Coffinsgrave had become trapped within crystal statues. At any other time such a scene would have looked beautiful, almost picturesque in fact. Nothing in Coffinsgrave moved. Nothing except the figure on the opposite side of the street. A figure cloaked and hooded and who was being escorted from above by a large, scruffy black bird.

Chapter 18

DEEVILMON'S ACCOMPLICE

'Look!' said Violet, pointing at the hooded figure hurrying down the street. Whilst remaining safely hidden within the shadows of the igloo entrance the children watched in silence as the mysterious character hastily made their way along the cobbled path, weaving deftly between the frozen statues and appearing to head towards a narrow side-street whilst all the time being escorted from above by the scruffy black bird.

'I really can't believe I didn't see this coming!' whispered Audrey suddenly, but more to herself than to the others. 'I've been such an idiot!' she said, angrily.

'What *are* you on about?' said Norman. 'Nobody could have seen this coming, Audrey, not you, not me, not even Barnaby Katobi.'

'What I don't understand is how you knew which potion to drink,' remarked Brian, puzzled and glancing briefly over his shoulder at the rows of coloured drinks. 'There must be hundreds of different potions in here!'

'We needed to drink one of Willy's anti-freezing potions,' said Audrey. 'Because that's the antidote to the potions that were stolen from his shop.'

'What?' scoffed Norman, incredulously. 'You're seriously trying to tell us that the freezing potions which were nicked from Willy's

Snow Shack did all this?' He gestured to the frozen scene of chaos outside.

The hooded figure on the other side of the street paused momentarily as if something had suddenly disturbed them, glancing briefly up and down the cobbled path and then in the direction of the igloo before deciding that they had, in fact, been mistaken and continuing onwards.

'Shhh! Not so loud, Norman!' snapped Audrey, anxiously. 'You're right; the freezing potions alone couldn't have done all this.'

'Then perhaps a magician did it?' suggested Brian. 'A warlock maybe?'

'Well, I guess a really, really powerful magician or warlock might have been able to do something similar,' conceded Audrey. 'But I really don't know of any, do you?'

Brian, Norman and Violet all shrugged.

'No, I think there's a much simpler explanation,' remarked Audrey gravely. 'I think the whole of Coffinsgrave is like this, don't you, frozen I mean? And for Willy's potions to have had such an effect then they would definitely have needed some form of conduit.'

'Some form of what?' asked Brian, having never heard of such a word before.

'Conduit,' repeated Audrey, watching as the hooded figure on the opposite side of the street carefully negotiated their way around two monsters which, moments earlier, had accidentally bumped into each other during the bedlam and had become frozen together so that their twelve legs looked like a partially collapsed rugby scrum. 'It means, er... channel.'

'Right,' said Brian, still confused. 'I still don't understand.'

'No, neither do I,' admitted Norman.

'Or me,' said Violet.

'Okay, imagine you're listening to some music in your room,' said Audrey, quickly becoming exasperated.

'Right,' said Brian.

'What sort of music?' asked Norman.

'It doesn't matter what sort of music!' snapped back Audrey, irritably. 'It can be any music! Now, what would you do if you wanted to play the music loud enough for everybody in the whole house to hear it?'

'I'd just turn the volume up,' said Brian.

'Exactly!' said Audrey. 'You'd amplify it! And that's what somebody's done with Willy's freezing potions.'

'You mean they've made it stronger somehow?' said Norman, in sudden realisation. 'So that it would affect more people?'

Audrey nodded.

'But how?' asked Violet.

'With Madame Shinny's Seeing Stone!' replied Audrey, staring out at the crowds of frozen people and monsters before her. 'Don't you see that's the reason why it was stolen?'

'Hang on, are you saying that Madame Shinny's Seeing Stone really is magical?' said Brian, doubtfully. 'That it really can see everything and everyone as Madame Shinny claimed it could?'

Audrey nodded. 'It was always Deevilmon's plan to steal the Cup of Ages because without it Deevilmon couldn't have become immortal. And with the exception of your granddad, Brian, it already has all the other Wizitches and the rubies that it needs too. But unlike Willy's freezing potions Deevilmon couldn't just steal the Cup of Ages. Oh no, Barnaby Katobi would certainly have ensured that such a thing was very well guarded. So instead, Deevilmon or, more likely, its followers stole Willy's freezing potions and Madame Shinny's Seeing Stone. Individually, neither would be particularly significant, but when combined... well, you can see for yourself,' she remarked, pointing at the motionless fair.

240

'Now, there's nothing stopping Deevilmon from stealing the Cup of Ages.'

'Except us!' replied Brian.

'And us!' said Sam, peering into the igloo with Hadley standing behind him, waving at them happily.

'Quickly, get inside before Waghorn sees you!' exclaimed Audrey, pointing towards the hooded figure on the opposite side of the street.

'You mean Beatrice Waghorn?' asked Sam in some surprise, attempting to spot her through the frozen statues whilst being shoved unceremoniously into the igloo by Hadley.

'Yes!' said Audrey.

'How come she isn't frozen like everybody else?' asked Sam, puzzled.

'Never mind that,' said Norman. 'How come you're not frozen like everybody else?'

Hadley pointed to one of the rows of potions and, in particular, a broken line of glasses filled with a light blue liquid. The sign at the very end of the row, which was half covered in magical snow, read, 'Anti-freezing potion – 2 bronze pieces'.

'You've drunk an anti-freezing potion too?' asked Brian, in surprise.

'When?' asked Violet.

'It's not my fault!' protested Sam. 'I was thirsty! And whilst you were setting up your stall this morning we popped in to see Willy Googalak. He's sort of a relative of Hadley's, on his mother's side. You see, Hadley's mother's father's sister…'

'Skip to the end,' pleaded Audrey, impatiently.

'And, well, we drunk one of those blue potions when Willy wasn't looking!' said Sam, awkwardly.

Hadley mumbled something whilst pointing to a row of green potions behind Violet.

241

'Oh yes, and we drunk one of those too,' said Sam, kicking his taller companion in the leg when he thought the children weren't looking.

'Any others?' asked Audrey.

'No,' replied Sam.

But Hadley pointed again.

'Apart from that brown potion' said Sam, kicking Hadley in the leg even harder this time and in full view of the children. In return Hadley just gave Sam a shove, sending him flying into a rack of furry hats that all began to growl rather disagreeably at him. 'But I wouldn't recommend that particular potion,' he added. 'When you go to the toilet it turns your—'

'Waghorn's disappearing up that alley,' interrupted Norman.

'Come on, let's follow her,' said Brian, leaving the igloo and running across the street before ducking behind a stall which had been partially flattened by an enormous four-legged monster.

'Do you think that's wise?' asked Audrey, taking a puff from her inhaler and following hurriedly.

'It's like you said,' replied Brian, cautiously peering over the fallen monster. 'There's nothing stopping Deevilmon from stealing the Cup of Ages now!'

'Except us,' exclaimed Sam.

'Exactly!' replied Brian.

The children and the two monsters followed the hooded figure up through the alley and then into the street that it adjoined. This new street was mostly empty although its cobbled path proved a little difficult for Norman's wheelchair. However, with Hadley helping to push Norman over some of the more difficult and uneven cobbles the hooded figure ahead of them was never out of sight for long.

Eventually, the road reached a junction and the children watched warily from inside the entrance to a shop as the figure ahead of them hurriedly turned left. Once again the children and the two monsters followed whilst always ensuring that they remained just out of sight from the scruffy black bird that continued to flap and hop from building to building high above them.

Soon they reached a Soobius Station, which normally at this time of day would have been quite noisy and busy with lots of people travelling to and from work during their lunch hour or perhaps making their way towards the fair. But at that very moment the Soobius Station wasn't noisy or busy at all. It was quite the opposite in fact. It was deathly quiet. Nothing within it moved. Everything and everyone was frozen. The magicians, the warlocks, the monsters, even the bookcases and the very books within them had been consumed by ice.

Unsurprisingly, the hooded figure did not venture inside and, instead, continued weaving their way through the crowded street of frozen people before disappearing down another alley.

'Is every Soobius Station like this, do you think?' asked Sam, amazed.

Audrey nodded and took another puff from her inhaler.

'If you ask me I reckon the whole Soobius System is frozen!' remarked Norman.

'Don't be ridiculous, the Soobius System stretches across the entire world,' pointed out Audrey. 'Deevilmon couldn't freeze the whole Soobius System even if it had a million of Willy's potions. No, I think it's just this part that's frozen, the part that's connected to Coffinsgrave, and that's why Waghorn's not using it.'

'Then where do you think she's going?' asked Brian, curiously.

But before Audrey could reply the figure they were following unexpectedly glanced over their shoulder, forcing the children and the two monsters to suddenly duck into the nearest street and out of sight.

'That was close!' gasped Violet, peering round the front porch of a shop called 'Earwax Candles'.

'Did she see us?' asked Norman.

'No, I don't think so,' replied Violet.

'Phew!' said Sam.

Hadley mumbled something unintelligible.

'So where do you think Waghorn's going?' asked Brian again.

'I honestly don't know,' replied Audrey, staring with some disgust at a small and prickly-looking monster that she had very nearly tripped upon. No bigger than a dog, and with silver-tipped quills covering its entire back, two of its four rear legs were cocked over a lamppost allowing it to relieve itself which, evidently, it had been doing quite happily before being frozen to where it stood. 'I had assumed,' said Audrey, side-stepping around the small, prickly monster, 'that Waghorn would be heading towards the Committee Chambers.'

'Why?' asked Norman.

'Why?' repeated Audrey irritably. 'Because that's where the Cup of Ages is kept! Honestly, don't you listen to anything I tell you?'

'And is she?' asked Brian. 'I mean, is Waghorn making her way towards the Committee Chambers?'

'No,' replied Audrey matter-of-factly. 'That's what's so strange. The Committee Chambers are behind us. Waghorn's heading in completely the opposite direction!'

'Come on,' warned Violet. 'She's heading into the next street!'

The children and the two monsters followed the hooded figure down a further two streets and another alley before they eventually came to a halt again. This time the mysterious figure had paused in front of a tavern, a tavern that had a large, severed claw hanging above its door which seemed to drip endless and magical blood onto the cobbled street below.

'Oh my, that's the Dragon's Claw!' exclaimed Violet, taken aback.

'What's she doing here?' asked Audrey, curiously.

'Look, she's going inside!' whispered Norman, and they all watched as the hooded figure glanced briefly up and down the alley before entering the tavern.

'We've got to follow her!' said Brian.

'What?' cried Audrey in alarm. 'It might be a trap, Brian! She might have seen us. You don't know for certain that she hasn't, or maybe that horrible bird of hers has seen us and right now Waghorn's secretly waiting inside to catch us all!'

'Where is her bird, by the way?' asked Norman, peering up at the magical sky just as it began to rain flashing green clothes pegs. 'Anybody see where it went?'

Hadley mumbled something and gestured with an enormous hairy arm to a window, partially open just above the tavern's door.

'It's flown in there!' said Sam, pointing and jumping up and down excitedly.

'Well, there's no need for all of us to follow her into the tavern. I guess Audrey could be right. It might be a trap,' conceded Brian. 'But I've got to know what she's doing in there!'

'Then I'll come with you,' said Violet.

'But—' began Brian.

'You can't go in there alone, mate,' agreed Norman.

'And I know the Dragon's Claw inside out,' remarked Violet. 'If it is a trap or if something does go wrong then at least I know where the best places are to hide and where all the exits are; Waghorn certainly doesn't!'

'Okay,' said Brian, albeit reluctantly.

'And we'll keep a look out,' suggested Norman.

'If we see anything suspicious we'll warn you,' said Sam.

'How are you going to do that?' asked Brian.

Sam thought for a moment. 'Hadley will hoot three times like a tawny owl, won't you?' he said, turning to his taller and much furrier companion.

Hadley mumbled something back at him.

'What do you mean you can't do an impression of a tawny owl?' asked Sam, disappointedly. 'Okay, what about a barn owl? Or a screech owl? Oh, you can't do any owl impressions! Well, why didn't you say so to begin with? Right, what about a ferocious grizzly bear? No? A wolf perhaps? A pincer spider? A jingle snake? How about a baby dragon? Well, what can you do then?' he asked, quickly becoming exasperated.

Hadley grunted.

'A kettle!' exclaimed Sam in amazement. 'Are you serious?'

Hadley appeared to shrug.

'Okay then. Well, if we see anything suspicious, Brian, Hadley will do an impression of a... boiling kettle,' said Sam.

'An electric or a gas kettle?' asked Norman, trying hard not to laugh.

But before Sam could clarify exactly what type of kettle Hadley could do an impression of Brian and Violet had already made their way to the front door of the Dragon's Claw. Slowly, Brian turned its handle and a moment later both he and Violet were inside the tavern.

When Willy's potions had been used to freeze Coffinsgrave the bar of the Dragon's Claw hadn't been particularly busy. There had been a few customers standing or sitting on stools and a few more seated at some of the unclean tables but on the whole the tavern had been fairly quiet. As Brian and Violet closed the door behind them they spotted Elfrida Gillibottom standing behind the bar like a waxwork in a museum. She, just as everyone else within the tavern, was perfectly still. Elfrida, it seemed, had frozen just as she had been pouring a tankard of ale for a customer. The watered-down liquid clearly hadn't been affected by the freezing potion, for as it had reached the lip of the tankard it had overflowed, pouring onto the floor and forming a winding pool of smelly ale that had spread completely around the bar.

'Can you see Waghorn?' whispered Brian, scanning the room for any sign of the hooded figure they had been following.

Violet shook her head and pointed to the stairs behind the bar. 'Let's head up to the next level,' she suggested.

But as the children wandered between the frozen customers Brian suddenly spotted movement towards the rear of the tavern. Immediately he grabbed Violet, dragging her behind a table where two men had been sitting and sharing a drink, their grinning faces now locked in permanent and eerie laughter.

Very slowly, Brian and Violet peered over the edge of the table, searching the bar for any further movement. And sure enough, seated in one corner was a man dressed in purple, wearing a matching hat and covered in dust.

'It's Major Bloodlock!' exclaimed Violet.

'What's happened to him?' asked Brian as they made their way towards his table. For just like everyone else within the Dragon's Claw he too appeared to be frozen solid. Only he wasn't. Not entirely. Somehow Major Bloodlock was able to move. Every now and then he would suddenly and unexpectedly change position just like a person sometimes jumps on screen in very, very old black-and-white films. One moment he was sitting, staring directly ahead of him, the next he was standing up and gazing at Brian and Violet.

'What's happened to him?' asked Brian again, concerned as the major attempted to open his mouth as if to try to say something. 'Why hasn't this happened to anybody else?'

'Well, I guess Willy's freezing potion affects ghosts differently,' replied Violet, bending her head nearer to the major's lips in an attempt to hear what he was trying to say.

'What?' exclaimed Brian, shocked. 'What did you just say?'

'I said I guess Willy's freezing potion affects ghosts differently,' replied Violet.

Brian stared at Major Bloodlock just as he jumped back to a seated position again, which resulted in a plume of dust falling from his hat and on to the table in front of him. Brian opened his mouth to say something, anything, but just like the major before him no words actually left his lips.

'You did realise that Major Bloodlock was a ghost, didn't you?' asked Violet, frowning at Brian in some surprise.

'No, actually… no, I didn't,' replied Brian, his voice suddenly returning. 'I don't believe in ghosts. Or, up until now, I didn't. I didn't think they were real. Besides, I thought ghosts were meant to be transparent. You know, like you could see straight through them and they dragged chains along the floor and stuff?'

'You've been reading too many books!' remarked Violet. 'No, the major was killed years ago. Don't know how or by what exactly. He doesn't like to talk about it. Ghosts can be like that, you know? But because of the way the major died it means that he's trapped here in the Dragon's Claw. Has been for years and years! The major can't leave. Can you imagine having to see and listen to the Gillibottoms every morning, noon and night of every day? I think he's had it worse than me, poor fellow!'

'And that's why he's always sitting in the same chair at the same table wearing the same clothes and drinking exactly the same tankard of ale,' said Brian, realisation finally dawning upon him.

'Exactly!' said Violet. 'He can't actually drink the ale, though, because he's a ghost, of course. He says he just likes the smell of it.'

'And that's why he's always covered in dust!' said Brian. 'Because he can't leave the tavern, because he just sits in the same chair all day every day. He must really get bored!'

'Look!' exclaimed Violet, taking a step back and staring at the major in surprise. 'What's he doing?'

Major Bloodlock had changed position yet again. But this time he had extended his arm and with an outstretched finger had marked a faint line within the dust upon the table top. A split second later he had jumped again and using the same finger had added another, second line so that it almost began to look like a letter.

'I think he's trying to tell us something!' said Violet.

'It's the letter H!' exclaimed Brian, staring at the table after the major had scratched a third line into the dust.

'But what does it mean?' asked Violet, watching as the old ghost quickly added three more lines to create a second letter.

'It's the letter P!' remarked Brian, puzzled. 'Hang on though, that doesn't make any sense. The letters H and P don't make a word, do they? What are you trying to tell us?' Brian asked the major.

Once more, the old ghost's lips parted but just as before no words left his mouth. Instead, the major jumped again but this time his outstretched hand knocked over the tankard of ale that had been sitting upon his table, which rolled across it and clattered noisily to the floor. Above them Brian and Violet heard sudden footsteps.

'Quickly, we've got to hide!' exclaimed Violet, panicking.

'Hide where?' cried Brian.

'In the kitchen!' suggested Violet, pointing to behind the bar. 'Come on!'

The two children raced into the kitchen, closing the door behind them only just in time. For at the very same moment the hooded figure they had been following emerged from a flight of stairs and silently surveyed the bar and its frozen customers for the source of the unexpected noise.

By now Brian's heart was pounding painfully in his chest and when the hooded figure began walking towards the kitchen door behind which he and Violet were hiding his heart began to beat faster still. Brian, his eye pressed to the keyhole, was certain that they were about to be discovered. But as the hooded figure grasped the handle to the kitchen door the sound of a tankard being kicked across the floor immediately made them stop and stare in the direction of Major Bloodlock. Within seconds the hooded figure was standing over the old ghost as he now continually began to jump and change position. Finding the empty tankard lying nearby, the hooded figure tapped it with one of their feet. Seemingly satisfied that this had been the noise that they had heard, the hooded figure turned on their heel and disappeared outside, slamming the tavern door behind them.

Cautiously, Brian and Violet emerged from the kitchen and quickly made their way over to the major, who was now standing up but no longer moving. It seemed that Willy Googalak's freezing potion had finally overcome him.

'Do you think Major Bloodlock's okay?' asked Brian, concerned.

'I think,' began Violet, 'that freezing a ghost takes a lot longer than it does anything else.' She touched the old man's arm, which now felt very cold and stiff.

'Well, whatever the major was trying to tell us we'll never know now,' said Brian, disappointed. 'What do you think HP means?'

'Dunno,' said Violet with a shrug.

'Come on, let's find the others,' said Brian, opening the tavern door ever so slightly and watching as the hooded figure hurried down the street, accompanied once again by the scruffy black bird that had reappeared above the rooftops. 'We've got to see where Waghorn goes next.'

Brian and Violet rejoined the others, who had been hiding within the shadows of a building opposite, and as they secretly followed the hooded figure Brian and Violet related everything that had happened to them whilst in the Dragon's Claw. Nobody had any idea as to what the letters HP meant (except for Hadley, but his suggestion was far too rude) or why the hooded figure had even entered the tavern in the first place.

'Where do you think Waghorn's going next?' asked Norman a few streets later.

'I don't know,' replied Audrey, peering curiously around a flight of steps as the hooded figure turned right and disappeared between two shops. 'But that alley she's just gone down leads into the square where the Diefromen attack took place,' she remarked, pointing to some damaged and partly wrecked buildings just ahead of them.

Cautiously the children and the two monsters followed the hooded figure into the market square which, unsurprisingly, was practically empty. The Diefromen attack had destroyed or ruined many of the shops and buildings, not to mention a lot of the actual stone square itself. They hid within a partially damaged shop front which was missing its front door and all its windows and watched in silence as the hooded figure hurried past the statues of both Sir Rodney Applegate and Lord Benfleet, both of whom were frozen too, before entering what was left of Abner Antiques.

'Why is Waghorn going in there?' whispered Norman, as they all left the burnt-out shop and quickly made their way across the square, stopping only when they had reached another, less damaged shop a few doors away from the antique shop.

Remarkably, Herbert's Magical Hardware Store had survived the Diefromen attack relatively intact. Like many of its neighbours it was missing its front door and one of its windows, but otherwise it seemed to have suffered only minor damage and appeared to have been able to reopen almost immediately, for inside there were a number of customers all of whom were standing perfectly still, frozen solid.

'Abner Antiques was practically destroyed during the attack, wasn't it?' remarked Violet.

'Yeah, it was,' agreed Brian.

'So what could Waghorn possibly want in there, then?' wondered Audrey aloud.

Norman, who had been peering up at the rooftops, suddenly announced, 'Her bird's disappeared too. I can't see it anywhere, can any of you?'

They quickly scanned the buildings and the rooftops but it appeared Norman was right; the scruffy, black bird seemed to have disappeared. And so too, for that matter, had the mysterious hooded figure, for as the children and the two monsters waited patiently amongst the frozen customers within Herbert's Magical Hardware Store the hooded figure did not reappear.

'I'm going to see what she's up to!' said Brian eventually, and before anybody had a chance to stop him Brian had already dashed over to the partially collapsed front wall of Abner Antiques and peered inside. What had, a few days ago, been a shop almost overflowing with two floors of unusual and wondrous antiques now looked like the inside of a furnace. Everything was scorched and blistered or, in some cases, so badly burnt that it had become unrecognisable. Although the upper level of the shop was still standing it was terribly burnt and it seemed clear that some furniture had fallen from it, collapsing on to other antiques below and destroying them. Strangely, the Door of Pealing, although quite scorched itself, still seemed to be in one piece. The hooded figure, however, that the children had watched enter Abner Antiques was nowhere to be seen.

'What a mess!' remarked Audrey upon seeing the inside of the antique shop; Brian had beckoned them over once he was satisfied that the coast was clear.

'And what a way to die,' added Norman, staring at all the burnt furniture inside. 'Poor old Barrington Abner! Burnt alive! Where do you think they found him?' he asked, eagerly.

'Norman Crabtree, why would you want to know something like that?' exclaimed Audrey, reproachfully. 'I think it's bad enough knowing somebody actually died in here. I certainly don't want to know where they found the poor man. Gives me the shivers just thinking about it.'

'Where's Waghorn?' asked Violet.

'Dunno,' replied Brian with a shrug. 'There's no way she could have got out through the back, though,' he said, gesturing to all the fallen furniture from the upper floor which was blocking the door.

'Then where did she go?' asked Violet.

Hadley mumbled something and pointed to the Door of Pealing.

252

'Don't be ridiculous!' cried his smaller companion. 'That's the most stupid idea I've ever heard!'

'What did Hadley say?' asked Brian.

'He said maybe Beatrice Waghorn went through that door,' he replied, pointing to the Door of Pealing and slapping his forehead with one of his hands.

'Oh my!' exclaimed Audrey suddenly, making everybody jump. 'That's it! Hadley's right!'

'What *are* you talking about?' asked Norman.

'Don't you remember?' said Audrey, excitedly. 'On the opening night of Abner Antiques, Barrington Abner himself said that this was just one of four Doors of Pealing that he owned!'

'So?' said Brian.

'So we know where the second one is, don't we, because we all used it?' said Audrey, pointing to the upper floor. 'But I wonder where the third and fourth doors are?'

'What, you think they're here somewhere too?' suggested Norman.

'I definitely think the third door's here,' replied Audrey. 'Up there probably, on that floor above somewhere, and that's where Waghorn's gone. That's why we can't find her. She's been using the third Door of Pealing to travel back and forth to Deevilmon.'

'But the doors were Barrington Abner's,' pointed out Brian.

'So she was probably blackmailing him,' replied Audrey. 'Forcing him to help her.'

'And when he didn't want to do it any more she killed him,' said Norman, nodding in agreement.

'Exactly!' said Audrey.

'So what now?' asked Violet.

'We've got to find that third Door of Pealing,' said Brian, taking a deep breath and stepping into the eerily free-standing door before him. Immediately the world about him began spinning madly, but the sensation of being trapped within some sort of magical

253

whirlwind did not last long. In a matter of seconds his journey was over and, just as before, Brian found himself standing on the upper level of Abner Antiques, although this was now so badly burnt that, in some places, he could see right through the floor and into the shop below.

By the time the others had arrived Brian had already discovered a set of footprints within the soot and ash which appeared to lead from the second Door of Pealing towards the opposite end of the room. Because a large proportion of the floor had collapsed the children and the two monsters, especially Norman in his wheelchair and Hadley who was so big and heavy, had to be particularly careful as they followed the winding path of footprints through what was left of the antique furniture. Eventually, however, they arrived at the rear of the shop where, strangely, the footprints ended abruptly in front of a large and badly burnt wooden chest.

'Where'd she go?' asked Norman, puzzled.

Curiously, Violet tugged at the lid to the chest, trying to pull it open, which proved quite difficult as the wood was badly warped from the fire, making the lid particularly stiff. But with Hadley's help she finally managed it and they all stared in some surprise at the flight of stone steps that disappeared down inside it.

'How is that even possible?' asked Brian, peering into the chest in astonishment.

'It must be some sort of Expandobox,' explained Violet, climbing onto the first step.

'And I bet the third Door of Pealing is at the bottom,' said Norman, excitedly. 'But how am I going to get down the steps in this?' He gestured to his wheelchair irritably.

Hadley mumbled something and in one swift movement had scooped both Norman and his wheelchair up into his massive hairy arms. With Sam not far behind him, he followed Violet into the chest and down the stone steps.

'Hey, are you okay?' asked Brian, concerned as Audrey, breathing heavily, climbed into the wooden box and also began descending the stone steps.

'My chest just feels a little tight,' she complained, taking a long deep breath whilst at the same time taking two puffs from her inhaler. 'It's nothing. It happens a lot. Especially when I'm a little nervous.'

'You sure you're going to be okay?' asked Brian, unconvinced. 'Only you're still getting over that asthma attack you had when the Diefromen—'

'Listen,' interrupted Audrey as she took another puff from her inhaler. 'There's nobody else now, is there? I mean to stop Deevilmon. It's up to us, isn't it?'

Brian nodded.

'Then I'm coming with you,' she said, stubbornly.

Although steep, the flight of stone steps was not particularly long and they ended, somewhat unexpectedly, within a damp half-moon tunnel that was partially covered in a green and brown moss of some description. From the ceiling water dripped upon the tunnel floor, forming large puddles, whilst mounted at regular intervals along the walls were torches that burned brightly.

By the time Brian and Audrey had caught up with the others the tunnel had expanded and opened up into a small cave which was completely covered in some sort of leafy vine. At the cave's centre, almost as if it had grown out of the very earth itself, was a spiral stone staircase which twisted upwards to connect with a simple and rather unremarkable brown wooden door.

'Is that the third Door of Pealing?' asked Norman.

'What else could it be?' replied Brian.

'Where do you think it goes?' said Norman, as Hadley scooped both him and his wheelchair up again into his huge shaggy arms.

'I don't know,' replied Brian. 'But there's only one way to find out,' and he began making his way gradually up the stone staircase.

When he reached the top Brian peered nervously through the open door and at the cave floor below him, which seemed an awfully long way down. If he was wrong, if this wasn't the third Door of Pealing and was just a normal door after all then he was going to step into it, fall straight through it and probably break every bone in his body. But Brian really had no other choice. He closed his eyes and stepped forwards.

Seconds later and feeling very disorientated indeed Brian staggered out from the other side of the door. His head was spinning madly and it took a few moments before he could finally take in his new surroundings. Behind him Hadley, who was carrying Norman, emerged from the fourth Door of Pealing quickly followed by Sam, Violet and Audrey. It seemed that they all had been transported to some sort of stone chamber which had no windows and a very high ceiling. Opposite was an archway which led into a corridor.

'Where are we?' asked Norman as Hadley set him upon the floor again.

'I don't know,' replied Brian, passing under the archway and into the corridor. Like the chamber before it the corridor had no windows, but it did have a number of further archways cut into its right wall.

As Brian reached the first archway and with the others following close behind he heard voices coming from somewhere below them. Cautiously, he peered around the first stone arch and stared in both fear and amazement at the sight that greeted him.

The corridor that they were in appeared to surround the top of a huge and hexagonal candle-lit chamber. From six of the arches a staircase led down to a large arena below where twelve vertical cells were somehow magically suspended in midair. The iron cells were not particularly big, with each one holding probably only a single prisoner who, due to the small size of the cell base, had no choice but to constantly stand. It was only when Brian stared more closely at the cells that he guessed the prisoners inside were probably the kidnapped Wizitches, although from his vantage point behind the arch he couldn't be certain.

In the centre of the six-sided arena was the hooded figure that the children and the two monsters had been following. This figure was knelt before another, much larger creature, a demon whose whole body including its face seemed to be made up from some form of black ever-changing mist.

The figure, who had been kneeling so reverently before the demon, spoke, although Brian could barely catch the words. 'Deevilmon... Master, I... I regret that I could not find the children. They were not to be found in the fair or the tavern...'

Immediately the demon raised one of its arms, and as it did so the swirling black mist which formed it temporarily detached itself from the creature's shoulder and then reformed again whilst the hooded figure kneeling before it fell suddenly silent. 'No matter,' said the demon, whose deep and rasping voice seemed to fill every part of the chamber, and with a clawlike finger it pointed up at the arch that Brian was hiding behind. 'For it would appear that they have found us!'

The hooded figure turned about and, whilst looking up at the corridor that surrounded the hexagonal chamber, slowly pulled back their hood.

Immediately, Brian let out a gasp and staggered backwards, refusing to believe what he had just seen.

'What is it, Brian?' asked Audrey, watching terrified as the colour quickly drained from his face.

'I-it's not Waghorn,' he stammered, using the wall of the corridor for support as he felt his legs grow weaker.

'What?' said Norman, confused.

'The hooded figure we were following,' said Brian. 'It's not Waghorn.'

'Not Waghorn?' repeated Violet. 'Then who is it?'

'It's... it's my granddad,' replied Brian.

Chapter 19

BACK FROM THE DEAD

The demon laughed terribly. It laughed for so long that Brian did not think that it would ever stop. Its unpleasant, gurgling voice reverberated all about the chamber, forcing Brian to place his hands over his ears in an attempt to block the sound from penetrating any further into his head. But it did not work.

Within the corridor that surrounded the chamber more demons suddenly appeared, one after the other. Although much smaller than the huge demon below they were formed by the same swirling black mist so that trying to discern their exact shape and size proved almost impossible.

'Bring them to me!' demanded a voice from below.

Although their bodies seemed to be fashioned from an almost insubstantial vapour the demons were still, somehow, able to push and shove the children and the two monsters unmercifully down one of the flights of stone steps and into the hexagonal arena below. At one point Hadley, who had picked Norman up in his wheelchair and was carrying him, almost slipped and dropped him.

Upon hearing the sound of the children's arrival the twelve prisoners being held captive within the suspended cells turned their heads instinctively in their direction. But none of them could actually see the children. For concealing each prisoner's face and covering most of their head was a crude, metal mask which, apart from a small rectangular hole cut into its lower half that, presumably, allowed its captor to breathe, was completely solid.

'Bring our guests a little closer,' commanded Deevilmon once the children were stood before it.

The smaller demons ushered the children and the two monsters further forward whilst Brian's granddad took his place at the demon's side. As terrible and frightening as Deevilmon was, Brian had felt surprisingly little fear as he had descended the flight of stairs into the arena below. Instead, he just felt resentment. For kneeling obediently, almost reverently, next to the demon was his granddad. A Wizitch who had sworn to rid the world of demons but, instead, had seemingly turned against the Order, joining and aiding Deevilmon in the demon's bid to become immortal. But why?

'How lovely to have *visitors*,' remarked Deevilmon, who somehow managed to make the word *visitors* sound much more like *prisoners*. 'Why, if I had known you were coming I would have arranged suitable accommodation for you all,' it said, gesturing to the cells suspended in midair. The demon's eyes, if that was what you could call them, glowed momentarily silver as it glided a little further forward. 'Although I see that one of you has been kind enough to bring his own cell with him.'

The demon peered down at Norman in his wheelchair with a curious fascination. 'How absolutely wonderful,' it remarked, as sudden wisps of sinewy smoke appeared to form the briefest of smiles upon the creature's face. 'Having to live your life in something like *that*? I mean, honestly, what's the point of living?'

Norman shifted uncomfortably in his wheelchair and lowered his head in an attempt to avoid the demon's gaze. He suddenly felt ashamed. After his accident three years ago he had said those exact words to his parents: *what's the point of living?* Of course, such a statement seemed ridiculous to him now. But at the time it had felt like the end of the world. His legs would not work and it was very likely that he would remain in a wheelchair for the rest of his life.

To him, his wheelchair was nothing more than a mobile prison, and after sitting in it for the very first time he had decided, right there and then, that his life was officially over! But Norman had been quite wrong. In no time at all, his dad had fixed and altered their house so that he could still go anywhere he wanted to. He'd even demolished the front and back steps, replacing them with a metal ramp so that Norman could still go outside in his wheelchair whenever he wanted. But, nevertheless, for the first six months after he'd been discharged from the hospital Norman had absolutely refused to leave the house, spending most days doing nothing other than constantly playing computer games.

It was only when he had been visited by Joseph, another boy in a wheelchair (via a meeting secretly arranged by his parents), that Norman, albeit reluctantly, had finally agreed to join the local football club. Up until then he'd had absolutely no idea that wheelchair football clubs had even existed, let alone actual leagues! After joining Homefield United as a defender and helping them to achieve second place in the league in his very first season he had then joined a local table tennis club and also began playing badminton every other Thursday evening after school. In fact, he was probably more active now and more involved in various sports than before his actual accident. Not that he didn't still enjoy playing computer games as well!

'You won't get away with this!' cried Norman resolutely. 'You won't get the Cup of Ages!'

The demon cackled, its voice echoing eerily all about them.

'But I already have the Cup of Ages,' declared Deevilmon, smiling unpleasantly and beckoning to one of the smaller demons to float forward. From somewhere within its ever-shifting form the smaller demon removed a simple and rather plain-looking metal cup with, set upon its outer edge, a number of red stones. However, it did not escape any of the children's attention that at least one of the precious stones was missing. For, as Deevilmon paraded the Cup of

Ages victoriously before them, it was quite plain to see that there was a much larger gap between two of the rubies than there should have been.

'You appear to be missing a Wizitch stone,' stated Audrey, pulling the inhaler from her jeans pocket and taking two puffs from it which, in turn, instantly relaxed her chest, which had been gradually growing tighter ever since their descent into the hexagonal arena.

'What a very observant girl you are,' remarked Deevilmon unpleasantly. Then, handing the Cup of Ages back to the smaller demon, it drifted a little nearer to Audrey who was, rather unexpectedly, finding it more than a little difficult to keep hold of her inhaler. It had, quite literally, assumed a life of its own and she watched in fright as it shook and rattled within her hands before magically springing free from her grasp and flying into one of the demon's outstretched palms. The enormous demon stared at the tiny inhaler curiously as the shifting black mist that formed its other hand began briefly to envelop it.

'I don't think you'll be requiring this again,' said the demon, cruelly. And as the mist started to dissolve it was clear that the inhaler had been completely crushed so that it was now as flat and as thin as a sheet of writing paper.

Audrey stared in horror as the demon dropped the flattened inhaler, which clattered noisily to the floor before her. Then floating towards the twelve cells suspended in midair, Deevilmon briefly peered into each one before pushing them so that for a moment they, very gently, rocked backwards and forwards.

It was only as Deevilmon did this, forcing each prisoner inside their cell to suddenly grab at the rusty metal bars surrounding them for support, that Brian noticed something very odd indeed. He had assumed that each of the cells contained one of the kidnapped Wizitches. It made sense. After all, there *were* twelve Wizitches and magically suspended in midair above him were twelve cells. And

261

within each cell was contained a single prisoner. But his granddad, unlike the other Wizitches – if it was them being held captive – was not amongst them. And that made thirteen in total. Not twelve. So had Deevilmon kidnapped somebody else, wondered Brian? And, if so, who was it?

'You're quite right,' agreed Deevilmon, turning to face the children and the two monsters. 'There is still a Wizitch stone that I have yet to acquire. For if I had it now then you would certainly be knelt before me just as a dog kneels before its master. One of you has it. And let me assure you that before this day is over you will give it to me. Preferably of your own free will. It would not be wise, I think, to make me force you to give it to me.'

'But we don't have the stone!' cried Audrey.

'We don't even know what it looks like,' added Norman.

Deevilmon began to laugh, its unnatural gurgling voice echoing all about them. Then, very slowly, the demon began to descend towards the children, its shape constantly shifting so that its size was never exactly the same from one moment to the next. It stopped only when its dark, swirling face was mere inches from Brian's.

'But Brian knows what it looks like, don't you?' said Deevilmon, twisting and extending its head so that its neck began to gradually encircle him.

'W-what?' stammered Brian, frightened and confused. 'No, I don't. Why would I know what it looks like?'

'Because it's your granddad's stone that I am missing,' replied Deevilmon, as it extended its neck even further, enabling it to weave its way about the children as though it were some sort of gigantic black snake.

'Well, if it's my granddad's Wizitch stone that you're missing then why don't you just ask him for it?' said Brian bitterly, nodding towards his granddad who, even now, was still kneeling obediently upon the stone floor of the chamber.

Appearing to ignore Brian's suggestion, Deevilmon shifted its shape yet again so that, all at once, its neck and head suddenly returned to, more or less, their previous size. 'You see,' the demon began, 'when each of the Wizitches was brought here—'

'Scrobbled, you mean!' said Audrey.

Suddenly, Deevilmon disappeared, reappearing almost instantly behind Audrey. 'Interrupt me again, Miss Jenkins,' rasped the demon, making Audrey jump, 'and I will kill you here and now. Am I making myself clear?'

Audrey nodded, albeit reluctantly.

'Good,' said Deevilmon, rematerialising almost immediately next to Brian. 'Now, as I was saying, when each of the Wizitches was brought here they very kindly all gave up their Wizitch stones to me…'

Straight away Audrey opened her mouth ready to argue that the Wizitch stones had, in reality, probably all been stolen rather than being simply handed over to Deevilmon as the demon had suggested. But the dreadful look upon Deevilmon's face as Audrey opened her mouth and its dire warning moments earlier meant that she, instead, closed her lips without uttering even a single word.

'However, as Miss Jenkins has clearly observed, the Cup of Ages is presently incomplete,' remarked the demon, as an unmistakable sense of irritation crept into its voice. 'A single stone is missing. Your granddad's stone, to be exact, Brian. Now, as I'm sure you're aware, the twelve Wizitch rubies were fashioned many years ago into various trinkets to be worn by the Wizitches which, as I'm also sure you know already, enhance their powers. Some of these stones were concealed within rings and broaches, others within a pendant made to hang from a necklace; one was even placed within a pocket watch. Your granddad's magical stone was held within a ring that he wore on his little finger of his right hand, was it not?'

Brian nodded in reply, although he still didn't understand. His granddad was here, knelt before him. No, not knelt before *him*, knelt before Deevilmon. If Deevilmon wanted his granddad's ring he had but to ask or, rather, simply take it from him.

'Unfortunately, when we *invited* your granddad and grandmother to join me here,' continued Deevilmon, gesturing to the arena with an enormous swing of its arm which momentarily detached itself from the demon's shoulder, 'there was, rather regrettably, a little... how should I put this... scuffle, during which your granddad's ring may have slipped off his finger. I say *may* because I do not know for certain. It's possible, although rather unlikely, that he was somehow made aware of my desire for the Wizitch stones and, perhaps, gave his ring to somebody that he trusted for safekeeping.'

'So it was you in Stermon Passage!' exclaimed Brian in sudden realisation. 'It was you who almost choked me to death. You were looking for my granddad's ring! You thought I had it, which is why you broke into our room in the Dragon's Claw and turned my granddad's house upside down searching for it!'

Deevilmon appeared to nod. 'You're quite right, it was your granddad's ring that I was seeking, but it was not I who was in Stermon Passage, Brian.'

The demon turned towards the figure still crouched so reverently upon the chamber floor. 'Time, I think, to lose the disguise,' said Deevilmon. And with that Brian's granddad stood up, grasped the underside of his chin and with a tremendous effort pulled the Mirrormask off his face.

Brian, Norman, Audrey and Violet all stared in amazement. They couldn't believe what they were seeing. The figure before them was dead! Burned alive! And yet, standing before them and gulping down a potion that he had retrieved from within the folds of his cloak, was none other than Barrington Abner, back from the dead!

'It was me in Stermon Passage that morning!' announced Abner.

264

'B-but you died…' stuttered Audrey, pointing at the antique shop owner in amazement.

'…in the fire…' added Brian, in complete disbelief.

'…during the Diefromen attack,' said Violet.

'Yeah, you were all burnt and stuff. Like one of my dad's sausages that he always overcooks on our barbecue,' remarked Norman, grimacing at the thought.

Abner threw the empty glass bottle, from which he had consumed the potion, upon the chamber floor. It broke instantly and what little liquid had been left inside quickly disappeared down into the cracks between the slabs of stone. 'That wasn't me in the fire, my boy,' he replied, almost jovially, and as he spoke his voice immediately changed from that of Brian's granddad back to his own.

The sudden surge of relief that Brian had felt as Abner had removed his disguise, knowing that his granddad hadn't betrayed him or turned against the Wizitches, quickly gave way to a sudden swell of fury. How could he have been so blind, fooled so easily? Why had he not seen past Abner's disguise? But then another, more urgent, question struck him, which he asked aloud. 'If it wasn't you who died in the fire, then who was it?'

Deevilmon roared with laughter, its unpleasant voice, once again, echoing all about the chamber. It drifted nearer to Brian, the demon's form constantly changing, shifting its shape until, eventually, they were face to face. And the demon rasped, 'Can you not guess?'

Brian took a step backwards, almost tripping over his own feet. He shook his head. He suddenly felt afraid, more afraid than he had ever felt before in his life. It had been the way Deevilmon had said those words, *can you not guess*, almost as if Brian should know who it was that had died in the fire. He glanced first at Abner, who was now holding what appeared to be a wand in his right hand, and then back at Deevilmon before he repeated his question, 'Who was it?'

Deevilmon smiled cruelly. 'It was your mother, Brian.'

Immediately Brian felt his legs begin to buckle, as if the bones inside them had somehow been removed. The world about him began to spin and he staggered backwards. If it hadn't been for Violet, who was standing beside him, Brian was sure that he would have passed out. Instead, and with Violet's help, he managed to remain upright although he was absolutely certain that he was going to be sick.

'I can assure you that she died very painfully,' announced Deevilmon.

Brian tried to reply but found that his mouth was dry, like a coffin full of old bones. He coughed once, twice before finally stammering, 'Y-you're lying!'

Deevilmon only laughed even more.

'Y-you didn't kill my mother!' spluttered Brian, shaking his head, disbelievingly. 'W-why would you?'

'No, you're quite right,' said Deevilmon, nodding in agreement and turning to face Barrington Abner. '*I* didn't kill your mother, Brian. But… you see, Abner here was absolutely convinced that she had your granddad's ring, that your granddad had given it to her for safekeeping. And when she kept saying no, when she kept denying that she had it, well…'

'Do you recognise this, my boy?' asked Abner, having removed a thin, golden chain from one of his pockets. He dangled it, tantalisingly, from the tips of his fingers. Hanging from the chain was an oval locket held shut by a tiny ivory clasp.

Brian recognised it at once. 'That's my mother's,' he cried, clenching his fists furiously.

'Yes, indeed it is… or was,' agreed Abner, studying the chain somewhat idly whilst all the time keeping his wand firmly trained upon the children and the two monsters before him. 'It had a rather pleasant picture inside it. A photo of you, your father and mother I believe. Taken upon a beach, very nice. Although in the photo you were a little younger, I think. I got rid of it, of course. Instead, I

266

replaced it with something more appropriate. A keepsake, something to treasure. Would you like to know what I put inside, Brian?'

But Brian didn't reply. He already knew that Abner was going to tell him anyway no matter what answer he might give.

Abner grinned wickedly. 'Your mother's final moments,' he said. 'Inside her locket I placed your mother's last few seconds of life! The very moment she died, in fact. And I captured it just for you. Something to remember her by. It's a little brief, I grant you, but what better way to remember your mother than to be able to share in her final few moments, her agonising screams, her cries for help and her pathetic begs for mercy? In a way it will almost feel like you were there, Brian.'

Then Abner undid the locket's clasp and pulled it open for everyone to hear.

This time Brian's legs did buckle and he collapsed upon his knees, consumed in grief. It was his mother's voice, just as Abner had said it would be, but he did not recognise it. It did not sound like his mother. It did not sound like anybody. All that came out of the locket was an almost endless cascade of screams and cries of agony. It was unbearable. And when, finally, the screams did finish the silence that replaced them felt even more unbearable.

As Abner closed the locket and threw it upon the floor so that it landed at Brian's feet, tears were pouring uncontrollably from Brian's eyes and no matter how hard he wiped them with the heels of his hands he could not stop their flow.

'You see, Brian,' continued Deevilmon as though Brian's anguish were insignificant, 'Abner's methods of extracting information, although admittedly quite antiquated, are remarkably successful. And such extraction will, on most occasions, result in death, which in your mother's case is exactly what happened. I was grateful really; not as grateful as your mother, I don't doubt, but by the third day her constant screams and wails were really quite tiresome.'

267

Brian wiped his nose with the back of his hand and struggled to his feet. Grief was still coursing through his veins but it was rapidly being replaced by something else, something even stronger. Anger.

'You must understand, Brian, that it was only by your mother's death that it became apparent that she was, in fact, telling us the truth. She really didn't have your granddad's ring! Can you imagine?' said Deevilmon, pausing momentarily and smiling unpleasantly. 'After tolerating all that pain and after enduring all that suffering your mother really had been telling the truth after all. I think that's absolutely marvellous.'

Brian stared at the huge demon, his grief having been almost completely consumed by rage, 'How did...'

'...I fool everyone into thinking that your dead mother was, in fact, Barrington Abner?' said Deevilmon, finishing Brian's question for him. 'It was remarkably easy really. A simple magical spell and a Mirrormask were all that was needed to allow Abner to alter your mother's appearance to his. Although she was already dead, Abner saw to it that your mother's body would be so badly burnt within the fire that identification would prove practically impossible, which, of course, it did.' Deevilmon's lips curled at the sides of its mouth as it spoke to form a huge and nasty grin. 'And with Abner's sudden disappearance everybody naturally assumed that it was he who had died in the fire.'

Abner continued, 'I simply used the exact same spell and another Mirrormask to transform myself into an identical copy of your granddad. I had hoped to discover where your granddad's missing ring was.'

'But you can see my dilemma now, I'm sure,' remarked Deevilmon. 'For if your mother didn't have your granddad's Wizitch ring then who *has* got it? Certainly none of those fools on the Coffinsgrave Committee! Abner, disguised as your granddad of course, has already searched their homes and places of work and questioned them. I doubt very much that your granddad would have given it to either that bookshop owner, Newtblaster, or Rimhorn the shopkeeper at Kinsgbury's. So I have little choice other than to assume that he gave it to you.'

'But I don't have the ring,' said Brian, shaking his head.

'Well then, let me make this very simple for you, Brian,' snapped Deevilmon irritably, as what passed for its eyes glowed momentarily silver again. 'If you don't have the ring, tell me who does or, on the count of three, Abner here will kill Miss Jenkins, won't you Abner?'

'Gladly, my master,' replied Abner, raising his wand dangerously at Audrey.

'One!' barked Deevilmon.

'But I don't know who's got it!' repeated Brian, frantically.

'Two!'

'You're not listening to me!' cried Brian, desperately. 'I don't know who's got my granddad's ring!'

'Then your friend Miss Jenkins is going to die,' replied Deevilmon, matter-of-factly. 'Three!'

Chapter 20

THE NORSIP BALL

'Wait!' cried Sam frantically, leaping in front of Audrey and waving his hands as Abner's wand was about to explode in a shower of deadly light towards her.

Abner glanced at the small, wellington-booted monster suspiciously and then at Deevilmon, who raised a black, swirling arm to indicate Audrey had won a reprieve, albeit a temporary one. Abner looked disappointed but he did not lower his wand.

Sam breathed a massive sigh of relief and then, turning towards his much bigger companion, said, 'Now, what did you just say?'

Hadley grunted something unintelligible back at him.

'What do you mean, you've got it?' replied Sam.

Hadley shrugged and mumbled something else which, just as before, was completely incomprehensible to everyone except, of course, his smaller friend.

'Got what exactly?' snapped Sam, quickly becoming exasperated.

Hadley immediately began rummaging within his fur and a few moments later had removed a large plastic football trophy from under his left arm. This, however, was clearly not what the monster had been looking for because he dropped it on the floor without a second's thought. The football trophy was soon followed by a bottle of bubble bath, a pair of smelly shoes, a large glass bottle crammed full of eyeballs (which, unnervingly, all appeared to be moving and staring excitedly at their new surroundings of their own free will), some sweet wrappers, a dustbin lid and a stapler which, when Hadley added it to the growing pile upon the floor, kept leaping about and trying to bite everybody's feet.

Eventually, Hadley found what he had been looking for. He gave a grunt of satisfaction and held out his right hand. There, hidden amongst his knotted, straggly fur, was a golden ring and set within it was a round blood-red ruby.

'That's my granddad's ring!' exclaimed Brian, his eyes widening in complete surprise.

Sam grabbed Hadley's hand, pulling it lower, so that he could get a better look. 'Brilliant!' he snapped irritably, upon seeing the ring. 'That's just brilliant! And where, exactly, did you get that from!'

Hadley shrugged and pointed to the folds of his fur hanging from his left arm.

'No, you great hairy oaf,' said Sam, kicking him in the leg. 'I mean where did you find it?' he demanded, trying unsuccessfully to disentangle his foot which had now become caught within his taller companion's straggly fur.

Hadley grumbled something in reply.

'What do you mean are you in trouble?' replied Sam, hopping about annoyed. 'Of course you're in trouble! We're all in trouble! That's what Deevilmon's been looking for!' He jabbed a finger first at the ring and then behind him at the demon as he spoke. 'Where did you get it?'

Hadley replied with a number of unintelligible grunts and groans.

'What do you mean you found it?' snapped Sam, finally tugging his foot free from Hadley's enormous hairy leg only to find that his wellington boot had come off and was now lost somewhere inside.

Hadley grunted again.

271

'You're saying you found it on the floor in Brian's living room the night we collected him?' exclaimed Sam in disbelief. 'What were you thinking? This is actually worse than the time you *accidentally* found the Green Dragon Diamond three weeks after it was reported stolen from the Museum of Mysterious and Magical Artefacts or when you just *happened* to discover Professor Snalegrinder's wooden leg a year to the day after it went missing when we visited him in the HAPPI or that time when you *miraculously* came across that ancient map to the Lost City of Santtila after it had been—'

'Enough!' cried Deevilmon irately, as it floated menacingly towards Hadley. 'Give me the ring!' Then, turning to Abner, it added, 'Watch them closely. Any sudden movements and you know what to do, don't you?'

'Oh yes, my master,' Abner replied, willingly.

A moment later one of Deevilmon's hands had engulfed Hadley's outstretched palm and when the wisps of black, sinewy smoke had disappeared so too had the Wizitch ring.

'Immortality is mine!' laughed Deevilmon, holding aloft the final stone that the demon had been so desperately searching for. Then, turning to Abner again, Deevilmon said, 'Now you can kill them!'

'What?' screamed Audrey, aghast.

'With pleasure, my master,' said Abner, grinning in anticipation and waving his wand as it began to explode in a dazzling ray of light.

It was then that a number of things all happened at once. From behind Brian a high-pitched howl erupted. At the same time he was roughly pushed aside as Violet leapt past him. Only it wasn't Violet. Not completely. The lower half of her body had changed and, indeed, was still changing before his very eyes. Her feet had become twice as large with toenails as long as claws. Her legs had stretched, grown more muscular and were now covered with dark and thick bristly hair. As she fell upon all fours and bounded towards Abner her upper body began to rapidly expand and her arms were stretching and swelling massively.

Abner didn't know what to do. The sight of Violet's sudden metamorphosis had taken him completely by surprise. He stumbled backwards in sudden panic, aiming his wand first at Audrey and then at Violet and then back at Audrey again. By the time he had fired his wand at Violet it was already too late. His spell missed her completely. Hitting, instead, the twelve prison cells suspended in midair, which all plummeted to the floor with a crash, their doors magically unlocking of their own accord and springing open. When Violet landed upon Abner's chest, seconds later, knocking and pinning him to the floor, she had completely changed from a girl into a massive Jackerbot. Now completely covered in thick bristly hair and feathers, Violet howled again and growled fiercely as long drips of sticky drool fell from the teeth within her beak and all over Abner's face.

At the same time as Violet's sudden and shocking transformation figures had begun to unexpectedly appear within the corridor that surrounded the chamber above them. But they were not demons. It was the scruffy, black bird that Brian recognised first. For it was flapping just above Beatrice Waghorn as she emerged from one of the arches and onto the nearest staircase, closely followed by Barnaby Katobi, Gordon Grubshackle and all the other members of the Coffinsgrave Committee.

'Kill them!' roared Deevilmon at the smaller demons angrily as Waghorn and Katobi both fired spells that exploded upon the wall just behind the demon, sending splinters of stone flying in every direction.

'V-Violet's turned into a J-Jackerbot!' said Norman in disbelief, pointing dumbly at the four-legged creature which still had Abner pinned to the chamber floor. 'How did she...' but Norman's next question was drowned out by a second explosion, this time coming

273

from behind him, as Helga Braithwaite began battling one of the demons that she had encountered whilst descending one of the flights of stairs.

'Yes, she's a shapeshifter,' cried Sam over the sudden roar of flame as a number of glowing balls of fire thundered over their heads, hitting and then magically passing through Deevilmon's chest before exploding behind it in a shower of sparks.

Audrey pointed to a number of Wizitches who had clambered out of their cells and were now wandering blindly about, completely oblivious to the battle that had erupted about them. 'They're going to get themselves killed unless we help!' remarked Audrey, 'Come on, we've got to get their masks off!'

'What do you mean she's a shapeshifter?' repeated Norman, frowning at Sam.

Hadley mumbled something in reply.

'Didn't you know she was a shapeshifter?' shouted Sam in some surprise as another spell exploded above their heads.

'What *is* a shape—'

'Norman!' Audrey scolded. 'It's hardly the time for a quiz!'

'But—' argued Norman.

'Look!' cried Audrey, urgently.

Norman followed Audrey's gaze and stared in alarm as one of the demons began rushing towards a Wizitch who had managed to escape from their cell and was now struggling futilely to free their head from the metal mask that it was still encased in.

'Quick, give me a push,' Norman shouted at Hadley as he hastily lined up his wheelchair to intercept the demon.

Hadley grabbed the handles to Norman's wheelchair, which immediately began to buckle under the monster's fierce grip, and then, with a huge push, he sent Norman hurtling across the chamber floor almost as if his wheelchair were being propelled by a jet engine.

By the time the demon realised what was happening Norman, who was shouting 'CHAAARGE' at the top of his voice and waving a fist angrily, was almost upon him. Looking rather like a cavalry general on his shiny metal steed, Norman's plan to stop the demon from attacking the wandering Wizitch almost worked.

Unfortunately, Norman had completely forgotten that the demon was not actually made from anything solid. So when he collided with it seconds later, rather than stopping the demon in its tracks as he had planned, Norman instead passed straight through it, crashing into the opposite wall of the chamber so hard that one of the wheels to his wheelchair completely snapped off which, in turn, sent poor Norman sprawling upon the floor in a great, messy heap. Dazed and with a nasty cut upon his jaw, Norman glanced back at the others and slowly raised his right hand. Clutched within it was a small and rather plain-looking metal cup. The Cup of Ages.

A howl of pain from behind them made Brian and Audrey suddenly whirl around. Even though Deevilmon appeared not to have physically touched Violet she had somehow been forced off Abner and thrown against the chamber wall. As she clambered back onto her feet and shook her head groggily Abner immediately sat up. There, lying upon the floor and just a few feet from him was his wand. He lunged for it.

'Oh no you don't!' cried Audrey, sensing what Abner was attempting and diving for the wand herself. She skidded across the stone floor, ripping her jeans in the process, in a desperate attempt to reach the fallen wand before the antique shop owner. But she wasn't quick enough. Abner reached it first and as he wrapped his fingers around one end and began whispering the words to a magical incantation green sparks began to fizz and splutter from it.

But Abner never got to finish his spell. Instead, he shrieked in agony as Audrey, now standing above him, brought her foot down painfully upon his hand not once but twice, forcing Abner to drop his wand yet again. Then, seizing the opportunity to scoop up the

275

wand herself, Audrey quickly grabbed it and immediately went to throw it to Brian. But suddenly she felt somebody grab her hair, jerking her head back painfully. Audrey screamed and twisted about. It was Abner and his face was absolutely furious. His eyes were open wide and bloodshot and still watering from the pain she had inflicted upon his hand when she had stamped on it.

'GIVE... ME... MY... WAND!' he screamed, almost hysterically, spit flying from his mouth as he desperately tried to snatch the wand away from Audrey. But Audrey was having none of it. She wriggled and twisted and with a well-timed elbow managed to hit Abner in the stomach, winding him, albeit momentarily. As his grip upon Audrey's hair slackened it gave Audrey just enough time to wrench herself away from him and throw the wand to Brian.

He caught it in the very same moment that Violet, having recovered from being thrown against the chamber wall, crashed into Abner with such force that all thoughts of reclaiming his wand were driven from his mind. The antique shop owner was knocked off his feet and sent sliding across the stone floor, his face scraping upon its hard surface and his cloak being torn from his shoulders, its contents spilling out of their secret pockets and tumbling everywhere.

As Brian raised his arm, aiming Abner's wand at Deevilmon, the anger of his mother's death began to surge within him like the lava of a volcano just before it erupts. His hand was shaking badly as he stared up at the massive demon, watching as it continued to deflect spell after spell from the members of the Coffinsgrave Committee, their spells bouncing into the chamber walls, ceiling and stairs sending stone and rubble flying everywhere.

As Brian looked about him it seemed that most of the other, smaller demons had already been defeated or had fled to wherever it was that they had originally come from, as only Winifred Hogfoot and Mellisant Melchant were left battling two particular devious demons who kept disappearing and reappearing whenever a spell was fired at them. But even these were eventually defeated when

276

Benjamin Brewster and Barnaby Katobi assisted in the attack. A dazzling, curving beam of light fired from the end of Barnaby Katobi's walking stick caught one of the demons around its neck as it briefly reappeared, instantly beheading it. The demon shrieked and immediately disappeared. The only evidence that it had just been there seconds earlier was a faint swirling mist which quickly disappeared too.

Mellisant Melchant meanwhile was positioned on one of the six flights of stairs that surrounded the chamber, firing an assortment of purple and green bolts of spinning light up at the remaining demon who, managing to avoid each attack, was slowly but surely edging nearer and nearer to her. Then, just as Mellisant attempted another, different spell the demon seized its chance and lunged at her!

If it hadn't been for Benjamin Brewster firing his ruler at the exact same moment that the demon pounced upon Mellisant then it would surely have caught and killed her. But, instead, the demon was struck by a shower of silver sparks that had burst from the tip of Brewster's ruler, which immediately took on a life of their own and began to encircle him. Faster and faster the silver lights spun until, with a sudden and very loud bang, they all exploded in an enormous flash of light like a rocket on Bonfire Night and when the flare of light eventually subsided the demon was nowhere to be seen.

Brian began to edge slowly forwards, towards Deevilmon. His hand was still shaking dreadfully as he lifted the wand and pointed it at the demon. Deevilmon glanced down at him oddly and, for the briefest of moments, it seemed to Brian that a tiny look of unease passed across the demon's face. Whether this was due to the fact that it was now completely alone, for each and every one of its demon servants had been defeated, Brian couldn't be sure. He had the strangest feeling, however, that it had more to do with the sight of Abner's wand clutched in his hand.

If it had indeed been a look of unease upon Deevilmon's face it disappeared almost instantly when a spell fired from the end of

Winston Zillion's ballpoint pen almost hit the demon full in the face. But once again Deevilmon somehow deflected the spell, forcing it back at Zillion, which immediately sent him diving for cover as it hurtled back over his head like some sort of magical boomerang.

As Zillion's spell exploded behind him, sending dust and stone flying in every direction and knocking poor Gordon Grubshackle off his feet, Deevilmon began hastily fashioning a strange and dark circle of vapour within the air before it. Tendrils of thin, sinewy smoke which had previously formed the demon's hands and arms quickly began to merge together, forming an ever-changing ring of black, swirling mist that was only broken by a sudden crackle of what appeared to be red lightning.

'ICE-FLIC-ERR,' roared Deevilmon and all at once the circle of black mist plummeted to the floor, its edges splashing upwards as it hit the massive slabs of stone beneath the demon, almost as if it were in reality some sort of liquid, whilst all the time constantly expanding. The circle of black smoke rushed past Abner and Violet and shot past Sam and Hadley before suddenly exploding in an enormous wall of red and orange flame directly behind Brian and Norman. And although the circular wall of fire did not feel particularly hot to their skin Norman's wheelchair, which unfortunately had been caught within it, quickly began to melt.

They were trapped! Outside, and clearly casting spell upon spell at the wall of flame with very little success, were the Coffinsgrave Committee whilst on the inside of the wall of flame were the children and the two monsters. They watched as Deevilmon drifted over towards Abner and, with its arms and hands reformed, scooped up what looked like a black, metallic ball. Brian guessed it must have fallen from one of the antique shop owner's pockets when his cloak had been torn from him for there were various other items lying nearby.

'I would not do that if I were you!' warned Deevilmon, nodding towards the wand that Brian was still pointing at the demon.

'And give me one reason why not?' said Brian, bitterly.

Deevilmon appeared to smile and held up the black, metallic ball it had just picked up. 'After losing your mother it would be a shame, I think, for you to lose your father too. Don't you agree?'

'What are you talking about?' spat Brian.

'It's a Norsip Ball,' remarked Audrey, staring up at the round, black orb that had magically begun to levitate just above one of Deevilmon's hands.

'Yes, a Norsip Ball is indeed what it is, Miss Jenkins,' said Deevilmon, nodding.

'And what's a Norsip Ball?' asked Brian, irritably.

'Don't you remember?' said Norman, who, after seeing his wheelchair begin to melt, had decided it was probably a very good idea to crawl as far away from the wall of flame as he possibly could. 'We saw one in Abner Antiques on the night it opened.'

'It's what some monsters call a Prison Ball,' added Sam.

Hadley grunted.

'That's right,' agreed his smaller companion, 'dark warlocks would use them in the old days to trap and keep their enemies in.'

'You're saying that my father... that you've got him trapped inside that Norsip Ball?' said Brian, lowering Abner's wand ever-so-slightly.

Deevilmon smiled unpleasantly.

'But how do I know that you're telling the truth?' asked Brian.

Deevilmon whispered something, a command which Brian, as hard as he tried, could not catch, and Brian watched in silence as the Norsip Ball suddenly began to unscrew itself ever-so-slightly. Almost at once a thin threadlike ray of silver light burst from it, which throbbed and pulsed as if inside the Norsip Ball were an actual living, beating heart. And it was then that Brian heard the voice, very faint at first, as if its owner were far, far away. But the voice, whoever it belonged to, was growing stronger and as it did so Brian immediately recognised it.

279

'Dad?'

'Brian?' came the anxious reply from the Norsip Ball. 'Brian, is that you?'

'DAD!' cried Brian as tears, once again, began to fill his eyes. It was all he could do not to run at Deevilmon right there and then and try to snatch the Norsip Ball away from it.

'Brian!' shouted the voice, sounding overjoyed. 'Brian, is it really you?'

'Yes,' replied Brian, wiping away his tears. 'It's me, Brian. Dad, Mum's been—'

'Where are you?' interrupted the voice, suddenly concerned. 'Are you all right?'

'Yes, Dad, but Deevilmon—'

'You've got to warn Katobi,' interrupted the voice again, suddenly growing fainter.

Already the Norsip Ball was beginning to close.

'What?' replied Brian, confused.

'You've got to warn Katobi,' the voice repeated again, urgently. 'Do you hear me, Brian? There's a... traitor.' And then, in barely a whisper, 'You must warn... Katobi.'

'I know,' shouted back Brian. He could barely hear his dad's voice now. 'It's Abner. It's Barrington Abner.'

'Now do you believe me, Brian?' asked Deevilmon, grinning, when the Norsip Ball had closed.

Brian nodded and through clenched teeth said, 'Now give the Norsip Ball to me!'

Deevilmon laughed. 'And if I don't?'

'Then I shall kill your accomplice,' replied Brian, matter-of-factly and flicking his wrist so that the wand he was holding now pointed at the antique shop owner lying upon the floor, still being guarded by Violet.

Audrey gasped. 'Brian, you can't do that! You just can't. It's wrong. That's murder!'

'She's right, mate,' agreed Norman. 'No matter what Abner may have done you can't kill him.'

'But he killed my mother!' spat Brian, furiously. 'He doesn't deserve to live!'

'I know,' replied Norman. 'But you're better than that, mate. You're better than him!'

Audrey stepped a little nearer to Brian and placed her hand upon his trembling arm and immediately she could feel the terrible rage that burned within him. 'Brian,' said Audrey softly. 'You can't do this. You really can't. If you kill Abner then you will become no better than him. Your mother—'

'My mother!' shouted back Brian, angrily. 'What do you know of my mother? You don't know anything!'

'I *know* that your mother would not want her son, her only son, to become a murderer,' continued Audrey calmly. 'No mother would. And neither would your father. If you do this, if you kill Abner, then what will become of your father, Brian? Who will save him? Who will rescue him? Do you want to lose both your parents? Because that's what will surely happen if you kill Abner.'

'But he killed my mother! He doesn't deserve to live!' cried Brian again, as the tip of the wand he was holding began to erupt in sparks.

'Quite right!' agreed Deevilmon. 'He really doesn't deserve to live, does he? And as I have no further use for Abner myself then I shall kill him for you.' And with that, a coil of red and orange flame leapt from the wall of fire that had been surrounding them and at once began twisting about the children and the two monsters as if it were, somehow, alive and seeking out the antique shop owner just as a snake hunts for its meal. When it inevitably found him, seconds later, the screams that poured from Abner's mouth as the burning ribbon of flame engulfed him were both dreadful and frightening. Abner's struggles were futile and in a mere matter of seconds all

281

that remained of the antique shop owner was a pile of smouldering ash.

'Nobody deserves to die like that!' growled Violet, returning to stand next to Brian.

Deevilmon simply laughed and turning towards Norman said, 'Now, I believe you have something that belongs to me: the Cup of Ages. Return it to me or I will kill each and every one of you!'

'You'll just kill us all anyway,' replied Audrey, 'whether we give you the Cup of Ages or not!'

Deevilmon laughed again. 'You're right again, Miss Jenkins. And you shall be the first to die.'

Brian raised Abner's wand towards the demon again.

'And what do you think you're going to do with that?' said Deevilmon, mockingly. 'You do not have the ability or the power to defeat me, and even if you had your actions would condemn your father too. Do you really want to become an orphan so soon in life, Brian? Now give me the Cup of Ages!'

'No!' replied Brian.

'Then so be it,' remarked Deevilmon. And, just as before, a sliver of twisting, burning flame suddenly burst from the wall of fire, this time directly behind Audrey and headed straight towards her. In the same moment a jet of silver light erupted from the end of Abner's wand, hitting the massive demon full in the chest. A clearly shocked Deevilmon seemed to momentarily lose some of its substance, for the dark black, sinewy smoke that formed its huge body began to fade and separate whilst the ring of flame that had been encircling them all began to drift apart. Large holes started to appear within it. At first most of these were too small or too high to physically pass through but soon others began to emerge. One very large hole appeared towards the base of the wall, just above the stone floor, which allowed two of the Coffinsgrave Committee to jump through it and join the children and the two monsters in their fight on the other side.

No sooner had they done this, however, than Deevilmon seemed to recover and as it did so, so did the wall of flame which immediately returned to its previous height and intensity, once again barring anybody else from passing through it.

'Something's wrong!' cried Brian, who was struggling to keep a grip upon the shaking, wriggling wand, even when using both hands. The beam of light which had burst from its tip was not having the same effect upon Deevilmon as it initially had, quite the opposite in fact. Deevilmon now seemed to be absorbing it.

'You are not strong enough to defeat me!' roared the demon as it began to draw nearer to Brian.

'I can't... I can't stop him!' stammered Brian, feeling suddenly exhausted and watching helpless as Stanley Clutterbucket and Kuchinska Chang , who had passed into the circle of flame when it had briefly begun to collapse, shot various spells at Deevilmon. The demon easily deflected these straight back at them, forcing the wizards to dive for cover.

'You foolish boy!' boomed Deevilmon triumphantly as the beam of light from Abner's wand began to grow rapidly weaker. It was starting to shrink, sputtering in places as though the power inside it was dying. 'You alone cannot defeat me!'

'But he is NOT alone!' cried Norman courageously, dragging himself towards Brian so that he could reach up and place his hand upon his friend's. And, as their fingers touched, Abner's wand seemed to suddenly explode! The beam of light that had poured from its tip but which had rapidly begun to fade instantly erupted again, forcing the enormous demon to retreat. Deevilmon was no longer absorbing the light. Instead the light seemed to be absorbing Deevilmon.

Audrey was next. She ran over to Brian and placed her hand upon Norman's. And once again this seemed to somehow increase the power within the wand that Brian was struggling so furiously to control. All three children could feel it begin to throb and vibrate as, all at once, a second, curling beam of light shot from its tip, twisting about the first and wrapping itself around Deevilmon, forcing the black mist that formed the demon's body to dissolve.

When Violet, who had now returned to her human self, placed her hand upon Audrey's it seemed to Brian that it was this final act that was the catalyst to Deevilmon's eventual fate. He, Brian, hadn't been strong enough to stop the demon, to defeat him. His grief and the anger raging inside him over his mother's death and his father's capture had been too much. He hadn't been able to control the magic within Abner's wand. If he alone had battled with Deevilmon then Brian would have most certainly lost. He knew that now. But between them, by joining forces, he, Norman, Violet and Audrey had made a difference. And that difference, as small as it might have been, was just enough to defeat the enormous demon.

Brian watched as Deevilmon, shrieking terribly now, wrestled fruitlessly with the twisting beam of light that had clung about it. A swirling maelstrom of black vapour had begun to envelop the demon and it looked to the children as though Deevilmon were trapped within a magical tornado. Bolts of silver lightning began blasting from within it, sending splinters of stone falling from the walls, and large cavernous cracks appeared within the stone floor. Suddenly there was a terrific burst of light which was followed by an absolutely thunderous explosion. Brian instinctively let go of Abner's wand and shielded his eyes. When he uncovered them a few moments later the magical maelstrom and Deevilmon had both completely disappeared. And so too had the Norsip Ball inside which his father had been trapped. It was nowhere to be seen.

Chapter 21

A BIRTHDAY PARTY TO REMEMBER

It was late September and almost two weeks had passed since the children's battle with Deevilmon. After the demon's defeat Brian, Norman, Audrey and Violet had been immediately admitted to the HAPPI along with the Wizitches and all the other hurt and wounded. It was a miracle that nobody had actually been killed. The Wizitches, although given very little food and water during their time in captivity, were, to everyone's surprise including their own, remarkably well. Nevertheless, they still required a number of days of rest and care in one of the HAPPI wards. Poor Stanley Clutterbucket, who had been accidentally struck by a rogue spell during his confrontation with one of the smaller demons, had to be kept in an isolation room for almost six days. His whole body had erupted in lots of nasty-looking green boils which kept bursting and staining his pyjamas with a disgusting yellow pus that smelt like the contents of a troll's toilet. Needless to say poor Stanley didn't receive many visitors.

For Norman and Audrey their recuperation within the HAPPI meant that they finally got to see and spend some time with their parents again, and although Brian was extremely happy for them both he couldn't help but feel slightly angry and bitter that he could not do the same. Of course, his grandparents visited him every day too but that just wasn't the same. He hardly knew his grandmother and his granddad. The person who he had thought was his granddad had, in fact, turned out to be Barrington Abner in disguise. Brian felt deceived, foolish and betrayed.

Violet, meanwhile, had been receiving even more visitors than he, Norman and Audrey put together. Quite apart from all the curious doctors and nurses who would call upon her during the day, she was also being visited by various members of the Coffinsgrave Committee who, more often than not, would escort her via the Soobius System to meet other and more important warlocks and magicians who would stare, open-mouthed and in amazement, as she transformed herself from a girl to a Jackerbot. As Violet herself said after one such visit, being a shapeshifter, it seemed, was quite a big deal!

During his stay Brian took to wandering the hospital, usually during visiting hours and mainly to avoid the company of his grandparents who, even though their hearts were in the right place, would irritate Brian by constantly asking him the same questions upon each visit: was he feeling okay? Was he eating his meals? Was he sleeping all right? More often than not Brian's wanderings would take him to one of the upper floors of the hospital and, in particular, to the Monster Ward where Sam and Hadley were recuperating.

'Wotcher, Brian,' said Sam, waving enthusiastically when he spotted Brian standing inside the entrance to the Monster Ward a few days after they had been admitted.

Hadley grunted and waved excitedly too. He, much like Willy Googalak when the children had visited him in the hospital, had an absolutely enormous bed due to his massive height and weight, which groaned very unhappily each time the monster either sat up or rolled over.

'What are you doing up here?' asked Sam in some surprise. 'It's visiting hours, you know? Won't your grandparents be coming to see you?'

'Probably,' replied Brian, miserably.

Hadley mumbled something unintelligible.

286

'I don't know what's the matter with him,' replied Sam in a hushed tone. 'I'll ask him.' Then, turning to Brian, he said, 'What's up?'

'You mean apart from my mother being murdered, my father being kidnapped and having to live with my grandparents whom I hardly know?' said Brian, matter-of-factly.

'Oh, right. Yeah, sorry,' replied Sam awkwardly, and he climbed out of his bed so that he could give Brian's knees a hug. Brian, meanwhile, noticed that, even in bed, Sam still wore his wellington boots.

'You got your other wellington boot back then,' said Brian, wanting to change the subject.

'Eventually!' replied Sam, tugging the hair on Hadley's arm painfully until his taller companion tried to hit him. 'It took almost an hour.' He opened the door of a cupboard that separated the two monsters' beds and gestured to the inside. Unsurprisingly, it was crammed full of things that Brian guessed must have been retrieved from the folds of Hadley's fur. He couldn't see everything inside it for the cupboard was too full but he spotted a pack of candles, some playing cards, a tennis ball, a couple of books, a frying pan with a hole in it and a rag doll which was clearly enchanted as it kept making very rude hand gestures at him.

Hadley grunted a few times.

'What did he say?' asked Brian, sitting on the edge of Hadley's bed and giving the rag doll a rude hand gesture back before shutting the cupboard door upon it.

'He, er.... said that you do realise that your grandparents love you, don't you?' replied Sam, a little embarrassed, his face turning red.

'Oh,' said Brian, taken aback, and then, after an uncomfortable silence, he added, 'It's just that I... well, I... miss my mum and dad.' And he started to cry.

'Now look what you've gone and done, you great hairy oaf!' scolded Sam, jumping up onto his bigger companion's bed and trying to give Hadley a kick but missing him completely so that the wellington boot shot from his foot and flew through the air, landing on the head of the patient in the next bed who, up until then, had been sleeping peacefully.

Brian openly sobbed. For the first time since Deevilmon's defeat he just cried. Like a river that had burst its banks tears poured down his cheeks and no matter how many hugs he got from Sam or very heavy pats on the head from Hadley he was unable to stop. Suppressing his grief as he had been doing ever since he had learned of his mother's death was neither good for him nor for anybody else. He had become irritable with the slightest thing annoying him. And he had grown to loathe visiting hours when Norman's and Audrey's parents came to visit. Where was *his* mother? Where was *his* father? It just wasn't fair!

In those first few days after being admitted to the HAPPI Brian only felt truly comfortable in Sam and Hadley's company. His grandparents loved him, he knew that. They were, after all, his father's parents. But Brian didn't know them, and that was half the problem. Norman and Audrey meanwhile were caught up in the excitement and relief of knowing their parents had survived being scrobbled and held captive by Deevilmon, whilst Violet, who most days was out visiting a warlock or witch, was hardly ever in the hospital except at night when she finally returned to get some sleep. So Brian found himself visiting Sam and Hadley every day. He didn't mind their bickering or their arguments or the fights that broke out between them when the three of them played Monster Snap (a game in which playing cards depicting various unpleasant monsters, when laid on top of one another, would often magically jump up and suddenly fight each other to the death or at least until one of them was torn in half). And neither Sam nor Hadley seemed to mind too much when something one of them said or did would

288

suddenly trigger a memory within Brian of his mother or father which, in turn, would upset him and make him cry. The two monsters would simply give him a hug and, when Brian felt better, suggest another game of Monster Snap with a promise that they wouldn't argue or fight which, of course, they never kept.

The funeral for Brian's mother took place almost a week after everyone had been discharged from the HAPPI. Everyone, that is, except Stanley Clutterbucket, who although now fully recovered from his 'Bursting Boils' had developed a rather nasty case of Cluckinitus. Cluckinitus and spells like it were simple, small incantations that were sometimes hidden within larger spells, causing the receiver no actual harm as such, just a huge amount of embarrassment. In Stanley Clutterbucket's case every fourth word he uttered turned into the very loud CLUCK of a chicken. This made any conversation with Stanley very difficult indeed and yet, at the same time, extremely funny.

Meanwhile, and much to Audrey's relief, the giant black slug that had been wrapped about her broken arm ever since the Diefromen attack suddenly dropped off. Finally Audrey was able to remove her sling and, even though her arm felt a little stiff, she was able to use it again as though nothing had ever happened.

It had been decided in case anybody should ask, which inevitably they would, that a false account be created of how Brian's mother had suddenly met her death. With Brian and his grandparents' agreement the Coffinsgrave Committee decided that, as unpleasant a task as it was, the suggestion of a car crash be used. They couldn't very well say that she had been killed by a demon and his accomplice. Of course it was only natural that a number of other relatives and friends would also ask after Brian's father, and those who did were to be informed that, although he survived the car crash that killed Brian's poor mother, he was presently in intensive care within a hospital somewhere whose name they couldn't quite remember.

Barnaby Katobi gave a reading at his mother's funeral; so did Brian's granddad, which Brian found particularly hard to listen to and very upsetting. Unfortunately, neither Sam nor Hadley could attend the funeral as the sight of two monsters sitting at one end of an aisle would, no doubt, have caused a bit of a panic amongst the congregation. But sitting with him in the front row were Norman, Audrey, Violet and, of course, his grandparents and for the first time since their battle with Deevilmon Brian was extremely glad that they were all there with him. After the service everyone who had attended the funeral returned to his grandparents' house (now magically repaired after the Diefromen attack and being ransacked) where both friends and relatives drank copious amounts of tea and coffee and ate from enormous platters of ham, cheese and cucumber sandwiches that his grandmother had made. Later that evening, when the last of the guests had left, Brian's grandmother was rather disappointed to see so many of her rock cakes and slices of sticky toffee pie had remained untouched.

Three days after his mother's funeral Brian's grandparents' house was once again full to bursting, but unlike the previous and understandably sombre event this time it was full of children, wizards, witches, magicians, warlocks and monsters who were all dancing the conga and singing loudly at the tops of their voices! The occasion? Violet's birthday party.

Audrey had suggested arranging a birthday party for Violet almost as soon as they had been admitted to the HAPPI. Of course, Brian didn't realise it at the time but Audrey's idea enabled him to focus on something other than his battle with Deevilmon and the death of his mother. Yet at first he didn't want to get involved. How could he help plan a birthday party when he was still grieving? But Audrey was persistent and each time Violet was whisked away to meet another important wizard or warlock she and Norman would congregate around Brian's bed to discuss their plans and ideas.

Violet didn't know when her birthday was or exactly how old she was and neither did the Gillibottoms, not that they really cared. The children guessed that she was a similar age to them, perhaps a bit older. After careful consideration Audrey had decided that the 21st September was a good a date as any to celebrate Violet's birthday and, after obtaining Brian's grandparents' permission to hold the party at their house, she had secretly sent the invitations out.

So, at just before one o'clock on the afternoon of the 21st September Brian, Norman and Audrey, along with everybody else who had been invited to Violet's birthday party, watched in a nervous silence as one of the bookcases in Brian's grandparent's living room suddenly began to empty itself. A few moments later Violet stepped out of it.

'SURPRISE!' cried everyone at the tops of their voices.

'Oh my!' squealed Violet in absolute delight, when she saw how many people were there to greet her, all of whom were clutching presents and singing, 'Happy birthday to you. Happy birthday to you. Happy birthday dear Violet. Happy birthday to you!'

As the well-wishers finished Violet's birthday song with a few added 'whoops' and 'hip-hip-hoorays' Barnaby Katobi also emerged from the bookcase, which then began to magically close behind him. As well as the walking stick which he always carried Brian noticed that he was holding a small and rather battered brown briefcase.

Violet didn't have many friends. Indeed, until she had met Brian, Norman and Audrey she hadn't had any friends at all. Audrey, therefore, had decided that it would be a good idea to invite all the children who, like them, had been taken to the Halls of Blooskstoof when the Wizitches had been kidnapped by Deevilmon in the hope that, by the end of the party, Violet would have made a lot more friends. The Hyland sisters had been the first to arrive along with their younger brother, Adam. Adam, who had caught a nasty cold the week before, was sneezing so often that, in the end, Brian's granddad decided to cast a spell with his screwdriver so that each time he was about to sneeze a handkerchief appeared out of nowhere to cover his nose and then wipe it for him before magically disappearing again. Next to arrive had been the Ellis sisters, then the Norris brothers, who were swiftly followed by Lucy Adams and then Jade Saliba who arrived at the party with two of her fairy friends sitting on her shoulders. Brian had never seen fairies so close up before and, try as he might, he couldn't help but stare. That is, until Jade, and then the two fairies themselves, told him that he was being rather rude. Amazingly the fairies looked just like normal human beings except that they were a lot smaller, obviously. And that they also had very thin and crystal clear wings.

As the children quickly swarmed around Violet, all thrusting their different-coloured presents into her arms, fireworks began exploding above them on the living room ceiling which had been bewitched by Brian's grandmother earlier that morning. There were 'oooooh's and 'aaaaaah's from some of the smaller children as streaks of green, yellow and red sparkling light shot up the walls and exploded above them, showering the children in a mass of magical, twinkling sparks.

'Anybody for tea?' interrupted a voice, forcing the children to drag their eyes from the ceiling and towards the large enchanted teapot that was now floating in midair next to them.

'Pardon?' replied Brian, staring at the teapot, surprised. By now many of the adults, including Barnaby Katobi, had disappeared downstairs into the dining room where Brian's grandmother had prepared quite a spread of sandwiches, crisps, cakes and other party food.

'Anybody for tea?' repeated the teapot enthusiastically as Brian stared at its porcelain spout which was gradually beginning to look more and more like a long, thin nose, whilst above this and on either side of it two large eyes had appeared which blinked back at him enquiringly. The pair of lips that had magically materialised beneath

292

the spout then added, 'Only your grandmother does have rather a lot to do, so she asked me if I would see if anybody would like a cup of tea.' The teapot gestured behind herself to where a long line of enchanted cups on saucers had been following obediently.

'You haven't got anything fizzy, like lemonade?' asked Norman, idly picking at what was left of the scab on his chin, which had been badly grazed during his battle with Deevilmon. However, and much to Norman's huge disappointment, it hadn't needed any slug stitches.

'Stop picking that scab!' snapped Audrey, irritably. 'It's absolutely disgusting!' She screwed up her nose unpleasantly. 'You've probably got bits of it under your fingernails and everything. Yuck!'

'Very unhygienic,' added the teapot with a tut.

'All right! All right! I don't need a lecture from you *and* the teapot,' grumbled Norman, placing his hands upon the wheels of his badly buckled wheelchair. Unfortunately, during the battle with Deevilmon, Norman's wheelchair had been quite badly damaged and even though it had been repaired with a number of different magical spells the left wheel still didn't turn quite as smoothly as it should have.

'Tea?' suggested the teapot again pleasantly, as a cup and saucer suddenly appeared under her spout, trembling excitedly in anticipation.

'No thanks,' said Norman, wheeling himself out of the living room and towards the small flight of stairs that led to the dining room below where, one by one, each step was magically disappearing into the floor and then reappearing at the top of the landing again just like an escalator in a department store. Brian, Audrey and Violet duly followed, but only once a very excited Violet had opened some of her presents.

They found Norman about half an hour later wearing a red paper hat, blowing a whistle very loudly and leading a conga dance of about twenty people and monsters that included Sam and Hadley into and out of their cardboard Expandobox, which had been stretched so high that it now touched the dining room ceiling. In front of him Norman was being accompanied by a floating set of drums, a trumpet and a clarinet which were all playing quite happily of their own free will. As the end of the conga line passed them by Audrey, quickly followed by Violet, grabbed hold of the last person and with Norman still leading the dance they disappeared back into the Expandobox.

Brian, meanwhile, weaved his way through the crowded dining room and into the kitchen where he almost tripped over an enchanted mop and bucket that were enthusiastically clearing up some spilt tea. At the far end of the kitchen it was snowing and it was here that Brian spotted Willy Googalak attempting, rather unsuccessfully, to pour himself a cup of tea; it seemed his massive fingers were far too big for the cup's very tiny handle and he had ended up dropping it on the floor, sending tea splashing in all directions. Brian gave the yeti a wave before grabbing himself a couple of sausage rolls from one of the plates that were levitating by the kitchen window and escaping into the garden.

He sat down on the bench outside the back door, glad to be away, albeit briefly, from the noisy crowd inside his grandparents' house. But even as he munched on his sausage rolls he could still hear the drums banging away at the front of the conga and Norman blowing his whistle as though it had been surgically attached to his lips.

When he had finished eating Brian's thoughts wandered, not for the first time that day, to his mother and very soon he found himself holding her gold locket which he had now taken to wearing about his neck. He desperately wished she was here and enjoying the party with him. At Brian's own request his granddad had placed a 'Galesin' spell upon the locket's clasp so that it would never accidentally open. He very much doubted that he would ever want to hear its contents again but he wanted to keep the locket, if for nothing else, so that he had something to remember his mother by.

'You all right, Brian?' asked his granddad, stepping out of the kitchen and watching as Brian hastily tucked the locket back under his shirt. 'Sorry, that's a bit of a silly question, isn't it?' he remarked, sitting down next to him. 'After everything that's happened.'

'It's okay,' Brian lied, idly kicking at the floor with one of his feet.

'Your mother...' began his granddad

'It's just... it's just that there's a few things I still don't understand,' interrupted Brian. He really didn't want to discuss the death of his mother. Not here. Not right now.

'Like what?' asked his granddad.

'Like what happened to everyone who was frozen by Willy Googalak's potion and Madame Shinney's Seeing Stone, for one thing?' asked Brian.

'Apart from them all waking up very cold and a few people finding themselves in some, er, rather embarrassing positions nothing really untoward happened to them at all,' replied his granddad. 'The spell that was cast to merge Willy's potion with Madame Shinney's Seeing Stone wasn't permanent. In fact, I don't think it lasted for more than about thirty minutes. Thankfully, there were no long-term ill effects. Your father made sure of that.'

'My father?' said Brian, in some surprise.

'Yes, of course, that's why he was kidnapped, Brian. Don't you see? That's why he was, and still is, being held prisoner by Deevilmon. As well as being able to sense a demon's presence he, like you, also has the ability on occasion to use another magician's Fizzlestick.'

'But why weren't Waghorn and all the other Coffinsgrave Committee members frozen like everybody else?' asked Brian, puzzled.

'Beatrice had had her suspicions about Barrington Abner for quite some time, long before I or any of the other committee members suspected anything untoward. She attempted, more than once, to warn Barnaby Katobi and the other committee members about him, but when her concerns fell upon deaf ears she then, instead, sent me a warning. That letter you found on the first day you arrived,' explained his granddad, unfolding and handing him a piece of paper that he had retrieved from his trouser pocket.

Unlike the last time Brian had seen the letter, when only a few words could be made out, this time the whole contents of the letter had been magically revealed. In a spidery and golden handwriting the letter read...

Henry,

I fear time is running out. The sightings of demons are increasing every day and I now believe, without a doubt, that the portal has been breached. I have warned the Committee but, even now, they refuse to accept the possibility that Deevilmon has returned. Have you noticed the road signs? Is it merely coincidence that such an odd occurrence has happened on every street where a Wizitch resides?

Perhaps, if we can meet tonight and visit the Committee together? I feel certain that they will listen to you. But if they do not, if they choose to ignore the evidence presented to them, then I am certain that there will be grave consequences indeed.

When Brian finished reading Waghorn's letter he frowned and said, 'But that still doesn't explain how Waghorn and all the other Coffinsgrave Committee members didn't freeze like everybody else.'

'Well, like you, Beatrice had guessed that the potions stolen from Willy Googalak's Snow Shack was no random robbery,' explained his granddad. 'She did quite a bit of investigating, I can tell you. And, although she was in no way certain why anybody would want or try to freeze the inhabitants of Coffinsgrave, she was positive that it would be on a day during the Coffinsgrave Fair when so many people would be in one place at one time. Not all the committee members were convinced though. Especially when Beatrice couldn't even provide them with an acceptable reason as to why anybody would attempt such a difficult spell. However, the majority of the committee members, who had previously ignored Beatrice's fears over the Wizitches before they were kidnapped, agreed to take a slightly modified and longer-lasting anti-freezing potion just in case she was right, which she most certainly was.'

'Okay, but then how did the Coffinsgrave Committee members find us?' asked Brian. 'I mean, to get to Deevilmon we ended up in what was left of Abner's antique shop and climbing into one of his trunks and then up a staircase...'

A bark from the kitchen which was swiftly followed by the appearance of a rather nervous black and white cat at its door suddenly caught Brian's attention. Much smaller than a usual cat and made out of what appeared to be china, it was most definitely enchanted. Brian watched as it glanced up at him before, all at once, speeding away from the kitchen, through his legs and down towards the shed at the end of the garden. It was closely followed, seconds later, by a brown china dog which, although slightly smaller than the cat, was nevertheless barking madly at the top of its voice.

'You have Claw to thank for Beatrice finding you,' said his granddad.

'Claw?' repeated Brian, having never heard of the name before. 'Who's Claw?'

'Beatrice's crow,' replied his granddad. 'She gave him a small draught of the anti-freezing potion too and it was he who was sent to follow the figure that Beatrice spotted wandering through the streets whilst everybody else was frozen.'

'We thought *that* was Waghorn!' admitted Brian.

His granddad laughed. 'Why in the world would you think that?' he asked, amused.

'Well,' began Brian, watching as the china dog at the end of the garden began encircling the shed where he guessed the china cat was probably now hiding, 'she's not very nice, is she?'

His granddad laughed again. 'Beatrice not very nice? Well, let me tell you this, Brian: in an emergency Beatrice would be the first person that I would call upon. You know, don't you, that she's taken Violet under her wing?'

'What do you mean, under her wing?' asked Brian, shocked.

'Violet is no longer going to be living with or working for the Gillibottoms,' said his granddad. 'Instead she will now be living, albeit temporarily, with Beatrice.'

'Does she know?' asked Brian, flabbergasted.

'I believe Barnaby Katobi was going to tell her earlier today,' replied his granddad. 'Best not mention it, though, until Violet does. I don't doubt that the Gillibottoms didn't treat her quite as well as they should have done. Perhaps not quite as badly as Audrey suggested, though.'

'Audrey told you about the bruises and everything, then?' asked Brian.

'Oh yes, she certainly did!' replied his granddad, with a sigh, and he rolled his eyes upwards. 'On more than one occasion. And Barnaby Katobi too, and anybody else from the Coffinsgrave Committee who would listen for that matter.'

'But Violet always had so many bruises!' argued Brian. 'Every day we saw her she would always have fresh bruises on her arms and face.'

'Violet's a shapeshifter,' said his granddad, matter-of-factly. 'And a very young one at that. Extremely rare! Each and every time she shifts it really does take a great toll on her body, Brian. Her bones are forced to expand and her skin stretches incredibly which, in turn, can and will cause quite horrendous sores and bruises all

298

over her body, poor girl. But I do not doubt that there is also some credibility to what Audrey told us.'

'How did the Gillibottoms take the news?' asked Brian with a wry smile.

'Violet is not a blood relative,' replied his granddad. 'The Gillibottoms had no choice in the matter, which is exactly what Barnaby Katobi told them. Violet, of course, was also consulted. Barnaby Katobi couldn't very well remove her from the Gillibottoms unless she wanted to leave also.'

'But to leave and go and live with Beatrice Waghorn!' remarked Brian, clearly appalled at the very idea.

Brian's granddad laughed out loud. 'Brian, you make poor Beatrice sound like some kind of demon! I think you'll find that she and Violet will get on much better than you anticipate.' Then, as an afterthought he added, 'They are, after all, not too dissimilar.'

Brian was just about to ask his granddad what he meant when a paper bag was thrust under his granddad's nose.

'Giraffe, anybody?' asked Aldwinkle, who had removed the white paper bag from a pocket within his cloak. Brian stared at the small, crumpled bag in some alarm, for its contents seemed to be doing their very utmost to escape.

'No thank you, Addison,' said Brian's granddad, shaking his head politely before adding, 'I'm trying to give them up.'

'What about you, Brian?' offered Aldwinkle, almost thrusting the wriggling bag up Brian's nose. 'The strawberry-flavoured ones are particularly nice'

Brian peered cautiously into the bag that Aldwinkle was now offering him. Inside it were about a dozen miniature giraffes. All different colours and all jostling each other and stretching their necks as far as they possibly could, desperately trying to see over the edge of the bag.

'It's all right, they don't bite,' chuckled Aldwinkle, seeing the look of hesitation upon Brian's face, and he plucked a brownish giraffe from the bag himself which, as soon as it was finally free from the bag, froze like a statue before Aldwinkle bit off its head. 'Oh dear,' he remarked, wrinkling his nose up in disgust. 'Cardboard flavour.'

'I'll... er, have one later,' said Brian, who, after seeing the unpleasant look upon Aldwinkle's face, really didn't like the thought of chewing on a cardboard-flavoured sweet himself. What other disgustingly flavoured giraffes were trying to escape, he wondered? 'How are your legs, Mr Aldwinkle?'

'All completely back to normal, thank goodness,' replied Aldwinkle, bending up and down a few times proving to Brian and his granddad that both his broken legs were now successfully healed. 'Been meaning to ask you, Henry,' he added, taking another bite from the giraffe so that it was now missing a leg as well its head. 'Something's been bothering me.'

'Has it?' said Brian's granddad.

'Yes,' replied Aldwinkle. 'Something's been bothering me since our encounter with Deevilmon. What do you suppose Brian's father meant when he referred to a traitor? Do you think he was referring to Barrington Abner?'

'Why, don't you think he was referring to Barrington Abner, then?' asked his granddad.

Aldwinkle shrugged and bit off another of the giraffe's legs. 'I suppose so,' he mumbled, and then, more to himself than to anybody else, he added, 'He surely couldn't have meant anybody within the Committee?'

'Henry dear, Barnaby Katobi is going to make an announcement,' said Brian's grandmother, looking rather puffed and red-faced and peering round the side of the kitchen door, clutching a tray of rock cakes. 'Come inside. You too, Addison, and you too, Brian dear.'

Brian got up and followed his granddad and Aldwinkle back into the dining room, via the kitchen where, it seemed, Willy Googalak had at last successfully poured himself a cup of tea, albeit within a rather large saucepan.

'Ladies and gentlemen and boys and girls,' began Barnaby Katobi, smiling pleasantly and hanging his cloak upon an invisible peg somewhere a little to his left. Then, placing his briefcase at his feet, he coughed and cleared his throat and the room quickly fell silent. 'Before Miss Armstrong's party gets into full swing I do have a couple of announcements to make. Firstly, I would like to thank Henry and Doris Pankhurst for hosting today's party. You really have outdone yourself, Doris,' said Katobi, smiling and gesturing to the tables laden with sandwiches and the trays of cakes and chocolate biscuits that were floating about the room. 'As usual your rock cakes really are... er...' Katobi faltered momentarily as he struggled to find the right words, before finally settling on '...particularly nice. Wouldn't you agree, Hadley?'

Hadley appeared to wipe something hidden somewhere deep within his fur, presumably his mouth, and burped loudly, which made all the children giggle. Sam kicked him hard in the ankle.

'As you are no doubt aware,' continued Katobi more gravely, 'there was, rather regrettably, an attempt made recently to steal a magical artefact known as the Cup of Ages. Thankfully the robbery was thwarted and this was, in no small part, down to the bravery of four particular individuals who I am very pleased to say are here with us today. I do not, however, refer to any warlocks, magicians or even witches for that matter, although there are many here who played their part in ensuring the Cup of Ages' safe return. The four particular individuals to whom I am referring are four children whose names are Brian Pankhurst, Norman Crabtree, Audrey Jenkins and Violet Armstrong.'

Although the children's names were known to most, if not necessarily all at the party, their revelation nevertheless resulted in tremendous amounts of cheers and applause from everyone present.

301

'Now, where are you all?' asked Katobi, searching amongst the crowded dining room for the four children. 'Would you please raise your hands? Excellent! And if you could just make your way to the front. Thank you.' He cleared his throat again before continuing. 'Now, I'm quite sure you've all noticed Mr Crabtree's poor wheelchair. Regrettably, it was very badly damaged during the battle to retrieve the Cup of Ages and although it has been repaired with numerous magical spells it has nevertheless developed, for want of a better term, a bit of a limp. Therefore, and in recognition of Norman's courage during the battle to retrieve the Cup of Ages, it gives me great pleasure to award him this!' And as Barnaby Katobi said the word '*this*' he lifted his cloak from the invisible peg to reveal a brand new silver wheelchair.

Norman's jaw almost hit the floor, 'It's a Lightning 72!' he gasped in amazement, wheeling himself a little nearer to it to get a better look. 'It's the best enchanted chair on the market! It's got self-propulsion, a fifteen-minute flight time, can store up to four cups of your favourite drink inside the arms and everything!'

'Your new wheelchair does come with one very important rule, however,' said Katobi, staring at Norman whose mouth was still hanging open wide in wonder. 'The optional extras that come pre-installed, and I particularly like the massage facility by the way, can only be used within Coffinsgrave or a similar magical environment. Do you understand? *Not* the outside world.'

Norman nodded dumbly and ran his fingers adoringly around one of the sparkling, silver wheels whilst mumbling repeatedly about the chair being able to store up to four cups of his favourite drink.

Not entirely sure if Norman had actually understood what he had just said Katobi re-emphasised, 'With the exception of matters of life and death, Master Crabtree, you must not, under any circumstance, use the optional extras in the normal and everyday world. Oh, and it also comes with a manual…'

With a puff of smoke and a flash of light a gigantic book suddenly materialised on Norman's lap; it both looked and weighed as though it were, in actual fact, a large-print special edition of the hugely popular 127-volume encyclopaedia entitled *Magic, a Brief History*.

'That's the quick set-up guide,' remarked Katobi. 'Three cheers for Norman!'

When the cheers, whistles and clapping had finally begun to subside Katobi raised his hands and said, 'I know I am delaying the party and for this I apologise greatly but there is still one more duty that I need to perform.' Then, turning his attention to the other three children, as well as Norman, he said, 'In a world where there is much to fear and where bravery seems to be a thing of the past you four children have proven, beyond any doubt, that friendship and your faith and determination in each other can overcome the most insurmountable odds. I and my fellow committee members, the Wizitches and the men, women, children and monsters of Coffinsgrave owe you a huge debt of gratitude. A debt which I do not think we can ever repay you...'

'Free drinks at the Snow Shack next Tuesday!' shouted Willy Googalak from the kitchen.

'Apart from free drinks at the Snow Shack next Tuesday, obviously,' added Katobi, smiling. Then, bending down to pick up his briefcase, he said, 'I would like to award each of you Bravery Medals...' But his briefcase wasn't there. Katobi frowned. '...Medals such as these have not been awarded to anybody in over one hundred years...' he said as he hastily began searching behind and in front of him but to no avail. '...A Bravery Medal is the highest award that the Coffinsgrave Committee can bestow... I say, has anybody seen my briefcase?' he asked, as his face turned slightly grey with fright. 'Only the medals were inside it and they're really quite valuable.'

Brian smiled. Standing opposite him were Sam and Hadley. And there, under Hadley's left arm, just protruding slightly from within his tangly fur, was what looked suspiciously like the handle to a brown leather briefcase...

THE END

Lightning Source UK Ltd.
Milton Keynes UK
UKOW031540260912

199692UK00010B/15/P